DIRTY DEAL

CRYSTAL KASWELL

Copyright

This is a work of fiction. Similarities to real people, places, or events are entirely coincidental.

DIRTY DEAL
Second edition.
Copyright © 2015 Crystal Kaswell.
Written by Crystal Kaswell.
Previously published as *The Billionaire's Deal*
Cover by Hang Le

Also by Crystal Kaswell

Dirty Rich

Dirty Deal - Blake

Dirty Boss - Nick

Dirty Husband - coming in 2020

Dirty Desires - coming in 2020

Sinful Serenade

Sing Your Heart Out - Miles

Strum Your Heart Out - Drew

Rock Your Heart Out - Tom

Play Your Heart Out - Pete

Sinful Ever After – series sequel

Just a Taste - Miles's POV

Dangerous Noise

Dangerous Kiss - Ethan

Dangerous Crush – Kit

Dangerous Rock – Joel

Dangerous Fling – Mal

Dangerous Encore - series sequel

Inked Hearts

Tempting - Brendon

Hooking Up - Walker

Pretend You're Mine - Ryan

Hating You, Loving You - Dean

Breaking the Rules - Hunter

Losing It - Wes

Accidental Husband - Griffin

The Baby Bargain - Chase

Inked Love

The Best Friend Bargain - Forest — coming in 2020

Standalones

Broken - Trent & Delilah

Come Undone Trilogy

Come Undone

Come Apart

Come to Me

Sign up for the Crystal Kaswell mailing list

About This Book

He'll dig her out of debt... if she submits to his terms.

Kat Wilder is struggling. She waits tables to support her little sister, but the money never goes far enough. She needs help, fast, or she's going to lose their home.

Enter Blake Sterling. The tech billionaire offers Kat a lifeline. A million dollars for her hand in marriage. A million dollars to don designer dresses, smile at paparazzi, stare into his eyes like she's madly in love. As long as she keeps up the ruse, she secures her family's future.

It's a good deal. Even if Blake is arrogant, impossible to read, and insanely handsome. How can someone so cold leave her so hot? When she's with him, she's on fire. There's something about his dirty demands... her body begs her to obey.

She can play his wife. But can she fall into his bed without falling in love with him?

A sexy Cinderella story.

Please Note: *Dirty Deal* is a revised and expanded

version of a work previously published as *The Billionaire's Deal.*

Chapter One

The manager takes one look at my discount heels and my loose pencil skirt and shakes his head.

"Sorry, but the position is already filled." He leers at my chest. Raises a brow. *Maybe you'd like to fill a different position.*

I swallow the insult rising in my throat. "Do you know when you'll be hiring again?"

"It might be awhile."

"Keep me in mind. I have a lot of experience." Not so much the kind he's looking for. But I do know how to wait tables.

He takes my résumé but keeps his eyes on my chest. "Sorry, honey, but we're looking for something specific."

Yeah, I bet.

I take a not-at-all-calming breath. This guy is nothing. He's not going to make me lose it. I've dealt with a thousand entitled jerks worse than him.

I'll deal with plenty more tonight.

It comes with working at a nice place.

I nod a *thank you* and walk out of the restaurant slowly.

I keep my steps casual. Easy. Well, as easy as I can in these shitty heels.

The air outside is freezing. Even by March in New York standards. The white sky is heavy with grey rainclouds.

Usually, I like the drizzle. I like the temperamental weather—the snowy winters, the rainy spring, the humid summer, the crisp fall.

Right now, not so much.

I dig into my purse for my phone. Lizzy will cheer me up. She always does.

With my next step, I bump into something solid.

No. Someone. Soft wool wraps over a hard body.

My leg catches on his. I think it's a his.

My ankle shifts.

Shit.

I throw my hands in front of my face to catch my fall.

Ow. The concrete smarts. And it's fucking cold.

"Are you okay?" a deep voice asks.

So that's a him. Very him. His voice is masculine. There's something about the steady timbre. Something that makes me forget I'm splayed out on the ground, damp concrete wetting my skirt.

"I'm fine."

His shoes are nice. Leather. Designer. Expensive. His slacks fall at exactly the right place. They're grey. Wool. And they're covering long legs.

His black wool coat falls at mid-thigh. It's buttoned. It's hiding his torso. It's hanging off his strong shoulders.

He's looking down at me, his blue eyes filled with… with something. I'm not sure. It's hard to do anything but stare back at those eyes.

They're beautiful.

And he has this square jaw. The kind of jaw that belongs on a sculpture.

Or a Disney prince.

He's the hottest guy I've seen in months.

And I'm splayed out on the concrete staring dumbstruck.

Awesome.

"I... Um... You should watch where you're going." I pick up my purse and slide it onto my shoulder.

He leans down and offers his hand.

Okay.

I guess he's a gentleman.

That's weird, but it fits him, what with the whole Disney prince vibe.

I take his hand. It does something to me. Makes the air sharper, more electric. Sends heat from my palm, down my arm, through my torso.

It's a strong hand, but it's smooth.

And that suit—

And that *I get what I want* look in his eyes.

I know this guy. Well, I know his type.

He's pure money.

The kind of guy who has the world at his fingertips.

"I really am fine." I pull myself to my feet. Or maybe he pulls me. Either way. I take a step towards the corner—the subway is only a few blocks away—but my ankle isn't having it. Fuck. That hurts.

His grip on my hand tightens. "Sit down." He nods to the bench behind us. "If you can walk."

"I don't need your help."

"Oh, really?" He raises an eyebrow and nods to my shoe as if to say *put it on then.*

Oh.

I'm not wearing a shoe.

For some reason, my foot isn't cold.

None of me is cold.

He's just so…

Obnoxious for telling me what to do.

And incredibly, painfully appealing.

I shift my weight to my other ankle, but I can barely balance. "I have to get to work."

"You'll get to work. Trust me." He slides his arm under mine, like a human crutch, and he sets me on the bench.

His touch is comforting.

It should be scary—this guy is a stranger. I don't even know his name.

But it's not.

It's soothing.

Tender.

But that doesn't mean anything.

It's just that it's been so long since anyone has touched me with any care or attention.

I take a deep breath. It does nothing to slow my heartbeat. "What's your name?"

"Blake. You?"

"Kat."

Those piercing eyes find mine. He presses his fingers against my ankle. "It's sprained."

"I've dealt with worse."

His stare is penetrating. It demands an explanation.

But why?

He doesn't know me.

He doesn't have any obligation to help.

He's someone and I'm no one.

He's not even going to remember me tomorrow.

Still, I want to wipe away the worry in his eyes. "I ran cross-country in high school."

He nods with understanding.

"I can't work on a sprained ankle."

"What do you do?"

"I'm a waitress." And I can't afford to not work.

I stare back at Money Guy. Blake. His expression is still streaked with concern. He's not going to leave me alone until he's sure I'm fine.

And I can't exactly make a quick exit. Not with my ankle this fucked up.

"I'll ice it when I get home. I promise." Ibuprofen will have to get me through my shift tonight. I've played through the pain before, back when I ran all the time instead of every so often.

"I'd feel better if you went to the E.R."

I press my lips into a customer-service smile. "Not happening."

"Where do you work?"

"It's not far. I can walk."

"I'll walk you." He slides my shoe onto my foot.

His fingers graze my ankle.

His touch is soft. Tender. Sweet. Like we're old lovers, not strangers.

It wakes up all my nerves.

I want those hands on my skin.

Under my skirt.

Tearing off my blouse.

Sliding my panties to my knees.

I swallow hard.

I don't think about sex like this. And certainly not with strange, rich men who insist on walking me to work.

Blake.

Money Guy.

He certainly has the tall and handsome thing covered.

If things were different, if Lizzy wasn't home, if I didn't have to work, maybe I'd invite myself out with him.

We could have dinner. Drinks. A night at a hotel. The kind with security. So it's safe.

I could finally punch my v-card.

But things aren't different.

I can't waste time with strange men.

Even rich ones.

I rise to my feet. "I can walk myself." I take a step to prove it. The first is fine, but the second makes me wince. Maybe I can't work on this. Fuck.

He slides his arms under mine, offering himself as a crutch again.

This time, I take his help without protest.

"You really shouldn't work on that." His voice is steady. Impossible to read.

"It's really none of your business."

He nods and walks with me. "It was my fault. I wasn't paying attention."

"You can admit that?"

"Should I not?"

"No." I take a few more steps. It's not so bad. I'm off tomorrow. With rest, ice, and plenty of over the counter painkillers, I'll be okay. "Just… I serve a lot of guys like you."

"Handsome?"

He… he's joking. I think.

I try to find the meaning in his expression, but I get lost in his beautiful eyes.

"Business types," I say. "Guys who are used to getting what they want."

"And they want you as dessert?"

"Sometimes." I get a lot of phone numbers. But that's normal. All the girls at the restaurant do. "They don't usually take no for an answer."

"And I?"

"I guess you're the same." I manage to put my full weight on my foot. It hurts, but it's tolerable. We turn the corner. It's not too far now. "Those guys... they don't like to admit anything is their fault. Even if they order the wrong entree. Or forget to say 'hold the onions.'"

"I know the type." He raises a brow.

We cross the street. I'm moving faster now. New Yorker fast. I nod to the restaurant two blocks down. "I'm there. I've got it." I step away from him.

He pulls his arms back to his sides. "I'm not different."

He pulls something from his back pocket and hands it to me.

It's a business card.

His voice is that same steady tone. "Give it a few days and let me know how you're doing."

"You mean how my ankle is doing?"

He holds my gaze. There's something in his eyes— some tiny hint of vulnerability. I look at the pavement, then back to his eyes. That vulnerability is gone. Replaced by pure determination.

"That's my personal number. Text or call anytime." He takes a step back. "Be careful."

I nod. "Thanks."

He turns, walks around the corner, and he's gone.

I look at the business card.

Blake Sterling. CEO of Sterling Tech. They're huge. Lizzy is obsessed with them. Uses their web services exclusively.

Blake is the CEO of one of the biggest tech companies in New York.

And he wants to know how I'm doing.

Chapter Two

Work drags on forever. By the time I collapse on the subway, my ankle is throbbing.

Two people squeeze onto the bench next to me, a woman and a man in their 30s.

He wraps his arms around her waist.

She climbs into his lap.

The two of them mash their mouths together like they're competing in some sort of face-eating contest.

I scoot to the edge of the bench, but it doesn't help me escape their groans.

It's almost sweet how badly they want each other. It must be nice to need someone so badly you're willing to dry hump on the L train.

Is Blake into that kind of thing?

No. He's far too polite to screw in public.

But then, it's always the quiet ones...

I let my head fill with ideas about the stoic CEO. Images form in my mind. A short comic strip.

A sketch of him standing there in that suit. Blake stepping onto the subway, his eyes streaked with confidence.

Blake ordering some pretty woman to strip out of her coat and plant on the bench.

It's been forever since a comic has floated into my mind. Since any image has floated into my mind.

Once upon a time, I spent all my free time drawing. I wanted to be an artist.

But that was before the accident.

That was back when I had the time and space to think about things like hobbies and guys and sex.

I'm so lost in thought I nearly miss my stop.

The horny travelers are still going at it.

I fight the jealousy that rises in my throat. I want to lose myself like that.

I step onto the platform as lightly as possible. My work shoes—thick, black, non-slip sneakers—soften the blow. But not enough to ease the ache.

Usually, I relish my walk home. The Manhattan skyline is gorgeous against the dark sky. Silver steel and yellow fluorescent bulbs against a brilliant blue. It's a color that belongs only to New York City.

I pass rows and rows of brownstones. A few trendy restaurants. People smoking on their stoops. Cars circling the block for a space.

It's quiet by our apartment. I climb the porch and check the mailbox. Angry red letters read *past due*. The bill for the mortgage.

It's a steal compared to rent anywhere nearby—our parents bought this place before Brooklyn was an It Spot—but it's still too much. I could afford it if I got a job like the one I lost out on today. I could even help Lizzy with school.

Right now…

Ankle first. Then my future.

There's a bunch more junk mail. Electricity bill. *From New York University.*

Lizzy's letter.

It's thick. Legal-pad sized.

She got in.

This must mean she got in.

I rush inside even though I'm limping. "Lizzy!"

Her bedroom light flicks on. She pulls the door open, and wipes her sleepy eyes. "You're supposed to be the one who warns me it's a school night."

I wave the letter.

"What? Hold on." She steps into her room and returns wearing her trendy black glasses. Her eyes go wide. "I can't open that."

"You have to." This is the best news in forever. Lizzy got in. That means she can stay here. With me. My best friend, the one person I trust, can stick around.

"No." Her eyes pass over the return address. Her lips press together. "You open it. Please, Kat." She presses her palms together. "I can't. I can't even think."

"Are you sure?"

"Have I ever asked for your help when I wasn't sure?"

"Have you ever asked for my help?"

She laughs. "I never have to."

It's true. I'm a little… overbearing. I know that. But I can't help it. Lizzy almost died that day three years ago.

It's cheesy, yeah, but I really do feel lucky she's alive.

Alive and ready for an awesome future.

She deserves it.

I tear the envelope open and unfold the letter. *Dear Ms. Wilder; We are proud to offer you acceptance—*

My heart swells. Warmth spreads out through my body.

She got in.

Everything is going to be okay.

We'll make it work. Somehow.

"You're not saying anything." Her fingers curl around my wrist. "Is it bad? Tell me it's not bad."

I shake my head. "It's good. Really good."

She scans it carefully. "Oh my God." A smile creeps onto her face. "Kat! I... I can't believe it!"

"I can." I wrap my arms around my little sister. She works so hard. She deserves it.

"But we can't afford this. Not unless they're offering a full ride. And NYU doesn't do that. It's not like if I got into Columbia."

"We'll find a way to afford it."

"Will we?" She stares back at me, studying my expression. It must be obvious I've got nothing, because she sighs and crushes the letter into a tiny ball. "I still have Stanford and USC. And there are bunch of SUNYs."

And other schools far, far away. "We'll find a way to cover your tuition."

"It's not the end of the world. The school in Albany is great and only a few hours on the train." She moves towards her bedroom. "It's okay, Kat."

My heart sinks. It's not okay. Nothing about it is.

One of us is going places.

One of us is destined for great things.

Lizzy is going to the best school she gets into. Period.

"There's a way. We just haven't figured it out yet." I'll do whatever it takes.

———

BLAKE IS SITTING IN MY SECTION.

He's in another designer suit.

His blue eyes are still icy. Impenetrable.

He still looks like a guy who can snap his fingers and get anything he wants.

12

He's here. That makes him yet another rich customer. I can handle that.

I make my way to his table. I'm a little slower than normal. My ankle is still aching.

He looks up at me. "Did you ice your ankle?" His voice is cool, but there's something in it. Compassion.

"And rested all day yesterday." Not that it's any of his business. "Can I get you something?"

"Whiskey. Rocks."

"You'll get that faster at the bar."

"I prefer here."

"Sure. I'll have that right up." I step back with my best customer-service smile.

His lip corners turn down.

His eyes go to his watch. Then to his cell phone.

Okay…

I guess he doesn't like smiles. Fair enough. I don't like smiling at assholes all day either.

I punch his order into the Aloha and stay busy rear-ranging salt and pepper shakers. The place is dead this time of day. There are only a few other people here.

And Blake is looking at me.

There's something in his eyes. Like he wants something from me. Like he's sure he's going to get it.

I head to the bar, grab his drink, and drop it off. "Enjoy."

"Wait." His voice is demanding. Sure.

"I have—"

"I'm the only person here." He pulls out the chair next to him. "Have a seat."

"This isn't Hooters. Waitresses don't sit with customers."

"Should I have a word with your manager?"

"And say?"

"That you're kind enough to sit to help a poor, confused patron navigate the lunch menu."

"Yeah? Do you not know the difference between filet mignon and ribeye?"

"Say I don't."

"Okay." I swallow hard. That chair is inviting. My ankle is killing me. And his gaze is intoxicating. "I only have a few minutes."

He nods.

I take a seat. Cross my legs. Smooth my black jeans.

"How's your ankle?"

"Fine." It will be fine. Eventually. "I appreciate your concern, but I don't need your help."

Those piercing eyes find mine. "You don't know how I can help."

His voice is low and deep and impossible to read.

I'd ask who the hell he thinks he is, but he's a tech mogul. He knows exactly who he is.

His hand brushes mine. "I have an offer for you."

"What kind of offer?"

His fingers curl around my wrist.

It feels so good.

I want that hand everywhere.

I want his touch everywhere.

I take a deep breath and exhale slowly.

This guy has a sway over me. I don't understand it. But I'm not going to give into it.

Not right now.

He draws his other arm over the side of his chair. "You were interviewing for a job the other day."

I clear my throat. "Keep that to yourself."

He nods. "Is this a profession you enjoy—waiting tables?"

"We can't all be tech CEOs."

"True." He leans a little closer. Those piercing eyes find mine. "You're a very beautiful girl."

There's a flutter in my stomach. Then somewhere below it. "Thank you."

"And polite."

"Uh… Thanks?" What's he getting at?

"I'm looking for someone like you."

What? "For…"

"It's a job. Unorthodox—"

"I'm not a whore."

"And I'm not a john. I don't pay for sex."

"What? You'd pay for the time and we'd happen to sleep together? I wasn't born yesterday. I know how this goes."

His grip around my wrist tightens. "No."

The word stops me in my tracks. It's strong. Confident. Sure. I feel it in my bones.

No. He doesn't want to pay me to sleep with him.

I shouldn't believe him, but I do.

He stares back into my eyes. "I want to fuck you, Kat. But I'm not going to pay you for that. It's going to be because you want me."

My cheeks flush. "I…"

"It wasn't a question." He lowers his voice to a whisper. "That other restaurant is a nicer place. You'd make more."

I nod.

"You need money?"

"You could say that."

"I have money." His voice lifts. Back to that confident, unshakable tone. "And I want you. For six months. A year maybe."

"You want me to what?"

"I want you to marry me."

Chapter Three

I want you to marry me.

What the fuck?

What the actual fuck?

I stare back into Blake's eyes.

They're still beautiful and blue and dead serious.

I fold my arms over my chest. "You don't even know me."

"I need a wife. And I want it to be you."

"But…"

"We'd start dating, get engaged, get married. After a few months, we'd divorce and go our separate ways."

"Why?"

His eyes turn down. "I can't explain."

"Then I can't agree."

"I'm willing to meet your price. Whatever that means. Think about it. You could graduate college debt free. You could buy an apartment in the Village. You could spend the next ten years in Paris." He pushes himself to his feet. "Whatever you want, I can make it happen."

"I… I've never even had a boyfriend." I press my lips

together. "I don't know how to be a girlfriend, much less a fake wife."

"It's like your job. You smile and convince people you like them."

So he does know something about the service industry.

Blake pushes himself to his feet. "Think it over. Call or text me anytime. I need someone soon, and I want it to be you." He pulls a hundred-dollar bill from his wallet, places it on the table, and leaves.

———

At home, I pour my thoughts into my sketchbook. It's an old habit. One I've ignored for a long, long time.

It feels good putting pen to paper. Even if my drawing is only okay.

I need practice. And training. Art school isn't cheap.

But if I have a blank check?

That could be the end of the mortgage.

It could be Lizzy's tuition.

It could be anything.

God, the thought of destroying the mortgage, of being free of that monthly obligation…

Blake may be an ax murder. He may be a jerk. He may be criminally insane.

But he's not lying about being a billionaire tech mogul.

There are pictures of him in a few dozen news articles. He made quite the stir when he founded Sterling Tech as a teen. He turned down a few million dollars for his company then.

Now, it's worth a thousand times that.

And he owns a lot of it. It's not clear how much, but it's enough that he could pay off the mortgage and finance Lizzy's degree.

But marrying him?

It's ridiculous.

I hide his card in my desk drawer.

————

FOR A WEEK, I IGNORE BLAKE'S CARD. I GO TO WORK. I hustle my ass off. I smile at assholes who leer at my chest and hint that they're staying nearby.

Sunday, I get home late. And lacking tip money.

My shower fails to wash away the tension of the day. Usually, I'm good at grinning and bearing it. But now that I'm considering the possibility of not waiting tables…

Of being able to breathe?

I find Blake's card.

If he's really willing to make all my problems go away…

That must be worth six months of my life.

I have to ask.

Kat: It's Kat. I'm considering your offer but I'm not particularly negotiable.

Blake: I'm at the office.

Kat: I'll take the subway.

Blake: I can send a car.

Kat: I'd rather do it my way.

Blake: As you wish.

He sends the address.

————

BLAKE'S BUILDING IS ALL STEEL AND GLASS. IT'S LITTLE pockets of yellow light framed by silver metal.

It's the tallest skyscraper on the block.

And it's beautiful. Downtown is always quiet at night. It's always still. The only movement is the wind.

I step into the old-money lobby. My heels squeak against the marble floor. My reflection stares back at me from the mirrored walls. She looks tired. Worn.

At least my boobs look good. This is the most flattering dress I own. I dig my lipstick from my purse and apply another coat. It helps add color to my face, but it does nothing to chase the exhaustion from my eyes.

The security guard behind the desk waves me through. I step into the massive elevator and press the **PH** button. Penthouse. Blake's office is the penthouse floor. The entire floor.

I've never been to a penthouse. Do they really exist?

I'm not convinced.

The shiny doors slide together. My reflection stares back at me. She looks even more uncertain than she did a minute ago.

That's no good. I'm here to negotiate.

I'm holding the cards. I'm not sure what Blake sees in me—he could have any woman he wants—but I don't care. He wants me for this *job*. I need to use that to my advantage.

Ding.

The elevator doors slide open.

A bright sign greets me. *Sterling Tech* in luminous white. It's the only light in the lobby.

My heel squeaks against the hardwood floor. This place is beautiful. The steel and glass of the city on one side. The deep blue of the river on the other.

That royal blue—the mix of indigo and fluorescent bulbs— fills the cloudy sky. It never gets dark here. Not really. Certainly not dark enough for the stars to shine.

Yellow light peeks out from under an office door. The one in the corner.

When I move closer, I see the chrome sign. *Blake Sterling.*

I move towards it. Knock softly.

"It's open." Blake's voice flows through the door.

I take a deep breath and turn the handle. It's cold. Metal. Like him. Well, like what I know of him.

He's standing behind his desk. It's one of those trendy desks that changes positions. His computer is like Lizzy's. Two screens. A fancy keyboard. A vertical mouse. A mesh ergonomic chair in the corner.

He moves out from behind the desk.

His eyes find mine. "Have a seat." He nods to the couch to my right, then moves to the bar in the corner. "What do you drink?"

Shit. That's a lot of top-shelf stuff. "What do you have?"

"Anything you want."

"Really? What if I want iced rooibos tea with a hint of lemon and a splash of lime vodka?"

"Then I'll get it." He stares back at me. "Is that what you want?"

No. I want money. And understanding. And his hands on my body.

He's not even touching me and I'm on fire from the proximity. His blue eyes are so intense. And his voice is so strong.

He drips power.

Is he like that when he fucks?

I want to know.

It's ridiculous— I never think about sex. I certainly never think about kinky sex. But my head is filling with all sorts of images of Blake.

Him staring at me with that demanding look in his eyes, ordering me to strip out of my coat. To sit. To wait at his beck and call.

Him pinning my wrists to the bed.

Throwing me against the wall and tearing off my panties.

"Kat?" His voice is soft. "What do you drink?"

"Gin and tonic."

He nods and gets to work mixing drinks.

I take a seat on the plush leather couch, fold my legs, smooth my dress.

Blake crosses the room. He sits next to me. His fingers brush mine as he hands over my cocktail.

The light touch sends desire racing through my body. I want those hands on me. I want it more than I've wanted anything in a long, long time.

It doesn't make any sense.

But the closer he gets, the less I care.

I haven't kissed anyone since high school. I haven't even thought about dating since the accident. And now there's a tall, handsome man next to me. One who looks at me and says he wants to fuck me. Who says it with confidence. Like it's normal to admit your desires in a crowded restaurant.

I take a long sip. The drink is smooth, crisp. Nothing like the gin I have at home.

But it doesn't cool me off.

Not at all.

I try to hold Blake's stare. "Your office is nice."

"Thank you." He takes a long sip of his whiskey. "Would you like a tour?"

"Sure."

After another sip, Blake sets his drink on a side table. He stands and offers his hand.

Again, my body buzzes as our skin connects.

I swallow hard. Suck a deep breath through my teeth. He wants to fuck me. I want to fuck him. We can do that. After we negotiate.

I follow him into the main room. It's still a big, wide open space. The view is still gorgeous. But it doesn't call my attention. Not with him this close.

He reaches for a light switch.

"Don't," I say. "I like the dark."

He raises a brow. *Really?*

"The view goes forever. See?" I move to one of the tall windows and look out at the Hudson. The deep blue water flows away from the city.

There's Midtown, all tall and silver and iconic. The Empire State Building is its usual shade of white. It stands out against the dark sky. It promises all the secrets of the city.

I've lived in Brooklyn all my life. I've always looked at Manhattan from afar. Considered it a place to work or visit. A place I'd never afford.

But here, the view... god, it's intoxicating. I want to move into this office and draw the city twenty-four seven.

"You love New York." His voice is even. Like it's a meaningless observation.

"Of course. I was born and raised here. You don't?"

"I lived upstate until college."

"You prefer the quiet suburbs and the trees?"

"The city is easier."

"That's it? It's easier?"

He nods. "My meetings are here. My office—"

"You spend all your time in your office, so what's it matter?"

"No."

"No?"

He half-smiles. "I also have an office in my apartment."

I laugh. "With windows?"

"They look out on the park."

"And you're too busy looking at your computer screen?"

"Worse."

"What could be worse than that?"

"I have blackout curtains."

That is worse. I'm not sure if I want to laugh or shake my head in horror. Blackout curtains blocking the park— "That's wrong."

He nods. He actually looks happy... happyish. He's teasing me. Maybe. I think.

"I guess you're used to the beauty of the city. But I never get tired of it." The Empire State Building is my favorite. Sure, it's a cliché, but it's famous for a reason. I can't tear my eyes away from it.

Okay, that's not true. I'm staring to keep from staring at Blake. His intensity does something to me.

Or more... it undoes something in me. That part of me insisting on keeping my clothes on.

Ahem.

"Would you like to work here?" he asks.

"Doing what?"

"I can find an entry-level position for you. Any department you want."

"Better for your wife to work in an office than in a restaurant?"

"You want to keep waiting tables?"

"I haven't thought about it." I don't mind my job, but it's not fun either. It doesn't bring me joy or fulfill me in any way.

"Appearances are important."

I stare back at him, trying to figure out where this judgment is coming from. Is it him or someone he knows? It must be someone else. Blake is doing this for someone. Not for himself.

But he doesn't seem like the type who cares what anyone thinks.

I take another long sip. It's still crisp and refreshing. It still fails to cool me off.

Ahem. I need to keep this conversation... well, a conversation. "People treat me differently if I'm in my restaurant gear."

"Worse?"

"Sometimes. Sometimes there's this wage slave solidarity. If I'm at Duane Reade or Staples or something. People will complain about their long day or their bosses if they can tell I'm on my way home from work."

Blake studies me. It's like he's a scientist and I'm an animal at the zoo. His eyes pass over me slowly. "You're a smart girl."

"What convinced you—my cleavage?"

He says nothing.

I just stop myself from rolling my eyes. "Next thing I know, you'll be taking off my clothes and telling me how smart I look in my lingerie."

"I wouldn't waste me breath if you were in lingerie."

I swallow hard. "Of course. I just mean—" I clear my throat. "You don't know me. Or that I'm smart."

"You posted about your college acceptances on Facebook."

"That was a long time ago," I say.

"But it's still there. Even though you haven't updated your page in two years." He makes eye contact. "You were accepted to two Ivy League schools, to three SUNYs, to NYU."

"And?"

"You could have done anything with your life, but you stayed here."

"Do you also know about my parents?"

"Yes."

"Then you know why I'm here." How the hell does he know that? I guess it's easy enough to find with a quick Google search. But still... I don't like it. Even if I did my own sleuthing.

"You value family."

"Yes."

"You're smart."

I open my mouth to object—Blake doesn't know anything about my intellect—but he's already on to his next point.

"You're beautiful."

My cheeks flush. "Thank you."

"You have terms."

I nod.

"What are they? What exactly do you want?"

Chapter Four

You have terms. What are they? What exactly do you want?

It's a complicated question.

For the last three years, I've been surviving. I haven't let myself want anything more than a roof over my head and three hot meals a day.

It's overwhelming, opening myself up to possibilities.

I press my palm against the window. It's cold. Sleek. Unbending. "What would we even be doing?"

His hand brushes my shoulders. Then my cheek. He tilts my chin so we're eye to eye. "I'll introduce you to everyone as my girlfriend. We'll get engaged. Then we'll have a quick wedding. You'll be on my arm at dinners, for weekend trips, at some family functions."

"How am I supposed to convince people I'm in love with you? I don't even know what that looks like."

"Look into my eyes."

I do.

"Like you love me."

Okay... I try to imagine a guy I'll love one day. A real husband. Him hanging my art on the walls, much to my embarrassment. Taking me up to the top of the Empire State Building on my birthday. Kissing me under the cherry blossom trees.

"Perfect."

It is? I'm just thinking… but I'm not going to talk myself out of a huge chunk of change. Still— "I don't want to lie to anyone, much less everyone."

His eyes are on fire. "My intentions are good."

"That and three dollars will buy you a cup of coffee."

"You have integrity."

"Is that a compliment or an insult?"

"What do you think?"

I don't know. He's intense. Hard to read. Appealing.

I finish my last drop of gin and tonic then unbutton my coat. Blake slides it off my shoulders and takes it into his arms.

He leads me back to his office and hangs it on his door.

The space seems smaller.

He's too close.

But then, I want him closer.

I want his body pressed against mine.

"Why do you need me?" I might be talking him out of this, but I have to know. "Why not find some girl who wants to be your girlfriend?"

"That wouldn't be fair."

"Because…"

"She'd have expectations." He slides his suit jacket off his shoulders. "I don't fall in love. I never have, and I never will."

"How old are you?"

"Twenty-six."

"And you're already sure you'll never fall in love?"

"Yes."

Okay… I guess I'm not going to argue with him. He

knows what he wants. I know what I want. And that doesn't include falling for an emotionally unavailable rich guy.

He takes my glass and pours another round of drinks.

I sit on the plush couch and watch him roll his sleeves to his elbows. His forearms are so fucking sexy. How can forearms make me this hot?

I take a deep breath.

Blake moves back to the couch. He hands over my drink and sits next to me. "What are your terms?"

God, it's so hot next to him. My body is buzzing. It's begging me to strip out of this dress and slide into his lap.

But that's lust.

I can survive six months of lust.

Hell, I really, really want six months of lust.

"The mortgage to my apartment." I take a deep breath, attempting my best *I'm as badass and confident as any tech executive* voice. "I want it paid in full."

"Done." He says it like he's agreeing to coffee.

"You don't even know how much is left on it. What if it's three hundred thousand dollars? Or half a million?"

"Send me the bank information, and it's done."

"Like that?"

He nods. "What else?"

I struggle to form a coherent thought. The mortgage, done, like it's nothing.

That can't be possible. That payment has been a thorn in my side for the last three years and it will be gone. Done.

"My sister got into NYU. She's worked hard to keep her grades up. She deserves to go to whatever school she chooses without six figures of student loans."

"Elizabeth?"

"Lizzy. You..."

"She's your friend on Facebook. I didn't look you up, Kat. Not beyond the normal search."

I'm not sure we agree about what constitutes a normal search. But it's not like I can talk.

"Sterling Tech selects scholarship students every year. She placed in a math competition last year. Is she studying STEM?"

"You don't know?"

"Not yet."

I nod. "Computer science or programming. I forget the difference. She wants to study artificial intelligence."

"Done."

"What?"

"We'll offer your sister a scholarship. A hundred percent of her tuition anywhere."

What? I... I must be hearing things. "You..."

"I can make it official right now."

"No, that's okay..." A hundred percent of her tuition. Covered. "What if I say no?"

"You won't." His hand brushes mine. It sends heat racing through my body. "Is there anything else?"

No. That's all I want. It's all I've wanted— Lizzy taken care of.

But I can't admit that. Not when I can get more.

"I... I want to go to college too."

Blake nods. "You'll sign a prenup. When we divorce, you'll get a million dollars, less what's left on your mortgage."

"A million dollars?" I... Uh...

"Kat. You okay?"

No. This... this is absurd. I stare back at Blake. "A million dollars?"

He nods.

"But... why?"

"I told you. I need someone and I want you."

But… uh…

I take a deep breath and exhale slowly.

Blake is worth a lot. A million dollars is nothing to him. Not compared to the price tag of a regular divorce.

This is what makes sense for him.

It's logical.

It's actually reasonable.

His fingers brush my wrist. "You can stay at your place for now, but I'll need you to move in soon."

"No. I'm staying with my sister."

"Fine. You'll stay with her until we marry."

I nod. I'd rather stay with Lizzy forever, but it wouldn't look right.

"I'll pay your expenses. Starting tonight."

"That isn't necessary."

"Kat. You're my girlfriend now. We're madly in love. Do you really think I'd force my girlfriend to fend for herself?"

"Yeah. It's called independence. You have heard of feminism?"

He chuckles. "You have heard of my charity?"

"No. That's a douchey thing to say."

"It's for domestic violence victims."

"Oh. That's… less douchey." And unexpected.

"It's okay. I know how I appear."

"It doesn't bother you?"

"Most people's opinions don't matter to me."

"So then why are you—"

"Some people's do." He stares back into my eyes. "I'll send over a credit card tomorrow. Treat yourself. Buy whatever you'll need to feel comfortable."

"I'm comfortable." I'm not exactly sleeping on

Egyptian cotton and dining on steak, but I am comfortable enough.

"You're a beautiful girl, Kat. I want to tear off that dress. But there are people in my life who aren't nearly so…"

"They're judgmental assholes?"

He half-smiles. "Exactly."

"And you keep them in your life because?"

"Because they have other traits I value. You're more than welcome to show up to an event in jeans and a t-shirt. She…" He shakes his head. "But you'll get looks. If you don't want that kind of attention—"

"I get it." All his rich friends look down on the poor H&M shoppers. I guess I can do a little shopping spree if it's for keeping up appearances. I could certainly use new clothes. I haven't bought much since the accident.

His fingers brush the hem of my dress. "I'm never going to love you, Kat. But while we're together, I'll make sure you don't want for anything."

"What about… it's not like I can have a secret boyfriend on the side," I say.

"You want to fuck me."

"Yes." My cheeks flush. "Not necessarily today. But eventually."

"This part is real." He leans a little closer. His hands slide over the sides of my chest. Over my shoulders. "But you need to understand something, Kat."

"What?"

His eyes fix on mine. "I do things a certain way."

I swallow hard.

"I'm always in control."

"You mean… with, um…"

"When we're together, you're going to follow every one of my commands."

"Oh. I… um… I've never…"

"You're a virgin?"

"Yes." My cheeks flush. I swallow hard. "I don't date."

"Good. I want to be your first."

My chest flushes.

"But I have to warn you—"

"Yeah?"

"I'm going to wreck you for other men."

I open my mouth to speak, but words refuse to fall. He's so… I… uh.

"I'll say it a thousand times. I'm not paying for sex. I'm going to fuck you because you want me. If you don't, if you change your mind—"

"I do. I… I want to try it that way."

"Good. I want you tied to my bed." He pulls the strap of my dress aside slowly. "I want you at my mercy."

I want to be at his mercy. It's scary how much I want to be at his mercy.

I barely know him.

But I want him in control of my body.

It's scary how much I want him in control of my body.

I lean into his touch.

His lips brush my neck.

It's soft. Tender. Hot as hell.

I let my eyelids flutter together. I surrender to the sensations forming in my body.

Blake pulls my dress off my shoulders. He cups my breast, over my bra. Kisses a trail from my lips to my collarbone.

Objections form and dissolve on my tongue. I force myself to hold onto one of them. "We haven't agreed to anything."

"Is there anything else you want?"

"How long will this be? Is it indefinite?"

"Six months. A year, max." The strength drops from his voice. It's hurting. Something about this hurts him.

"Is there an out?"

"I'll only accept a full commitment."

A year with a man I barely know.

That's a huge gamble. But it's worth it for the end of that awful mortgage. For an education for Lizzy. And for me.

A million dollars.

That's enough to travel the world. To get a fine arts degree. To start my own comic studio.

That's... everything.

"Okay." I offer my hand.

He shakes. "I'll have my lawyer draft a contract. We'll sign tomorrow."

"Okay."

He stares deeply into my eyes. "This will move fast. You'll need to be ready by next week."

"I can do that."

"There will be cameras when we announce our engagement. You can wear what you want, but if you need help finding something, my assistant—"

"Okay." I nod. As much as I don't like the idea of being a doll, I don't know fancy parties. I don't want to look out of place. It's going to be hard enough convincing the world I'm Blake Sterling's girlfriend looking the part.

"I'll pick you up Saturday morning at nine a.m."

Jesus, that's early for someone who works mostly nights. "As long as you bring coffee."

He brushes my hair from my shoulder. "When you're with me, I'll take care of everything."

"Coffee?"

He nods.

"Food?"

He nods.

"What else?"

He runs his hands over my bra. "Clothing."

"Oh, that stands for clothing, does it?"

He nods.

His lips close over mine. It's magic. Like one of those scenes in a movie where fireworks explode over a pretty pink castle.

His lips are soft. Sweet. Commanding.

I run my hands through his hair. It's short. Thick. Neat.

His hand slips into my bra.

His fingers brush my nipple.

Fuck, that feels good.

I'm shaking. It's been a long, long time since anyone has touched me like this.

No. No one has touched me like this, like I'm a gift they want to unwrap.

I groan against his lips. Slide into his lap. Details fade to the back of my mind. They're so much less important than my body against his.

I dig my hands into the soft fabric of his shirt until I can feel the hard contours of his muscles.

Desire overwhelms me.

I've never wanted anyone this much. I never even knew you could want someone this much.

He tugs at my dress, but he's pulling it back on, back over my shoulders.

My head is spinning. He's not... but he... he can't stop now.

I'm pent up.

I'm going to explode.

"It's late," he says.

I blink a few times, but he's still staring at me with that

same impenetrable look on his face. "What else?" I ask. "Besides food, coffee, and clothing?"

"You'll come when you're with me, Kat. I'll make sure of it."

"But not tonight?"

"Not yet." He shifts off the couch. "I'll walk you out."

"I can walk myself."

I reach for my coat, but Blake is already holding it.

His fingers brush against my neck as he helps me into my coat.

Heat floods my body. It's everywhere. I can barely stand.

But we're not having sex tonight.

I... I don't get it.

I squeeze my purse. This is for the best. I've only known him a week.

Blake walks me to the elevator. He waves his key card in front of the door. "I'll have one made for you."

"Sure."

"My driver will take you home. If you need anything, call."

"I'll be fine."

His stare is intense. "Anything."

My stomach flutters. He can't mean sex. He just sent me out of his office with my dress falling off my shoulders.

I clear my throat and step into the elevator. "Goodnight."

He nods.

The doors slide closed, and I finally exhale. Almost home. It's a quick ride to the ground floor. As promised, there's a sleek limo waiting out front.

The man standing in front of it nods. "You must be Ms. Wilder."

I nod.

"Jordan." He offers his hand.

I shake.

"It's lovely to meet you." He opens the door to the backseat and motions *after you*.

I slide inside.

It's not like the limo I took to Junior Prom. It's sleek. Dark. Black leather and soft suede.

The minibar is stocked with tiny bottles of top-shelf stuff—brands I've never heard of. I crack open a mini bottle of gin and take a long sip. It's good.

But it's not doing anything to help with my frustration.

It's only winding up the tension inside me.

Letting down all the walls protecting me from my libido.

The door closes. Jordan speaks into his earpiece. "Understood, sir." The partition rolls up with a quiet whir.

I'm as good as alone.

My phone rings in my purse. Blake. What the hell?

I answer. "Hello."

"I said anything, Kat."

"I was there."

"You want something."

My heart races. Of course I want something. He's not an idiot. "Yes."

"So ask for it."

Heat rushes through me, collecting between my legs. "I…"

"Take off your underwear. I want to hear you come."

Chapter Five

My cheeks flush, but I can't blame the alcohol.

I'm hot everywhere.

Take off your underwear. I want to hear you come.

I… Uh…

I can't strip in the back of a limo.

Even if I'm more or less alone.

"Kat?" His voice is a command. It's *now*.

I let out a heavy exhale. "I can't."

"You want to come?"

"Yes."

"Put the phone on speaker."

I do. I set it on the bench next to me. The limo is already moving. It's not far to my place. We're right by the Brooklyn Bridge.

Is ten minutes enough time for this?

It's not like I take my time when I masturbate.

But this is different.

It's for him.

"Kat." His voice drops an octave.

"It's on speaker." I squeeze my knees together. It does nothing to temper the heat racing through me. I'm achy.

I can't believe it, but I want to strip right here.

I want to touch myself for his listening pleasure.

His voice flows from the speakers. "Don't make me ask again."

My fingers curl around my panties. I lift my hips and slide them to my ankles.

"Done," I breathe.

"Good girl."

It should annoy me, but it doesn't. It makes me hotter. It makes me even more desperate for release.

"Spread your legs."

I slide my knees apart. It shifts my pelvis up. Cold air hits my tender flesh. It wakes up my nerves. It winds me tighter.

"Take off your bra," he demands.

I roll my dress to my chest, unhook my bra, and slide it off my shoulders.

My nipples tighten.

I'm stripping for a voice on the phone. No, for Blake. For a man with all the money and power in the world.

I like that he has the power to snap his fingers and destroy me.

I like that I'm out of my fucking mind.

I want to forget the rest of the world. I want to forget everything but his demands.

"Good." His voice gets heavier. "Play with your nipples."

I squeeze my eyes closed and imagine him here, touching me the way he touched me in the office.

Slowly, my thumbs brush my nipples. I draw circles. Soft ones. Then hard ones.

A groan falls off my lips. Then another. It's almost like

he's touching me. But, fuck, I really wish it was him touching me.

His breath gets heavier.

Needier.

He's the one in control, but I'm doing something to him too. I'm driving him out of his mind too.

"Bring your hand to your thigh," he says. "But don't touch your cunt. Not yet."

I stroke the inside of my thigh. Closer and closer and closer. But not quite there.

My breath speeds. Desire courses through me. I need release. I'm desperate.

"Kat."

"Yes."

"I said not yet."

I move my hand back to my knee, tracing circles around it. I can't wait any longer. I need to come. I've never needed to come this badly.

"Back to your thighs," he says.

No. Now. I need release now.

It's torture dragging my hand to my thigh. Stroking my skin as softly as I can stand it.

But it's a beautiful torture.

"Now," Blake says. "Slowly."

My fingertips brush my clit.

It's intense. I'm wound up. Sensitive.

I do it a little harder.

A little longer.

Fuck.

That feels so good.

A groan falls off my lips.

I lean back on the bench seat.

And I touch myself with that same speed. That same pressure.

Then faster.

Harder.

Mmmm.

I need to come. I need my groans in his ear. I need everything.

His voice gets hard. "Slowly."

No. Faster. Harder. Now.

I force myself to slow. I force my touch to lighten. My fingers brush my clit with soft circles. It's agony. Delicious, beautiful agony.

Pleasure wells up inside me. My sex tightens. I'm close. So fucking close.

I keep up those slow circles. I wind myself up. Tighter and tighter and tighter.

His breath gets heavier. Needier.

He's sitting there in his office, listening to me touch myself.

And I…

I really fucking like that.

It deepens the ache inside me.

My hand takes over. I move faster. Harder.

Pleasure pools in my core.

The tension is too much too take. I'm so close.

"Come for me, Kat."

Yes.

My next stroke is faster. Harder. It only takes a few flicks of my finger, and I'm there. Agony fades into bliss. Pure, deep, blinding bliss.

The tension inside me unfurls as I come. My groans echo around the limo. Pleasure spills to my fingers and toes. I feel so fucking good.

I collapse on the bench seat. Spent. Satisfied.

"Fucking beautiful," he growls.

I try to find words, but they refuse to climb my throat.

"I'll let you go." Satisfaction drips into his voice. "Sweet dreams."

"You too."

The phone clicks.

I catch my breath, then I push myself up. Get back into my dress. Stuff my cell into my purse.

I'm not in control of this.

Not at all.

It's terrifying.

But it's thrilling too.

———

AT TEN THE NEXT MORNING, THERE'S A LOUD KNOCK ON the door. I nearly drop the graphic novel in my hands. The slick plastic cover—the same on every other library book I've ever borrowed—is slippery.

Lizzy is at school.

Nobody comes by this early.

That must be Blake's assistant. With our paperwork.

I rise to my feet and move to the door. "Hello."

"Hello, Ms. Wilder. I have something for you."

I pull open the door.

A friendly man in a suit smiles at me. He hands over a sleek black briefcase. And a cup of coffee. "Mr. Sterling said you'd appreciate this."

Blake is sending me coffee.

From his assistant, but still.

I take a long sip. It's more bitter than I like it, but it's still good. Rich. Strong. Bold. Like him.

"Thank you." I nod goodbye and move back inside the house.

I fix my coffee with a little cream and sugar and take another sip. There. That's perfect.

43

I guess Blake did say he'd take care of me.

It's a strange thought. For the last three years, I haven't let anyone help me. I've been taking care of myself. And of Lizzy.

Half of me wants to let go of every ounce of that control.

The other half wants to hold onto it as tightly as I can.

I take another sip of my coffee. I let it warm me from inside out. I let it push my thoughts away.

This is coffee.

It doesn't have to mean more than coffee.

But what's in this briefcase—

The paperwork makes everything official.

A non-disclosure agreement forbids me from sharing details of our arrangement with anyone.

There's a credit card in my name. The bill goes right to Blake.

The contract stipulates our terms.

Starting today, I am Blake's doting girlfriend. I'll clear my schedule for him whenever he needs me. He gets approval of all my public appearances and social media.

Within the next three months, we'll marry. I'll sign a prenup. He decides when we'll divorce, but it will be by the end of next year. I'll get a million dollars for my trouble.

He'll pay off the mortgage as an advance.

My incidentals go on the credit card. They're to be "reasonable."

But I'm pretty sure Blake's idea of a reasonable allowance ends in a lot of zeros.

No more shitty generic coffee.

No more library books.

No more crappy running shoes.

No more serving rich assholes.

I'll be smiling at them instead. But at least they'll be the ones sucking up to me.

I pick up my cheap Bic pen and I sign on the dotted line.

I'm signing away my freedom.

But I'm getting a hell of a lot in return.

———

I PUT IN MY TWO WEEKS' NOTICE.

I tell Lizzy I'm dating a new guy. A rich guy.

She presses for details, but I keep my lips zipped. I don't know what to tell her. I don't want to lie to my sister. But I need to say something. She needs to know I'm quitting my job because we're set.

I think it over all week.

I fail to come up with a cover story.

Saturday morning, Blake's limo pulls up at nine on the dot.

Thankfully, Lizzy is still asleep. I leave a note on the kitchen table and make my way outside.

It's a beautiful day. Yellow sun. Bright blue sky. Crisp, clear air. The skyline is beautiful. Awake. Alive. Inviting.

Jordan is standing on the stoop. He nods hello. "Nice to see you, Ms. Wilder." He opens the door and motions *after you*.

I slide inside.

Blake is on the opposite bench. He's wearing slacks and a blue, collared shirt. His sleeves are rolled to his elbows.

He almost looks casual. But in an untouchable Blake kind of way.

"Good morning." He nods.

"Good morning." I try to pry my eyes from his forearms, but I fail. God, he really has nice forearms. And I can't bring myself to look him in the eyes. Not after what we did… what *I* did last time I was in this car.

He hands over a cup of coffee. "How do you take it?"

"Cream and sugar."

He holds up a nondescript paper bag. "I have a few different options."

I grab it. It's warm. And it smells like—

I tear it open.

Bagels.

Plain. Sesame. Onion. Cinnamon raisin.

I grab the latter and pull it apart. "My favorite." I dig out cream and sugar. But how am I going to fix my coffee while we're moving?

"Here." Blake offers his hand.

I nod.

He takes my coffee and my packets. He sets the cup on the bench seat and peels the plastic lid open. Somehow, he fixes it without spilling a drop.

His fingers brush mine as he returns my java.

It's the same as last time. My body lights up. It wants those hands.

But then…

Maybe today.

Maybe I'll get them today.

"Thank you." I take a long sip of my coffee. It's perfect. This is the perfect breakfast.

He takes the plain bagel and tears off half. "It's going to be a long day."

I nod and take a bite. Mmm. Chewy, sweet, spicy perfection.

"Let me know if it's too much."

"What?"

His eyes pass over me slowly. "Everything."

———

BLAKE'S ASSISTANT, ASHLEIGH, A PRETTY BLACK WOMAN IN a designer outfit, guides us through an exclusive department store. She fills her arms with expensive things and leads me into a fitting room.

It starts with underwear. She measures me for a bra and brings a dozen in my size. Some are sexy, lacy things. Some are comfortable. Practical.

Then it's cocktail dresses. The first is backless and black. It's smooth. Sleek. Expensive.

Ashleigh takes a long look at me. She cocks her head to one side, assessing me.

It's weird. I feel like a doll.

But I also feel like I'm on *America's Next Top Model*, waiting for the judges to assign a look for my makeover.

You'd look fierce with highlights. We need to bring out those eyes of yours. Sometimes they look green. And sometimes they look blue. But they always look gorgeous. And I want them to pop.

"What do you think?" she asks.

I take in my reflection. The dress is beautiful. It hangs off my slim body, creating the illusion of soft curves.

I usually curse my slender frame. Between running and stress non-eating, I stay pretty thin.

It's a popular look in Manhattan, but it leaves me lacking in the T&A department.

"I love it," I say.

She beams. "Perfect. Let's stick with this for the party. Black is always classy. Blake gave me specific instructions. He wants to make sure you're comfortable with your wardrobe. I have another dozen dresses for you. And a bunch more casual wear. Or you can start looking yourself."

I don't know anything about clothes. I should accept

her help. I should learn how to accept help. "Let's see them."

She smiles. "Excellent." She calls out to the main room, where Blake is waiting. "Mr. Sterling, we're going to be a while. You may want to get a coffee."

"I'll wait," he calls back.

She shakes her head. Lowers her voice. "He always needs everything just so." She steps backwards. "Strip for me, sweetheart. I'll be right back."

I nod. It's strange, stripping for a stranger, but I'm getting used to it.

I strip and hang the dress.

A few moments later, Ashleigh returns. She helps me into another dress. A long, purple one, with a deep v-neckline.

It's racy. Sexy. Daring.

It's the kind of person I want to be. "I love it."

She smiles. "Perfect. But I do need a few more, ahem, conservative things. Mr. Sterling's sister is very…"

"Judgmental?"

She nods. "Keep that between us. Even if he knows better than anyone."

She helps me into the next dress—powder pink chiffon, knee length, fitted, scoop neckline. She points to a pair of strappy silver sandals.

I step into them and take in my reflection.

God, it's like something out of a dream. Like I'm Cinderella getting ready for the ball.

Ashleigh tilts her head, taking me in again. She motions to my hair. "What about this?"

"What about it?" I've never done anything with my hair. It just hangs there. Limp, flat, refusing to hold a curl. It's not a particularly pretty shade of medium brown, but it's not bad either. It suits my complexion.

"We can style all sorts of fun updos. Ponytails are always chic. Or a bun. Or we could try something bolder. These dresses, they're loud. You want your hair and makeup as loud. Do you know how to do makeup?"

Uh… "A little."

"I'll make an appointment for you. For lessons."

"No. I'll schedule it." That actually sounds fun. I can take Lizzy. She's way more into girly stuff.

"Perfect." Ashleigh motions to my dress. "Strip for me again, sweetie. I have more for you."

I do.

She leaves and returns with another outfit. A regular outfit. Or rich people regular. Designer jeans. A cashmere sweater. A camisole that costs more than all my shoes combined.

I try it on. Then another similar outfit. Then another.

We go like that forever. An hour at least. Or maybe two.

By the time I'm done, I'm tired and hungry. My dreams of judges complimenting my smize (a smile with your eyes) are gone. I am a doll. I exist for someone else's benefit.

She pulls my dress too tight.

"I got it," I snap.

She bites her lip and forces a smile. *Difficult customer.* "Maybe you'd like to talk to Mr. Sterling."

"Okay." Maybe I'll ask why I need a new wardrobe. Even though I know the answer.

She leaves and returns with him.

The space is too small for the three of us.

But then I want him closer.

I want every inch of him pressed against every inch of me.

Blake's eyes find mine. "Take half an hour, Ashleigh."

"Mr. Sterling, your lunch meeting—"

"I have time."

She clears her throat. "You have thirty minutes. Exactly."

"Go." He shoots her a demanding look.

She obeys.

So I guess I'm not the only woman in his life who follows orders.

He pulls the curtain closed behind her.

The entire dressing room is reserved for us.

It's just me and Blake here.

Even so, I feel exposed.

Blake's fingers graze my hips.

He turns me around so I'm facing the dressing room's mirror.

I watch the reflection as he unzips my dress. It slides off my shoulders and falls to the floor.

Here I am, nearly naked, and he's fully dressed.

He has all the power here.

It doesn't annoy me.

It makes my sex clench.

"What are we…" I sigh as his fingers graze my lower back. "What are we doing?"

"We have thirty minutes."

"To…"

"You're not that naive, Kat. You know exactly what I'm doing."

"Oh."

"I'm not going to fuck you."

My teeth sink into my lip. I can't believe how badly I want him fucking me in this tiny dressing room. It's driving me wild.

"But I am going to make you come." He unhooks my bra and slides it off my shoulders. "Now plant your hands on the mirror and do exactly what I say."

Chapter Six

My heart thuds against my chest.

I force myself to face the mirror.

To plant my palms against the slick surface.

"Watch." He strokes my cheek with the back of my hand.

I stare back at his reflection. I watch as he drags his fingertips down my neck, across my chest, over my sides.

He moves closer.

His lips brush my neck.

A soft kiss.

Then he's sucking on my skin.

He drags his hands over my stomach, my chest, my thighs.

Slowly, his hands settle on my breasts.

He toys with my nipples with his thumbs.

He draws a line of kisses up my neck and over my shoulders.

Then he's pressing his crotch against my ass.

He's hard.

I can feel him through his slacks. Though my panties.

And I want that. I've never touched a guy before. Not below the waist.

But I want my hands around him.

I want him in my mouth.

Inside me.

I want him in ways I've only read about.

Fuck, his fingers feel good on my skin.

I lean into his touch.

Soak up every flick of his thumbs. Every soft circle. All the heat of his mouth.

Pleasure pools in my body. His touch makes me achy. I shift my hips, rubbing my ass against his crotch until he's groaning.

His hands go right to my hips. "Stay."

The command makes my sex clench.

I nod. I want to stay for him. I want to follow every one of his orders.

He drags his hands over the waistband of my panties. Then lower. Lower. Lower.

He strokes me, pressing the silky fabric against my clit. It's smooth. Slick.

Too smooth.

Too soft.

I need more. Harder. Everything.

But he's patient.

I arch my back a half inch. It presses his hand against me. But it's not enough.

He doesn't relent.

He keeps his touch soft. Slow.

He gets me shaking.

Panting.

Finally, he slides my panties to my knees.

I kick them off my feet.

I'm naked.

And he's dressed.

And the sight of us makes me wetter. Hotter.

He makes eye contact through the mirror. "You're nervous."

"A little."

"Do you remember what I said last time?"

"You said a lot of things."

"Not true." He smiles. Just barely.

"A few things." I take a deep breath and study his expression. It doesn't offer any insight. "About the terms or about how if I want something, you'll give it to me? But last time, you sent me home. I know I didn't ask, but you obviously knew."

"Kat."

I bring my gaze back to his. "Yeah?"

"What do you want?"

A shiver passes through me. "You."

He places his palm on my lower back. "How?"

"You said we're not having sex."

"I said I'm not fucking you right now."

My lips press together. I hate this edict. It's awful.

"But I will. Tonight."

"So…"

"How do you want to come, Kat? On my lips? On my hand? On yours?"

"Uh…" I try to find the words to respond, but I can't. I'm too caught up in his dirty talking. How does he do that?

"How?"

"I don't know."

"You want me to decide?"

I do. I nod.

"Good. I'm in charge of this. Of your body. Of your orgasm."

My breath catches in my throat. I should hate it, but I don't. I want that.

My body goes into overdrive. It's pleading for mercy. For release. For everything.

"I want that," I say.

"Good."

He slides his arm around my waist and holds my body against his.

The fabric of his suit is rough against my skin. But it feels good. Like exactly the friction I need.

His hands hover over my inner thighs. His expression stays patient. Like he could wait a million years for me to do as he asks.

A sigh escapes my lips. Half irritated, half desperate. My body is buzzing, shaking. He needs to touch me. Now.

"Please," I say.

Nothing.

I press my palms into the mirror, undoing the arch in my back.

His fingertips brush my inner thighs. Barely. It's enough to send a wave of pleasure straight to my sex.

He strokes my thighs a little harder. A little higher.

I press my eyes closed, taking in every touch, every breath.

His fingers brush my clit.

Fuck.

That feels so good.

Want races through me. Yes. There.

He brings one hand to my chest and toys with my nipples. I arch my back, pressing my crotch against his hand.

A sigh of pleasure falls from my lips.

My body is pure anticipation.

My universe is pure anticipation.

Blake draws circles around my nipples with his fingertips.

His other hand strokes me. It's so soft I can barely feel it. But that only winds me tighter.

A moan escapes my lips.

He strokes me. Harder. Faster. Then it's perfect. Yes.

I groan. It's too loud. But I don't care.

I don't care about anything but his hands on my skin.

I let my eyelids fall together.

My teeth sink into my lip.

He strokes me, faster, harder, more. An orgasm rises up inside me.

Almost.

There.

The next flick of his fingers sends me over the edge.

The pressure inside me unravels.

It spreads to my fingers and toes.

My world goes white. Nothing but pure, deep bliss.

I blink my eyes open. I watch him watch me.

He's intense. In control. Demanding.

And satisfied.

I can feel his cock against my ass.

He's hard.

But he's satisfied too.

I… I don't quite understand.

But I'm not complaining.

———

I SPEND THE AFTERNOON IN THE MAKEUP DEPARTMENT, attempting to understand the YouTube tutorials that load on my phone. A salesgirl takes pity on me and teaches me how to do a full face.

I even manage to recreate the look myself.

Sort of.

Even so, I make an appointment to come back for a proper lesson. With Lizzy. It's on an afternoon I know she's free.

I meet Blake for dinner at Lotus Blossom, the restaurant that rejected my job application without a second glance.

He makes a show of parading in front of the asshole manager who ignored me.

The place is packed, but we get a table instantly. It's right by the window. With a gorgeous view of Fifth Avenue.

The city is as beautiful as always. Blue bleeds into yellow and cream.

Blake slides his arm around my waist. It's a protective gesture. Sweet, even. But is that for show? Or does he really want to keep me safe?

I'm not sure.

He pulls out my chair. "After you."

I sit, fold my legs, press my palms into my chiffon dress. The pretty pink one. I feel like a fairytale princess in it.

Blake takes his seat. Opens his menu. Takes a quick glance.

I bury myself in mine. Anything to avoid conversation. I have no idea what I want to say to him. We've got nothing in common. But he's going to be my husband.

It's weird.

A waiter drops off water.

I read the menu three times, give up on using it as a distraction, and down my entire glass instead.

Blake's eyes find mine.

I stare back. Try to force a smile. I want to get lost in his eyes. I want to go back to his place and fuck him senseless.

"Kat."

"Yes?"

"This only works if we're honest with each other."

"I'm honest."

"You're annoyed."

"I'm tired. Hungry. Wanting…" I clear my throat. "My sister hasn't answered any of my texts. I don't know where she is. Your assistant seems to think my hair isn't good enough, and my face is sticky from all this makeup."

He nods like my complaints are reasonable.

Maybe they are. I'm lucky, but I'm tired too.

This is surreal.

My new clothes are beautiful. I'm now the proud owner of a bunch of high-end makeup. And I'm dining with the sexiest man in the room.

I fold my arms in my lap. "You like me all cleaned up?"

"Yes, but I liked you before." He reaches across the table, offering his hand. "Look at me, Kat."

"I am."

"Like you love me."

I draw a circle on his palms with my fingertips. Make my eyes as big as they'll get. Part my lips like I'm desperate to kiss him. "Like that?"

"It's good. But I need more."

I slide back into my chair, pulling my arms to my sides. Gaga couples can't be gaga all the time. Especially not when they're starving and waiting to order.

People get into fights. Isn't the passion the whole appeal of a passionate love affair? Passion isn't just long, desperate kisses and bodies thrashing together in ecstasy. It's screaming and fighting and slapping too.

"Kat."

"Yes?"

"Have you ever loved anyone?"

"No. I already told you that." And he said my look was perfect. What's changed in the last week? I dig my nails into my thighs. "Maybe you should show me what you want."

He slides out of his seat and kneels next to me.

Heads turn.

He is in the perfect position to propose. He lifts himself up, so he's a few inches from me. His eyes get wide, soft. His lips curl into a tiny smile.

Warmth spreads through my body. It's not like before. It's not a desperate heat. It's in my chest, not between my legs.

Blake takes my hand and rubs the pad of his thumb against the skin between my thumb and forefinger.

I look away—this is too intimate—but he reaches for me.

His fingertips graze my cheek. It's a feather-light touch.

It makes me warm everywhere.

It makes me dizzy.

It's bright in here. Loud. But, somehow, I can't hear or see anything except him. I can't help but stare into his eyes. That look is pure affection. It's love. I almost believe it. No, not almost.

I do believe it. Warmth swims to my stomach and cheeks. He loves me.

But he doesn't.

This is all pretend.

He leans closer. Closer.

His lips are an inch from mine. It's not like before. It's not carnal.

It's sweet.

His hands slide into my hair. My eyes flutter closed. I forget everything except the feeling of Blake's lips.

They're soft. Sweet. With the faint taste of lemon.

58

He pulls back and brings his mouth to my ear. "It's pretend, Kat. It's all pretend."

I nod like I believe him. "I know."

"Can you do that?"

I don't know. But I already agreed to it. I nod.

He shifts back to his seat. His eyes stay glued to mine. "Good."

"What?"

"The way you're looking at me. I believe you."

"Oh, yeah, of course." I press my palms against the chiffon, but the fabric does nothing to absorb the sweat. We nearly had sex in a dressing room. I shouldn't be nervous over a kiss and a few sweet glances.

But I am.

I am staring at him like I love him.

And I'm going to keep doing it without falling in love with him.

Somehow.

Chapter Seven

The limo ride back to Blake's place is slow and not at all fun.

He quizzes me on the biographic details of his life. It's not personal. It's facts, plain and simple.

His father died when Blake was fourteen, he went to Columbia at sixteen on a scholarship he didn't need, he graduated at nineteen. His company was up and running by the time he could drink legally in New York State.

It's like reading a Wikipedia entry. Even when he tells me about his hobbies, he lists then without tone or joy.

Blake plays chess and watches sci-fi films, but they don't seem to make him happy. Is Blake ever happy? I don't know.

He claims he loves his daily workouts.

That he gets all the satisfaction he needs from work.

That he takes great pleasure in cooking elaborate dinners in his free time.

But I'm not sure I believe it.

Blake never looks happy. Not with me.

By the time we arrive at his building, I'm grieving for the loss of joy in his life.

I've had it hard the last few years. But I do find pockets of happiness. Brunch with Lizzy. A great graphic novel. Running around city streets. Catching snow on my tongue. Lingering under the cherry trees. Sketching.

He leads me through his building's sleek lobby. Straight to the shiny silver elevator in the back.

He hits the *penthouse* button.

The doors slide together.

The elevator moves slowly. There isn't enough space in here for how much I want him. It's sucking up every ounce of oxygen.

Finally, the doors slide open.

We move through the hallway. He pulls out a key, unlocks his apartment door, and holds it open for me.

"Thank you." I step inside.

It's huge.

Four times the size of our place. It reeks of money.

Hardwood floors. Black leather couch, stainless steel appliances, thick oak table, floor-to-ceiling windows.

There's a balcony. An enormous balcony overlooking the park. I move towards it without thinking.

"Careful," he says. "It's cold out."

Somehow, Blake beats me to the sliding door. He pulls it open. Cold air rushes inside.

My dress blows in the wind. It would be gorgeous in a panel—a girl alone on the balcony. Or a girl with a beautiful man, her dress blowing behind her, his hand under her chin, his eyes on her.

Like he loves her.

Like she loves him.

But that part is fake.

Blake reaches up to turn the heating lamp on. It glows bright orange.

I move towards the edge of the balcony. The railing is cold against my hands. Against my waist.

I peer over the edge.

That's a long way down.

My knees wobble. His hands go right to my sides.

He pulls me backwards. "Careful."

"Girl overboard. That would raise your insurance. And the whole death could be an accident or suicide or homicide thing." His swanky pad would be perfect on an episode of *Law & Order*. The setup is classic. The rich guy who always gets what he wants. The pretty young woman found dead in a cocktail dress and heels. A wisecrack about an unfortunate ending to a party. Hell, it writes itself.

His hands dig into my sides. "I'd hate to lose you."

"Because I'm useful?"

His hands slide down my hips, all the way to the hem of my dress. "Because I'd hate to lose you." His fingers skim the outside of my thigh. "You can admit you're nervous."

"I'm just kidding."

He drags his fingers up my thigh, until they reach the outside of my panties. "You're scared."

My eyelids press together.

The wind rushes around me. It blows my hair in every direction.

Yes, I'm scared.

But it's not the sex that scares me.

It's everything else.

The possibility of falling in love with him. Of losing track of what's pretend and what's real.

Of him breaking my heart.

"Kat?"

"A little."

He drags his lips over my neck. Slides his hand under my dress. His fingers dig into the straps of my thong. "Have you ever heard of a safeword?"

"Yes. Do we really need that?" Is it getting that intense? I'm not sure if I can handle anything intense enough to require a safeword.

"It never hurts." His breath warms my earlobe. "I'm going to make you feel so much that you're going to want to scream *no, I can't take any more*."

"How do you know that?"

"I've done this before."

I can't argue with that. And it never hurts to be cautious. "Okay."

"How about *chess*?"

I can't help but laugh. "Chess?"

"Yes."

"Because it's the only thing you do besides work?"

"Because it's easy to remember and hard to confuse." His fingertips graze my neck. "Do you have another word in mind?"

"No, I guess chess is fine."

"Good." He brings one hand to my hip. The other goes to my lower back.

His fingers close around my zipper.

Slowly, he undoes my dress and pushes it off my shoulders.

Cold air hits my skin, but it does nothing to temper the heat racing through me. I'm on display for anyone on a nearby balcony. Anyone at the park.

For him.

The thought makes me hotter.

There's a power in being looked at. I never noticed it before. But I can feel Blake's gaze on my skin. Even with him behind me.

He unhooks my bra and tosses it aside.

He slides his hand over my chest, cupping my breast and rubbing his thumb against my nipple.

Mmm. He's way too good at this.

I lick my lips. Tilt my head. Press my neck against his mouth.

He scrapes his teeth against my skin. It's soft. A tiny burst of pain. But that only wakes up my nerves. It makes everything sharper.

Blake lets out a low grunt as his hands find the edges of my panties. He bends to slide them to my ankles.

I step out of them. Somehow, I stay upright. These heels are sturdy. Comfortable even.

"I'm in charge now, Kat. All you need to do is feel."

My sex tightens. My body gets light.

The thought of giving up control terrifies me.

And thrills me.

I... I don't know if I can do this.

But I want it so badly.

It's on my tongue. *Chess.*

It's a strange thought. And a strange word. But I can't give up now. I have to do this. I want to.

"I... what if I can't handle it?" I ask.

"You can."

I don't know why, but I believe him.

"Do you want me to fuck you?"

"Yes."

"Do you trust me with your body?"

I don't know. "I think so."

"Then listen. And breathe. Okay?"

I nod. I can do that. Probably.

His hand slides around my waist. "Come with me."

I follow him inside.

He closes the door behind us. Stops. Stares at me like I'm a painting hanging in a museum.

He studies every inch of my body with wide-eyed appreciation.

I've never felt particularly beautiful or desirable.

But I do right now.

Right now, I feel like the most beautiful woman in the universe.

His gaze meets mine. "Are you on birth control?"

"No," I say. "I don't date."

"I'll make you an appointment."

"I can handle it."

"I'm clean. I'll send you the test results if you'd like."

"Okay."

He leads me into a bedroom.

It can't be his. Everything is too clean, too warm, too feminine. The bed is dressed in white cotton sheets. A chiffon curtain covers the window. It's the same pale pink as my dress.

Blake opens the drawer and pulls out a condom. "Sit on the bed."

My head thinks up all sorts of objections, but my body cuts through every one of them.

His voice gets low. Rough. "Now."

I plant my ass on the bed. It's firm. An expensive foam mattress.

Palms flat behind me, I lean back.

Blake's brows raise. His gaze moves over me slowly.

"You're fucking gorgeous." He reaches into the dresser and pulls out something black. "You own my thoughts, Kat."

"I do?"

He nods. "I keep drifting off during meetings. Thinking

about splitting you in half when I should be thinking about numbers. It's a disease, but I don't want a cure." He shuts the dresser drawer. "Lie down, arms above your head."

The expression in his eyes commands me.

I obey immediately.

I shift onto my back and lift my arms.

He shifts onto the bed. His knees plant outside my thighs. His crotch presses against mine.

It's not enough.

I need more of him.

Blake reaches for my hands and ties a black rope around them. Then he ties the rope to the railing of the headboard.

He tests the strength of the knot. "Okay?"

I nod.

"What's the safeword?"

"Chess."

"Good."

He slides his jacket off his shoulders. Then the tie.

I shift back, testing my mobility. My legs are free. I can do whatever I want with them.

But my arms are in place.

I'm at his mercy.

It's equal parts scary and intoxicating.

I can't see him from this position, but I can feel him.

The warmth of his body. The weight of him shifting the bed. The sound of his breath.

Buttons undo. Then a zipper. Pants hit the ground.

He comes into view. One hand plants outside my shoulder. The other brushes hair behind my ear.

His eyes lock with mine.

It's sweet.

Caring.

Then his eyelids are pressing together and his lips are on mine.

He tastes so good.

Desire collects between my legs. He's been teasing me all day, offering this all day.

I need him to make good on his word.

I need him. Period.

His hands slide down my chest. His thumbs brush my nipples. Then he's dragging his hands lower.

Below my belly button.

His lips follow his hands' path.

He kisses my neck. My chest. My stomach.

Lower.

Lower.

Almost.

My breath catches in my throat. No one has ever been this close to me. I don't know how it's supposed to feel. If I'm doing everything right.

His fingers curl into my thighs.

He pins my legs to the bed. "You smell fucking amazing." His voice is a low growl. It's raw. Animal.

It's the complete opposite of the Blake I know. That guy is an uptight suit. This one is completely undone.

My body relaxes as he groans against my thigh. He wants this too. He must. He has me tied up. He has me under his control.

I squirm as he drags his lips up my thigh. My legs fight his hands.

He pins me harder. Digs his nails into my skin. It hurts, but in a way that feels good.

He moves closer.

Closer.

There.

He runs his tongue over my folds. His mouth closes on my left side. He sucks hard.

Pleasure overwhelms me. It's intense and it's unlike anything I've ever felt before.

He's warm. Wet. Soft. But hard too.

I…

Uh…

Fuck.

My legs go slack.

I try to reach for something but my hands are bound. There's no way for me to contain the sensation. All I can do is feel it.

He draws shapes with his tongue. A circle, a triangle, a star, a heart. Romantic. The thought dissolves into the air.

Everything else fades away.

Everything fades into pleasure.

I'm at his mercy.

And he's taking me so fucking high.

He flicks his tongue against me. Soft. Then hard. Fast. Slow.

Pleasure jolts through me. It's intense. It's almost too much to take.

He licks me again. Again.

My legs fight his hand. But he's got me pinned. His nails sink into my skin. Harder. That hint of pain pushes me higher. It makes everything more intense.

An orgasm builds up inside of me.

With the next flick of his tongue, I come.

I shake. I shudder. I groan.

He pulls back for a moment, then his mouth is on me again. He licks me with long, fast strokes.

It's a lot.

It hurts.

But in a good way.

"Blake." I groan his name again and again. It's the only word in my universe. He's the only thing in my universe. His lips. His groans. Those strong hands.

He winds me up. He pushes me all the way to the edge. I'm so close I'm going to snap. It's too much. It's more than I can take.

Then I'm there. The pressure inside me releases. Pleasure spills through my body. It knocks me over like a wave.

My muscles relax.

I sink into the bed, shaking as I come down.

Blake pushes himself onto his knees. He looks down at me the way a lion looks at its prey.

Like he's going to devour me.

Fuck, he really is a sight to behold. He's tall and broad, with chiseled muscles. And his, he's...

I've seen plenty of naked guys in figure drawing classes. But never hard.

He unwraps the condom and rolls it over his cock. I force my eyes to meet his. But it's too intense. It's too intimate.

No. It's just intimate enough.

I understand this Blake.

I understand exactly what he wants from me.

And I trust him to give me what I need.

He arranges my legs flat against the bed again. Then he brings the weight of his body against mine.

I soak up the feel of him as I sink into the foam mattress.

He spreads my legs wider. The tip of his cock strains against me. The rubber tugs for a moment. Then that fades and all I feel is his warmth.

He slides inside me.

Fuck.

It's intense.

Not painful, not really. Just intense. Like I'm so full I'm going to burst.

But that feels good in its own way.

Blake plants his hands outside my shoulders. He pushes into me. He goes deeper.

The discomfort fades.

I'm just full.

Whole.

Instinct takes over.

I arch my hips to push him deeper.

I go to bring my arms around him, and my wrists catch on the restraints. I'm not in control. Blake is.

It makes my sex clench.

Which makes him growl.

His lips press against my neck. Then his teeth. A soft scrape. Then a harder one.

It hurts, but in a good way. Like he's claiming me. Like I'm his.

His hips shift against me.

He moves faster. Harder. It hurts for a minute, then it feels so damn good.

I arch my back, meeting his movements, pushing him deeper.

It feels so good.

So right.

This is why people write pop songs. This is why people go to war. This is why people hand over their body to a near stranger.

This is everything.

His nails scrape against my thighs.

It hurts, but that's not what grabs my attention. No, it's this animal version of Blake.

I let my eyelids press together.

I surrender to sensation.

Everything mixes together—pain, pressure, pleasure, need.

His breath speeds. His thighs shake.

His lips part with a sigh.

He's almost there.

I don't know how I know, but I do.

He's about to come and it's the most beautiful thing I've ever seen.

It spurs me on.

The tension in my sex winds tighter.

He moves harder.

Faster.

There.

The pressure inside me unwinds as I come. It spills through my pelvis, my thighs, my stomach. I feel it everywhere.

Then he's there, moving faster and harder, groaning against my neck.

Groaning my name.

He tears at the sheets as he comes. His cock pulses inside me. His muscles stiffen then relax.

He's mine. It's only for a brief moment, but I feel it as clearly as I've ever felt anything.

When he's done, he collapses next to me. His expression is calm. Relaxed. Spent. I've never seen him like that. I like it. A lot.

He slides off the bed, discards of the condom, and returns.

His gaze hardens as he gives me a long once-over. "Are you okay?"

I nod.

He unties me. He's careful about checking my wrists, stretching them, pressing his lips against them.

Then he pulls me into his arms and plants a kiss on my lips.

It's soft. Sweet, even.

Then he pulls away. Climbs off the bed. "You can stay as long as you want."

"Thanks." He takes a step towards the door. "Make yourself comfortable. Jordan will take you home whenever you're ready. If there's an emergency, I'll be in my office."

I nod like it's normal he's fleeing the scene. "Sure."

"Goodnight." He steps into the hallway and pulls the door closed.

Okay…

I've never had sex until now, but I'm pretty sure that's abnormal behavior.

His terms are clear. The affection is fake. The carnal desire is real. I don't get soft kisses and sweet whispers when we're alone. And I don't want them.

It's better keeping things separate.

I climb off the bed and examine the room. There isn't much besides the bed. The bookshelf in the corner is packed with never-before-read classics. Books for show.

The attached bathroom is gorgeous, all stainless steel, Italian marble, and an enormous tub with jets and imported bubble bath.

I run the water until it's just right then climb in. This thing is practically a pool. It's the tub of my dreams. But I can't relax.

Something feels off.

Once I'm clean, I climb out, wrap myself in a towel, and return to the main room.

My clothes are folded on the couch. Not the pink chiffon dress but the jeans and t-shirt I wore this morning.

The apartment is quiet. Moonlight flows in through the

big windows. A sliver of yellow light flows out from under the door in the corner. Blake's office.

I guess I inspire him. Something like that.

I plant on the couch and try to get comfortable. This is a beautiful apartment, but I can't see any of that.

I can't see anything but that closed door.

It's locked and I'm not welcome there.

I'm not welcome anywhere but his bed.

Chapter Eight

Lizzy stares into the vanity mirror as she brings the pencil to her waterline. She draws a perfect line of espresso. "See? Easy."

Uh...

The makeup artist doing our lesson looks to me. "What do you think, Kat? Are you ready to try it again?"

How can drawing on your face be this hard? I'm not exactly Picasso, but I'm well above average when it comes to pen to paper.

Lizzy hands over the pencil.

I cross and uncross my legs. I stare at my reflection in the vanity mirror as I bring the pencil to my eye.

I trace the line along my lashes. The top. Then the bottom. It's not too bad. A little messy. But close.

"All we need to do is clean it up a little." The makeup artist picks up a brush with an angled tip. "Close your eyes."

I do.

She runs the brush along the line I drew. "Okay. Open."

I stare back at my reflection. That looks better. A lot better. More smudged and sexy than smudged and amateur. "Can I try?"

"Of course." She smiles.

I line my other eye then I pick up the brush and trace my work. My blending isn't quite as expert as hers, but it looks alright.

"I like it," Lizzy says. "It's sexy."

"Yeah?" I ask.

"Like you're walking home from your one-night stand." Lizzy picks up a tube of red lipstick. "Try it with this. Screams sex appeal."

"It's too red," I say.

"Guys like red." Lizzy looks to the makeup artist. "Right?"

"Yes, but honestly, guys don't know anything about makeup. My boyfriend is always telling me how pretty I look without makeup when I have a natural look going. It doesn't matter how many times I tell him I'm caked in product. He keeps insisting." The makeup artist scans the rows and rows of lipstick. She grabs something in a deep berry. "Let's try this. It's a little cooler. Not quite as bright. I think it will suit you."

I take the lipstick, pout, apply two coats. It's dark and rich, like a glass of red wine. Or a raspberry. Between the lipstick and the smoky eye, I look like an adult. Like a sexpot, actually. Like I'll be the one driving Blake out of his mind.

"Oh. I'm going to find one." Lizzy smiles at the makeup artist. "Do you think you have any palettes in purple? Shimmery or matte."

"I'll check." She moves to another row.

Lizzy turns to me. "Are you going to fess up?"

"To?" I play dumb. The berry lipstick really is working

for me. I can see it smudged on Blake's lips. Or his neck. Or his collar. Or just below his belly button.

"Since when do you care about makeup?"

"This is fun, isn't it? The lesson."

"Yeah." Lizzy looks back at her reflection, checking her shimmery purple eyeshadow. "It's awesome. For me. But you... no offense, Kat, but you look sorta confused and frustrated."

"It's not my skillset."

"Don't you work on Tuesday nights?"

"I quit."

"What?" She stares back at me. "Can we—"

"Yeah. I arranged something. I can't explain. But trust me, it's good."

"And it has something to do with your sudden interest in makeup? And the limo that was waiting the other day? Why was there a limo?"

"I'm dating someone with money."

"Oh."

"What do you mean 'oh'?"

My sister stares back at me with a knowing expression. "You have a sugar daddy. Right on. It's about time, Kat. You deserve a break."

"No. It's not like that." Okay, it's not unlike that. "We're serious." About getting married. Not about loving each other.

"Okay, sure. That's why you didn't come home the other night. And why you had that satisfied, just fucked expression when I got home from school the next day."

"I plead the fifth."

"Who's Mr. Rich Guy?"

"A guy I met at work."

"Oh my God, that's so *Pretty Woman*."

"She's a prostitute!"

"Whatever. It's still romantic. You have a picture?"

No. We should have pictures. Everyone takes selfies nowadays. Or at least vacation photos. "You know what he looks like."

"He's famous?"

"Sort of. He's..." I fold my arms. "Don't freak out, okay?"

"I never freak out."

That's true. But still... this news is weird. Ridiculous. I take a deep breath and exhale slowly. "He's Blake Sterling."

Lizzy's eyes go wide. "Sterling Tech Blake Sterling?"

"Yeah."

"Oh my God. He's a legend. He's amazing. Have you seen any of his code? Have you been to the office? Tell me you'll take me to the office!!!"

"I can probably arrange that."

Lizzy grabs my wrists. She squeals. "You're amazing. Oh my God." Her eyes go to my neck. "That hickey. That's from Blake Sterling."

"It's..." I adjust my hair so it's covering said hickey. "It's nothing."

Lizzy laughs. "I'm glad you're finally dating. You've been different the last week. Happier."

"Yeah?"

"Satisfied." She laughs. "Is there some reason why he bought you all those new clothes?"

"Sorta."

"You know I could have helped pick stuff out."

"We went during the day. You have school."

"I have a life too. And I'm a senior. This semester doesn't even count."

"Still. You should be learning."

"I learn all the time."

"I have to say this. I'm your legal guardian."

She nods *fair enough.*

"You can help today."

"Yeah?" Her eyes light up.

"I have an appointment booked at a salon. For my hair. But I don't really know what I want to do."

"What are you trying to do?"

"Look like I belong with Blake Sterling, I guess."

"Like a fancy, rich slut?"

"Not exactly."

"More classy?" She laughs.

It makes me warm all over. Lizzy is always bright. She's the sun in my sky. She's been through so much, but she's still hopeful.

Don't get me wrong. My little sister is cynical as all hell. She can be grumpy or prickly or flat-out anti-social. But she always makes me laugh. She's just… fun.

And she's doing well. With that scholarship, she'll be able to go to any college she wants. She'll have the kind of bright future she deserves.

"I have an idea," Lizzy says. "It's very rich, classy, artsy broad. Perfect for you."

"I trust you."

TWO HOURS LATER, I'M STARING BACK AT A NEW ME. IT'S not a radical change. Lowlights. Layers with a soft wave.

With my hair done and my makeup perfect, I actually look the part of the rich guy's girlfriend.

Lizzy squees as she takes in my new do. "It's perfect. And it's so you. Classy and pretty."

"I'm bright?"

"Yeah. You're really positive. Like compulsively."

Maybe. I'm glad I convince her of that. "You don't think it's too dark?"

"No. It's good."

The buzz of my purse makes me jump.

"Oooh. Is that loverboy?"

Probably. I don't text with anyone besides Lizzy and Blake. I used to have a handful of friends, but I haven't had the time or energy to stay in touch. For the last three years, I've been hanging out with Lizzy. Just Lizzy.

I pull my cell from my purse.

Sure enough, it's a text from Blake.

Blake: I need to talk to you. Come by my office tonight. I'll be here until midnight.

"Booty call?" Lizzy waggles her brows.

I play-swat her. "No. Just a regular call."

"Let me see then."

I do.

She smiles as she reads the text. "That's absolutely a booty call."

I don't think so. Even if it is— "So what?"

"So nothing. I'm glad you're finally getting some."

"Where did you learn to talk like that?"

"Books."

"No offense, but you don't read."

She laughs. "Okay. TV." She takes a step backwards. "You need to go now?"

"No. After dinner. My treat. Whatever you want."

"Greasy noodles?"

"Sure."

"But not here. We need to go to Chinatown and get the good stuff."

I nod. "Wherever you want."

———

AFTER A LONG, GREASY, MSG-FILLED DINNER, LIZZY AND I part ways. I take the subway downtown.

It's empty. Again. I guess it's always empty this time of night.

I take a minute to admire the beauty of the city, then I go straight to Blake's office.

Once again, it's empty except for him. I go straight to his open door and knock.

"Kat. Come in."

"How did you know it was me?"

"Who else would it be?"

"The janitor."

"His shoes don't squeak."

My cheeks flush. "I guess I should get new shoes. Better ones."

"If you'd like." He steps out from behind his desk. His eyes pass over me. They start at my hair, linger over my chest, stop at my cheap boots. "Those suit you."

"Cheap and not as waterproof as advertised?"

"Artsy."

"How do you know I'm artsy?"

"You stop and stare at beautiful things every few minutes."

"Oh." I guess I do.

"I can arrange lessons if you'd like."

That would be awesome. But— "I can handle it."

He motions to the couch. "Would you like a drink?"

"Sure." I drop my bags—my purse and the department store bag packed with four hundred dollars of makeup—in the corner and take a seat on the couch. It's strange, the way Blake offers to take care of everything. I'm tempted to take him up on all his offers.

But then where will I be when this is over?

Will I even exist or will I be some amalgamation of Blake's desires?

He fixes our drinks and brings them to the couch.

The brush of his hands still lights up my body. It's funny. We had crazy, rough, animalistic sex a few nights ago, but I still feel like we're strangers.

He's still treating me like a colleague.

"Thank you." I take a long sip of my gin and tonic. It's just as crisp and clear as last time. "Is everything alright?"

"Not exactly." He takes a long sip of his whiskey. His gaze moves to the window that looks out on the city. The silver moon peeks out from behind a skyscraper. "There's a party on Friday."

"One we're attending together?"

"Yes. A company event. But my family will be there as well."

"You have a family?"

He looks at me like he's not sure if I'm joking. "Of course."

"No, I only meant... you haven't really mentioned them."

His hand brushes the outside of my thigh. "I want to announce our relationship at the party."

"Oh. Okay."

"And to ask you to marry me."

"Already?" It's only been a week. Not even.

He nods. "Things are moving faster than I'd hoped."

"What things?"

His gaze goes back to the window. "We'll need to move up our timeline. Get married next month."

"Next month as in April?"

He nods. "That is the month after March."

I think he's teasing me. Maybe. "Is that really plausible?"

"If we tell everyone we've been dating in secret." He looks me in the eyes. There's something in his expression. A sadness. "I hate rushing this, but it's the only way."

"What do you need from me?"

"I made a document. More of my history. A fake history for us. I need you to make one for yourself. Tomorrow. Email it to me. I'll have it memorized."

"We could just hang out. Get to know each other. That kind of thing."

His smile is sad. "There isn't time." He leans in to press his lips to mine. "This is faster. Easier." He finishes his last sip of whiskey, stands, brings the glass back to the bar. "I'm going to be busy the rest of the week. I'll send a car for you Friday."

"Okay."

He turns so his back is to me. "You're welcome to hang out in the office, but I need to get back to work."

"Oh. Sure." He's kicking me out of here too. And this time all he got from me was a kiss.

"I'll email the document to you."

I nod. "Sure. I'll see you Friday."

"Goodnight, Kat."

"Goodnight." I turn and leave and spend the subway ride thinking about the sadness in his eyes.

It's something bad.

But what?

Chapter Nine

Blake's fingers graze my back. They press the silk of my dress into my skin.

He rests his hand on the curve of my waist.

It's possessive. Sweet. Loving.

Of course, that's all a lie.

No, the possessive part is real. I think. But the rest of it—

I force my lips into a smile.

I lean into his touch.

He turns to me with wide, bright eyes. He stares at me like he's madly in love with me. Like I'm his favorite thing in the entire world.

I swallow hard.

This is a lie.

He doesn't love me. I don't love him. Yes, I have all the facts in his *about me* memorized, and he knows all of mine, but that's surface level. We don't understand each other. Not when we're dressed.

I press a French-manicured nail into the pad of my thumb. I think about sitting next to Lizzy, gossiping about all the obnoxious customers at Pixie Dust, the boutique where she works. I think about our dinner this evening, the one at the cute place around the corner, with the waiter who always gives me extra pancakes.

When I look back to Blake, I forget everything.

I think about his smile and his eyes and his shoulders.

I think about his body on top of mine.

I think about the sadness that creeps into his expression.

And how badly I want to wipe it away.

He leans in to whisper in my ear. "You're perfect."

My breath catches in my throat. I'm perfect. At pretending. Only I'm not. Not really.

He pulls back and turns to a man in a navy suit.

Blake offers his hand. The guy shakes.

He turns to me. "You must be Kat."

I nod. "I must."

"I've heard a lot about you." He offers his hand.

I take it. Make my grip as strong as I can. "Kat Wilder. It's nice to meet you." I offer my best coquettish grin. Has Blake really mentioned me? We've only been faking dating a week.

"Declan Jones." He pulls his hand back to his side. "Blake undersold your beauty."

I press my lips into a smile. "Thank you. I've heard so much about you." Okay, I skimmed his name in that little document that explained Blake's entire life. Declan is a San Francisco tech guy.

"And where is your date?" Blake asks.

"I'm here on business, my friend. No dates. But I'm glad you volunteered to entertain me." Declan smiles. "Things didn't work out well with Grace. Different lifestyles."

"That means she wasn't okay with him seeing other

women." Blake raises an eyebrow as if to challenge his friend.

Declan shrugs with false modesty. So the guy is a bit of a player. No surprise. All that matters is that he's buying into this whole ruse.

I have to admit, it's convincing. Blake is the quiet, protective boyfriend, and I'm the pretty young thing he needs on his arm.

Blake bids his friend goodbye and turns to another man. He's tall, with a strong jaw and deep, intense eyes.

"Should I know him?" I whisper.

Blake shakes his head. "No. He's not a friend."

"Then why's he here?"

"You know the old expression. Keep your friends close and your enemies closer."

This time, my smile is real. "You have enemies?"

"More like competitors. That's Phoenix Marlowe. He's the owner of Odyssey."

"I'm barely computer literate."

"It's a new artificial intelligence program. Very cutting edge. It could disrupt the entire industry." He shakes his head. "Listen to me, using lingo. Forgive me."

"Okay." The sincerity in his voice makes my knees weak.

"I should introduce your sister, but…"

"But?"

"He has a reputation."

"You're protective of Lizzy?"

He nods. "She's family now."

I stare back at him. He means it. So something about our impending marriage is real. He really does believe we'll be family. At least for a while.

"He's handsome." He really is. "Not as handsome as you, but—"

"I'm not jealous."

"No? What if I go on and on about how I'd like to tear off his suit?"

Blake stares back at me with a *try harder* expression.

"How I'd like him to tie me to his bed?"

"Would you?"

"Maybe." No.

Blake's eyes narrow. He is jealous. He shakes his head, refusing to admit it. "Then I'd have to find somewhere private right away. To remind you of how badly you need me."

Yes. I like this plan. I nod. "You should."

But we're cut off by another friend.

I smile through our introduction. Then another. Then a dozen more.

It gets to be a routine. Blake announces me. The guy says something about how I'm too beautiful for Blake. I laugh. Clutch Blake's arm. Insist he's the only one for me.

He holds me tighter.

His voice gets lower.

Like he really is jealous.

Like he can't stand other guys looking at me.

A woman in her mid-twenties cuts in. "Blake."

He remains steel. "This is my sister, Fiona."

She nods hello. Presses her dark hair behind her ears. "Kat, isn't it?"

I nod. "It's nice to meet you."

She nods as she shakes. "Yes... it's... interesting." Her voice trails off. She doesn't believe our story, but she doesn't dwell on it. She turns to her brother. "Mom wants to meet your girlfriend. She said something about how she hopes you finally care about more than getting between a woman's legs."

His mom said that?

That's weird…

Or maybe that's Fiona talking. There's something about her posture. She's on edge. Jealous? Or doubtful? It's hard to say.

Either way, I need to sell this.

I hold Blake tighter. "It's funny. Our relationship started out purely sexual. It was… mind-blowing. I'll spare you the details. But Blake is so sweet." I turn to him. Stare into his eyes. Cultivate every ounce of affection in the world. "I couldn't help myself. I fell head over heels."

He runs his fingertips over my chin. "Kat…" His voice is soft. Sweet. Pure affection.

Pure love.

He leans closer.

Closer.

His lips brush mine.

He kisses me like he's madly in love with me.

My stomach flutters. My knees knock together. My entire body is light. I believe it. I believe every drop of it.

I rise to my tiptoes.

I slide my arm around his neck.

He presses his palm into my lower back to pull me closer.

I kiss back harder. Pretend or not, his lips are perfect against mine.

Fiona scoffs. "Get a room."

Blake pulls back. He throws his sister a *fuck you* glance. "Where's Trey?"

She plays with her wedding ring. "A conference."

There's a sadness in her expression.

Her husband is off somewhere and Blake is throwing our relationship in her face. That must hurt.

Even if she seems… unpleasant.

"He couldn't be bothered?" Blake's voice is all protective older brother.

It makes my knees weak. First looking out for Lizzy and now for his not particularly kind sister. It's charming.

"Mom is tired today. Put in some face time before your speech, okay?" she asks.

"It's under control."

"No, now. I'm not sure she's going to make it through your speech." She looks me up and down, picking me apart. "Where exactly did you and Blake meet?"

I stare back with my best *I'm madly in love with your brother* look. "I bumped into him on my way out of an interview."

"Oh? You work. That must be a refreshing change, Blake," Fiona says.

Irritation flares in his expression. Okay, there's a hint in his eyes. But that's a lot for him.

"What do you do?" Fiona asks.

"I'm a waitress," I say.

Fiona fights something. Judgment. Or maybe solidarity. I'm not sure.

She looks to her phone. Frowns. "It was nice to meet you but I need to make a call."

Something passes between her and Blake. It's pure sibling magic. I do the same thing with Lizzy.

When their gaze breaks, she turns and leaves. Her steps are heavy. Frustrated.

And my heart is racing.

I'm still floating from that kiss.

It was pretend.

But none of this feels pretend.

Not anymore.

I grab a champagne flute from a passing waiter.

It's amazing. Sweet. Bubbly. Fruity.

I tilt the glass back, but Blake grabs my wrist.

He leans in to whisper. "Slow down."

It's a good idea. I need my wits about me. I need my inhibitions at full force.

I nod. "Of course, honey."

He presses his palm against my back as he leads me through the crowd. Everyone waves or nods.

Most look at me the way Fiona did, like they're assessing me. Deciding if I'm the love of his life or a disposable piece of arm candy.

I keep my eyes on the decorations. Sleek, abstract art in gold and silver. Totally incomprehensible, just like Blake.

We make our way to a row of seats in the corner of the room. There's a woman sitting in the corner, nursing a glass of champagne.

She's in her forties. Or maybe her fifties. I've never been good with ages. She's thin. No, she's tiny. Like she's disappearing.

She's pretty, well-dressed with perfect hair and makeup, but there's something off about her. She's pale. Not typical New York in the winter pale. It's more like she's ill.

Color spreads over her face as she sees Blake. Her eyes light up. Her lips curl into a smile.

She looks me over. Not like everyone else. Like she's happy to see me. Like she wants me to be good enough for Blake. To be everything for Blake.

She stands slowly.

Blake rushes to help her, but he's too slow.

She shakes her head. "My son has always been very protective." She turns to me. "You must be Kat."

"Yes." I struggle to meet her gaze. She has the same intensity that Blake does, like she can read my mind. "I've heard so much about you."

"Oh, you're so sweet to lie. If I know Blake, well, I doubt you've heard much about anything."

I smile. A real smile this time.

"Call me Meryl. And, please, none of that Mrs. Sterling crap. If you insist, it's Miss. Can't have any eligible bachelors thinking I'm off the market."

I go to shake her hand, but she hugs me instead.

Her head is pressed right up against my chest. Meryl is on the shorter side, and I'm wearing towering heels under my dress.

She laughs. "Ah! I see why my son likes you."

"Mom." Blake clears his throat. For a second, he sounds like a teenager complaining that his parents are embarrassing him.

It's incredibly endearing.

She laughs. "My son. It's not his fault, but he thinks I'm too old to notice these things." She turns to Blake. "One day you'll be in your late forties. You'll still be noticing breasts."

Blake's cheeks flush. Holy crap. His mom *is* embarrassing him. It's so normal.

Meryl shakes her head. "Dear, do you need to sit? Those heels look excruciating."

"I'll be fine. I'm on my feet all day."

"Really? What do you do?"

"I'm a waitress." I brace for a snarky comment. Meryl seems nice, but people with money, you never know if they look down on the commoners.

"Isn't it supposed to be *server* nowadays?" she asks.

"It's all the same, really." Though I'm not doing it anymore.

"You call shit roses, it still smells like shit." She laughs. "I used to wait tables at the nicest place in town. That's where I met the late Mr. Sterling."

"Oh?"

She nods. "You should have seen him. He dressed even

better than Blake does. He was so flashy with his platinum watch. When Orson—"

"Orson, really?"

"I'm afraid so." Her smile lights up her entire face. "When he came into the restaurant, it was a commotion. All the girls wanted that table. It was the dream to marry a rich customer. Best way to get a better life. But I hated the asshole."

"How did you two end up married?"

"I've embarrassed Blake too much already."

Blake is still red. It's amazing. I can hardly believe that he's capable of any kind of shyness.

I lean closer and lower my voice to a whisper. "I won't tell."

"It started off as sex. It was about the only thing we had in common. We got caught up in the passion. Then I... well, Blake knows this story. I got pregnant. It was a surprise, but it was wanted. I'd always dreamt of being a mother. We married immediately. Things were different then. People didn't have children out of wedlock." She finishes her last drop of champagne and moves towards the nearest waiter.

Blake fusses over Meryl. He takes her glass. Shoots her a concerned look.

She shakes her head. "I'd better let you go, dear. I'm sure Blake wants to show you off."

"Likely."

She studies my expression. "I wouldn't fault you if you were after his money or his looks."

"I... Uh... It did start that way. Physically, I mean. But Blake's..." I look at Blake in the hopes he can rescue me from this conversation, but he's still finding another glass of wine. "He's wonderful."

"Really? He's always seemed... uncompromising."

"Sometimes. But I… I trust him to take care of me." At least that's not a lie. Not technically. I trust him to get me off. And that's taking care of me. In a way.

"Be patient with him. His father wasn't a good man. It's no excuse, but…" She shakes her head as she falls into her thoughts.

Blake arrives with two fresh glasses. He hands one to his mom and one to me. "Give us a minute."

I nod. "Of course. It was lovely to meet you."

Meryl nods. Neither of them speaks until I turn, and even then, it's too quiet for me to hear.

Even so, I can tell they're talking about me.

I can tell they're sharing a secret.

Chapter Ten

The bathroom is as beautiful as the rest of the hotel ballroom. The floors are marble. The mirrors are ornate. Modern art lines the walls.

I turn the shiny fixture to cold and splash my neck.

It helps.

A stall door opens behind me. Footsteps move closer.

I focus on applying another coat of lipstick. That berry color. The one that makes me feel like a sex goddess.

Fiona steps up to the mirror. She stares at the sink as she washes her hands. Her eyes are red. Puffy.

She's been crying.

She looks to me as she grabs a paper towel. "I'm surprised Blake let you off his leash."

I force myself to smile. That might be a threat or it might be sincere curiosity. Either way, I'm selling myself as madly in love. "He can't exactly join me here."

"Hmm."

"He is protective."

"Try having him as an older brother."

"I can imagine."

"Every guy at our school was afraid to date me. They thought Blake would kick their asses."

"Would he?"

"What do you think?"

"Excuse me?"

"He's your boyfriend. You don't know how he reacts to jealousy?"

"That was a long time ago."

"Mhmm." She brushes her dark hair behind her ear. "No. Blake isn't violent. Well… not usually."

I swallow the question that rises in my throat. There's something she isn't saying. Something I'm not supposed to know.

She gives me another once-over. "I have to say. I didn't expect him with someone like you."

"Like me how?"

She pulls her lipstick from her clutch. "Blake is married to his job. He's worse than my husband. I always imagined him with someone who was the same."

"I love my work too."

"Waiting tables?"

"I'm an artist. I have a lot to learn. It keeps me busy."

She nods, accepting my story. Or maybe that's an *okay, whatever you tell yourself* nod. I'm not sure.

"Blake makes time for me." That's true. Sort of. "He wants to change things. He knows he won't be happy unless he does."

"I hope you're right. But you know what they say about men and change?"

"No. I don't."

"That's it. They don't."

Deep breath. This is a test and I need to pass. "I guess time will tell."

Fiona bites her lip. "Or does it not matter to you?"

"Excuse me?"

"You're a waitress. He's loaded. It doesn't take a genius to figure out he's got *meal ticket* written on his forehead."

"It isn't like that. I love Blake." God, this is a terrible confession of passion. I force a smile. I think of the things that make my heart race. The accident. The skyline against the sunset. The spring's first flowers. "He... he's not like anyone I've ever met. He makes me feel safe. He makes my knees weak. He's..."

She snaps her purse shut. "I hope you are telling the truth. For your sake. Because if you're not... you're going to regret using him. I'll make sure of it."

"I appreciate that you're looking out for him." Really, it's sweet. Even if it's at my expense. "I hope you enjoy your night." I drop my lipstick in my purse and I saunter out of the bathroom.

Conversation whirls around me. It's loud.

Everyone is looking at me the same way Fiona was.

What's he doing with her?

And what's she doing with him?

Someone that young—she's looking for a meal ticket? Just look at her dress.

You think she's a hooker?

Okay, I'm imagining things. I think.

It's funny. I never thought people would be looking at me thinking I was too pretty to be with someone.

It's almost nice.

But Blake isn't after my looks.

He's after my—

No, he's not after anything.

This is all bullshit.

I find a waiter and grab another flute of champagne. The bubbles burst on my tongue. They lift me higher. They make the room effervescent.

Now where is my adoring boyfriend?

He's not in the corner where he was earlier. Neither is Meryl.

I wander around the party, looking for him. But I don't see him anywhere.

Oh. There's a quiet balcony up ahead. That's perfect.

Someone steps into my path. Declan, Blake's old friend.

"Hey, Kat. Blake is about to give his speech."

"I'm just going to get some air," I say.

He pats my shoulder. "Nonsense." He leans in close and whispers, "I have it on good authority that he mentions you in it."

Oh.

We're moving up the timeline.

That must mean…

I swallow hard. "Of course."

I follow him into the main room. Grab another glass of champagne and drink quickly.

This is too fast.

I'm not ready to be a fiancée.

Declan pats me on the back. He nods to a small stage. Blake is standing there. He's holding up his own glass of champagne like he's about to give a toast.

He scans the crowd. His eyes rest on mine. They fill up with love.

Like this is real.

His smile spreads over his cheeks.

That's how I know it's fake.

Blake doesn't smile.

I press my nail into my palm.

He doesn't love you.

He'll never love you.

This is all pretend.

"I know we're all very excited about the new Photos feature. I'd love to praise the dev team—you're all fantastic—but this is a party." He lifts his glass. "Let's skip to something interesting."

Everyone laughs. And lifts their glasses.

Blake finishes his in one long sip. It's not like him. Not like the Blake I know.

He wipes sweat from his brow.

That isn't like him either.

Blake doesn't get nervous.

His eyes meet mine. They fill up with something, something real.

The flutter in my stomach builds.

Lightness spreads through my fingers and toes.

I forget everything but those deep blue eyes of his.

"My priorities are different nowadays." He steps off the stage. "There's something, no, someone I love more than Sterling Tech."

The crowd parts until it's a straight shot between Blake and me. Good thing his mic is cordless, because I can't move a muscle.

He walks to me slowly.

He hands off his champagne glass.

The expression in his eyes is pure love.

I believe him.

I believe everything.

He takes my hand and strokes my fingers. "Kat, I love you more than I've ever loved anyone."

My stomach flutters.

This is pretend.

But my body can't grasp that.

My body is on fire. It's demanding him. Not just the heat of his touch, but the softness of his embrace.

"You make the happiest man alive." He drops to one knee.

I force my lips into a smile.

Blake pulls a ring box out of his pocket. "Will you marry me?"

It's a solitaire on a platinum band. Four carats, five maybe. Sleek, like everything else he owns.

The room goes quiet. Every ounce of attention is on us. I catch glances from his mother. Her mouth is hanging open, but there's no mistaking the joy on her face.

I go for a big smile. I throw my hands over my mouth like I can't believe my luck. "Of course."

His eyes stay glued to mine. He slides the engagement ring over my finger and rises to his feet.

Blake leans into a kiss. Our lips meet and fireworks explode inside my body. But it's fake. Everything but the ring is fake.

I'm engaged to Blake Sterling.

This is either the best decision I've ever made or the biggest mistake of my life.

Chapter Eleven

Lights flash. Cell phone cameras click. An actual shutter closes and opens.

We're a spectacle.

Of course we're a spectacle. A public proposal is always an event.

Blake is already at my side, his arm around my waist, his expression cool and aloof. If I didn't know better, I'd think he was a robot with only one programmed facial expression.

He's not. There's more to him, other shades. I've only seen them briefly, but I'm as sure of them as I am of anything.

Blake waves at the crowd. "If you'll excuse me, my fiancée and I would like to be alone. To celebrate."

Some people laugh. A few cheer. Everyone knows *celebrate* is code for *have crazy, hot, we-just-got-engaged sex*.

It's romantic. We're committing to forever. We're promising to proclaim our love in front of everyone. It's beautiful.

Except it's bullshit.

I force my lips into a smile. I force my gaze to my ring. It catches every bit of light in the room. It mocks my decision to choose money over integrity. Over honesty and love and affection.

I don't believe in karma, not usually, but I can't fight the sense I'm sealing my fate.

I'm mocking love. I'm mocking marriage. I'm mocking lifelong commitment.

My parents loved each other. Even after twenty years of marriage, they were madly in love. They still smiled and giggled like teenagers.

They even died together.

It was better that way. For them. They would have been lost without each other.

But for me…

It's been three years since the accident that killed my parents and left Lizzy in critical condition for weeks. I've been holding things together for three years, and I've never really found my footing. Everything is too expensive. And there's never enough time.

I need Blake's money. I know that.

But this gorgeous, expensive, showy ring makes me want to hurl.

It's the most beautiful horrible thing I've ever seen.

Blake's grip around my waist tightens. It's a little possessive, sure, but that part is for show.

I think.

The crowd parts for us. No, it's parting for Blake. He has that effect on people. They bend to his will.

Cool air hits my face as Blake pushes the doors open.

I lean into Blake's touch.

I soak up all his warmth.

And I hate that too.

My gesture is a lie.

I force my gaze away from the ring. We're at some fancy hotel uptown. The streets are quiet. The limo is parked at the curb. And, there, in front of it, are bare trees. But there are tiny white buds on the tree at the end of the street.

It's a cherry tree. It's almost the season.

Blake opens the limo door for me and helps me inside. Then he's on the opposite bench. He pulls the door closed. It shuts out the sounds of the party.

Soft white lights glow. This really is a beautiful limo. Sleek. Like all his possessions.

Like the ring.

Like me. I'm close enough to something he owns. A woman under contract. He doesn't strike me as the type who would think of his wife as his property, but you never really know. Rich people are awfully entitled. The men especially.

I sink into my seat. The leather is freezing against my exposed skin. The entire world feels freezing. Like there isn't a shred of love or warmth left.

"Kat."

He's just as cool as the leather. As the air. "What's wrong?"

"Nothing." I smooth my dress. Cross my legs. Try to look at anything besides the ring.

"Something." His voice is sincere.

Does it really bother Blake that I'm upset? He got what he wanted. This is all what he wants.

He takes a seat next to me. Presses his thigh against mine.

He leans in to whisper. "Tell me."

His breath warms my skin. It's the only warm thing in the universe. I can focus on how much I want him, how much my body demands his.

That's real.

And, right now, I need real.

His lips brush against my neck. My body reacts instantly.

My back arches of its own accord.

My legs part.

My tongue slides over my lips.

"You're overwhelmed." He whispers it in my ear like it's a dirty promise.

"I know how I feel. I don't need you explaining it to me." My body whines at my protests. It doesn't want to talk. It doesn't want feelings. It wants his hands and his mouth and his cock.

He pushes my hair aside with a gentle touch. Then it's his lips on my neck. He kisses me. Softly. Then harder.

"Tell me I'm wrong." His fingers skim the bare skin on my back. They settle on the top of my zipper.

"Do you even care?"

His eyes turn down. He actually looks hurt. I think. His expressions are all so similar. "I want to make this as easy as possible for you."

"You wouldn't want a difficult wife?"

"No." He undoes my zipper. "I like you, Kat. I want you to be happy."

"Really?"

"I don't lie when we're alone."

Happy is a tall order, given the circumstances. "That isn't going to happen. Not with all this deception."

He nods with understanding. "You don't want to think about it."

It's more a statement than a question. I nod anyway. I stare into Blake's blue eyes. They're still beautiful and deep and impenetrable. "Distract me."

His lips curl into a half-smile. He nods. "Close your eyes."

I do.

He turns me so I'm facing away from him.

He pushes my dress off my shoulders.

It falls to my waist.

I'm topless— this was one of those can't-wear-a-bra-under-it dresses.

I'm exposed. On display.

It makes my sex clench.

I still like it. I still like feeling dirty. Blake still seems to know my desires better than I do.

His hands skim my back, sides, torso. He draws circles around my nipples.

My thoughts float away. They're off in some corner of my brain. Desire is taking over the rest.

I need him.

Now.

Faster than now.

I arch my back, pushing my breasts into his hands. He nips at my ear. And his hands, oh his hands.

"Are you on birth control?" he asks.

I nod. "The shot." As promised, he sent me his test results after our last conversation.

He tugs at my dress, lifting my ass so he can slide it to my feet. "You remember the safeword?"

"Yes."

He tugs hard at my panties. They strain against my hips until the lace fabric snaps.

Blake's lips find mine. His kiss is commanding. Possessive.

It wakes up every nerve in my body. It gets every part of me screaming for more of him.

I shift my hips. I tug at the fabric of his suit jacket. I kiss him back as hard as I can.

His pulls me onto his lap. I can feel his erection through his slacks. Fuck, it feels so good, knowing he's hard because of me. There's something instinctive and visceral about it.

I want my hands around him.

I want him coming from my touch.

Or my mouth.

I have no idea how to touch a man beyond late night gossip sessions back in high school. But I don't care that I'm inexperienced. That I may make a fool of myself.

I want him too badly to care.

He drags his lips down my neck, over my collarbone and chest. His mouth closes around my nipple. He sucks hard. Soft. Then it's short flicks of his tongue. Long ones.

I surrender to the sensations forming in my body.

His soft, wet mouth.

His strong hands.

The cold leather against my thighs.

The strain as he spreads my legs.

His thumb against my clit.

Pleasure wells up inside me as he rubs me. It pushes out that last nagging thought, the one reminding me about the weight on my left hand.

Then he's teasing me with one finger. I rock my hips to meet him deeper but he teases and teases and teases.

Finally, he slides his finger inside me.

Damn. That feels good.

It's not as intense as last time, when it was his cock inside me, but it's still fucking amazing.

He rubs me, sucking on my nipples as he fucks me with his fingers.

It's so much sensation. I can barely take it. But this time, my hands are on his skin. This time I can touch him.

I tug at his tie and toss it aside. I undo the top two buttons of his shirt. My fingers skim his chest. He's hard and strong against my palm. And warm.

The whole world is warm.

I dig my nails into his skin. He sucks harder. Strokes harder. Pushes deeper.

The pressure inside me winds tighter. I tug at Blake's hair. I shift my hips. I let out a heavy groan.

Everything unfurls as I come.

"Blake." I pull him closer. I groan his name.

Bliss overwhelms me. Every part of me feels good. Home. Safe. Satisfied.

Blake wraps his arms around me.

I blink my eyes open. Stare into his baby blues.

He's the Blake I understand. The one who only wants my body. Who only brings me pleasure.

If only we understood each other like this all the time.

He runs his fingers through my hair and leans in to press his lips to mine.

I kiss him harder. I need all of him. Not just his body, but the rest of him too. He's going to be my husband. I need more than great sex. I need something else to hold onto.

He drags his lips to my ear. "Turn around." His voice is a demand. "Hands against the back of the seat."

I shift off him, plant my knees on the bench, and press my palms against the slick leather.

He positions himself behind me. His zipper undoes. My tongue slides over my lips reflexively. I want so badly to touch him or taste him. Something. Anything.

But I'm still at his mercy.

No, I like being at his mercy.

I want it.

And I want more.

I want everything.

For the first time in my life, I'm greedy.

His fingers dig into my hips. He holds me in place as he drives into me. It's one hard thrust. I get the full force of him.

Just him. No condom. Nothing between us. Well, between our bodies.

My eyelids press together.

He feels so good. Warm and hard and mine. Like his body was made for mine. Like we're both exactly where we belong.

"You need to come on my cock." His voice is heavy. Almost desperate.

I nod. I need to come on his cock. I need it more than I've ever needed anything.

He holds me in place as he fucks me.

He goes hard. Deep. It hurts, but in a good way. In a fucking amazing way.

Pleasure wells up inside me. I tug at the seat. Curl my toes. Groan against the leather.

It spurs him on. Gets him going deeper. Groaning lower.

He slides his hand between my legs to stroke my clit.

Fuck.

It pushes me right to the edge. Almost…

I arch my back, shifting my hips to meet his thrusts.

His nails dig into my skin. A warning that he's in charge. I moan some kind of affirmation. He's in control. I love him in control.

A few more thrusts and I'm there. All that pressure unwinds. My sex pulses as I come. I groan his name. I rock my hips. I try to do something to contain the intensity of it, but it still knocks me over.

My knees shake.

My hands slip.

Blake helps me up. Holds me tighter. Only he's not Blake now. He's that animal version.

His groans are low and deep.

His movements are rough. Hard.

He moves faster. Deeper.

It hurts, but in a good way.

His breath gets ragged. His groans get higher. His nails dig into my skin.

Then he's there. I can feel his orgasm in the way his cock pulses, in the way his groans run together, in the way his nails scrape my flesh.

When he's done, he pulls back and zips his slacks.

I collapse on the bench seat. I'm naked. He's dressed.

I hold onto my satisfaction for as long as I can. Maybe he'll never love me, but he will fuck me senseless. That's more than some people get.

It's not enough, but it's something.

Chapter Twelve

Somehow, I get back into my dress long enough to get from the garage to the elevator to Blake's apartment. He says nothing until we're in the bathroom and then it's only to ask if I'd like anything to eat or drink.

He draws a bath. Half of me wants to scream *I can do this myself*. The other half wants to fall into his arms and let him take care of me forever.

There's something comforting about the surrender. About letting go of all the thoughts bouncing around my head. I want to be better at it.

I want to be able to let go. To let someone else take care of me. Someone I trust.

I'm just not sure if that's Blake.

I split the difference. He leaves to fetch me a snack, and I wait in silence until the tub is full enough, then I slip into the sudsy water.

It's perfect. Hot but not painfully so. Big bubbles that smell of lavender and peppermint.

One by one, my muscles relax. The day washes away.

The pain of pretending washes away. Everything is perfect and warm and sweet.

Blake returns with a tray of snacks. Grapes, berries, crackers, cheese, and dark chocolate.

He's in jeans and a t-shirt. It's weird. But hot too. He wears cotton well.

I move to the edge of the tub. "You look normal."

"And usually?"

"You're in a suit. You wore a suit when we went shopping."

"I wore slacks and a collared shirt."

"Okay, you were business casual. Most people wear something like that." I draw a circle around his outfit. "Isn't that how programmers usually dress?"

"I don't program much these days."

I pop a raspberry into my mouth. I never buy berries. Too expensive. It's better than I remember. Tart, sweet, perfect. "Do you miss it?"

"At times."

"Did you love programming?"

"I love some things about it."

"Like…"

"There's this feeling of accomplishment when you get a program to work. A satisfaction. Nothing compares."

"You like being in control of the computer?"

"That's part of it. It's more the sense of accomplishment."

"What do you do now? Besides programming?"

"Lots of meetings. Executive-level decisions. It's important, but it's not as satisfying."

"You could let someone else run your company."

He stares back at me in horror. I think. "What do you love about art?" He takes a strawberry and sucks the juice from it. "We've never talked about it."

"We don't talk much."

"True." His voice gets light. Well, for Blake.

"I love all of it. But I love graphic novels the most."

"Comic books?"

I nod.

He half-smiles. "You do realize I started a tech company at sixteen."

"And you were inspired by Batman or something?"

"No. He's too violent."

"Iron Man?"

"Do I strike you as snarky?"

I laugh. I'm pretty sure that's a joke.

It is. Blake is actually smiling. God, he has a nice smile. It makes me feel warm all over.

"I don't really read comic books," I say. "I'm not into superhero stories. I like graphic novels about people and relationships. My sister always says it's boring girl stuff."

"You love her a lot?"

"Of course. Don't you love your sister?"

He nods. "She's difficult, I know. If she was—"

"It's okay. I get it. What's the deal with her husband?"

"Trey? He's not a good man."

I arch a brow. "That's not a good explanation."

"It's not my secret to share."

Fair enough. I sink my teeth into the chocolate. It's perfect. Rich. Sweet. Satisfying. "What do you do for fun?"

"Chess."

"*Chess*?"

"That too." He glances at the plate. "Do you want something more substantial?"

"Not in the bath." I push back to the wall—the tub really is that big. "I... I want to know why we're doing this."

He nods. Then nothing.

"That was your cue to start the explanation," I say.

He nods to a glass of water. I roll my eyes but I drink the entire glass.

"Don't do that," he says.

"Follow your instructions?"

"Roll your eyes."

"Or what? Will you punish me for being bad?"

"I'm going to do what I can to respect you, Kat. I expect the same from you." His gaze is intense. "Understood?"

"If you want respect, then respect me. I asked you for something. You didn't reply."

He stares back at me.

I can't hold his gaze. My eyes go to my ring. It's still catching all the light.

"You like it?" His voice is soft. Almost like he actually cares about my reaction.

"Does it matter?" I do like it, though I'd like it a lot more if it was from someone who cared about me. If it symbolized love instead of bullshit.

"Yes." He kneels next to the bath, bringing us eye to eye. "It suits you."

"I'm expensive and showy?"

"You're beautiful and understated." He offers his hand. "I want this to be easy for you."

"It will be easier if you stop saying that. And if you explain." I dip my head into the water. I feel cleaner instantly. Like the bath is washing away all the hair product and makeup. All the stuff that makes me Blake's pretty, fake fiancée and not Kat.

Blake stares at me, studying me.

I wipe the makeup from my eyes. "Why did you ask me to marry you?"

"The same reason I asked you to play my girlfriend."

"Helpful."

"I wanted to make someone happy."

"Who?" I squeeze shampoo into my hands and lather.

Blake motions *come here*. When I move closer, he combs the shampoo through my hair.

"I can do that," I say.

"Let someone else help you for once."

"I don't need help."

"Accept it anyway." He runs his hands through my hair. It's soft. Gentle. Loving. "You remember my mother?"

"Meryl. Of course. She was sweet."

"And weak. She could barely stand." His voice is soft. Hurt. "She's not supposed to drink with her medication, but at this point, I don't think it matters."

I don't like the sound of that. "Why not?"

"She has liver disease." He shakes his head. "I should have convinced her to quit drinking. This wouldn't have happened."

"You're her kid. You can't convince her to do anything."

His eyes go dark. "I could have. She knew better. We all knew better."

"Maybe she... maybe there are treatments." Oh. It hits me all at once. There are no treatments. This whole charade is for his mother's benefit. It must be because—

"She's dying, Kat." He presses his palm against the porcelain. "We thought she had a year, but things took a turn for the worse. Best case scenario, she has three months."

My stomach drops. Meryl is a sweet woman. Loving. It's not fair.

But then I gave up on life being fair a long time ago.

I offer Blake my hand. "I'm sorry."

"Thank you." He takes it. "She's always worried about

me. After my father, it makes sense, but I don't want her to die worrying."

"What about your father?"

He ignores my question. "We need to sell this. We need to convince her we're madly in love."

"Why not tell her the truth?"

He looks me right in the eyes. "She thinks her marriage cursed us. She's still guilty she stayed with him."

"But why?"

This, too, he brushes off.

I stare back at him for a few moments, but his expression stays a wall. He isn't going to explain.

I dip my hair, rinsing out all the shampoo and most of the product. When I surface, Blake is waiting with a bottle of conditioner.

He runs it through my hair. "If you have any objections, I'd like to get them out of the way."

"You're pretty much at my mercy," I say. "I mean, you've already proposed to me. You can't find a new fake girlfriend now."

His fingertips graze my forehead. "I want you. Not anyone else."

"You're stuck with me."

"No, I want you."

I pull back and duck my head into the water to rinse the conditioner. Thoughts swirl around my brain. Objections. Encouragement. That voice that screams *you still need his money*.

I barely know Meryl, but I know enough to want her happy.

Even if it's a lie. A lie that makes you happy must be better than a truth that hurts you.

Tension builds between my shoulders. It doesn't feel

right. It feels like more bullshit. "So we're... what, we're going to get married ASAP? So she's there?"

He nods.

"How are you going to plan a wedding that fast?"

"I could have a wedding planned tomorrow if I wanted." His voice gets low. "Money can buy just about anything you want."

"It can't buy me." Not my core. Not my love. Not my will. If I'm doing this, it's because I believe it's the right thing to do.

Something in him changes. He nods. All steely and determined. "You've already signed a contract."

"And you've already said you want me. Just me."

He nods. "You're a good negotiator."

"Maybe. I just want to survive this." I bite my lip. "My sister will hate me for lying to her."

"Your sister will understand." He stares at me with big, earnest eyes. "This is for her future too, isn't it?"

It's the first time I've seen him this earnest.

"Does your mother mean that much to you?" I ask.

"She means everything to me."

But lying to her...

Blake is right.

I already agreed to this.

But if he really does need me, I'm the one holding the cards.

I don't know Meryl. I don't know if she'd prefer a comforting lie over a hurtful truth. I have to trust that Blake does know her. That he's making the right choice.

I know my sister.

And she's not going to take lying. "I have to tell Lizzy. I tell her everything or I walk."

He stares back at me. "She's a kid. She'll gossip."

"She won't. And either way, I'm not negotiating this point."

Blake stares into my eyes, picking me apart.

"I want her to meet you. I want you to be friendly."

He nods. "I'll find a break in my schedule."

"Okay." I offer my hand.

He shakes.

Now this is on my terms too.

———

I ARRIVE HOME AT 3 A.M.

Lizzy is sitting on the couch with a worried look on her face.

"What the hell?" She pulls her phone from her pocket and opens her web browser to a gossip site. "*Tech CEO Blake Sterling Engaged to Everyday Girl*." She makes eye contact. "Quite the fucking compliment."

"It's a school night," I say.

"I'm not going to school tomorrow. I won't hear the end of it."

She stares at me like she's looking for a crack, something she can use to get me to confess.

I'm back in jeans and a sweater. Most of my fancy clothes are in Blake's apartment. He'll probably want me there soon. Until his mom... I don't even want to think it.

"We don't lie to each other. That's the deal, remember?" she says. "The two of us against the world, because the world is obviously against us."

"Of course." That's what I told her after the accident. When I realized how screwed we were. "It's still us against the world. I promise."

"Are you going to tell me what's going on here?" she asks.

"In the morning. I'm too tired to think straight."

"Kat, now. I'm not going to be able to sleep. This doesn't make any sense."

"In the morning. We'll get pancakes and walk around the gardens."

"I got this today." She goes to the kitchen table and picks up an envelope. "A scholarship from your boyfriend's company. Excuse me, your fiancé's company."

"That's great."

"Kat, you know I'll be happy for you. I'll support you in whatever this is, but only if you tell me the truth."

My chest tightens. That's what I want. Only I also want her respect. And I'm not sure I deserve it. "Okay, I promise."

"How the hell did you get me this scholarship?"

"You earned it."

"Bullshit." She slams the paper against the table. The whole thing shakes, and her glasses fall off her nose. The tough look on her face drops. "Okay, so I'm not pulling this off."

"You'd make a great bad cop." I take a seat at the kitchen table. "He suggested it. Said you'd be perfect for it no matter what, since you're a woman in STEM."

She wipes her glasses on her t-shirt. "I mean no offense by this, really, but did he suggest this while you were on your knees?"

"Really?"

"Really? I'm not the one suddenly engaged to a freakin' billionaire."

My sister thinks I'm a whore. Or maybe I am a whore. I'm fucking Blake because I want him. But the rest? He is buying something from me. Something that shouldn't be for sale. "We have an agreement. It has nothing to do with you."

"So he hasn't been your secret boyfriend forever?"

"No."

"You're not in love?"

"No."

"But you are having sex? I mean, I know you are. You keep showing up with a satisfied look on your face."

"We are. But that's not what he's paying for. I know how it sounds—"

"You don't have to explain." She folds the letter. "You deserve a break, Kat. And he's hot. Whatever he's paying for... I don't care. As long as you're happy. And as long as it's for you."

"It's for us."

Her expression gets serious. "Don't do this for me."

"You already have the scholarship. It's done."

"Kat! Will you fucking listen for a minute?"

"I am."

"No, you're not. I know you're obsessed with solving all our problems, and I appreciate that. I really do. But I'm an adult. I can handle things too. I can find a scholarship. Or take a loan. You've already sacrificed a lot for me. I can't take you giving up anything else."

But... this is for us. It needs to be for us or what the hell is the point of it?

"Kat?"

"Just take the scholarship."

She folds her arms.

"It's done, already. And this is for me too. I quit my job. Now, I'll have time to draw and run and live my life. And I'll be able to finally go to school. You're right. I want a break." Not as much as I want Lizzy doing well, but I do want it. "And I like Blake. I want to get to know him. And to sleep with him."

That gets her smiling. "It's that good?"

"Yes. But we're not talking about that—"

"Oh my God, we so are!" Her smile widens. "Let me see the ring." She takes my hand and stares at the enormous rock. "You know, his company is worth like ten or twenty billion dollars."

"I know."

"They have this side project. A chat bot they're testing on their IM program, to see if it can fool users. It's really cool." She releases my hand.

Figures my nerdy little sister is more interested in chat bots than in my fake wedding. Even if both are imitations of human connection.

"He wants to meet you. You could show him your chess bot," I say. "He loves chess."

Her cheeks flush. "I couldn't. That's like you showing your sketchbook to van Gogh or something."

"You really should go to sleep. It is a school night."

"And I'm skipping. It's public school. I can call in sick for myself. And there's no way I'm sleeping until I get all the details. About this arrangement. And about sex with a hot billionaire." She gets up and turns on the kettle. "You want black or green tea?"

"You can't tell anyone."

"I won't. I promise."

Chapter Thirteen

Once upon a time, before the accident, I would spend weekends exploring the city with my friends. It was exciting just to get out of Brooklyn.

It felt like there was an adventure waiting around every corner.

The last three years, I've been sorely lacking adventure. I work, I read, I play video games with Lizzy.

Whatever happened to what I wanted to do? When I was seventeen, my life was wide open with possibilities. Art school to turn my doodling hobby into a career. A state university to study something practical. English or business, maybe. My best friend, Belle, asked me to take a gap year to travel Europe with her.

It was such an exciting thought. The two of us zipping around Europe, taking in the sights, flirting with different guys in every country. After the accident, all that went out the window. Everything I wanted or needed went out the window. Taking care of Lizzy and keeping us afloat came first.

And now…

I have no idea how to spend my afternoon off. Lizzy and I had a long, chatty brunch, but now she's at work (she refused to quit) and I'm wandering around the park by myself.

I should be ecstatic that the weight around my neck is gone. No more waiting tables. No more mortgage hanging over my head. No more struggling with bills.

I am relieved.

But I'm restless too.

Like I don't have a direction.

What the hell am I supposed to do with my time?

I pull my coat tighter as I lean in to examine a rose-bush. Right now, it's all leaves and thorns. It's all the protection and none of the beauty. None of the life.

I'm the same. I've ignored my hobbies, my friends, my dreams. For three years, I've been a machine. Work. Sleep. Taking care of Lizzy.

What if there's nothing else to me?

What if there's no Kat when you strip away the girl desperate to get by?

I close my eyes and try my best to recall a typical week before the accident. School. Homework. Cross-country. I loved losing myself in a long run as the city whizzed by me.

In high school, I took every art elective I could. I was utterly indiscriminate. My parents discouraged art school. Wouldn't pay the bills. But the bills won't need paying soon. I can go to school, get a master's, take a job I love that pays crap. I can ask Belle to give me another chance and pay for a year in Europe.

This money is options.

This money is freedom.

This money is security.

I spend the rest of the afternoon loading up on art books and supplies. The smell of sharpened pencils recalls so many nights spent drawing. I buy one of everything in every color. Markers, ink pens, pastels, watercolors, graphite pencils, acrylics, oils, canvases. Being in the store makes me dizzy. Something about it feels so right.

A call from Blake interrupts my bliss. When I answer, he's all business.

"We're meeting my family tomorrow. I'll send a car to your apartment at four-thirty," he says.

A surge of irritation passes through me. He could ask. He could pretend like he cares that I have my own priorities.

"You're supposed to meet my sister," I say.

"Trust me. You don't want to bring her to dinner. Not with Fiona's mood."

Deep breath. I have to push back to get what I want from Blake. "Then meet her tonight. Come over for dinner."

"I'm entertaining a friend."

Since when does Blake have friends? I bite my lip. No backing down now. "Bring him."

"I'll make reservations for four. Eight o'clock. I'll send a car to pick you up at seven-thirty."

"Good." I'm not sure which of us won that argument. Or if it was an argument. "I'll see you then."

"You too." The phone clicks.

I'm getting what I want, but, somehow, I don't feel victorious.

———

LIZZY IS NOT IMPRESSED BY THE CAR SERVICE. SHE SITS with her arms folded over her chest, her eyes on the window. "Is all this fuss necessary?"

"It's faster than the subway."

"The subway is better." She stares out the tinted window, her lips curled into a frown. She's upset, yes, but I don't think it's about Blake.

It's something else.

"You okay?" I ask.

"You know I don't like being in a car."

"We *can* take the subway."

"No. I'll be fine." She squeezes her purse so hard her knuckles turn white.

Lizzy is strong, but she's like me in her inability to admit she needs help. She used to love being in a car. It was a rare treat. But since the accident, she gets quiet and skittish in autos.

I don't blame her—she almost died in the backseat of a car.

But I have no idea if it's a slight annoyance or a crippling fear.

She's silent for the rest of the ride. As soon as she steps onto the concrete, the tension falls from her shoulders. She sighs with relief.

"It looks like a nice place." She nods to the restaurant. "You think the food's good?"

"Probably."

"You think they'll card Mr. Blake Sterling's guests?"

Oh, hell no. I shoot her a death glare. "Not funny."

She laughs. "It's actually really funny. You look like a cartoon character. Like your head is a balloon that's going to pop."

I'm too overprotective. I know that. But she's all I've got. "Don't talk about alcohol at dinner, okay?"

"Why?"

"It's a sore subject. Trust me."

"Okay."

I follow her inside. The restaurant is dark in a romantic way.

I nod hello to the hostess. "Kat Wilder. I'm meeting—"

"Of course, Ms. Wilder. Your party is in a private room." She grabs two menus and leads us upstairs.

The room is impressive—a table big enough for eight people and tall windows that let in the intoxicating mix of sky and steel.

Blake is sitting opposite Declan, the guy I met at the company party. He must be the friend. I guess he's visiting.

Blake stands. "We're fine. Thank you." He takes the menus from the hostess.

She nods and disappears back down the stairs.

Blake offers Lizzy his hand. "Blake Sterling. You must be Lizzy."

"Yeah." She shakes his hand. "It's nice to meet you. About time, really, with you engaged to my sister."

"You can't blame me for wanting to keep her to myself," Blake says.

She shoots me a *nice line* look. "You can't blame me for objecting."

"No. Anyone would want Kat around." Blake motions to his friend. "Declan Jones. Too much of an ass to introduce himself, apparently."

Declan makes his way to Lizzy. They shake. "Nice to meet you." He turns to me. "And nice to see you again, Kat. I thought Blake was fucking with me when he suggested we invite two more people to our dinner."

Lizzy laughs. "Kat doesn't ever go out with me either."

They share a knowing look at our expense.

Blake pulls out my chair. His fingertips skim my neck as I take a seat. It makes me warm and hot at once. It's sweet and possessive. Affectionate and sexual. But which part is real and which part is fake?

I turn to Declan. "Have you ever met one of Blake's girlfriends?"

"A girlfriend? Blake? No. He's never had one." Declan shoots Blake a wink. "Maybe not even a girl-space-friend. You should have seen him in college. Girls went crazy for him. He was a legend—the kid with the company, the one who ignored female attention. There was a bet in our class. A bunch of women thought they'd be the first to seduce Blake. They'd come up to him with gaga eyes and offer to blow him right in the computer lab."

Blake's cheeks flush red. "It wasn't that explicit."

"It was worse. It got to be a thing—who was hot enough to tempt him away from his work? But no one ever did," Declan says.

Blake is actually blushing. It's amazing. I want to capture his expression forever. I want to draw it in a million panels and a billion portraits.

"I wasn't exactly a monk," Blake says.

Declan laughs. "He can't have you thinking he didn't get laid."

Blake motions to me and clears his throat. "I'm trying to convince her I'm a gentleman."

Lizzy laughs. "Kat is the same with guys. She always thinks they're friendly. There's this waiter who's always flirting with her, but she insists it's just professional courtesy."

"Is that so?" Blake shoots me a knowing look.

"He's just being nice," I say.

"He invites you to meet him after his shift all the time. And he gives you free drinks," Lizzy says. "He's cute too. You should have taken him up on it when you had the chance." She smiles at Blake. "Well, maybe not as cute as your fiancé."

She and Declan share another knowing look.

This is flirting.

I swallow hard.

No way in hell is my sister hanging out with an entitled player.

There's a knock on the door. A waiter steps inside and takes our drink orders. Lizzy sticks with her usual Diet Coke.

I relax into my seat.

This almost feels like a normal dinner.

Blake turns his attention to Lizzy. "Kat tells me you're a programmer."

"Nothing of your caliber, but yes," she says.

"What languages?" Blake asks.

"Work at dinner?" Declan asks. "You have more game than that, Sterling."

"It's fine." This is one time I'm happy to suffer boredom. I want Lizzy and Blake connecting. I want her on board with this plan instead of tolerating it.

"I mostly do Java and Python," Lizzy says. "But I'm learning C++."

Blake leans over, unzips a bag, pulls out a laptop, and sets it on the table. "You want to see any of the Sterling Tech code?"

Her eyes go wide. "Uh, yeah. If you're sure that's okay."

"We'll call it a family secret," he says.

She nearly jumps out of her chair and kneels next to the laptop. "The chat bot has always been my favorite thing."

"Kat told me you're interested in A.I."

"That's like saying a fish is interested in swimming."

Blake smiles.

I melt.

———

PROGRAMMING TALK SLOWS TO A MINIMUM. BLAKE OFFERS Lizzy an internship for next summer. Declan matches the offer. It takes everything I have not to throw my drink on the floor and scream *no way in hell is my sister working with a flirting player*, but I manage to keep my mouth shut. The guy is nice. Flirting isn't a crime.

It's a nice dinner. Blake and Lizzy actually seem friendly. And the way he kisses me goodnight... I can feel the affection in it. Some of it is real. He does care about me.

Lizzy waits until we're seated on the subway to talk. She shifts in her seat, still bouncing from her caffeine high.

"I can see why you like him." She takes a slow breath. "But you have to be careful. He'll rip your heart out like it's nothing."

Chapter Fourteen

After another long day I struggle to fill, I take the subway to Blake's building. There's a key waiting for me with the doorman. Apparently, my fiancé is still at work.

I settle into the big, empty room.

The sun is sinking into the sky, casting soft orange light over the den. It doesn't suit the space. The light is warm, inviting, alive. This apartment is sterile. Lifeless. Dull.

It's a beautiful room, but it looks more like a model house than a home. There isn't a single crumb out of place. The tile is shiny, the appliances are sparkling, the floor is spotless.

I settle onto the plush leather couch and fish my new sketchbook from my purse. It's pocket-sized. Well, purse-sized. Perfect for capturing what's in my head. I'm not sure what I'm doing with my life now that I'm not getting by twenty-four seven. This will help me figure out what's in my head. What I want.

The park really is beautiful in the sunset. I sketch the view. The buildings across the park start as rectangles. I add detail—the shadows, the windows, the satellite dishes on the roofs—until they take on life.

It's not a technically great drawing, but it's a start.

The door opens and Blake steps inside. My attention goes straight to him.

He's in his suit, all tall and stoic and handsome.

Those blue eyes of his make my heartbeat pick up.

"You're early," he says.

I nod. "I felt like being here."

Blake moves closer. He sits next to me, examining my sketch over his shoulder.

This isn't good work. It's not worth showing off.

I flip my sketchbook closed and slide it into my purse.

"You can draw. I don't mind." He brushes a stray hair behind my ear. "We don't need to leave for a while."

"Okay."

"Have you taken a look at your room?"

"My room?"

He motions to the sex room.

"It's mine?"

"We're engaged."

"Don't engaged couples share a bed?"

"Call it your office. You'll need space for your art. For school. For whatever you'd like to do."

"What if I'd like to shop and get manicures?"

"You wouldn't."

"But what if I would?"

He stares at me, picking me apart. "Then you'll need space for your wardrobe."

"Are you teasing me?"

He shrugs *maybe*.

He is teasing me. And it makes me warm. But then it also makes me want him more. Want *this* more. His affection is real. A part of him cares about me. And that's confusing.

We're getting divorced in six months.

I can't fall in love with Blake.

I can't get confused.

"Are you telling me I should change?" I ask.

"Were you planning on wearing that?"

I'm in jeans and a sweater. Not exactly a nice outfit, but the kind of thing people wear to dinner at a parent's house. "Why? Does your mother have a problem with women who shop at H&M?"

"No. But Fiona will have a comment."

"I'll put on one of my dresses."

"It's up to you."

"Is it? You seem insistent."

"No." His fingers skim my leg. "I want to protect you from my sister, but I'm not sure it's possible."

"She hates me already?"

"She doesn't think you have good intentions."

"She's right."

"No. Your intentions are good. They just aren't love."

I guess that's true. "Maybe... well, I don't know anything about you. Not really." I move off the couch. There aren't many places to go in this enormous apartment, at least not in the way of furniture. I take a seat on a stool in the kitchen. "This would work better if we really did love each other. As friends." More than that is out of the question. And contemplating the possibility of it is confusing.

"What would you like to know?"

"Something important," I say. "Something your fiancée would know."

"You know everything important. The documents I sent over with Jordan—"

"That's all stuff anyone could find online. What about the Blake behind the suit and the steel expression?"

The steel expression softens. He slips out of his suit jacket, undoes the top two buttons of his shirt, and pulls it open. He points to a thin scar running across his chest. It's light. Faint. "See this?"

I nod.

"I tell people I fell out of a tree. You'll see at my mother's house. None of the trees are sturdy enough to climb."

"What happened?" I ask.

"My parents were fighting. I stepped in. My father hit me instead."

My stomach flip-flops. That's something a lot of people wouldn't know.

It's awful, but Blake's expression is still stone.

It's matter of fact.

How can he be so calm about his dad hitting him?

I force myself to hold his gaze. "How old were you?"

"Twelve."

All the breath leaves my body at once. Twelve? That's nothing. A child.

He moves towards me. "It was a long time ago. It doesn't hurt me anymore."

"Yeah, of course." I force a smile. "Thanks for telling me. I hope you're not... Well, if you want to talk, we could talk." I try to decipher the look on his face but it does me no good. "I know that talking isn't really our thing. Or your thing. You're very quiet and all. But, yeah, um... I could listen if you ever wanted to talk. And I could talk, too." My cheeks flush. "If you want."

"I appreciate that."

"Thank you for telling me. Really. You can tell me things like that, but I meant more like... a hobby or your favorite book. Something like that."

"*1984*."

"Really?"

He nods. "Funny, I know. My company is basically Big Brother."

"You don't have personal access to that, do you?" My cheeks flare. "You couldn't see my search histories or emails. Could you? You could, couldn't you?"

He nods. "I haven't. I won't. If I ever want to know something about you, I'll ask."

I study his expression. Inscrutable as usual. He's probably telling the truth. I don't think he lies to me.

"And you?" he asks.

"What about me?"

"What's your favorite book?"

My cheeks flush. "You'll laugh."

"Have you ever seen me laugh?"

Now, I'm the one laughing. "Come to think of it, no. Not a full-on belly laugh. I'm going to have to make more stupid jokes. Do something to get an expression on your face."

He is unblinking, as usual. This time, I'm pretty sure he's trying to mess with me.

"It's Botox, isn't it?" I ask. "The secret to your youth and your lack of expression. I bet it's Botox."

That elicits a smile. He really does have a beautiful smile. It lights up the room.

"It's a graphic novel," I say. "*Ghost World*. It's about these teenage girls who live in a small town. There are all these little vignettes of their lives as they start to grow up and realize their ideas about the world are wrong."

A smile. It's a full-fledged smile. It's all the way to his cheeks.

"It sounds perfect for you."

"It is. And you, um, do you like graphic novels? Or

comic books? I know you're a programmer, but you've never actually mentioned anything geeky. Not even something that's really mainstream like *The Avengers* or *Star Wars* or something."

He stares back, unblinking.

"You don't even… Well, I guess, except for *1984*, I don't know much about what you like or do. Except work. And chess. You work and you play chess and you read *1984*." A comic book version of Blake filters through my brain. He's as built as any superhero, but his superpower is work. Every page, he's at a computer, in a business meeting, or playing chess in a new, fantastical location.

"Kat."

I'm back to attention. "Yeah?"

"What's your favorite book that isn't a graphic novel?"

"You mean a book where all the pages are words?" I ask.

He nods.

"*Brave New World.*" I wink.

He holds my gaze. "Are you mocking me, Miss Wilder?"

"Definitely. I mean, obviously, if I was going to go dystopia, I'd go with *The Hunger Games*." I rack my brain for a book I really love, one that will make me sound mildly sophisticated. Nothing comes. "*Ghost World* is my final answer."

He opens the fridge, pulls out a bowl of fruit salad and two forks, and makes a motion that can only mean *eat*. "You're sticking to your guns. I admire that."

"Thanks." I pick up a fork and stab a berry. The fruit salad is all berries. Blake has been paying attention. "I was writing a graphic novel back in high school. I might finally have time to work on it now."

He moves closer. Three inches away. One hand slides

around my waist, pulling up the fabric of my sweater. The other traces the outline of my lips. He brings his fingers to his mouth and licks them clean. He leans closer. Closer. My eyelids press together.

His lips make contact. It's not like any of our other kisses. It's not some big thing for show. It's not a smoldering kiss designed to make my panties wet. It's sweet. Caring even.

That's a lie.

But I'm starting to believe it.

———

AFTER AN HOUR OF CONVERSATION, WE DRESS IN SEPARATE rooms and take the elevator to the parking garage.

Pretty, made-up Kat stares back at me through the mirrored walls. I'm still not expert with makeup, but I look pretty good. And my dress is beautiful. Elegant. Way too much for a family dinner, really.

I make my way into the limo with careful steps. Blake follows.

The door shuts behind us, locking us into our own little world.

He nods to a bottle of champagne in the ice bucket. "The same one you liked at the party."

"The party where we had our joyful engagement?"

"Don't say things like that."

"Why? We're alone. This is the part that's real. That's what you told me."

He stares at me. "Fine. Get it out of your system now."

If I didn't know better, I'd swear I'd hurt his feelings. "That's okay."

The car starts and pulls out of the parking garage. Once we're on the street, its movements become one comfortable blur. No wonder rich people take these things everywhere. You really do forget you're in transit.

He shifts. We're on different bench seats. They're perpendicular. I have to turn if I really want a good look at Blake.

There's so much to his face. The strong jaw, the sharp line of his nose, the gorgeous blue eyes.

That bit about eyes being the windows to the soul— total bullshit. They're not the windows to Blake's soul. I stare into those eyes and come up with nothing. I don't have a clue what he's thinking or feeling.

If only I could crack that gorgeous head open and pry into his brain. It shouldn't interest me this much. He's closer to a boss than to a boyfriend.

"Penny for your thoughts?" I bite my tongue. That's a terrible line. And it's cheesy as hell.

His expression stays neutral. "We need to announce our wedding date tonight."

"Already?" My palms get clammy. This whole marriage thing is still a weight on my chest. I can do it. I will. But it makes me feel sick."

"The last Friday in April. I booked a ballroom at the Plaza. Very exclusive."

"I'm not getting married in a hotel ballroom."

Surprise fills his blue eyes. "Why not?"

"It's awful and stuffy and not at all my taste."

"What's the difference?"

"You want people to believe this or not?" I smooth my dress. "I'm getting married in a park."

"It will be cold in late April."

"I'll get a dress with sleeves."

"It might rain."

"Then it will rain," I say. "And since the season lines up, I'd like a park with cherry blossom trees."

He smiles. "You like them?"

"No, I want to get married there because I hate them." The sentence leaves me out of breath. Talking to him is impossible. Sarcasm isn't helping. It's not my strong suit. "Of course I like them. They're gorgeous."

It's not like our last ride in this limo. I trust him to understand.

"Before the accident, we would go to DC for a weekend every April just to look at the trees. My parents got all sweet and romantic. I thought it was gross back then, Mom and Dad kissing under the flowers. And I didn't understand my mom's lecture either. Every time, it was the same. 'Life is short. You need to take time to enjoy it.'" I press my back into the seat. Move my eyes to the floor. "I was a stupid teenager. Life felt long. I couldn't wait until I'd finally graduate high school, then college. I couldn't wait to be independent. Funny how quickly I became independent."

A tear wells up inside me. I squeeze my eyelids together until it retreats. This is waterproof makeup, but I'm not crying in front of Blake. He's all walls and defenses. I can't let down mine.

"It must be hard being the woman of the house." His voice is steady but there's a certain sweetness to it. Almost affection.

"Everything worth doing is hard." I meet his gaze. Smile. "I'm getting married under the damn cherry blossoms. You won't stop me."

"Are you sure you wouldn't rather save that for your real wedding?"

"Positive." Tension flares between my shoulder blades. "We'll be legally married. Our families will attend. I'm sure I'll be in a very expensive dress. That's plenty real."

"I'll get Ashleigh on finding you a dress. Tell her what

you like and she'll find something for you." He looks at something on his phone. "She'll text you about setting up an appointment."

"I want to bring Lizzy."

He nods. "You should."

"Good." It feels like a victory, him suggesting my sister support me.

"Will she be your maid of honor?"

"Of course. And your best man?"

"I don't want one."

"No?"

He shakes his head. "I don't trust anyone enough."

"That's weird."

"And I'm not."

"You're a control freak."

"True."

"I, um… with the wedding, we need to make sure we find a way to agree on things. Compromise is the key to any healthy relationship. Even a fake one."

His lips spread into a full-blown smile. Then, I can't believe it. He laughs. His entire face lights up. His eyes are bright. He's always been attractive as all hell, but that laugh, those bright eyes.

Somehow, he's even more gorgeous when he smiles.

"Noted," he says.

"Who are we inviting?"

"My family. Your family."

"That's it?"

His expression softens. He moves closer. "You object?"

"No. That's perfect. I just expected a big show from you after last time."

"This is for Meryl, not for anyone else."

It's sweet, really. A big fat lie for his dying mother.

Chapter Fifteen

The house is more modest than I imagined. Two stories. Four bedrooms. A walkway lined with rosebushes.

I squeeze Blake's hand as we move towards the door.

My heart is racing. My stomach is flip-flopping. I'm not sure I've ever been this nervous. Lying at a party is one thing. But sitting down with his mom and lying to her face?

I'm still not sure if I'm capable.

Blake squeezes back. It's too sweet, too comforting. I need to banish all the ideas floating through my head, the ones about this being real.

The door is open. He turns the handle and motions *after you.*

I step inside. It's warm. And it's beautiful. Pictures line the staircase, pillows decorate the couch, books overflow from a shelf against the wall.

We move into the kitchen. Meryl is nursing a glass of wine. Fiona is sitting with a man in a suit. He's in his 30s and he's not really here. His attention is all on his shiny iPhone.

He's the picture of a Wall Street guy. Similar attire, but he's so different from Blake.

It's hard to explain. This guy radiates a certain self-importance. Blake is arrogant, but there's a kindness behind his eyes.

Blake takes my coat and hangs it, and his, on a rack. He greets his family with a nod. "Kat, this is Trey, Fiona's husband."

Oh. Of course. That explains a lot. I'd doubt the possibility of marriage for love if this guy was my husband.

Trey looks up from his phone for a split second. He nods. "Nice to meet you."

Meryl catches my gaze. She shakes her head as she nods to Trey. "What are you two drinking? And don't say you're driving. I saw the limo pull away. What does the poor driver do while you're here?"

"Earn his salary." Blake plants a soft kiss on my cheek. "I'll get drinks."

Meryl holds up her mostly empty glass. "Wine is on the counter."

Blake frowns but takes her glass. I guess there's no sense of objecting to drinking harming her health. Not if she's dying.

My stomach drops. I force my lips into a smile. Half my thoughts go to the warmth on my cheek. I can still feel his lips. The other half go running in the other direction. The *stop getting caught up in your own lie* direction.

"Have a seat, sweetie," Meryl says. "I remember working in a restaurant. I was always desperate to get off my feet."

I sit. "Actually, I'm not working at the restaurant anymore."

Fiona smiles. "Oh?"

"I quit. To focus on my art." Sort of.

Fiona nods like she understands. "It was the same when I started my clothing line. I had to leave my purchasing job at Saks."

Meryl smiles at her daughter. "I'm sure you could help Kat. Teach her about running her own business."

"I don't know anything about art." She offers me a remorseful smile.

I can't really get a read on her. Does she actually want to help me? Or is she reveling in being withholding?

Everything falls from Fiona's expression as Trey's phone rings.

He nods to his cell. "Excuse me."

She fights her frown, but she doesn't quite get there. She watches her husband leave the room like he's taking her heart with him.

I get the feeling this isn't the first time he's bailed on a conversation for a call. Even the first time tonight.

"My son is a lot of trouble. I hope he's making it up to you," Meryl says.

Right on cue, Blake returns with drinks. Wine for Meryl. Whiskey for him. Gin and tonic for me.

His fingers brush mine as he hands over the glass.

It's the same. My body buzzes with desire. Already, I want to be alone with him.

I take a long sip of my gin and tonic. It's delicious, but it isn't refreshing.

Blake shoots his mother a *really* look. "That isn't appropriate dinner table conversation."

"Oh, please. You know I wouldn't mind." Meryl looks to me with a smile. "Dinner should be ready shortly. But if you're hungry, there are snacks in the fridge."

"I'm fine, thank you." I finish half my drink. It warms my throat and pushes away the *you shouldn't do this* voice in my head.

Fiona stares at her half-full glass of wine. "I'm surprised Blake hasn't offered to help you." She looks to Trey's empty seat. "Trey is the one who offered the seed money for my clothing line. He was very supportive."

Regret streaks her expression. The guy taking a call outside is clearly not supportive. He's one of those wealthy guys who writes a check instead of tending to his wife's emotional needs.

I don't know the asshole, and I already hate him.

My gaze goes to Blake. Damn. He's good at this. There isn't a single visible reaction on his face. The man is the picture of cool.

But then, he always is.

"I'll do anything for Kat. Anything." He runs his fingers over my cheek. Stares at me like we're in love. "But her independence is very important to her. She wants to make her own way."

"Admirable, but sweetie—" Meryl takes quite the sip of wine. "Take the poor fool's money if he's offering it."

"It will be our money soon." Blake smiles. "We set a date. The last Friday in April."

"You're not asking for a prenup?" Fiona tries to wipe away the shock on her face but doesn't quite land at a neutral expression.

Blake raises a brow. They share a look of understanding. It's pure sibling telepathy.

"I don't want to hear those words again," Meryl says. "And I do not want to hear a single figure."

Fiona frowns. "But Blake could lose the company if they divorce."

"What did I say?" Meryl squeezes her wineglass.

Fiona flushes red. She stumbles over her words. "I only want to help him protect himself."

"And how did that prenup work for you?" Meryl asks.

"That's different. He had more money," Fiona says.

"I am signing a prenup." I try my most confident voice. "It was my idea. I don't want Blake thinking I'm in this for his money. I may be young, but I'm not naive. I know marriage doesn't always work out. I'd rather we have these details ironed out now than later."

Meryl stares at me the way Blake does. She picks me apart, assessing the weight of every single word. "You're a fool, sweetie, but an admirable one."

I smooth my dress. "Thank you. I think."

She laughs. "It's a compliment." She looks to Blake and Fiona. "My kids, they don't get it. They think marriage is about protecting your assets. It's not. It's about finding a partner who will hold you up when you need that. It's about finding someone who you need by your side. Someone who will support you."

I swallow hard. Marriage should be all those things. It should be everything.

Right on cue, Trey walks into the room. "Fi-fi, sweetie, I have to go."

Meryl shoots Fiona a *see* look.

Fiona frowns. "Can't you stay for dinner?"

He leans in to plant a kiss on her check. "I wish I could, but this is an emergency." He looks to Meryl. "Meryl—"

"Don't bother." She shakes her head. "This is the example I set for you. Hell, at least you're leaving."

Somehow, this doesn't hurt Trey.

He looks to Fiona and whispers something. She narrows her eyes and furrows her brow.

Trey stands and takes a step towards the door. "I'm sorry, Meryl. I'll see you next week."

Meryl clears her throat. "Have a safe drive."

Trey kisses Fiona goodbye and steps out of the room.

Everyone is quiet until the door slams shut and a car outside turns on.

Fiona addresses Meryl. "He's trying to be supportive."

"He's an asshole."

"So was Dad."

Meryl lets out a heavy sigh. She stares at her wineglass like it holds all the secrets of the universe. "If you do this to Kat, I swear to God..." She looks at me. "Some family to marry into."

I swallow hard. "Blake is sweet."

Meryl makes eye contact with him but speaks to me. "This is what money gets you—the pursuit of more money."

"I'm not like Trey. And Kat isn't like Fiona," Blake says.

"Fuck you." Fiona folds her arms.

"Not everything is an insult," Blake says.

They exchange hostile looks. There's something knowing about it. Like there's no way for them to let anyone else in.

They seem to hate each other and love each other in equal measures.

Meryl's voice softens. She offers Fiona her hand. "You didn't know better, sweetie. You were just a kid."

Fiona pulls her hand into her lap. "I was nineteen."

"Exactly. You're better off without him," Meryl says.

"With nothing," Fiona says.

Meryl looks to Fiona. To Blake. Neither one of them is willing to challenge her. Something about her expression makes them stand down.

Meryl shakes her head. "What is with you two? Why is it always money? There's more to life than that."

Under the table, Blake squeezes my hand. He looks at me as if to ask *are you okay?*

I nod *yes.* I'm okay enough.

The room goes quiet. It makes the air heavy. I guess Blake and Fiona agree that everything is about money.

It's kind of sad.

I've never pitied rich people before. Not even for a second. Being broke sucks.

But it makes you appreciate what you have.

I have a best friend. Someone I love unconditionally, who is always going to be on my side.

I wouldn't trade my relationship with Lizzy for all of Blake and Fiona's money.

Fiona plays with her food. She looks to Blake and adopts her best sisterly voice. "Three and a half weeks is awfully fast."

Something passes between Meryl and Blake. Damn. This whole family has some kind of crazy telepathic power.

"We don't want to wait," Blake says.

Meryl looks at me as if to confirm. "Is that right?"

"It was my idea," I say. "I'm insistent about marrying under the cherry trees, and I don't want to wait another year."

Her expression softens. "I see."

"I'm very sentimental about them. It's always been a family tradition. Well, I don't want to bore you."

"And your family approves?" she asks.

"It's just me and my sister. My parents were in an accident a few years ago. They passed on." I press my lips together. I don't like thinking about it. It gets too many feelings whirring in my chest, and I don't have time to stop and feel them.

Or I didn't.

I guess I do now.

"Oh, I'm sorry, sweetheart," Meryl says.

"Thank you." I nod.

"You'll need help with the wedding," Meryl says. Her voice is packed with understanding. "How about I handle the reception? Just pick a color."

It's a sweet offer. "Pink."

Meryl smiles. "A girl after my own heart."

The kitchen timer rings. Meryl presses her hands into the table, but she struggles to stand.

Blake rushes to help her. She shakes her head like she can't stand the fuss.

"I'll get it," Blake says.

He motions to Fiona, another sibling secret. Whatever it is, it works. Fiona excuses herself and they put together dinner in the kitchen.

"Let them fuss," Meryl says. "Tell me, what do you like to do for fun?"

"Typical stuff. Movies, TV, hanging out with my sister."

"What about the stuff that isn't typical?"

I play with the hem of my dress. "I ran cross-country in high school, but I haven't kept up with it very well."

She looks at her glass wistfully. "Never cared much for running myself."

I nod. "Are you okay?"

"Fine. What about when you want to relax? After a run? You don't strike me as one of those girls who is mostly interested in parties and shopping. Though I did enjoy both in my day."

"I draw." I make my voice confident. I'm about to marry the woman's son. I need to seem like a strong, independent woman. Someone worthy of him. "I've been thinking about art school."

"Excellent. Art school. Yes, that would suit you. You'll have to stay in the dorms and drive Blake mad forcing him to visit."

"That would get him out of the office."

She smiles, but it's not the same as before. She doesn't quite have her strength.

Blake and Fiona finish setting the table. They bring in dinner on thick ceramic plates. It's homemade, a pot roast and side salads dressed with a dark vinaigrette.

"Thank you," I say to no one in particular.

I take Blake's lead when everyone starts eating.

Meryl picks at her salad. Fiona stares at her food like it bores her. I can't imagine she has much of an appetite after her husband's remarkable show of apathy.

She turns her attention to me. "Can I see the ring?"

"Oh. Sure." I place my hand over the table like I'm modeling the enormous rock. "It's beautiful."

"Tiffany?" Fiona asks.

Blake shoots her a *shut up* look.

"It looks expensive." She glances at her smaller but still impressive wedding ring.

"Don't be tacky," Meryl says.

"I'm admiring my future sister-in-law's jewelry." Fiona huffs. She squeezes her hands together like she's trying to stay calm. "Am I not allowed an interest in jewelry either?"

"What did I ever do to raise two children who care so much about status?" Meryl shakes her head. "What the hell are you going to do when I'm not here? You'll drown yourselves in your fucking money."

"Mom, that's not true," Fiona says.

Meryl pushes her plate aside. "Excuse me. I need some air."

Blake makes a move to follow her.

"Sit down. I'm fine. My only problem is the two of you. Finish your dinner, and clean up after yourselves. I know you both have people who do that for you at home." Her eyes turn down. The energy drains from her expression. "Have dessert and coffee without me."

"Mom." Fiona's voice breaks into a whine. "It's cold out."

"I grew up here. This is nothing. Please, let your poor mother have a chance to be alone." She grabs her coat off the rack and walks up the stairs.

For once, I can perfectly read the look on Blake's face. He's terrified.

Chapter Sixteen

Fiona excuses herself the second she's finished eating. She sulks on the balcony, speaking into her cell phone with hushed tones.

It's almost romantic, finishing dinner with Blake. He refills my drink as soon as I'm done. He offers me seconds of everything. He anticipates my needs before I even feel them.

When we're finished, he clears the table and returns with fresh drinks.

He really is a perfect gentleman.

A loving son.

Everything else might be bullshit. But I'm positive Blake adores his mother.

He slides his arm around my waist and pulls me into a tight hug.

His lips hover over my ear. "You're tense."

"I'm fine."

"Are you ever going to admit when you aren't okay?"

"Are you ever going to ask how I feel instead of telling me?"

His voice softens. "Are you alright, Kat?"

"No. I'm kind of tense. You might have noticed."

He lets out a tiny laugh. "You think I'm an asshole."

"If the asinine statements fit…"

"I'll work on asking."

"I'll believe it when it happens."

"Fair." He presses his lips to my neck. "I can get your mind off everything."

"I'm not sure what you're referring to, Mr. Sterling."

His voice drops to that demanding tone. "You are."

"Not at your mom's house."

He pulls back. Takes a long sip of his whiskey.

His eyes pass over me, slowly picking me apart, finding any hint of weakness.

Or maybe he's trying to figure out what I need.

Maybe that look is one of support rather than attack.

Maybe I'm reading him all wrong.

Blake offers his hand. "Come here."

I squeeze his fingers. They're warm. Comforting. I tell myself it's okay I find his touch this calming, but I'm not sure I believe it.

He leads me to the den. It's a cozy room with a TV, a couch, and a small table.

He motions *sit* then digs through the shelf and pulls out a box. Chess.

"I haven't played since grade school," I say.

"The rules are easy." He sits and arranges the pieces on the black-and-white board.

I sit across from him. "I haven't got a chance against you."

"I'll take a handicap."

"Is that right?" I ask.

"The simplest and most severe is removing the queen." He picks up the black queen and sets it on the table.

"Why is it the most severe?"

"The queen is the best piece on the board. It can move in any direction, any number of spaces."

"And to win I have to murder your king, right?"

A laugh. He's actually laughing. It's the best thing I've ever seen. It lights up those blue eyes.

God, those eyes are beautiful.

I clear my throat. So. Not. Going. There.

"What is so funny?" I ask.

"It's called checkmate. Or check."

"It's regicide, plain and simple, buddy. Don't sugarcoat it."

Blake smiles.

My knees go weak. His smile does things to me. It's incapacitating.

He explains all the movement rules, but I'm only barely paying attention. I'm too caught up in that smile.

It takes forever for me to get the rules. Bishops are on the diagonal, pawns go forward one, attack on the diagonal. Knights are some weird 2:1 angle and they jump. Rooks are horizontal and vertical. The queen can move in any direction, any number of spaces. And the utterly useless king can only move one space in any direction.

"That's bullshit," I say.

Another laugh. My heart races. My stomach flutters. The whole world feels warm and safe.

He's laughing at me. Teasing me. I'm like a kid in grade school again, desperate for the boy I like to pull my hair.

Well...

I do want *that*. But not here.

"Why is that?" His voice is light. Easy.

"The queen has all the power. She's a total badass. Why is this stupid game based around protecting a king who is hiding behind all his minions?"

"Think of him as a figurehead. And the queen as the one pulling strings behind the scenes."

"Yeah, I'll consider that." I look at the board. I'm white, the player who goes first. A pretty big advantage, apparently, but nothing compared to losing a queen. "Is that your attitude towards powerful women—you throw them away?"

He stares at me. His voice gets serious. Well, more serious. "I'm not going to throw you away."

"I'm not powerful."

"You are."

"You're right. I have a great power to deceive people. But you have that too."

He slides out of his seat and kneels in front of me. His fingertips graze my thigh, right under my dress. "You're capable of so much."

My heart does a backflip. "Like what?"

"You're captivating."

He slides his hand up my inner thigh. My eyes close instinctively. Want flutters through my body. I tug at my dress. My legs part. *Captivating.* I like the sound of that.

Blake leans closer. His lips connect with mine.

His tongue claims my mouth. His hand slides over my panties. Damn. I'm wet already.

I need him touching me. Even if this is the most inopportune place.

He kisses me harder. Presses his palm flat against me. He's so, so close to touching me properly.

"Jesus H. Christ!" Fiona shrieks.

Blake shifts back into his seat.

Fiona shakes her head. Wipes tears from her puffy eyes as she storms into the kitchen. She returns with a bottle of red wine. "You have an empty limo for that."

Blake leans in to whisper. "Are you okay alone for awhile?"

"Sure." It's sweet he wants to help his sister. Even if I'm not quite clear on their relationship.

He looks to her. "Grab another glass."

Fiona shoots him a *really, in front of your arm candy?* Look.

I push myself to my feet. "Will Meryl mind if I ask to join her on the balcony?" It's the perfect excuse to check on her. Ease the tightness in my chest a little.

"No. She likes you." Blake squeezes my hand. "But knock first."

Fiona sets the wineglass on the table. She looks like she's about to come apart at the seams. I know how that feels—I was walking around like that the year after the accident. It took a long time to feel anything close to okay.

I move to the stairs. They creak with every step. The hallway too.

I knock on the door in the corner. "Meryl. It's Kat. I'm looking to get some air, and Blake is preoccupied downstairs."

Footsteps, and the door opens. Meryl smiles. There's no strain on her face. No signs of her outburst.

She motions *come in*. I do. Her bedroom is clean but not freakishly so. Nothing like Blake's place.

I follow her onto the balcony.

It's cozy. We can see into the backyard. There are a few scrawny trees. And there are flowers just starting to bloom.

She leans against the wooden railing and looks up at the stars. "I hate to get didactic, dear, but take a look at these. You can never see them in the city."

She's right. The dark sky is dotted with them. I haven't seen this many stars since I was a kid. "It's beautiful."

"Yes. They make you think. They're like roses. They're too good as metaphors."

"True."

"You mind if I ask your age?"

"I'm twenty-one."

"A baby. Your whole life is ahead of you." Her sigh is wistful. "If you do marry Blake… you can't give up on your dreams. I know it's tempting, basking in luxury, spending all your time sunbathing in Cabo San Lucas, but that's not a fulfilling life."

My chest warms. This is the kind of talk mothers have with their daughters. Only I never got the chance. "I won't."

"I'm sorry about before. My kids mean well, but, quite frankly, they're idiots."

I laugh.

"Really. Fiona and that awful stockbroker. He's such an ass. Just like her father. Well, not quite. Thank God."

There's something about her voice.

Blake was casual about his father hitting him. Because it only happened once? Or because it happened all the time?

I stare back at Meryl, but it doesn't offer any insight. I have no idea what a battered wife looks like. Even if I did, Blake's father isn't around anymore. He died when Blake was a teenager. That was in his *about me* packet.

"Sweetheart, are you alright?" she asks.

"Oh. Just thinking."

She smiles. "I remember being young and in love. It's hard to concentrate."

"Yes." It is, but it's not the love. It's more the lust.

"Is art school what you want?" she asks.

"I don't know. The last few years, the only thing I wanted was for my sister to be okay. I haven't had the energy to think about the future."

"Is she ill?"

"No. She has a back injury, but it's not serious anymore." I run my fingers over the railing. "My parents died in a car accident three years ago. She was in the backseat. She was in the ICU for a few weeks, but she pulled through. After physical therapy, she was okay. She has most of her mobility."

"Is she in school?"

"She's going to NYU next year." I beam. Lizzy is going to be great. I'm so damn proud of her.

Meryl stares into her wineglass. "You must have grown up fast."

"I did what I had to do for my family."

She turns her attention to me, studying me the way Blake does. "Any art schools in mind?"

"Not yet."

"Make me a promise, dear."

I struggle to keep up my smile. Promises are not my strong suit. "Okay."

Her expression hardens. "Whatever happens between you and Blake, promise you'll go to school."

Above us, the stars shine. They offer all the possibility in the world.

I have that now. Well, as soon as I have the rest of Blake's money.

But I can't lie to Meryl. Not any more than I have.

I need to mean whatever I tell her.

Am I going to school? It's a new idea, but I like it. Four years to focus on what I want, to find my style, to find myself.

It's perfect. "I promise."

She smiles, softening. "You two don't have to get married on my account."

"We're not."

"He told you. I can tell. After my outburst or before?"

I bite my lip. Suddenly aware I'm not in a jacket. "Before."

"Don't rush on my account."

"That's not it. It's just… I want to do it now, before my sister leaves for school."

"Before she's an entire subway ride away?"

I laugh. "She'll be busy. And I want to do this now." Passionate, whirlwind romance. That's the story. I conjure up the image of something that makes my heart flutter, but the only thing that comes to mind is Blake. Damn. "I love him. I don't want to wait."

She studies me. "I'm sure you have the best intentions, sweetheart. But that kind of fire in your loins—I see the way he looks at you like he's undressing you—that never lasts."

"That's your son."

"Men. They're all the same. Always thinking with the head between their legs." She finishes her drink and sets her glass on the railing. Then all her attention is on me. "He's handsome. Rich. If he's good in bed—"

My cheeks flush. "Don't tell me you want to discuss that."

"No. I'm not that… evolved. But I know what it's like being young and in lust. It clouds things. Makes you believe you're in love." She leans in. "But dear, all the money in the world isn't worth a loveless marriage. Trust me on that. True love is priceless."

My heart thuds against my chest.

It's like she knows I'm lying.

Like she can see every lie I've ever told.

I take a step towards the door. I can't keep this up for any longer.

"Excuse me," I say. "I could go for some dessert. Would you like to join me?"

"No thank you. But help yourself. There's coffee and tea in the pantry. Even some of that almond milk everyone is drinking now."

"I think they've moved onto coconut milk."

She smiles. "Good to know. I'll get some of that next time."

"Thank you. For everything."

"Good luck."

I arch a brow.

"With school. It's a lot to consider."

"Oh. Of course."

She looks back to the sky. She's already lost in her own world.

I force myself to leave without another goodbye.

Downstairs, Blake plays chess against himself.

It's quiet. He's alone.

He glances up at me, most of his attention on the board. "I sent Fiona home in the limo. I'll call us a car whenever you're ready to leave."

"She okay?"

"She will be." He pats the spot next to him. "You want coffee?"

"I want that distraction you promised me."

He smiles. "Your wish is my command."

Chapter Seventeen

I get the hang of chess by the end of the second game. Even without his queen, Blake destroys me. The board is picked clear of white pieces except for the scared king cowering the corner.

The weight on my chest gets heavier. This is moving too fast. I met Blake two weeks ago and we're already planning our wedding.

Meryl doesn't want us to rush.

Can she really want us to lie?

Blake's phone buzzes. He picks it up. "The car is here." But he doesn't look happy about it.

I don't ask. Instead, I gather my things and follow him outside.

There's a black town car waiting on the street. It's normal compared to the limo. But it lacks privacy.

I want to be alone with him.

I want to surrender to him. To lose myself to the sensations he's creating in my body.

I step into the car, drop my purse on the ground, fold my hands in my lap.

Blake gives the driver instructions. There isn't any traffic right now. We should be in his apartment within forty-five minutes.

That's too long.

He makes me impatient.

There's an itch inside me. I'm desperate to scratch it.

Blake is all the way on the other side of the car. The middle seat is between us. It's only a few feet, but it feels like a million miles.

I don't get his head or his heart.

I need his body.

I need it pressed against mine.

I need to destroy every inch of space between us.

The car pulls onto the main road.

Blake's eyes pass over me. They light up with some mix of desire and curiosity. Am I a mystery to him too? It's hard to imagine. I feel like my heart is on my sleeve. But he looks at me like he can't figure me out.

He leans closer, so his mouth is hovering over my ear.

The warmth of his breath sends a shiver down my spine. My nerves wake up. They scream for attention.

His lips skim my neck. It's feather light, but I feel it everywhere. My sex clenches. My nipples harden. My knees knock together.

He kisses me harder.

His lips trail from my ear to my collarbone.

His fingers skim the neckline of my dress. "Unzip that."

"But—" I nod to the driver. Honestly, it doesn't bother me. No. It's more than that. I like the idea of the driver knowing. Of someone watching. It feels dirty. Wrong in the right kind of way.

"Now." He pulls my skirt up my thighs. "Don't make me ask again."

His voice is a demand. His eyes too.

There isn't a single part of me that wants to disobey.

I want to forget my thoughts. To forget everything but his words and his touch.

I reach behind me and pull the zipper down to my ass. "Take it off."

The driver looks at me through the rearview mirror.

My cheeks flush.

My sex clenches.

He's going to watch.

And I want him watching.

I just don't want the car crashing.

I look to Blake and slide my straps off my shoulders, one at a time. My dress falls to my waist. "Is that enough?"

"Take off your bra." His tongue slides over his lips as he gives me a long once-over.

I follow his orders.

I unhook my bra and drop it on the floor.

This is getting to be a pattern—me topless and him dressed.

On display for him and anyone else who happens to be around.

Blake's eyes fix on me. "You're fucking gorgeous. You know that?"

My cheeks flush. "Thank you."

Blake undoes his seatbelt. He moves into the middle seat and presses his lips into mine.

He palms my breasts, rubbing my nipples with this thumbs. They harden instantly. His touch lights me on fire.

Need. Blake. Now.

It's the only thing my body knows. The only thing it's ever known.

He takes my hand and places it on his thigh.

It makes me hotter. Needier. I want every inch of his skin. I want him every way I can have him.

It feels so good to touch him. Even with his slacks in the way. His legs are muscular. Strong.

He takes my hand and places it over his hard-on.

Yes.

Now.

Please.

He drags his lips to my ear and sucks on my lobe. It sends pleasure right to my sex. I lose track of what I want more—his mouth on me or my hands on him.

It's all of it.

Everything.

"Unzip me," he says.

Yes.

Fuck yes.

I need to touch him.

My breath catches in my throat. My heart thuds against my chest. My hands get clumsy.

I fumble over his belt. Finally, I get it. I undo his button and pull down his zipper.

I cup him over his boxers.

There's barely any fabric between my hand and his cock.

Desire shoots through me. I need to feel him properly. I start to wrap my hand around him, but he grabs my wrist.

"Not until I tell you," he growls.

He's that animal Blake again.

The one I understand. Who understands me. Who knows what I want better than I know it.

I nod. Not until he tells me.

His teeth scrape my neck. It's just hard enough to hurt. "Hands at your sides."

It's torture bringing my hands back to my sides. They want his skin. I need to touch him. I need it in my bones.

He nips at my neck. It's a soft bite. Then a hard one.

Pain shoots through me, waking up every nerve in my body.

Yes. I need this. He nips at the skin on my chest. Almost.

His lips brush my nipple. Light. Then harder.

He sucks on my nipple. No softness. It's so hard it hurts. Pleasure and pain whir inside me.

It's a lot.

But I still want more.

He toys with me, sucking, licking, biting softly. Then harder.

My instincts beg me to touch him, but I keep my hands at my sides. I tug at my dress. I squeeze my thighs together. I contain myself the best I can.

He moves to my other nipple and teases it mercilessly. It's this beautiful mix of pleasure of pain. Or need and satisfaction. I'm achy. Empty. Desperate to be full.

When he releases me, I'm panting.

His eyes lock with mine. He takes my wrist and guides my hand up his thigh, under his boxers, around his cock.

I wrap my hand around him. That's Blake in my hand.

I rub my thumb over his tip and he lets out a groan.

He grabs me by the hair, his palm flat against the back of my head. He wants my mouth around him.

And I want that too.

I have no idea what I'm doing, but I want it so badly.

I lick my lips reflexively. My eyes are begging him.

He nods, giving me permission.

I plant one hand on his thigh. He guides me into position.

My heart thuds against my chest.

My sex clenches.

I'm about to give Blake head in the back of a car and I don't have a single objection.

There's something wrong with me.

But I don't care.

I wrap my hand around his cock, wiping a drop of pre-come from the head.

I brush my lips against him. The skin is soft but he's so hard.

I try it again. Again. Until I find the spot that makes him groan.

Then I take him into my mouth.

He tastes good. Salt and something uniquely Blake.

His hands go to my hair. One cups the back of my head, holding me in place. It winds me tighter. All of it.

I slide my tongue around him. It feels so right, him in my mouth, him holding me in place, him utterly in control of how I bring him pleasure.

He presses his hand against the back of my head, guiding me over his cock.

He starts gentle. Then gets harder. Deeper.

Until he's so deep I'm gagging.

But that feels good too.

Blake's groan fills the car. I'm sure the driver is watching, but I don't care. That sound is music. That sound is poetry.

His hands tighten in my hair. He takes me deeper. Harder. I follow his motions. He shifts his hips, thrusting into my mouth, tugging at my hair as my tongue hits just the right spot.

Fuck, I love the way he pulls my hair.

I love everything about this.

He feels good in my mouth.

I run my tongue along every inch of his cock, testing his reactions. He shudders as I flick my tongue against his tip.

Perfect.

I do it again. Again. Again. He tugs at my hair a little harder. It spurs me on.

I slide my mouth over him and take him as deep as I can.

He leans back, holding me in place, as he thrusts into my mouth.

"Fuck, Kat..."

He goes harder. Harder. I'm stuck in place. At his mercy. Forced to take it as deep as he wants me to.

But I fucking like it.

His hand knots in my hair as he pulses. With the next thrust of his hips, he comes.

He's warm. Salty. A little sweet.

I catch every drop, swallowing when he's done.

"Fuck," he groans.

Something in Blake relaxes as I return to my seat.

The car slows to pull onto an off-ramp. We're almost back to his place.

I'm almost in his bed again.

I reach for my bra but Blake grabs my wrist.

"Take off the rest of your dress."

Desire shoots through me. I lift my hips to slide the dress to my feet.

He tugs at the strap of my thong. "That too."

I slide the panties to my feet. They fall over my dress.

Blake reaches for my coat and slings it over my shoulders.

I slide it all the way on and clasp all the buttons.

There's nothing under my coat but me.

Chapter Eighteen

The elevator is mercilessly slow.

I hug my chest, squeezing my coat closed. Blake slips his hand under it and strokes my outer thigh with his thumb.

I'm naked under here and he's touching me and there's a nice older woman riding the elevator with us. She's prim and proper. Exactly the type you'd expect in a building like this.

Finally, the elevator stops.

The doors pull apart.

She shoots us a curious look as she steps into the hallway. It's like she knows I'm naked under here. Maybe she does. Maybe it's all over my face.

The doors slide together.

We're alone. There's a camera in the ceiling, but we're alone.

Blake moves in front of me, blocking the view of the security camera.

He undoes the buttons of my coat and slides it open.

I'm naked in the elevator.

On display for him.

It makes me so fucking hot.

It's exhilarating.

He runs his fingertips down my body. Lips. Neck. Chest. Stomach. They stop just below my belly button.

Then lower.

Lower.

Almost.

His eyes stay glued to mine.

He shifts his hand another millimeter lower.

His expression stays intense. In control.

Ding. Penthouse. Blake's floor. His apartment takes up the entire floor.

We step into the hallway. He pulls my coat off my shoulders and lays it over his arm.

I'm naked in the hallway.

No one can see—you need a key card to access the floor—but still.

I'm naked in the hallway.

He opens the door and motions *after you*. It's absurd, him politely holding my jacket and opening the door for me after ordering me to strip and suck him off in the back of a car. With a driver watching.

He's the ultimate gentleman in the streets, freak in the sheets.

The apartment is dark. The lights of the city flow through the window.

I hug my chest reflexively.

Blake's hand slides over my shoulder. He presses the door closed and clicks the lock. "Hands at your sides. I want to look at you."

My breath hitches.

He stares at me, his eyes wide with lust. He likes what he sees. He likes looking at me.

And I like him looking at me.

It's a prefect arrangement, really.

"Turn around," he demands.

I do.

It's such a strange sensation. I'm exposed. Vulnerable. But I like it. I like him looking at me, thinking about me, wanting me.

He moves closer, placing his body behind mine. His lips on my neck. His hands on my ass.

His fingertips skim my sex.

It pours gasoline on the fire raging inside me.

"Turn around," he says.

I do. I slide my arms around his neck and press my lips to his.

He kisses back. It's hard. Hungry. Like he needs this as much as I do.

Like he needs me as much as I need him.

Blake slides his hands under my ass. He lifts me into the air and holds my body against his. I hook my legs around his waist and squeeze him with my thighs.

He carries me like I'm weightless.

We move into the bedroom.

He throws me back on the bed. I land with a soft thud. The foam mattress absorbs all the impact.

He doesn't play around.

He climbs on top of me and pins me to the bed.

The weight of his body sinks into mine. He's heavy and warm. His cock is straining against his slacks, pressing against my sex.

Fabric is between us.

Again.

I'm really starting to despise fabric.

He reaches for something—a length of rope with a cuff at the end. It's part of an under-the-bed restraints system.

He cuffs my hand and squeezes the rope tight. Then he does the same with my other hand.

My upper body is stuck in place.

I'm at his mercy.

But then, I was already at his mercy.

Blake drags his lips over my body. Mouth. Neck. Chest. Stomach. Just below my belly button.

His breath is warm against me. His mouth is inches from my sex. So. Damn. Close.

He nips at my inner thigh. I shift my hips, desperately trying to make contact. He ignores my plea, dragging his lips all the way to my ankle. He undoes the buckle of my shoe and slides it off my foot. Then there's something else around my ankle.

Rope. Another cuff.

He's gentle about sliding off my other shoe.

My breath hitches. My heart races. Nerves rise up in my stomach as he cuffs my other ankle. I trust him. But this is a lot.

I'm immobile.

I shift, testing the restraints. They're tight. I have a few inches of wiggle room at best.

He moves off the bed. A drawer opens. Then he's back on the bed, his crotch planted over mine.

He feels so good against me. It pushes all my nerves away. It pushes away every thought but *more*.

"Careful." He lifts my head and pulls something over it. A blindfold. "Comfortable?"

The world is dark. It sends my body into overdrive. Every inch of me is buzzing.

I need him to touch me.

Kiss me.

Fuck me.

I need everything.

"Yes," I say.

"Good." He shifts off the bed again.

There are sounds. Footsteps. He's leaving. What the hell?

I tug at the restraints but there's no give. I have no choice but to wait for him.

Anticipation fills me slowly.

My limbs, my chest, my stomach—everything gets light. Every inch of me gets desperate. A buzz spreads through my torso, down my legs, up my arms, all the way to my fingers and toes.

His footsteps get closer. He's coming back. He's going to touch me. I need him to touch me.

I can hear Blake undressing. A button shifting out of a hole. A zipper undoing. Pants dropping to the floor.

Tension builds inside me. It's like I'm climbing up a roller-coaster, desperately anticipating the release of the drop.

He shifts onto the bed. Parts of his body press against mine. An arm, a hand, his chest. His bare skin sends a shiver down my spine. We're close.

A cap is undone, and I instantly smell chocolate. My thighs shake. That must be...

He squeezes the bottle. His fingers slide over my lips. Chocolate sauce. Dark and sweet and just a little bit sticky.

I lick it off my lips, savoring the feel of it on my tongue. He squeezes the bottle again then slides his fingers into my mouth. I suck hard. I get every drop.

Blake draws a line over my collarbone, my breasts, down my stomach. I arch my back, buck my hips. It's the only movement I've got.

He straddles me. Fabric presses against my sex. Dammit. His boxers are in the way.

173

I shift to press my sex against his cock. He feels so good, so close, even with the fabric between us.

He pins my hips to the bed. "Not yet."

My breath hitches.

His commands fan the fire inside me, but I need him touching me.

Waiting is torture.

His breath gets harder.

Heavier.

Like this is killing him as much as it's killing me.

He drags his hands up my sides and over my shoulders.

His lips brush my skin.

He licks the chocolate sauce off my neck. With soft strokes. Then hard ones.

He moves down my body, licking every drop of syrup.

He stops at my nipples to suck hard. The pressure is so intense it hurts, but it's a good hurt. A fucking amazing hurt.

My back relaxes. I sink into the bed under his weight. I soak in the feeling of his tongue.

He traces his steps back up my neck like he's making sure to get every drop.

He kisses me. He claims me with his tongue. He tastes like chocolate and sugar and sweat. He tastes fucking good.

I gasp as Blake releases our kiss.

I arch my back like I'm begging him to take me to the edge.

He doesn't. He stays slow. He stays merciless.

He licks his way down my stomach, lapping up every bit of syrup. My sex clenches.

He's at my belly button. Then below it.

So damn close.

He sucks on the skin of my inner thigh then moves

down to my knee. Then to the other leg and back up again.

His teeth scrape my skin.

Almost.

So... close...

I shift my hips, begging him for release.

He nips at my inner thigh.

Lower.

Higher.

The other leg.

Higher.

Almost.

There.

His tongue slides over my folds.

My body screams with relief. His mouth feels so fucking good against me.

I relax into his touch. I let go of controlling any bit of this.

He sucks on my folds. Then scrapes his teeth against them. Not hard enough to hurt. Only hard enough to feel amazing.

He moves to the other side and does the same thing.

He tortures me with his mouth, winding me up, taking me closer, licking me up and down.

Pleasure shoots through me as his tongue flicks against me. There's no way to move. There's nothing I can do to contain the sensation.

I groan his name. But it's not enough. The intensity is overwhelming.

He licks me with a steady rhythm. It's exactly what I need.

Tension builds inside me. Faster and harder and deeper.

Almost.

He pulls back.

I cry out. "Please."

His teeth scrape my inner thigh.

"Blake..."

"Louder."

"Blake. Please... Blake. I need to come. Please."

He flicks his tongue against me.

"Blake. Please…"

He pins my pelvis to the bed, holding me in place as he licks me.

Pleasure builds inside me. It winds tighter and tighter.

Then everything unleashes.

My orgasm sends me into free fall.

My sex clenches. Pleasure radiates through my belly and thighs.

"Blake," I groan.

I come down, panting in a desperate bid to catch my breath.

He shifts. Fabric moves. He must be taking off his boxers.

Almost…

He pins my shoulders to the bed.

His knees nudge my thighs apart.

I can feel his warmth against my sex.

I arch my back, trying to meet him, but I'm not close enough.

He digs into my skin, shifting his weight into my hips.

Almost.

His tip slides over my clit. Over my sex.

He teases me.

Again.

Again.

"Blake." I arch my hips, pushing him deeper. "Please."

Still, he teases again.

Again.

"Please," I breathe. It's the only word in my head. *Please*. Please everything.

He teases again and again.

And again.

I'm ready to scream when he finally slides inside me.

It's fast. One hard thrust. It hurts, but it feels so fucking good. I feel so fucking whole.

Pleasure shoots through my limbs. I'm back on that ride, ready to climb all the way to the top. He's taking me there. He's taking me to another free fall.

He thrusts into me fast and hard. His breath catches.

He groans as he sinks into me.

My nipples scrape against his chest. He nips at the skin on my neck. Groans into my ear.

I can't move. I can't do anything but soak in the feeling of our bodies connecting.

And fuck, it feels so good.

All his skin against mine.

Him driving inside me.

With a few more thrusts, I'm at the edge. Then I'm there, my sex pulsing as I come.

I groan his name again and again.

I shake. I shudder. I rock my hips against him.

But it's not enough. I don't have time to come down. He's still driving inside me.

It hurts, but in a good way.

Blake fucks me.

There's no other way to describe it.

A groan overtakes him.

He goes harder.

Harder.

His nails sink into my skin.

His body shakes.

"Kat," he groans.

One more thrust, and an orgasm overtakes him. He comes inside me. He rocks into me as he spills every drop.

When he's finished, he collapses next to me. Kisses my neck.

A few shifts of his weight on the bed and he's taking off my restraints. The ankles first, then the wrists. I curl my body to wrap it around his.

Blake pulls off my blindfold. I blink my eyes open and stare into his.

"You okay?" he asks.

I nod as I sink into his touch.

Right now, I'm perfect.

I'm exactly where I need to be.

Chapter Nineteen

We take a long shower together. Blake rubs soap over every inch of my skin and rinses me off carefully. I return the favor.

It's the first time I've really gotten to touch him. His body is all hard muscles and perfect lines. He really is gorgeous.

After, he helps me into a soft terry cloth robe. It's as lush and luxurious as everything else in the apartment.

We move to the kitchen.

Blake pours two glasses of water and motions for me to drink.

I'm still not sure how to handle his commands. Part of me wants him taking care of me. Another wants to scream *I'm not a child*.

His eyes catch mine. He can sense the irritated half.

I turn and pull my robe tighter. I'm not sure I'm up for this conversation. Not right now.

His eyes stay glued to me. His stare is penetrating. I don't have to look at him to know. I can feel it.

My cheeks flush. "Yes?"

"Is something wrong?" His voice is steady.

"You're asking?"

"I'm trying."

That makes me warm all over. "I appreciate gestures, but I don't need to be told when to drink or eat or sleep or shower. I'm not into that."

"Noted."

My shoulders relax. Is it really that easy? Maybe our marriage won't be so bad. We're getting good at compromising.

"Are you hungry?"

"Starving." I finish my water and pour another glass.

Blake fixes a plate of fruit, cheese, and chocolate. My breath hitches as he slides a square between his lips.

I just had him.

How can I want him more?

I grab a piece of cheese and plop it in my mouth. It's good. Rich. Creamy.

My gaze shifts to the windows. Moonlight falls over the part. Meryl was right. We don't have any stars here. For the first time in forever, I miss their twinkle.

It's sad. This apartment is gorgeous, but Blake doesn't appreciate it. I don't appreciate it. The space is a curse. It gives him more room to lock me out.

"Are you here a lot?" I ask.

"No."

"You're at work?"

"Mostly."

"How many hours a week do you work?" I ask.

"A lot." His voice shifts to something contemplative.

"If you had to guess."

"Eighty. A hundred maybe."

Damn. That doesn't seem possible. I've worked hard the last three years, but nowhere near a hundred hours a week. That wouldn't leave a moment to spend with my sister.

"Why make all this money if you've got no time to enjoy it?"

"I enjoy work," he says.

"Are you sure? Maybe you're afraid of being away from work." I turn back to Blake and make eye contact. His stare is intense, but I manage to hold strong. "You're always in control."

"And it gets you off."

"Yeah." I swallow hard. "But it must get exhausting." I move towards him. Take a strawberry from his plate. "Don't you want to let go sometimes?"

He shakes his head.

"You need it, don't you?"

"Spare me the pop psychology."

"Is that why you're doing all this for your mom? Can't control that she's dying but at least you can control what she thinks of you?"

His expression hardens. "You don't know what you're talking about." But it's in his eyes. That's exactly what he's doing.

"I don't mean that you don't care. I know how hard it is to lose someone you love."

"This is what I want. That's what you need to know. You shouldn't waste your time looking for my motivation."

"What if it interests me?"

"Does it?"

"Yeah." I move closer. "You interest me."

"You're concerning me, Kat. You have doubts. I understand doubts, but I can't tolerate you backing out of this."

"What will you do?"

"I don't know. Not yet." His eyes narrow. *But something bad. Something awful.*

"What if your mom would rather have the truth?"

"She wouldn't."

"How do you know?"

"You've known her a few hours." He raises his voice. "I've known her my entire life."

"I'm not a child. Don't scold me."

His brow furrows. He digs his fingers into the marble. "Fine. You're an adult. You agreed to this. That's the end of the conversation."

"Blake... I..." Fuck. This is going all wrong. I'm not trying to question him. Not exactly. "I want to talk to you. Or at least... You can talk to me. It must be hard, your mom dying. I'm sure you have a lot to say. Well, a lot for you."

"No." He turns, crossing his arms over his chest, closing me out.

There's hurt behind his eyes.

His mother is dying. His sister is a mess. His father was horrible.

And he's shouldering all of that alone.

I want to help.

I want to take some of his burden.

My stomach flip-flops. Blake is a difficult boss. That's it. I can't start wanting in his head and his heart.

But it's too late.

I do.

I want to hold him all night.

I want to whisper words of comfort in his ears.

I want everything with him.

Not just sex. Not just pretending.

Everything.

I need to pull back. I need to protect my heart. I need to lock *him* out.

But I don't.

I move closer. "Your father. You said he hit you."

His voice gets harder. "I'm not discussing that."

"Okay."

"There's a lot to do for the wedding. I'll take care of it. All you need to do is show up."

I take a few steps towards him. "It's my wedding too. I want a say."

I place my hand on his back.

He shudders. His shoulders soften.

But he keeps his body away from mine.

His voice steadies. "What specifically?"

"I want to do it at the Brooklyn Botanical Gardens."

"I'll make it happen."

"What if it's booked?"

He shrugs, pushing me away. "I'll pull some strings." He turns and his eyes find mine. "Anything else?"

"I'll think about it."

He nods to the plate. "Eat something."

"Later."

Blake steps aside. "It's late."

"I want to sleep over." I bite my tongue. This is not locking him out. This is inviting him in. Demanding more.

I need to make a choice here.

I need to let myself fall in love with him.

Or I need to close him out.

The middle ground is going to kill me.

Blake stays turned away from me, but his voice softens. "Your clothes are in your room." He points to the room where we had sex.

"The sex room?"

"Yes. I have to get back to work."

"It's late."

"Even so." He moves towards the back of the apartment. His bedroom. "Help yourself to anything." He opens his office door.

"Blake?"

He turns back to me. His eyes meet mine. It's a quick moment, but I can feel everything in those baby blues.

The hurt of his past.

The fear of leaving his mom.

And something else. Something I can't explain.

Something I desperately need to understand. "Are we going on a honeymoon after the wedding?"

"Of course."

"Where?"

"It doesn't matter. We'll be spending it in the hotel." He opens his office door. "But you're welcome to pick."

"Oh."

"You don't want to spend a week coming?"

"No, I just. Forget it. I'm tired." I pull the robe tighter.

"Goodnight." He steps into his office. The lock clicks behind him.

I raid the fridge. The snack plate is no good. The smell of chocolate is mixing me up.

He doesn't even care about our honeymoon.

He's never going to love me.

I need to pull back.

But I'm not sure if I can.

I'm not sure if I can do anything to stop myself from falling in love with him.

———

THE OFFICE STAYS QUIET.

I stay restless.

I flip around the TV, unable to concentrate on reruns.

I stare at my sketchbook, unable to form a single line.

This is the perfect time to draw something. My junior year art teacher always told us to pour our emotions onto paper, but I don't know where to start.

Blake is intoxicating. He's fascinating. He's aloof, distant, and moody.

He doesn't believe in love.

A rerun changes to an infomercial. I go to the cable guide.

It's past midnight. I'd better call Lizzy and tell her I'm spending the night.

My bag is sitting on the kitchen table. I fish my phone out of it. There's a new text message.

From Fiona. Her number is programmed right into my phone. What the hell?

Fiona: I didn't mean to intrude, but this is the only way. I need to speak to you about your relationship with Blake. Immediately.

She sent it a few hours ago. I reply.

Kat: There's nothing to discuss.

Fiona: Yes, there is. Are you at his place?

Kat: I am.

Fiona: There's a coffee shop three blocks north. Meet me there tomorrow morning at nine A.M. Don't worry about what to tell Blake. He'll be at work by eight.

Kat: It's Sunday tomorrow.

Fiona: Exactly. He always works Sundays. You should know that. If you've really been together for months.

Kat: I'm busy.

Fiona: It will only take a few minutes. I promise.

I drop the phone. This is weird. There's no way Fiona could know about our arrangement.

Blake is discreet.

And she's caught up in her own problems.

But maybe I'm not that good at pretending.

Maybe she's great at snooping.

I need to hear her out.

Suddenly, I'm not hungry or tired.

I'm awake.

I'm restless.

I doodle in my sketchpad. Manic, angry, terrified lines. The TV murmurs in the background. It casts a soft glow over my paper.

It's a blur of sounds and light.

Sometime after two A.M., I resolve to sleep. But not in the spare room. Not in the sex room. Even if it's going to be mine.

I go to Blake's room. I heard him leave his office to go to his bedroom. I didn't look, but I heard the doors opening.

I knock softly. No sounds. I open the door and step inside. It's an ordinary room. A bed, a dresser, a laptop charging on the floor. He works in here, too. He's addicted.

Blake is sleeping in the middle of the bed, stretched out wide. He takes up most of the space. I climb in next to him and wrap his arm around my waist.

He stirs. "Kat. You shouldn't be here."

"I don't care." I nestle into him. "I want to be here."

He murmurs something I can't make out. He pulls me closer. His breath slows like he's drifting back to sleep.

It happens quickly.

I fall asleep in his arms.

Chapter Twenty

Eight A.M. comes too soon. The bed is cold.

Fiona was right. Blake's been gone for a while.

I dress, brush my teeth, fix my hair and makeup. There's coffee in the machine.

I take a few sips and discard it. I can't stomach anything today. I'm way too nervous.

My thoughts rush together. Somehow, I manage to wait until eight forty-five.

I practically run out of the apartment.

I take the elevator to the lobby and walk the three blocks to the cafe.

Fiona is sitting at a small table. She's picture perfect in her tailored shift dress. She has that trademark Sterling stone expression. What the hell happened to this family to make them all so good at hiding their emotions?

Her nostrils flare as she spots me.

She doesn't like me. I know that much.

But I need to know why.

"Grab a drink if you'd like, but I'd rather keep this quick." Fiona takes a long sip of her coffee.

"No, that's okay." I take my seat. I'm not in the mood for coffee. I'm already wide awake.

"I don't want you to think of this as an accusation." She purses her lips. "I'm sure you have a very good reason for what you're doing. Maybe you don't even realize you're doing it."

Her expression is strong, but her hands are shaking.

She pulls them back and folds them in her lap.

I pull my coat tighter. It's cold in here.

"I was like you when I met Trey. I was desperate to get out of my life any way I could. He was handsome and rich. He had a great apartment. He made me feel safe, but, deep down, I knew he'd never love me." She swallows hard. "I let myself believe I was in love, but I wasn't. I was in love with the idea of escaping. I was in love with the idea of someone taking care of me."

Deep breath. I need to sell this. "It's not like that. I love Blake."

"Maybe you do. Or maybe you just believe it. It doesn't matter. It won't last. The Sterlings are cursed. We can't love anyone."

"No." I swallow hard. That can't be true.

"I did the same thing you're doing. I ignored the signs. But Trey was never going to love me. He was never going to make room for me in his life." Her eyes get serious. "I didn't have options. Maybe if I had them, I would have done something else."

I press my palms into my thighs. Her expression is strong. Sure. She believes every word.

She's saying the same thing Blake does.

He's never going to love me.

He's never going to want more than sex.

He's never going to make room for me.

Fiona clears her throat. "I had you investigated. I'm

188

sure it was hard—that accident with your parents, taking care of your sister. I can see why you'd latch on to Blake."

I take a breath, willing an *I love him* to escape my lips. But I can't make the words happen.

They don't feel like a lie anymore.

Fiona unzips her purse. "I would have done the same thing. I did do the same thing and I had it much easier."

"I should go."

"This is no questions asked." She pulls something out of her purse. A check. She unfolds it and sets it on the table. "If you need money, here it is. It's more than enough to get you on track."

She pushes the check towards me.

It's for a hundred thousand dollars.

Holy shit.

"Take the money. Or don't. It's your choice." She stares into my eyes. "I know what you must think of me. I'm a bitch. I'm okay with that. But Blake has spent his entire life protecting me. This time, I'm going to protect him."

I push the check back. "I don't want your money."

"Then tear this in half right now."

I can't. My fingers won't move.

She's right.

I need options.

This is an option.

One that might spare me from a lot of heartache.

I'm already falling in love with Blake.

Can I really survive living with him?

Marrying him?

Proclaiming to the entire world that he'll be mine forever?

"Maybe you really do love him, Kat, but he's never going to love you. He's married to his job. That will never change." She stands. Her eyes get apologetic. "If you really do love him, if you can handle coming second every night, then tear that check up. Marry him. Get rich and bored waiting by the door every night."

I swallow hard.

She's telling the truth. Her truth at least.

I believe she's doing this for Blake.

Hell, I believe she's doing this for me.

I slide the check into my pocket.

Blake is never going to love me.

But I might be able to walk away before I'm in too deep.

I might be able to wipe away all this deception.

I might be able to survive this one.

I've made too many decisions on my own. I've done too much under pressure.

For once, I'm asking for help.

For once, I'm considering my options.

Chapter Twenty-One

The kitchen smells like coffee. It's warm, rich, nutty.

This place is warm. Cozy. Homey.

I wouldn't trade it for a dozen penthouse apartments.

I wouldn't trade it for anything.

"Earth to Kat?" Lizzy laughs. "You've been a space case lately."

"Sorry." I've spent the last few days drifting off. Drawing. Staring at the check. Asking myself if I can stomach taking Fiona's money. If I can survive not taking it.

I thought it would be hard avoiding Blake, but it's been easy. He's working. He's only texted to say goodnight. It's kind of sweet, the way he wants to be the last thought in my head.

But that gets me all mixed up.

It sends my thoughts racing in every direction.

Running, drawing, staring at the ceiling, walking around the city—they're all equally ineffective at bringing clarity.

I guess it's time to admit I need help.

"It's fine." She stirs sugar into her coffee and tests the

flavor. "You used to be like that all the time. Before the accident."

"That was so long ago."

"Yeah. It feels like it was another lifetime." She takes a long sip and sighs with pleasure. "Is everything okay?"

"Yeah." More or less. "It's a school day."

"It's early." She motions to the clock on the wall. "Besides, you need me more than I need school."

"Do I?"

She nods. "Something is up. You keep taking walks by the water. You only do that when you're worried about something."

"Do I?"

"Yeah. You do it every month before the mortgage is due." She presses her lips together. "We didn't get a bill."

"Blake…"

"Oh." Her eyes fix on mine. She's thinking something about me, but I'm not sure what it is.

"I know you don't like him."

"I don't like how he makes you feel." She traces the outline of her mug. "You've been in a funk since you got back from his place."

Accurate. "I'm thinking."

"About?"

"You should go to school. We can talk tonight."

"We can talk now."

My instincts demand I lie to her. Tell her everything is fine. It's just family drama. It's just stress about the wedding. But I can't do that. I need to bring her into this decision. "Okay."

She smiles. "Good. Let's go out. Get brunch. My treat."

"You don't want me using Blake's credit card?"

"Can't I treat without an ulterior motive?"

"I don't know. Can you?" I study her expression. She looks normal. Concerned.

"Well, since I'm treating, it's my pick. We can go to the place around the corner. The one that doesn't card."

"No way in hell."

She laughs. "Have I ever ordered a drink with a fake ID?"

"In front of me, no? But a grand says you've done it."

"Okay. Fair. But you know I'm messing with you, right?"

I know. But— "I'm your older sister. It's my duty to ruin your good time."

"You don't. You're a good time, Kat. Even when you're moping."

"I'm not moping."

"Uh-huh."

"I'm contemplating."

"Around the house, in your pajamas, all day."

"I need comfortable clothes to really consider things."

She laughs. "Whatever you want to tell yourself." She takes another sip of coffee then rises to her feet. "But put on clothes for this. Ones that aren't made of flannel."

"You know, I hear people in Portland wear flannel all winter."

"Are you in Portland?"

"Is Brooklyn that different?"

She laughs. "Do you ever see anyone in flannel?"

"Sometimes."

"When?"

"I bet we'll see someone in flannel."

"I bet it's less than one in ten." She moves towards her bedroom. "You'll feel better dressed. Trust me."

AFTER BRUNCH, WE GO TO THE BROOKLYN BOTANICAL Gardens. The spot of the future fake wedding, though Lizzy doesn't know that.

The cherry trees are decked with little white buds. In a few weeks, the flowers will bloom, fade to a soft shade of pink.

Then they'll float away on the breeze.

Lizzy takes a seat on a stone bench and folds her legs over each other. She stares at the manmade lake. "You want to tell me what's really bothering you?"

I do. And I'm going to. Just... I need to work up to it. I'm not good at asking for help.

She turns to me. "What's our deal?"

"Me and you against the world."

"Not Kat takes on the world all by herself." She adjusts her glasses. "We're partners. I want to help you. I want to be there when you need me."

"I know. I just..."

"I love you, Kat. Whatever it is, I'll do what I can."

Leaves catch on the breeze. The grass rustles. The lake ripples. "I don't know where to start."

"Anywhere." She pats the spot next to her.

I sit. She knows enough about my arrangement with Blake that I can jump straight to Fiona's offer. No. I need to start earlier. "Blake is doing this for his mother."

She arches a brow.

"She's dying. And, um, he doesn't want her dying thinking she ruined his chance at love."

"Why would she think that?"

"His father..." I press my lips together. That isn't my secret to tell. "He was a bad guy. She feels guilty about staying with him. At least, that's how it seems."

"That's sweet. Sort of. I mean, it's also kinda weird and controlling. But sweet too."

"He does have good intentions."

"But you, well—" she laughs. "Whenever you spend time with him, you either come home just-fucked and satisfied or upset."

I laugh too. "That's probably true."

"He already paid off the mortgage, right?"

"Yeah."

"We can handle the rest on our own. Really. I got in to Stanford. With a full scholarship."

"You didn't tell me."

"I was waiting until… I don't know. Until it felt right. Now it does."

I hug my sister. This is good news. Even if it means she might be three thousand miles away. "Wouldn't you rather stay in the city? Go to NYU?"

"Yes. And no. There are much better computer science programs. And there's… I might not even go to school."

"What?" That is not a possibility.

"I could get an internship. Start working right away."

"Lizzy—"

"I know you want to help, but this is my choice. I'll probably go with school. But I'm considering the other possibilities too."

I bite my lip. She's an adult. She should be able to run her own life. But this is supposed to be for us. What's the point of all this suffering if Lizzy isn't going to take Blake's scholarship?

If she's going to move anyway?

"Blake's sister thinks I'm a gold digger," I say.

"She thinks you're pretty enough to be a gold digger. It's practically a compliment," she teases.

"Maybe. She wants me to leave him." I pull the check from my pocket and hand it to Lizzy.

Her eyes go wide as she unfolds it. "Fuck. She really wants you to go away."

"We're supposed to get married here in three and a half weeks."

"Classy. Perfect for you."

"It's go-away money. She wants me to take this and never see him again."

She folds the check and presses it into my palm. "She must have some serious jealousy issues."

I shake my head. That isn't it. "She thinks I'm deceiving Blake. Or deceiving myself about Blake. Maybe I am." I tuck the check into a pocket in my purse. "She... she might even be doing it for me. Because she feels bad for me."

"Uh-huh."

"Really. Her husband was at dinner. He's one of those rich jerks who works nonstop. She thinks Blake is the same. That I'll also end up in a loveless marriage. Or as a young divorcee."

"You're too nice. It sounds like a controlling-bitch move to me."

"You're too cynical."

"Let's say that's true. What's in the middle?"

"I'm not sure. I guess it doesn't matter. She's offering me money to go away. I can take it. Or not."

"You get more if you marry him."

"Yeah." But I don't need more. I just need Lizzy okay. And she is. She doesn't even want this money.

"Do you want to marry Blake?"

My thoughts go straight to the two of us right here. Me in some beautiful lace dress. Him in a suit. Pink petals blowing around us. It's beautiful. Romantic. Sweet.

But it's not a lie. Not in my head.

In my head, it's real. He really loves me and I really love him.

That's what I want. Not yet. But one day. I want to really be his. For him to really be mine.

But it's not an option.

I play with the buttons on my coat. "I don't know."

"Don't do it for me. I will be okay."

"In California."

"We can't be together forever." She squeezes my hand. "You know that."

I know, but I still hate the thought of being three thousand miles from the only person who matters to me.

"I can't believe this. All because the guy almost broke your ankle." She laughs. "I don't know if you're lucky or unlucky."

"This is the best and worst thing that's ever happened to me."

"Forget feelings. Forget everything except the cold, hard cash." Lizzy pulls me off the bench and trots towards a tree blooming with little white flowers. "He's offering you the rest of a million dollars. If you go through with this wedding, you're set. You can do whatever the hell you want. It's all your money. Yours, Kat."

"Ours."

"No," she says. "It's yours. I'm not saying you can't buy me dinner sometimes. Or pay my share of the occasional trip to the Caribbean, but it's yours."

"Lizzy—"

"I'm not taking his money. This is for you, Kat. If you can't handle the fake marriage, then leave. Take his sister's money. Or tell them both to go fuck themselves. You'll be okay without their money. We both will."

Maybe. I was barely making ends meet before I met

Blake, but now that the mortgage is paid, a job waiting tables is plenty.

Or I can take Fiona's money. Use it to pay for college. To jump-start a better life.

I have options.

I try to imagine dumping Blake, convincing him I can't do this.

That weight sinks into my chest. It's an awful thought.

This means a lot to Blake. Yes, it's bullshit and he's lying to everyone who loves him, but he's doing it because he believes it's the only way.

He doesn't love me, but he does trust me.

Calling this off is breaking that trust.

I… I'm not sure I can do that to him.

Or that I want to.

But I do know something.

I need to talk to him. I need to look him in the eyes. I need to figure out if I can survive another six months proclaiming my love for him.

Lizzy checks a text on her phone.

"Can you handle dinner on your own?" I ask.

"Go get laid," she says. "I don't judge."

"That better not be a boy."

"And if it is?"

"He's meeting me before he takes you out." I pull out my phone and text Blake.

Blake: I'm at the office. It will be cleared out by seven. Come then.

It is the perfect place for a negotiation.

Chapter Twenty-Two

Downtown is quiet. Still. It's funny how quickly the streets go from bustling to empty.

The yellow fluorescent lights pop against the dark sky. The city is beautiful. I never tire of it.

I never tire of tilting my head upwards, gawking at the skyscrapers like a tourist.

They're tall. Powerful. Unmoving.

Shit. I'm comparing buildings to my fake fiancé.

He's taking over too many of my thoughts. Not just the ones about sex. But the ones about long walks and shared dessert and forever.

I hug my purse to my shoulder as I step into the building.

The security guard nods with familiarity. I'm not sure how he recognizes me—I've only been here a few times—but he does.

I nod back. I need all the pleasantries I can get right now.

I'm not sure what I'm going to say to Blake.

I know what I want, but it's not on the table.

Is it really possible to find a compromise with something this black and white?

I don't know.

But I'm not giving up on that possibility.

I step into the shiny silver elevator and push the *penthouse* button.

It flashes red. Damn key card. I fish it from my wallet, swipe it, and press the button again. Green.

His office needs a key for access.

It's so Blake.

My reflection stares back at me. It's just like last time. She looks tired. Scared. In over her head.

But last time worked out well. I got everything I wanted.

Maybe I can do the same here.

Ding. The doors slide open. I step into the lobby.

Once again, the floor is empty. Dark. Still. The light of the city flows in through the windows. The big, grey clouds feel close. Like I could touch them if I opened the window.

I go straight to Blake's office. Grab the handle. Try to turn.

It's locked.

He's here alone and the door is locked.

A panel forms in my mind. A cartoon version of Blake pulling open his chest to show off the walls around his heart. There are a dozen different locks. Each with a different key.

It could make for an interesting story. A girl on a quest, trying to figure out how to tear down each of those walls.

I steel myself as I knock. I'm not sure how this is going to go. Only that it's going to be difficult.

Blake pulls the door open. His blue eyes meet mine. They fill with a mix of concern and appreciation. He's glad I'm here. And worried it means something.

He's not wearing a suit.

He's in jeans and a long-sleeved t-shirt. It's tight on his broad shoulders and chest. It hangs off him perfectly. And those jeans…

Heat pools between my legs. I'm here to talk. Not to beg him to pin me to the couch and fuck my brains out.

He gives me a long once-over. "Gin and tonic?"

"You're not wearing a suit."

He chuckles. "I changed after you texted."

"Oh. For me?"

"Yes."

My heartbeat picks up. Blake is changing for me. It's not a metaphor. It's probably for comfort. But it feels like it means something.

"Do you want a drink?"

"Sure."

He moves to the bar and pours carefully.

I take a seat on the couch. Fold my legs. Smooth my jeans. Tap my heels together. These are nice boots. Expensive leather with good waterproofing. My feet are dry. Warm.

It's heaven compared to walking around the city with soggy socks.

It's the kind of thing that wasn't possible last month.

But creature comforts aren't enough anymore.

I need more.

He moves to the couch and hands over my cocktail. His eyes fix on mine as he takes a long sip of his whiskey.

"This is early for you." I let the alcohol warm my face and cheeks. "To stop working and have a drink."

"I figured it's important."

"Oh?"

"You haven't said anything but *goodnight* in three days."

"I didn't think you noticed."

He stares back at me. "Of course."

Of course? What the hell is that? I take another sip, but it doesn't offer any clarity. Or confidence. "I've been thinking."

"About?"

Wanting you to love me. Wanting this to be real. My inability to separate fact and fiction. "Everything."

He slides his fingertips over my neck. "What's one thing?"

I take a greedy sip, but it does nothing to refresh me. My eyes go to the shiny hardwood floor. It's perfect, spotless, pristine like everything in Blake's office. Like everything in his life. "Do you trust me?"

He answers immediately. "Yes." His voice is certain. Sure.

I force myself to stare back into his eyes. They're sincere. They're worried even.

I mean something to him.

I just don't know how much.

I fish the check from my purse. "Your sister thinks… well, I'm not sure what she thinks. But she wants me to go away." I unfold the check.

He reads it. "You want more?"

"No, I…"

"We have a deal, Kat. If it's not enough anymore—"

"This isn't about money." I squeeze the check with my thumb and forefinger. "I'll tear it in half right now if I have to."

His lip corners turn down. "You're showing off a check for a hundred grand. What else could it be about?"

Love. "Don't you care that your sister wants me to go away?"

"She's trying to protect me. In her way." His gaze shifts

to the window. "She's not taking the divorce well. You don't need to like her, but don't take it personally."

"Don't take go-away money personally?"

"It's more than she can afford. She must think you're valuable to me."

"Is everything a number to you?"

He arches a brow.

"Would I be less valuable if she'd offered me fifty grand?"

"That isn't what I mean."

"No? It sounds like it."

"If you want more money—"

"I don't."

"Then why tell me?"

"I trust you." My toes tap together. "You've been honest with me. But..."

"But?"

"Stop offering me more money. I don't want any more of your money."

"Fine." His voice is short. Frustrated.

"I want to talk about this. Like adults." I go to tear the check in half but my fingers won't cooperate. "You can't buy me. Your sister can't buy me. I'm not for sale."

I do it again.

This time, I manage a tiny rip.

I don't want Fiona's money.

I don't want anyone buying my allegiance.

Deep breath. I tear the check in half.

The paper flutters to the ground.

Fuck. There go my options.

"There's no shame in needing money." Blake finishes his whiskey and sets his glass on a wide table. "You can admit it."

I dig my heels into the hardwood. "Fine, I need the money. I'm not a billionaire. I don't have a tech company. In fact, I don't have a fucking penny to my name. It's just my sister and me. No one else will help. Is that what you want to hear?"

"If it's the truth."

"I need your fucking money. I hate that I need your money, but I do."

His stare cuts through me.

I turn away. Fuck this. Blake can't intimidate me.

I go to push myself up but he grabs my wrist.

"Don't," he says.

"Why? This is a business arrangement. Our terms are the same. There's nothing to talk about." There's no way to get what I want. Not like this.

His grip tightens around my wrist.

"We're not friends."

"Aren't we?" He pulls my body into his. "I care about you."

"You don't care how I feel."

"Yes, I do." His breath warms my ear. "I know this is hard for you. And I hate that. But there isn't another way."

"But you…" I don't know what to say. His voice is sincere. He does care about me. "How much?"

"How much?"

"Do you care about me? Am I a colleague? A friend? A lover?"

"I'm not going to fall in love with you." The words are easy. Like he's talking about the time.

My stomach sinks. "I don't know if I can do this without falling in love with you."

"Kat…"

"I know. You'll never love me. I understand." Sort of. He thinks he'll never love me. But he does care about me. And that's how it starts.

Blake looks me over. His gaze is softer. There's affection in it.

He picks the pieces of the check off the floor and sets them on the side table.

"You can still take Fiona's money."

"I don't want it."

"Good. Pretend like this never happened."

"She doesn't believe we're in love."

"She does. That's why she offered you this much. It's a test."

"That's fucked up."

"That's the Sterling family." He slides his palm around the back of my neck. Stares into my eyes. "I meant what I said. There's no shame in needing money. Most people wouldn't do as well as you have."

"Maybe."

Blake runs his fingertips over my cheek. "It must have been hard, holding everything together after your parents died."

I nod. It's still hard. It's still pent up inside me.

There's affection in his eyes.

Maybe we are friends.

Maybe that's enough. I don't need him being in love with me if he really does love me.

"How did it happen?" he asks.

"They were in a car accident."

"And that was it?"

"Yeah." I let my eyelids flutter together. "I was at a cross-country event when I got the news. I was thinking about the guy who asked me to Winter Formal. About my dress. About things that didn't matter at all."

Blake runs his fingers through my hair. I lean into his touch. I soak up every bit of it.

"You'd have liked the dress. It was black. Low-cut. It's

still in my closet somewhere. I don't think I've ever worn it."

He pulls me closer. Until I can feel his heartbeat. It's steady. His breath is too.

I sink into his arms. It feels good. Safe. Reassuring. I haven't had any reassurance. For three years, I've been the one telling everyone else *it's going to be okay*.

And now he's doing it.

I want that.

I want to collapse in Blake's arms.

I want him taking care of me.

"My coach came over." I swallow hard. "It was right before I was set to race. I was all high and mighty, wondering what could be so important. But there was this look on her face. Something was wrong.

"She took me to the tiny parking lot. She couldn't look at me. I couldn't look at her. I don't remember exactly what she said, just that I ran. I ran to the hospital even though it was miles away. I had no idea what had happened, if my family was alive or dead."

He holds me closer.

"I knew it was bad from the way the nurse looked at me. But it didn't feel real. It felt like I was watching the whole thing on TV. Mom and Dad were dead on arrival. Lizzy was in the ICU. I stayed with her for a while. I only went home to change and shower. I slept in the waiting room. It was only a few days, but it felt like weeks. I would have been completely alone. I wouldn't have had anyone."

A drop falls on my leg. Another. My hand is shaking. Gin and tonic is spilling over the sides of the glass.

Blake takes my hand and pries my fingers from the glass. He sets it on the floor then intertwines his hand with mine.

His eyes meet mine.

It's a look I've never seen before. Not on him.

It's like he does love me.

Like the only thing he wants is my happiness.

He brushes my hair behind my ear. "That must have been hard."

"There was no time for it to be hard. My parents didn't save for shit. They were in debt. Their life insurance was enough to get me through high school. Then to cover what my job didn't. But it wasn't enough."

"Were you eighteen?"

"Yeah. Thank God. We don't have any other family. Lizzy would have been in foster care if I didn't become her legal guardian."

He brushes the hair from my eyes. "It's okay to want a comfortable life."

"That was the last time I was free, that morning at the cross-country meet. It's not about the money, Blake. It's about the sense that I could do anything. I haven't felt that for a long time."

He nods.

"I want Lizzy to have that."

"Of course." He runs his fingers along my chin, tilting it so we're eye to eye. "You are free, Kat. I need you for a few months, but when we're not together, you're free to do whatever you want."

"As long as I keep up the right image."

"Your image is perfect." He stares into my eyes. "You're better than I ever imagined."

"At lying to people."

"If I was looking to fall in love, it would be with you." His hand brushes my cheek.

If he was going to fall in love it would be with me. What bullshit. He's not going to fall in love, so it's not going to be with me.

It's not a compliment. It's not comforting. Not unless I can convince myself it's more than a lie.

"Don't say things you don't mean." I slide to the other side of the couch.

"I never do." He moves closer. "I want you to feel better."

"I'm not going to feel better."

"I disagree." He pulls me onto his lap. Wraps his arms around my waist. "I'll get your mind off this."

"You can't appease me with sex," I say. "Is that the only way you can deal with people's emotions—pay them off or fuck them?"

His eyes flare with something I can't place. No, I know that look.

I'm right and he hates it.

He releases his grip. It makes me cold. Empty.

"You're right. I don't know how to make someone happy," he says. "But I do want you to be happy."

"Then don't say things like that. Don't act like you might love me."

He nods. "What do you want with my money?"

"I already told you."

"You want it for your sister. But what about for you?"

"What I told your mom. I want to go to college. Art school. I want to publish graphic novels. One day."

"Yours or others?"

"Both. I want to help people pour their soul onto the page. And share it with the world. I know it sounds cheesy. I guess it is. But that's what I want. I always thought I'd have to be an art teacher. Something like that. My parents were teachers. It's a good job. But not for me. I'm not good with people."

"You are."

"Maybe. But I prefer to work alone."

"That, I understand."

I can't help but laugh. "Do you have any friends?"

He arches a brow. "Is that an accusation?"

"No. I'm more… curious. You don't want a best man. There must not be anyone close to you."

"There isn't. Just my mother and my sister."

"Isn't that lonely?"

"I'm used to it." He looks up at me. "I know what you're going through taking on all that responsibility."

"Yeah?"

"My father wasn't just an asshole who drank himself to death. He took out his frustrations on my mother."

"Oh." My heart sinks. Poor Meryl.

"Once I was old enough to step in, he took them out on me." He looks at me. His voice fills with vulnerability. "I was fourteen when he died. I was relieved. The extra responsibility was nothing compared to how much I hated him."

"I'm sorry." My heart sinks for him too. I want to wipe his pain away. I want to prove that love doesn't have to be that ugly. I want to make the world a prettier place.

"Don't be. I'm glad he's gone."

"But I'm sorry you went through that. Love shouldn't hurt. Not like that."

He takes my hand. "It made me stronger. You lost parents who loved you. You lost something real. But it made you stronger."

I shake my head. "I'm not strong."

"You are."

A tear rolls down my cheek.

I miss my parents. There's still a hole in my heart. I never let myself feel it. I never let myself grieve the life I could have had.

Blake catches a tear on his thumb.

He leans in to press his lips to my forehead.

It's soft. Sweet. Loving.

I mumble into his neck. "I'm sorry you went through that."

"Thank you."

"What was it like? If you want to talk about it… You don't have to."

He pulls me closer. "I thought it was normal. That all houses were that full of hatred. My parents were always drinking. It gave her courage. It made him angry. It was a toxic combination. He'd threaten to hit her and she'd call him a coward. She'd dare him to do it."

"She was brave."

"But stupid." He drags his fingers through my hair. "I did the same thing when I stepped in. So he'd take out all his anger on me. The asshole didn't care who he hurt as long as he hurt someone."

I squeeze his hand. I don't know what to say. Only that I want to be here. To listen. To help him. To hold him.

"I didn't do enough to protect her or Fiona. I could have called the police. I could have cut his brake lines. I could have stopped him for good."

"That's a hell of a choice for a fourteen-year-old to make."

He shakes his head. His expression softens. His posture does the same.

It's like he's sinking into me.

I do the same. I melt into him.

We stay pressed together, breathing together, for a long time. The room is still. Silent. But it's comfortable.

I feel safe in his arms. Even with all this ugliness swirling around us.

He brushes my hair between my eyes. "I have a perfect distraction."

I wipe my eyes, willing my feelings back into the box where I usually stuff them.

"Or we can stay here."

I take his hand and rise to my feet. "Is it sex?"

He laughs. Actually laughs. God, it really is a nice laugh. He eyes crinkle. His cheeks spread to his ears.

He has a dimple.

It's the best thing I've ever seen.

I have my clarity.

I want to be by his side.

Whatever that means.

I take Blake's hand and follow him out of the room.

Chapter Twenty-Three

The roof-access door is locked.

Of course, Blake has a key.

He squeezes my hand as he unlocks the door and pushes it open.

Moonlight falls over the concrete stairs. I grab onto the cold, steel railing as I climb the steps.

There.

It's like I'm actually touching the sky. The tall buildings surrounding us look close enough to touch. The dark, grey clouds seem inches above me.

I feel like a superhero. Like I could bounce around these buildings, making the city mine.

It's colder than it was this afternoon, but it's not seeping into my veins. If anything, I'm hot.

The rooftop pool glows with an aqua sheen. It's a spot of brightness against the dull sky.

Light dances on the water. It casts strange lines over Blake's face.

He's watching me, studying my reaction. It's softer than normal. Sweeter.

"No one else has access to the roof," he says.

"So this is your private pool?"

"More or less."

He drops his keys on a little patio table. The guy maintains a pool on the roof of a damn skyscraper for kicks.

"Do you ever use it?" I ask.

"When I need to think."

"And how often is that?"

He smiles. Actually smiles. My heart goes into overdrive. It's like I'm a schoolgirl with a crush. Blake is smiling at me. Smiling. At. Me.

We're going to get married, and I'm atwitter over a smile.

I'm totally fucked.

"Your point is taken," he says.

"So I was right? You admit it."

He laughs. That's twice in one hour. It's a record.

He nods. "You getting in?"

"After you."

He pulls his t-shirt over his head.

I try not to gawk, but I can't help it. His body is a work of art.

There's no way I rejected his sexual advance minutes ago. That's impossible.

He slides out of his jeans. My gaze is drawn to his muscular thighs. His narrow hips. The cotton boxers...

I hate those cotton boxers.

I want to draw him from every possible angle. I want to capture every nuance of his body with my pencil.

"You look warm," he says.

"I'm fine."

He moves towards me. Unbuttons my coat and slides it off my shoulders.

I shiver but not from the cold. It's from the proximity. From his touch.

I pull my sweater over my head, then I reach for his boxers.

Blake shakes his head. He drops to his knees and unzips my boots. I step out of them, one at a time.

He lifts my foot to peel off my sock then does the same with my other leg.

His fingertips trail over the seam of my jeans, up my leg, over my sex, down my other leg.

Then back up again. He's careful about undoing my button and zipper.

He pushes my jeans—and my panties—to my ankles.

I step out of them. It's not nearly as graceful as his striptease. But it's effective.

I'm standing here in my bra.

He's in his boxers.

We've been naked together plenty, but this feel more intimate. More revealing.

Like we're finally showing each other our hearts.

He rises slowly.

He's inches away. Close enough we could kiss. Touch. Make love.

Silly me, it's not making love with Blake. It's fucking. He fucks. He doesn't love.

I send the word through a shredder and stuff it some place where it can't get to me.

Love isn't a part of this equation.

I'm going to come to terms with that.

Somehow.

I step back, undo my bra, and let it drop to the ground. I turn away, but I can feel Blake's gaze.

It sends heat racing through my body.

I move towards the pool and dip a toe. The water is warm. Inviting.

Blake slides out of his boxers. I can't stop myself from gawking. He really is perfect. He belongs in a museum. He should be an entire wing of the Met. He should replace David at Galleria dell'Accademia in Florence.

"Are you waiting for something?" he asks.

I shake my head.

Here goes nothing.

I jump into the pool.

Damn. That's intense.

The hairs on my neck stand up. I dunk my head. Underwater, everything is a blurry mess of blue-white.

The water rocks back and forth. There's a splash above me. Blake. He's in the pool with me.

I surface. He's five feet away, water dripping off his perfect shoulders.

He moves closer. "Distracted?"

I nod. "Thanks for listening before. And for talking… I almost believed you were my supportive fiancé."

His fingertips brush my chin.

I look up at him for as long as I can stand it. He's still intense, but there's a softness in his eyes. A sweetness.

My lungs work extra hard to find their next breath.

There's too much going on around me.

This pool is an oasis of calm. The eye of the storm, I guess. But it feels more like the storm itself. It feels like there's something raging inside me.

"I do care about you," he says.

"Yeah, I know we're not—well, I'm not sure what we are, but we're not lovers."

"I'll do anything I can to support you."

"What more could I ask for in a husband?" My voice

cracks. I dive back under the water. The chlorine stings my eyes.

I can just make out the edges of Blake's body. They're blurry but they're still perfect.

I push off the concrete and glide towards the deep end. When I come up for air, Blake is staring at me. Fixed on me.

He moves closer.

Closer.

His wet hair is slicked back. It suits him, really, but so far I've never seen anything that doesn't suit him.

"Kat." His voice is sweet.

"I'm fine, thanks. Just thinking how lucky I am marrying such a supportive guy as a ruse. Luckiest girl in the world, really."

He studies me, deciding if he believes me. He nods like he does.

"You've never been in love," I say.

"Never."

"Nothing?"

"Never anything more than lust."

"Yeah, of course." I squeeze water from my hair. "Me either. I want to, one day, but it's not really a priority. I have to think about school and a career." I press my lips together. "Do you think it's because of your parents? That what they had was love taking an ugly turn?"

"I don't bother dwelling on the why." He runs a hand through my hair. "I've never seen love go any other way. Look at Fiona and Trey. They're miserable."

"My parents were in love. They were happy."

"How do you know for sure?" he asks.

"I do. Love isn't something you know. It's something you feel." My heart speeds up. My breath follows suit.

"And it feels amazing. Warm and comfortable and perfect."

"You said you've never been in love."

Oh, yeah. I did say that. And it's true.

My cheeks flush. Heat spreads down my chest, through my stomach.

His stare disarms me.

It makes me feel even more naked.

I try to recapture my train of thought. "I've never been in love. But I have loved people. My sister. My parents. My grade school best friend. That feels good too."

His eyes stay fixed on mine. There's something on the tip of his tongue, but he swallows it down.

I dive under the surface and do a somersault.

The water is warm. Comfortable. It's everywhere, all around me. This is what love feels like. You're swallowed whole, but you know you're safe. You know it's going to be okay.

Not that I'm familiar with the concept.

Not that I'm falling in love with someone.

Not anything like that.

Chapter Twenty-Four

We spend twenty minutes swimming around the pool. Clouds get darker, greyer. A drizzle turns into a downpour.

I ignore Blake's suggestion we leave. We're already in the pool. Rain isn't going to hurt us.

The sky flashes white. Lightning. Thunder booms a few seconds later. Okay, no more playing around. I don't need to be told that a pool on top of a steel tower is a bad place to hang out during a thunderstorm.

Blake helps me out of the pool. He sends me into the staircase naked and gathers our clothes alone. He's trying to protect me, but I'd rather share the risk of electrocution. I'd rather we work like an actual team.

The roof door pulls open and Blake steps inside.

He's in his boxers. He's holding the rest of his clothes to his chest.

He pulls my sweater over my head. It soaks up all the water dripping off my chest and shoulders. I'm a little warmer. But it's not enough. I'm still cold.

I take the stairs one at a time. My hand stays on the cold metal railing until I need to push the door open.

Only it's locked.

Blake is the only one with a key to the roof, but the door still locks automatically.

It's fitting.

He positions himself behind me, his chest pressed against my back. He's wet. Smooth. Hard.

His body feels good against mine.

I want to lose these clothes.

To lose track of words entirely.

He slides his hand over my mine. His breath warms my neck. I suck a deep breath through my nose. I will my nerves to settle.

They don't.

Blake offers me my panties. "I don't want you caught on tape. Unless that's a fantasy of yours."

"No." I don't think it is. I blush as I pull on my underwear. "Thanks."

He unlocks the door and presses it open.

It's just as cold in here. Goosebumps spread over my arms. My nipples get hard. I hug my chest, but it doesn't do enough to warm me up.

"Are you hungry?" he asks.

"I could eat." I'd rather fill another one of my needs, but I could eat.

He takes my hand and leads me to a break area. It's as sleek and modern as the rest of the office.

There's a thick white table, a kitchenette with stainless steel appliances, and a rectangular black couch. It would look great as the background of a panel, especially with the cloudy window.

I imagine the shading. The way Blake would be in the shadows. A bit of an obvious metaphor—the unknowable guy stepping out into the light—but it works.

Blake drops our clothes on the table. He kneels in front

of a cabinet and pulls out a blanket. "We'll have to share." He hands it to me then points to the ceiling. "There are no cameras in this room if you want to change."

"Change?" I raise a brow.

He laughs. Actually laughs. "That too."

My heart thuds against my chest. My breath catches in my throat. I want his laugh. And his body. And his heart.

But the latter is out of the question.

I need to let go of the idea.

I'm trying.

But when he looks at me with those piercing blue eyes…

"Sit. Get warm." He nods to the couch.

It's a good idea. I toss my wet clothes on the floor and wrap myself in the blanket.

Blake fills a coffeemaker with water. "What do you want to drink?"

"Hot chocolate."

"Really?"

"You have a problem with hot chocolate?" I put my hand on my hip, but the gesture is impossible under the blanket.

Blake turns to me, taking in my attempt at a confident, badass look.

His lips curl into a smile. Then—oh God, it's happening again.

He laughs.

My whole body fills with warmth. It's wrong how good his laugh makes me feel. How much I want his happiness.

"Hot chocolate it is." He grabs mugs from the counter.

I take a seat on the couch, willing my body to relax.

It's not happening. My stomach is still light. My heart is still racing.

But my thoughts are coming together.

I pull the blanket over my head. It's quiet. Calm. And I don't have to watch my expression.

I'm tired of being under the microscope.

He moves towards the couch. "You're not good at sharing, are you?"

No. I'm not.

I pull the blanket to my shoulders.

He's standing in front of the couch, a mug in each hand.

"I guess not." I'm perfectly good at sharing some things. But not my feelings. Not my history. Certainly not my heart.

With the blanket, well, I'll do my best.

I take a mug. I shift so half the blanket frees. Blake sits next to me and pulls the blanket over our laps.

My eyes refuse to obey my commands. They fix on Blake's shoulders, chest, and stomach. He's still wet. It highlights the lines of his torso.

I want to draw him.

Realism was never my style, but it's the only way to capture the majesty that is Blake. A cartoon version could never compare.

Hell, a drawing could never compare.

Nothing compares.

I let my eyelids press together. I soak in the sound of the rain. The warmth of the mug. The smell of chocolate wafting into my nostrils.

When I open my eyes, I'm surprised by the darkness. The sky is ugly. Deep blue with big, grey clouds. The rain is hard, but the sound of it is beautiful. Like music.

"Kat?"

"Yeah?" I look into Blake's eyes, but it doesn't help with my nerves. I still want to get lost in those eyes.

"You okay?"

"Mostly." I sip my cocoa. It's instant, but it's soothing all the same. I take a long sip then set my mug on the floor.

I don't need chocolate and sugar.

I need him wiping away the rest of the world.

Blake watches me the way he always does. He'd make a great scientist. Or a judge. There's no telling what's going on behind those gorgeous eyes.

He offers his mug of coffee. I nod and take a sip. It's black. Rich. Bold. Vanilla.

My gaze shifts back to the window. To the rain hitting the glass. "I should get home soon."

"It's pouring."

"It's always pouring this time of year." I shift and the blanket slips off my shoulders, all the way to my waist. "I'm sure you have more work to do. I don't want to impose."

He sets his drink on the floor. "I like you here."

"Yeah, but you have to work. And I have to work too. I might be able to make some of the spring admissions deadlines for art schools. There are a lot of choices I've never really considered. My parents insisted I go to a regular school."

Blake's eyes stay on mine. He doesn't glance at my exposed torso. Respect or disinterest, I'm not sure. Everything about today feels different. Almost like we're really a couple.

That's a lie.

The reminder isn't hitting me today.

Explanations bounce around my head. Some things are real. Our sex is real.

Maybe this is real too.

I shift onto Blake's lap, my thighs outside his, my crotch over his.

He's warm. Safe. But that's not right. There's nothing safe about this.

He pushes my hair behind my ears.

I wrap my arms around his strong shoulders. I squeeze my thighs around him.

He presses his palm against my lower back.

It sends a shiver up my spine.

When I look back into his eyes, his curiosity is gone. He's shifting back to the Blake I understand. The animal driven by lust and control.

My eyelids flutter together as I kiss him. He tastes like coffee and vanilla. And like Blake.

I slide my tongue into his mouth.

He holds me tighter. Kisses back harder.

His hands slide to my ass. His nails dig into my flesh.

I moan into his mouth. I'm not giving up control this time. I need to touch him everywhere. I need to touch him on my terms.

He drags his fingers over my back and shoulders. Then they're on my neck. Digging through my hair.

Blake pulls back. His eyes find mine. "Get on your back."

I shake my head. "I want to touch you."

"We're doing this my way."

The commanding tone to his voice makes my sex clench. But I can't relent here.

I stare back at his eyes. "I want to touch you."

He nods. "You will. Trust me."

I do. That's the problem.

But this is a compromise. Of sorts.

I need to do this.

His way is fine. No, it's perfect.

I nod. "Okay."

I shift and pull the blanket out of the way. My body

sinks into his. I can feel him. He's hard under me. He's almost mine.

Blake grabs my hands and brings them to his shoulders.

I explore his chest with my fingertips. It feels so good to touch him. So much like he's mine.

He grabs my ass and pulls my body into his. His other hand goes to my hair.

He brings my head to his.

And he kisses me. It's hard, but it's sweet.

His way. I like his way.

I explore the nooks and crannies of his torso with my fingertips. There's a soft tuft of hair just below his belly button. I slide my hand beneath it and play with the waistband of his boxers.

He grabs my wrist and brings my hand back to his shoulder. A warning. Or a demand. I'm not sure.

He drags his lips to my ear. "Not yet." He plants kisses down my neck.

Every brush of his lips makes me shudder.

I'm desperate for more of him. For whatever he's willing to give me.

I rub my crotch against his. The friction of my sex against his cock is divine. Those damn boxers are in the way. They press into my tender flesh. They make everything harder. Rougher.

Pleasure knots in my core. I move faster. I groan into his ear.

He groans back against my neck.

His nails dig into my back.

It hurts, but in a good way. It's like he's marking me. Like I'm his.

He kisses me as he brings his hands to my ass and lifts my hips.

His hand brushes my sex.

I groan. I dig my fingers into his shoulders.

He strokes me with his finger.

My sex clenches.

My nipples tighten.

Desire collects between my legs as he rubs me.

I inhale every ounce of ecstasy.

I stare into Blake's eyes, commanding myself to hold his gaze.

It's intense, but I can handle it.

I can handle him.

I keep my eyes glued to his as he strokes me. As he pushes me closer and closer to the edge.

The pressure in my sex builds.

He takes me higher and higher.

Until it's all I can take.

My teeth sink into his lip.

I tug at his hair.

There.

The next flick of his finger pushes me off the edge.

I groan his name as I come.

I stare back into his eyes as my sex pulses with after-shakes. He makes me feel so fucking good.

"Come here." He presses his palm into my lower back. "I need to be inside you."

My nod is heavy. Needy.

He slides his boxers to his knees and brings his hands to my hips.

Slowly, he guides my body over his.

His tip strains against me. Then it's one inch at a time.

Fuck.

He feels so good inside me.

It's perfect.

Blake guides my body over his.

I shift up, until he's barely inside me, then down, until he's filling me.

With his hands on my hips, he guides me up and down.

He goes deeper.

Harder.

I press my hands against his shoulders for leverage.

I rock against him, rubbing my clit against his pubic bone.

Pleasure whirs inside me. It builds with every shift of my hips. With every brush of my skin against his.

He digs his nails into my skin. He groans my name.

His eyelids press together.

His brow furrows.

He's almost there.

I watch pleasure spill over his face as I fuck him. I drive him into me again and again. Harder. Deeper. Faster.

My eyelids press together.

All the tension in my sex winds to a fever pitch.

I come in torrents. Pleasure rocks through my body. Up my torso, down my thighs, all the way to my lips and eyes and nose.

Every part of me is buzzing. Every part of me is spent.

I turn my attention to Blake. His lips part. He groans. His eyelids press together.

His hands dig into my hips.

He pulls back. Rearranges our bodies.

He's standing behind me.

I'm facing away from him, my knees on the couch cushions, my hands on its back.

I arch my back, offering myself to him.

He grabs my hips.

With one swift motion, he drives inside me.

It's so deep it hurts.

But in a fucking amazing way.

"Blake," I groan. I arch my back so I can feel every one of his movements.

His grip tightens around my hips. His breath speeds.

He's close. He's losing control. He's mine.

He thrusts harder. Faster.

It's too much. But too much isn't enough.

I claw at the couch. "Blake."

He drags his nails over my hips. His cock pulses. His thighs shake.

"Fuck. Kat." He drives into me as he comes.

It sends me back over the edge.

My orgasm is fast. Hard. Intense. I claw at the couch as my sex pulses. Pleasure spreads through my torso. It spreads out to my fingers and toes.

He thrusts through my orgasm.

Then he's there too.

Groaning against my skin as he comes inside me.

Slowly, he untangles our bodies.

I collapse face first on the couch.

He pulls his boxers on. Sits next to me. Wraps his arms around me.

This feels so fucking good.

But he's not mine anymore.

He's back to the stuffed shirt. I understand this Blake better than I did.

But his heart is still locked tightly.

This time, I'm the one who pulls away.

I push myself off the couch. "Do you have anything I can wear home?"

"Of course." His eyes turn down.

If I didn't know better, I'd swear that's disappointment in his expression.

Does he really want me around?

Want our intimacy to last beyond our bodies being one?

It's hard to believe.

But it's tempting.

He shakes it off as he leads me to his office. There's a pair of sweats in the bottom of his filing cabinet. They're in his size, but the pants are drawstring. They work well enough.

Blake plants a kiss on my lips. "You're meeting Ashleigh at six tomorrow."

"I know."

"Good luck."

THERE'S A NOTE ON THE TABLE AT HOME.

At Sarah's to study for a test. Already had dinner. Love you, Lizzy.

I'm not sure if I believe her. She spends a lot of time at Sarah's. But Lizzy's eighteen. Going out is normal. Dating is normal. Sleeping with guys is normal.

She wants to be an independent adult.

That's normal.

Even if I hate it.

I change out of Blake's clothes and step into the shower. Warm water hits my head, my shoulders, my chest.

I shampoo, condition, and soap quickly. I don't want to be alone with my thoughts. I don't want to be alone, period.

When I'm done, I step into a robe, make a sandwich, and eat it by my computer.

There are so many art schools, but all of them want portfolio samples.

I haven't done any serious work since high school.

229

Some of that stuff is decent, but it has nothing to do with the person I am now.

Maybe that doesn't matter. It's a college application. It's not like I have to bear my soul to some nameless, faceless admissions officer.

Still.

I want to show off my best work. Not the work I happen to have lying around.

I grab my sketchbook and a pencil and draw Blake from memory. It's not perfect. It wouldn't immediately read as Blake. But I have captured that impenetrable look in his eyes.

That lock around his heart.

I turn the page and try making it into something different.

Before the accident, I dreamed of drawing graphic novels. Capturing something real about life between the pictures and the words.

It's funny. Back then, I had nothing to say, and all the time to say it. Now that I'm bursting at the seams, I barely have the energy to pick up a pencil.

That's going to change. After this ruse is over, I'll have time and energy in spades. All of it will go to what I want. For Lizzy *and* for me.

I try drawing a comic version of Blake. He has broad shoulders, round eyes, a strong nose, and a square jaw.

It's not quite right. I play with the eyes until they feel like Blake. There. It's not perfect, but it's a solid start.

I draw a cartoon Kat. Overdone waves of hair, tight cocktail dress, sky high heels. The fake Kat. Super-Girlfriend.

There's nothing about me in that portrait. Nothing real. I try my hand at the real Kat with her mess of hair, her casual outfit, her inability to open herself up. But that's not something I can draw. Not yet at least.

But I'm going to get there.

I may never unlock Blake's heart.

But I will figure out mine.

Chapter Twenty-Five

Ashleigh shakes her head. Irritation is written all over her face. "We spoke yesterday about this happening at six on the dot."

The salesgirl shoots back her best customer-service smile. "It's only 5:45, miss. Perhaps you'd like some champagne while you wait." She looks at me. "Miss Wilder?"

"No, thank you." I shrink into the corner. I'm not interested in this pissing contest.

She leans over the counter, whispering something to the salesgirl. Not my problem. This whole wedding gown ordeal doesn't have to be my problem, but I can't bring myself to put Blake in charge of this.

I doodle in my sketchbook—a four-panel comic of my arrangement with Blake. But how the hell am I supposed to draw the feelings whirring around inside me? Those don't fit on paper. They don't fit anywhere.

Four panels, all the same. Blake standing there, aloof and distant, with a wad of cash in his hand. *I can help you.*

It's sad. He doesn't realize he has more to offer than money. He doesn't realize how sweet he can be.

I check my phone. No word from Lizzy even though she's been out of school for hours.

I rip out the drawing of Blake and crumple it into a tiny ball. I'm not thinking about him anymore today.

This is about my dress.

This is going to be exactly what I want.

"Thank you, I will." Ashleigh sits next to me. She glances at the sketchbook. Her expression is curious. "Blake told me you're an artist."

"You could say that."

"Natalie is pulling the dresses for you. They were supposed to be ready." She slides out of her heels and rubs her feet. "Barely three weeks now. We need something off the rack." She takes a quick scan of my body. "You'll look good in anything but an empire waist. Do you have any style of dress in mind?"

I stare at her like she's speaking another language. "I haven't thought about it."

"Given the weather, we might want to avoid a train. I'm guessing you're not too keen on dragging mud."

"Okay." I draw a circle in my sketchbook. That seems reasonable.

She frowns, pulls an iPad from her purse, navigates to a wedding website, and takes me through the different dress silhouettes.

Except for the sheath, they all flare somewhere and most of them flare dramatically. There's A-line, fit and flare, trumpet, mermaid, ballroom.

She goes over the pros and cons of each, but it all flies in one ear and out the other.

Lizzy is better at this kind of thing.

But where the hell is she?

"Miss Wilder." The salesgirl, Natalie, calls us to the dressing room.

It's huge. There are four or five stalls arranged in a circle. Mirrors on every door. Double set of mirrors in the middle of the room. And a podium on a turntable.

A great display case for a trophy-wife-to-be.

Natalie points us to a pastel pink bench. The entire room is pink. It's the picture of love and romance.

"These are beautiful dresses." Natalie wheels a rack closer.

There are a dozen dresses in different shades of white, ivory, and blush. There must be miles of chiffon and lace.

"She wants something sophisticated," Ashleigh says.

"Of course."

Natalie pulls a dress off the rack. It's simple ivory chiffon. Gathered waist. Barely looks formal.

"She's not going to the beach. She's getting married." Ashleigh waves the dress away. "Something dramatic. They'll be under the cherry blossoms. It's the middle of spring. We want lace. We want something feminine. Innocent but sexy. Pretty. Cherry blossoms represent the mystery of female beauty."

Damn. I've never heard someone wax poetic about a dress before.

I clear my throat. "That's the Chinese interpretation of cherry blossoms. In Japan, they're considered a symbol of the transience of life."

"Right," Ashleigh says. "So something beautiful, delicate, and dramatic all at once."

Natalie nods and suppresses an eyeroll. It's fair. How can a dress be dramatic and delicate?

She brings over another dress.

It's optic white, heavy satin, and beaded all over. It sparkles like the sun.

Ashleigh shakes her head and waves it away.

"You look like Blake did that day at the department store," I say.

"God, that bad?" She offers Natalie a pleasant smile. "Kat, maybe you could explain what you want."

"I'm not sure. Something pretty." I rack my brain for the right words to describe a dress. If I want to be an artist, I'm going to have to get a hell of a lot better at design. I steal the words Blake used to describe me. "Something beautiful and understated."

Natalie pulls another dress off the rack. A strapless ball gown with a sweetheart neckline. The puffy skirt takes up half the room.

"That is the opposite of understated," Ashleigh says. She stares at her phone. Her brow furrows. "Excuse me."

Natalie shakes her head. "Would you like to try it on to get a feel for it?"

Not really. It's ugly. But trying it on is better than sitting here helplessly.

I nod *okay* and follow Natalie into one of the dressing stalls.

"Did you bring a long-line, honey?" she asks.

"A what?"

"We'll try it without a bra. Just to get a feel for it." She motions to the hooks on the wall. "Call me over when you're ready."

Okay. Getting almost all the way naked in front of a strange woman I've never met. That's normal.

I strip to my panties and leave my clothes on the floor. "I'm ready."

Natalie enters the room. "Turn around, sweetie." She helps me into the dress, zips me up, and clips the back so I'm squeezed in tight.

I glance in the mirror. The dress has a corset top. It's tight on my chest and waist and then poof—this is less like a skirt and more like a hemisphere. I trip over the organza on my way to the main room.

Ashleigh is back on the bench. She frowns with distaste.

Natalie shoots her a dirty look.

"Let's try something else," Ashleigh says. "Unless you like it, Kat."

I stare at my reflection. I look like a Disney princess gone very, very wrong. "It's not my favorite."

Natalie offers me another dress. This one is straighter. It has a slight flare just about the knee, a trumpet style I think.

I go back to the stall. Natalie undresses and dresses me. All I do is step in and out of the gowns.

I avoid the reflection until we're in the main room.

"Aw," Ashleigh squeals. "You look beautiful. And understated."

My eyes go to the mirror.

This dress is more my style. It's simple. No beading, no embroidery. Just a pretty lace with a flower pattern.

Ashleigh snaps a photo with her cell phone. She offers me a smile. "Why don't we try putting on a few accessories?"

"Okay." I stare at my reflection. I'm wearing a fucking wedding dress. I'm getting married. This is absolutely absurd.

It's an easy lie.

All I have to do is smile and act like everything is normal.

I let Natalie have her way with me. Veil. Necklace. Jeweled belt. Silver heels.

She turns me to the mirror, waiting for my smile. There's a way this is supposed to go. I'm supposed to jump and squeal and proclaim my eternal happiness.

I stare back at my reflection.

It's a beautiful dress.

I look beautiful in it.

But it doesn't feel right.

This doesn't feel right.

The bell dings. Door opens. "Hello."

Lizzy. She's here.

Normal. I have to act normal.

She wanders into the main room. Her eyes go wide when she spots me in the dress. "Oh my God, Kat. You look beautiful."

"Doesn't she?" Ashleigh studies her work with pride. "Lose the belt I think." She turns to me. "Do you like it?"

"It's nice," I say.

"Yeah, but do you like it? Is it the one?" Ashleigh asks.

Lizzy looks from Natalie to me. "It's really nice."

"It is," I agree.

"But it only matters what you think," Lizzy says. "It's your wedding, and you're in charge of what you wear."

"It's only a dress," I say. "And I've got it under control."

"Yeah. You always have it under control." Lizzy drops her backpack on the floor.

Is that an angry drop or a normal *this is heavy* one?

I don't know.

The dress is too tight. It's making it hard to breathe.

I reach for the zipper but Natalie stops me.

She motions to Ashleigh. "Can you help Miss Wilder change? I'll show—what's your name dear?" She offers her hand to Lizzy.

"Lizzy." My sister shakes hands with Natalie.

"Let's look at bridesmaid dresses, huh?"

"Okay. Unless you have that under control too, Kat."

I shoot Lizzy a death glare.

She knows how hard this is for me.

Why is she pushing me?

I move into the stall, but I can't get out of the dress. I knock. "A little help?"

Ashleigh joins me. She pulls the zipper down. "You really look beautiful."

"Thanks."

"Is there anything you want to talk about?" She lowers her voice to a whisper. "I've known Mr. Sterling a long time. He's... exacting."

"No, it's nothing. I'm just... This is moving really fast."

She nods. "He's a good man."

"He is."

"And he does care about you."

I step out of the dress. "What do you mean?"

"Your deal. He... I'm sorry. I thought you knew I knew." Her eyes soften. "Don't tell him I said anything."

"I won't."

"I've worked with him a long time. He's always been difficult." She grabs another dress. "But I've never seen him this demanding. He wants to make you happy. It's just... in his way."

She's right. I see the same thing.

But I'm not sure his way will ever make me happy. "I wish he wanted to make me happy in my way."

"If only men were that simple."

I nod. "Are they always this complicated?"

"I'm sure you know Mr. Sterling better than I do."

"Maybe."

She nods. "He is different when he talks about you." She zips the dress. "He really does care for you, Kat. Maybe it's not enough. But it's more than I've ever seen."

"You mean with other women?"

"He has me arrange some of his dates and weekends away. Not that he dates, exactly. It's more like—"

"No-strings-attached sex?"

"That's the impression I get." She pushes the door open. "Are you ready?"

"Yeah."

She leads me to the main room. "It's beautiful."

It is.

It's perfect.

I should be happy.

I should be crying.

God, if my mom were here, if I were really getting married, there would be major waterworks.

She would have loved this dress. It's gorgeous. A ball gown with a wide v-neck and a subtle flare. Lace sleeves go all the way to my wrists. There's a small bow right beneath the low v of the back.

It's perfect.

Ashleigh motions for me to twirl.

I do it.

I feel silly, but when I catch my dress whooshing in the mirror—

It's perfect.

I'm Cinderella getting dressed for the ball.

Ashleigh pins a veil to my hair and pulls its fabric behind my head.

There I am, the girl who will be standing at the altar opposite Blake.

A sob rises up in my throat. I try to push it down, but it won't go.

I wipe away a tear. Another.

I shake my head. *I'm okay*.

I have to pretend these are happy tears.

I have to be able to handle this.

"Excuse me." I rush to the dressing room and slam the door shut behind me.

"Kat." Ashleigh knocks on the door. "Are you okay?" She lowers her voice. "I can get that champagne."

"I just need a minute."

She moves away from the door. I slink to my feet, pulling my knees into my chest the best I can. The full skirt is in the way. Not even this is going right.

They're talking in the main room. It's that loud whisper. The kind of thing my parents did when we were kids.

They go quiet. Footsteps move closer. Someone knocks on the door.

"Kat, can we talk?" Lizzy asks.

I push myself to my feet. Wipe the stray tears from my eyes. "Okay."

I open the door and Lizzy steps inside. She's wearing a long pink dress. She looks great, grown up. My little sister is going to be my maid of honor.

Another sob rises in my throat. This time, I don't push it away. That's a lost cause.

I wipe my tears. I try to smile like I'm happy.

"Don't bullshit me," Lizzy says.

I drop the smile.

Lizzy shakes her head. "This guy is tearing you to pieces."

"That's not true."

She lowers her voice to a whisper. "Does he even care that this hurts you?"

I wipe away a tear. There's no sign Blake cares. But Lizzy is being shortsighted. "It's for a lot of money. I can stand being miserable for a while."

"Does he know how you feel about him?"

"I don't feel anything."

"Don't lie to me. Or yourself." She stares into my eyes. "You deserve better than this."

"I can't leave him."

"Why not?"

"Because I want to be with him."

Her eyes go wide. "Oh. Kat... I'm sorry."

"I... I have to do this. No matter how much it hurts."

"Why?"

"For his mom."

"It's sweet... stupid, but sweet." She reaches for the door. "Let's go home. Talk. Eat ice cream."

I shake my head. "I have to finish this." All of it.

"Just walk now, Kat. Don't put yourself through this."

"It's not that bad. It's just... This makes me think about Mom. About how much I miss her."

Lizzy tilts her head, assessing my words. "You swear?"

"I do."

"Okay. Let's go home anyway. I have a test."

"No. I want to stay."

"Will you be okay alone?"

"Yeah." Maybe.

"You promise?"

I nod.

She stares back like she doesn't believe me.

Still, she opens the door and steps into the main room. "I love you, Kat."

"I love you too."

I pick myself up and step into the main room.

Natalie and Ashleigh are waiting. Staring.

I nod goodbye to Lizzy.

She disappears out the front door.

"Do you want a picture in that dress?" Natalie asks.

"No, this one is perfect," I say.

Ashleigh nods. "Excuse me." She stares at her phone and walks into the other room, shaking her head.

She calls someone in there. Blake probably.

Natalie helps me change out of the dress. She has a sympathetic look, but mercifully, she remains silent.

I change back into my clothes.

Natalie leaves to rearrange everything. I linger in the dressing room as long as I can.

At least here there's no one watching me, no one doubting me, no one deciding what's best for me.

My reflection stares back at me. Just Kat in here. Not the billionaire's fiancée, not the older sister, not the would-be artist. Just Kat.

I'm still not sure who that is.

That front door opens again. The bell rings. Again. There's a low voice. Ashleigh makes some dramatic noise.

I let out a sigh. She called Blake.

Like he's my dad and I'm a misbehaving child.

Or maybe like she's concerned and doesn't know what else to do.

Either way, I can't shake the feeling I'm about to get a lecture about being on my best behavior.

I adjust my sweater and step into the main room.

Sure enough, Blake is standing there. He's picture perfect in his sleek black suit.

"Let's get dinner," he says.

My stomach rumbles at the mention of food. My heartbeat picks up as I stare back into his piercing blue eyes. "Okay."

Ashleigh throws him a *hurry up* look. "Natalie will freak if you see the dress."

"Of course." He almost smiles.

Enough pleasantries. I push out the door. Outside, the sun is setting. Orange light streaks across the skyline. It's beautiful.

But everything around me feels ugly.

Chapter Twenty-Six

We eat at a very expensive Thai fusion restaurant. It's pretentious. The decor is a mix of gold Buddha statues and photos of farmers in Thailand. Like any of them could afford the prices on the dinner menu.

I pick at my red curry. It's delicious. Fresh shrimp. Crispy vegetables. Fluffy rice.

But my tongue is apathetic.

Blake is sitting next to me, but he feels a million miles away. I'm not here. Not really.

I'm stuck in my head.

I'm trying to convince my feelings to recede. It's less than a month until our wedding. I can survive a month of pretending.

Blake brings a broccoli floret to his lips and bites off the head.

He has a perfect business way of eating. It's patient. Neat.

I suck iced tea through my straw. This place doesn't have a bar. But then that's better. I don't need anything clouding my judgment.

What is he thinking?

What goes on behind those gorgeous blue eyes?

He catches me watching and raises his brow. "Do you want to order something else?"

I stab a shrimp with my fork and eat it whole. "No."

"Ashleigh was concerned."

"About?"

"I'm not sure. I didn't ask her to spy."

I study his expression the way he studies mine. I'm sure there's more to see on my face.

Blake is still a mystery, but his concern is clear.

He does care about me.

"I don't really want to talk about it." I stab another shrimp and eat it whole.

He brushes the hair from my eyes. The same thing he did last time. It calms me.

It should be a crime for someone to be able to calm me down or wind me up as easily as he does.

He stares into my eyes. "Do it anyway."

"I always thought my wedding would be more... real."

He nods.

"And my parents... I always thought they'd be there." I stab a red pepper. "I miss them."

"I'm sorry."

"Lizzy... she thinks I'm stupid to let you push me around."

"Is that what I do?"

"Sometimes." I chew and swallow my food. Half a plate to go. I will my appetite to return. This time last month, I would have killed for a meal like this. "She thinks I'm doing it for her."

"Aren't you?"

"Yeah. But she doesn't want me to... She still has this idea that I try to stay in control of everything." I press my fingertips together. I do try to protect Lizzy, but that's my job. She's my baby sister, even if it's been a while since she's been a baby.

His expression is intense. "Do you want to talk about it?"

"No. You and your sister aren't exactly on the best terms. I'm not sure I want your advice."

"I'd like to help you."

"You are," I say. "That money is going to change my life."

"But more than that." He stares into my eyes. Brushes my hair behind my ears. "I want to make you happy."

My stomach flutters. Blake has no idea what he's doing to me. He has no idea how unfair this is.

I take a deep breath. "Don't do that."

"Do what?" His fingertips brush my neck. My shoulders.

"Don't say sweet things."

"I do want to make you happy."

"Don't."

It's just like the pool. I'm about to be swallowed whole but, somehow, I believe it's going to be okay.

"I care about you," he says.

I close my eyes, soaking in the feeling of his hands on my skin.

I want all of it.

All of him.

"Blake. Don't. If you're going to whisper something, whisper a dirty promise."

He presses his lips to my neck. Then my ear. "I want to make you come."

My sex clenches. That's more like it. "How?"

"Pressed up against the wall begging for more."

I nod.

He slides his hand up my thigh. "Is this all you want from me, Kat?"

"It's all I'm going to get."

"That isn't true."

"Are you ever going to love me?"

"No."

"Then yes. This is all I want."

He kisses my neck again.

It's soft and sweet.

But it's sex.

It has to be just sex.

If I'm not careful, I'll get my heart broken.

I clear my throat. "Let's order dessert."

His composure breaks for a second. His brow furrows. It's like he's trying to figure me out. He glances at my now mostly empty plate and nods.

"Then I'll take the subway home," I say. "I haven't narrowed down my school choices, and I'm sure you have a lot to do at the office."

He stares at me. "No."

"What do you mean no?"

"I mean you're not going home. You're coming back to my place."

"No."

"There's only one way for you to say no, Kat, and it's not that word." His expression hardens. "You're coming home with me tonight."

Can't he see I'm trying to protect myself?

Maybe he doesn't care. He doesn't need protection. He's cool and aloof and impervious to all the pain that comes with falling in love.

I push myself out of the booth. "I'm going home by myself." I hold his stare. "Now, if you'll excuse me, I'll be in the bathroom."

Blake's gaze is intense. I turn away, but I can still feel it on me.

I don't get it.

He says he cares about me. But then why is he teasing me? Why is he offering breadcrumbs? Why is he so fucking lovable?

I can't do this.

Not if he's going to keep dangling his heart in front of me.

Not if he's going to pretend as if he's offering more.

The bathroom is through a small hallway. I pull the door open and step inside.

It's nice. Expensive.

The counter is marble, the mirror is smudge-free, the sink is a porcelain rectangle.

I run the water and splash it on my face. No makeup today. Nothing to wash off.

I'm just Kat, or maybe the shell of Kat left by whatever Blake is doing to me.

The door opens. I stare at the mirror, trying to ignore it. This is a public restroom. These things happen.

"This isn't our deal."

What the fuck? That's Blake.

I rub my eyes and check again, just to be sure.

"This is the women's restroom," I say.

He glances at the space between the stall doors and the floor. No one else is here. It's quiet. It's clean. Hell, it's nice.

He goes to the main door and turns a lock.

His eyes pass over me slowly. His breath speeds. "Take off your clothes."

I step back, but I'm pressed against the sink.

His voice gets low. "Don't make me ask twice."

Chapter Twenty-Seven

Heat collects between my legs.

My cheeks flush.

I've been naked a lot today, but it was never in this context.

It was never this inviting.

I hold Blake's gaze. It's intense. Demanding.

He's somewhere between the Blake I don't understand and the one who makes perfect sense.

I'm not sure it matters.

I want to give myself to every Blake.

I want to surrender to every Blake.

It's just… I want more than the uptight Blake is willing to give me.

He takes a step towards me. "Kat. Now." His voice gets low.

It makes my sex clench.

It centers me.

This makes sense.

Everything else… Not so much.

I pull my sweater over my head and drop it on the floor.

His eyes fix on mine.

His pupils dilate.

He wants this as much as I do.

Needs it as much as I do.

Blake doesn't understand me either. Not the clothed version of me.

I toss my undershirt next to my sweater.

All the thoughts racing around my brain quiet. Right now, I'm Blake's and he's mine. That's what matters.

I unhook my bra and slide it off my shoulders. My nipples tighten. A shiver runs over my skin.

I've been on display before, but I've never been this exposed.

Heat rushes to my core. There's something perfect about this. I want him staring at me, thinking about me, lusting after me.

"Touch your nipples," he demands.

His gaze sends a shiver down my spine. I rub my nipple with my thumb.

I stare back into his eyes as I do it again.

Another shudder rushes through me. My breath hitches. My heart races. My entire body is buzzing.

I run my fingers over my nipples the way he does. My eyes want to close, so I can really soak in the sensation, but I force them open.

His tongue slides over his lips. He motions *come here.*

I take three steps towards him, until we're close enough to touch.

Blake grabs my hips. He pulls my body into his, crotch first. He's hard.

Fuck. It feels so good, him being hard. I'm never going to tire of it.

His hands slide over my shoulders and down my torso. He glides them back up my sides and over my breasts.

I gasp as he plays with my nipple. It's much better than my hand. So much better.

I fight to keep my eyes open, to keep them on his.

Heat rushes through my body. Every brush of his fingertips stokes the fire inside me.

Tension builds in my sex. I need him already. I need him desperately.

I rub my crotch against his, soaking in the feel of his erection against me.

He tugs at my jeans. "Turn towards the mirror."

I do. My neck presses against his face. He brushes his lips against it. Then it's teeth. Hard. Pain bursts through me, calling all of my attention. I grab at his suit jacket again.

"Not until I give you permission." He sinks his teeth into my neck, testing me. "Hands at your sides."

I tug at the sides of my jeans. Anything to keep my body cooperating.

Blake nips at my neck, my ears, my collarbone. It's the perfect bit of ecstasy. I feel the ache everywhere.

Conscious thought is long gone. He's all I know, all I want, all I feel. I close my eyes and soak in the sensation of his mouth, teeth, tongue.

I let out a low groan.

He tugs at my hair, pulling my head back and biting me again and again. My hands shake. They want so badly to touch him. I want so badly to touch him.

But I have to wait.

He brings his mouth to my nipples and sucks hard. It feels so good I can barely stand it.

Ecstasy builds inside me. My sex pulses. I'm desperate for a proper release.

Pain bursts through me as he bites my nipple. My hands reach for his hair, but I stop myself. Hands at my sides. Those are the rules.

Blake moves to my other nipple. He sucks and bites and licks. Pleasure and pain whir around inside me. It's so much sensation my legs go weak. There's nothing to hold onto.

"Unzip your jeans." He steps back to watch.

My body goes cold. It's screaming for him to stay closer. Right now, Blake is the only thing I need.

But I have to play by his rules. I let out a shaky breath and do as I'm told.

His eyes find mine. "Touch yourself."

I push my jeans to my knees. Then my underwear. My breath catches. I'm as good as naked.

Blake's pupils dilate.

My fingertips trail beneath my belly button. Almost.

I skim my clit lightly. I want so badly to come, but I want it from Blake.

"No teasing, Kat." His voice is low. "Touch yourself properly."

My sex clenches. I hold his gaze as I rub myself. Pleasure builds inside me. My cheeks flush.

I'm masturbating for him in a public bathroom, and I'm fucking enjoying it. What the hell has happened to my life?

"You want to come, Kat?" he asks.

"Yes," I barely breathe it. My finger circles my clit. I'm throbbing. Desperate.

"You want to touch me?"

God yes. I nod. "Yes."

"Come here."

I take a step towards him. Close enough to touch again.

"Closer."

I press my body against his. He drags his fingers over my hips, my stomach, my breasts. He pinches my nipples so hard I gasp.

He presses his lips to mine. His kiss is aggressive. Commanding.

Heat rushes through my body. Every part of me feels good. Feels his.

He pulls back, his lips hovering over my ears. "On your knees."

Hell yes. I slide to my knees, holding onto his hips to stay upright.

Blake looks down at me. He undoes his belt. Unzips his slacks.

My tongue slides over my lips. Almost.

"Kat, look at me."

I do.

"You want to come?"

"Yes."

"You want to suck my cock?"

"Yes."

"Then touch yourself." He slides his hand into my hair, holding me steady.

I bring one hand between my legs.

I stop holding back.

I rub my clit harder. Faster.

Pleasure builds inside me.

Almost…

With his free hand, Blake pushes his slacks to his knees. Then the boxers. They strain over his cock.

Want floods my body. I slide my finger inside my sex. Mmm. It's the next best thing to him.

He presses his palm against the back of my head, bringing me closer. I brush my lips against his cock.

He tastes good, like soap and like Blake.

I dig my hand into his hip to stay upright, but he pushes it away.

"Rub your nipples," he commands.

I press my knees into the floor. Nothing to hold onto. No way to stay upright.

I slide two fingers into my sex.

I rub my nipples with my other hand.

Pleasure floods my body. I'm close, but I can't come yet.

I can't come until I have him in my mouth.

Blake digs both hands into my hair, holding my head in place.

I run my tongue over the head of his cock, savoring the taste of him.

He presses his hands against my head, guiding me.

I take him into my mouth and suck on his tip.

He groans, holding me steady as he thrusts into my mouth.

He starts slow. Then he moves faster. Deeper. I press my tongue flat against his base, sucking on him as he fucks my mouth.

Blake groans. I slide my fingers deeper in a desperate attempt to match his pace.

Pleasure whirs around me. There's so much sensation I can barely take it.

He fucks my mouth. Harder. Deeper. I relax my throat, fighting my gag reflex.

I need to take him as deep as he'll go.

He tugs at my hair. His breath is heavy. Desperate. "Come for me, Kat," he groans.

I surrender to the sensations, matching his rhythm with my fingers.

Harder, deeper, faster. Pleasure pools inside me. It builds with every one of his groans.

Almost.

He tugs at my hair. The burst of pain pushes me to the brink.

My body is on fire. Everything is too much. Too much pleasure, too much pain, too much feeling.

Finally, I understand that idea. More is more.

And God do I need more.

I move faster. I suck harder. I pinch my nipple until I'm groaning. An orgasm rises up inside me. It's so tight, so hard, so damn good.

Bliss overtakes me as he fucks my mouth.

With the next brush of my fingers, I come.

An orgasm washes over me. My sex pulses. My thighs shake. It feels so fucking good.

I suck on him in some attempt to contain the sensation.

But it's not enough. I have to grab onto his hips to stay upright.

He looks down at me, holding me in place as he thrusts into my mouth.

Blake groans. His eyelids press together. His nails scrape against my neck.

With his other hand, he tugs at my hair. Harder. Harder. Harder. I groan against his cock.

It's more than a hint of pain, but it's perfect. That's how good he feels. That's how much he wants me.

"Fuck," he groans.

He launches into a final thrust as an orgasm overtakes him. He holds my head tightly as he comes in my mouth.

I wait until he's finished and swallow hard.

Blake releases his grip. I fall to my hands and knees, catching my breath. My heart is still racing. My body is still keyed up.

He offers his hands. I take them and he pulls me to my feet.

Blake helps me into my panties and jeans. His fingertips skim my hips, sides, chest, neck.

I meet his gaze. Still topless, but that's not why I feel exposed.

My cheeks flush. My attention turns to the floor.

He runs a hand through my hair, the same sweet touch from before. "You okay?"

I nod.

He adjusts his pants then kneels and helps me finish dressing.

His eyes find mine. "Ready to go home?"

I nod. This relationship might crush my heart, but my body demands more. It demands all of Blake, all the time.

It's the only way I can have him.

Chapter Twenty-Eight

We have our dessert on Blake's couch. Of course, he worked everything out so sticky rice and mango was waiting for us in his apartment. The man can pull strings I can't even fathom.

I flip around the channels. I settle on a *Grey's Anatomy* rerun, and he watches with a bemused fascination.

"What the hell is this?" he asks.

"It's an amazing soap opera where all the doctors and nurses are sleeping together. I used to watch it with Lizzy." Before I was too busy to commit to Netflix binge sessions.

"Why?"

"It's TV. It's fun. Don't you ever watch TV just to zone out?"

He stares at me like I'm crazy.

"No, of course you don't. You have three spare hours a week and you spend them all, what—playing chess?"

"No. I spend them fucking beautiful women."

"Really?"

He shrugs.

I laugh. Blake is making a joke. It's weird but perfect.

He scoops sticky rice with his spoon and slides it into my mouth. Sweet, creamy, hint of coconut. And, yes, damn sticky. Last time he was…

I dig my nails into my thighs so I won't react. I want to connect with him when we have our clothes on.

I lick the spoon clean. Blake raises an eyebrow as if to say *hmm, you really like that sticky rice.*

I flip him off.

He smiles. My heart thuds.

Fine. I get off on his smile. I can accept that. It doesn't mean we're serious.

Who wouldn't giggle over a perfect smile?

Especially when it's as rare as Blake's is.

"And you make time for this show?" he asks.

"Not this show in particular. But it's important to relax." I eat mango with my hands. The juice runs down my fingers.

Blake takes my hand and runs his tongue over it, lapping up every bit of juice. His eyes connect with mine. "You don't relax unless I force you to."

"I went to brunch with my sister." And spent the entire time stressed over that damn check. "It was very relaxing."

He stares at me like he doesn't believe me. "Take your own advice, Kat. What do you ever do that's just for you?"

"I don't know."

"You deserve to treat yourself." He runs his finger up my neck. "You deserve everything the world has to offer."

He looks at me like he's promising me everything, but I only want this. Him looking at me like I'm the fucking world, like I'm the thing he wants to explore.

Warmth rushes around inside me, collecting in my belly. It's not the racing heat of what happened in the bathroom. It's not about touching him. Not physically.

I clear my throat. "And what are you offering? Anything better than the world?"

His lips curl into a smile and then—thank God I'm sitting, because my knees go weak—he laughs.

It's a belly laugh. A perfect laugh. His eyes light up and that little dimple appears on his cheek.

He brushes a hair from my eyes.

His breath warms my ear as he leans closer. "Much better than the world."

"And what's that."

He nods to a box tucked away on the bookshelf. Chess. "The chance for victory."

"Yeah?"

"Unless you're afraid of a challenge."

You mean like surviving the next few months with Blake without falling to pieces? "Never."

He sets the game up on the coffee table. We play a dozen times. Same handicap for Blake—no queen. I manage to win a few times. But the truth is, my mind isn't on the strategy.

It's on him. His fingers gliding over the pieces, over his chin as he thinks. The cute look of frustration when he loses a piece. The way his eyes get big and bright. A new idea, something to excite him.

His smile.

That dimple on his cheek.

His laugh.

His perfect laugh.

My heart races. All this nervous energy over a board game. It's not like me. I hold my own with people yelling in my face, with six tables who all need me at once, with no way to pay next month's bills.

I hold my own.

"I should really get to bed." I yawn dramatically to sell my story.

Blake presses his lips into mine. "I'll go with you."

He's going to *sleep* with me? My nod is quick. Enthusiastic. My next step is closer to a skip.

I brush my teeth and change into a pair of pajamas from the dresser. My size, my style. I don't even care how he got them, who bought them.

Only that they're here.

That we're both here.

He pulls me onto his bed. His lips brush mine. It's softer and sweeter than any of our previous kisses.

He holds me until I fall asleep.

He holds me like he loves me.

———

I WAKE UP COLD. NO ARMS AROUND ME. NO ONE ELSE IN the bed. The apartment is quiet. Empty.

There's a note on the counter:

Went into work early. Will be home by 8 P.M. if you want to stick around. If not, take a cab and use my credit card. I insist.

Help yourself to anything.

- Blake

Home by eight. Nice and early. A solid twelve hours away.

I dig around the kitchen. There's coffee, tea, cereal, milk. That's about it. There's plenty to do in this area of town. Hell, I could spend the whole day in the park. I could spend half of it at the Met.

But I'm not rearranging my day around Blake. As nice as his place is, as much as I want to wander around Central Park, I'm not staying here.

I fix myself cereal and coffee and sit on the balcony. It's

warmer today, but there's still a chill. I wrap myself in a blanket and doodle the view in every direction.

I'll miss this apartment.

I'll miss Blake more.

I try to shut out the thought, but it sticks in my mind.

The only thing worse than staying with him is leaving.

Chapter Twenty-Nine

At five after eight, my phone buzzes.

Blake: Damn. You're not here. There goes hope you greet me naked.

My breath catches in my throat. That's how he wants me. Sitting around his apartment waiting to be ready the second he's home. What a goddamn cliché of a wife-to-be.

Of course, I wouldn't exactly mind greeting him naked. I certainly wouldn't mind him throwing me on the couch and fucking me senseless.

I shake my head.

I need to stem the feelings pouring from me.

We have a deal. It's business. I need to keep it business.

Period.

Kat: Maybe if you had offered to greet me naked.

Blake: Come over. I will.

Kat: I can't. I have to work on my portfolio. Columbia application is due next week.

My fingers hover over the phone screen. It's a half-truth. The application is due next week, but the portfolio isn't due for another month.

I need to figure out how to pull back before I dive in.
Somehow.

———

He invites me over or offers to meet somewhere to fuck me.

I dodge with excuses of work.

I almost feel like he wants me.

No, he does want me. Just not the way I need him to.

Blake: You must need a break by now.

Yes. Desperately.

Kat: I'm too tired to head uptown.

Blake: I'll come to you.

Kat: And fuck me with my sister in the next room?

Blake: No. And fuck you in my limo.

My sex clenches.

Blake: We have dinner reservations next Saturday. In midtown at six. With Mom and Fiona.

Kat: Have you ever heard of asking.

Blake: Will you join me for dinner?

Kat: Yes.

Blake: Please bring Lizzy. Mom wants to meet her.

Kat: Sure. For Meryl, not for you.

Blake: Of course. I'm not under any illusions about why you're doing this.

But he is. Because it's not just for Meryl. It's for him. Or maybe for me. Because *I* want to be around him. Just… I need to figure out how to be around him without falling harder.

Blake: Now, Kat, may I make you come in my limo?

Kat: Do we have to talk?

Blake: Nothing but dirty promises.
Kat: I'll be ready in fifteen.
Blake: Don't wear anything under your coat.

———

BLAKE IS SITTING ON THE BENCH. HE'S IN HIS SUIT AND TIE, the picture of confidence.

His eyes meet mine. They demand everything.

Dirty promises. We're only making dirty promises tonight. We're only making dirty promises forever.

"Take off your coat," he demands.

My body obeys before my head can step in.

I slide my coat off my shoulders.

I'm not quite naked. I'm in thigh high stockings and heels.

He eyes the tights with appreciation.

"They weren't under my coat. Technically," I say.

He half-smiles. He must appreciate technicalities. He would.

The limo pulls off the street.

I press my palms against my hips. I need to look confident.

This is for me. Because I want him. Because I want this distraction. Because I want my thoughts a million miles away.

He leans back, spreading his knees. "Lie down on the bench. On your back."

Slowly, I lower my body onto the cold leather seat.

He leans next to me. Brushes his fingers against my inner thighs.

His touch is light. A tease. I should be used to his teasing by now, but I'm not.

My body whines for more.

I stare up into his eyes. Demanding more.

Blake pulls a champagne bottle from an ice bucket.

He tilts the bottle away from me and pops the cork. It bounces off the ceiling and lands on the floor. Bubbles spill over the sides of the bottle.

A drop hits my chest. It's cold. Sticky.

Heat spreads through my torso. He isn't touching me. He isn't licking this drop off. I need that. All of it.

It's been too long.

Blake slides out of his suit jacket. "Arms over your head."

My body obeys immediately.

He holds the bottle two inches above my mouth and dribbles champagne over my lips.

I lick the bubbly. My tongue is greedy. All of me is greedy. I need the sweet, fruity drink. I need it obliterating every one of my inhibitions.

Blake draws a line of champagne over my body from my lips to my belly button then back up again.

He plants a kiss on my pelvis. Then it's his tongue on my skin, lapping up every drop of champagne.

He moves up my stomach. My chest. My neck.

He sucks at my skin to lap up every drop.

His fingertips skim my inner thighs. The tease makes me shake. He's taking too long. I can't wait. I'm already waiting for so much.

Then he kisses me and I have everything I need. Feelings are pouring from me to him. And back from him to me. Only I don't know what they are.

He needs me.

I need him.

I don't have a clue about the rest.

His kiss is hungry. Demanding.

When he pulls back, he's panting.

He looks down at me, some mix of affection and desire filling his eyes. "Comfortable?"

"Very."

He undoes his tie and holds it tightly.

He works slowly, wrapping my wrists and binding them.

I'm at his mercy again.

But then I'm always at his mercy.

"Please." I arch my back. "Fuck me."

"I'm going to fuck you so hard you see stars."

I nod. Yes. That. Now.

"But you have to wait."

No. I hate waiting. He always makes me wait.

His eyes stay glued to mine as he strips out of his shirt. Then the belt. The shoes. Socks. Slacks.

He slides his boxers to his feet.

My sex clenches. We're naked in here together. We're so fucking close to exactly where we need to be.

He wraps his hand around the neck of the champagne bottle. His finger slides over the rim.

Then it's his lips.

The teasing motherfucker.

He dribbles champagne onto my lips.

It's amazing, but it's not what I want.

My back arches. It's the only way I can plead. I like being at his mercy, but he's too fucking merciless.

Blake draws another line down my neck, over my breasts, down my stomach. This time, he stops at my belly button.

It's like he's promising to keep tracing that line with his tongue.

Like he's promising he'll finally give me what I need.

His tongue slides over my neck. Flat. Wet. Soft.

Pleasure whirs around me. My nerves wake up. My entire body wakes up. It's here. In this moment. Buzzing with desire.

He licks his way to my breasts. His tongue slides over my nipple. Then it's a flick. Pleasure shoots through me. He does it again.

Again.

Again.

Heat pools in my sex as he teases me. It feels so fucking good. But it's not enough.

I'm shaking when he releases my nipple. He drags his mouth over my stomach, lapping up every drop. He's slow about working his way down my body. His touch gets softer as he moves towards my belly button.

Then below it.

"Please," I groan. I part my legs as wide as they'll go.

"Beg me." He presses his hand against my hip, pinning me to the bed.

"Fuck me, Blake. Please, fuck me. I need your cock inside me. I need you coming inside me."

He leans down to take my nipple into his mouth.

Pleasure floods my body. "Please." I arch my back to push my breast into his mouth. "Please."

His teeth scrape against my nipple. His hands close around my thighs. Yes. Hell yes. Anticipation floods my body.

He drags his lips down my stomach, under my belly button.

Lower.

Lower.

There.

His tongue slides over my clit.

I lean back, relaxing into my restraints as he licks me from top to bottom.

His nails are sharp against my thighs. His tongue moves with utterly perfect precision. Every flick of it sends another wave of ecstasy through me.

Almost…

I press my thighs against his hands. His nails sink into my flesh. The burst of pain is enough to send me into overdrive. An orgasm rises up inside me. It gets tighter and better and harder. Then everything releases in one perfect wave of pleasure.

Blake moves fast. He plants his hands around my shoulders as he brings his body onto mine.

The weight of him feels so good against me.

He's warm.

He's hard.

He holds my hips steady as he thrusts into me.

It's hard. Deep. It's too fast, but it isn't fast enough. It's too much, but it will never be enough.

I arch my back and lift my hips to push him deeper.

He groans as our bodies come together.

He stares back into my eyes as he fucks me.

One hand presses my shoulders into the bench seat. The other holds me steady.

I surrender.

I lose myself in the movements of his body.

Every thrust makes me feel whole and needy at once. He feels so good inside me, but it's not enough. I need more. I need everything.

He moves harder.

Deeper.

An orgasm rises up inside me. I moan. I pant. I groan his name.

I thrust my hips to meet him, to push him deeper.

There.

Pleasure rushes through my body as I come. It knocks me down. My muscles relax. One leg slips off the bench seat. The other presses into its back.

Blake's hands are on my chin.

He's staring at me with that perfect mix of lust and affection.

He plants a desperate kiss on my mouth.

He presses his body against mine.

And he drives into me harder.

He slides his hands around my ass, pulling my body into his, pushing deeper.

It's like I'm his plaything.

Like I'm exactly what he needs.

He groans into my mouth. His nails sink into the flesh of my ass.

There. His cock pulses as he comes inside me, filling me, marking me as his.

He collapses on top of me. Presses his lips against my neck.

I catch my breath as he dresses and undoes the knot on my tie.

"I'd like you to come over." He takes my hand and presses a kiss against my wrist. "If you'd like."

"I have too much to do." I stare back at him. He means it. He wants me around. As much as I want that, it's the opposite of what I need.

"Of course." He nods and settles into the bench seat.

But he actually looks… sad.

We're silent as the limo drives back to my place.

It stops.

Blake slides my coat over my shoulders and does the buttons. He kneels in front of me and rolls my stockings onto my feet one at a time. Then the boots.

He drags his fingertips up my calves and over the insides of my knees. "I'll see you soon."

But which Kat will he want?

Chapter Thirty

Lizzy is not happy about this dinner.

Or about my continuing arrangement with Blake.

Or how I'm "lying to myself."

She spends the afternoon in her room making alternating claims of doing homework and picking out an outfit.

I knock at five. It's at least half an hour on the subway to Midtown. I don't want to make it harder for her by taking a cab.

My jaw drops as she pulls the door open. She looks so pretty. So grown up.

Her hair is swept into an elegant updo. Her makeup is soft and subtle. Her chic black dress suits her perfectly.

"You look beautiful," I say.

"Thanks. You too." She reaches for her purse. "Should we go?"

"In a minute." I take a long look at my sister. We've barely talked since the fight at the boutique. I miss her. I miss having camaraderie.

I check my phone for word from Blake.

There are a few days of *sweet dreams* texts. And there's a reminder with the restaurant's address. That's it.

Maybe he doesn't want me. I don't know. It's confusing.

I throw my sketchbook in my purse. It's a new habit. In case inspiration strikes. I still have a lot of work to do for my portfolio.

"Listen, Kat." Lizzy looks at her foot. Presses it into the ground. "Never mind. We should talk about it later."

"You sure?"

"Yeah, totally." She pulls the door open. "About the other day… I know I should have—"

"It's okay. I understand."

I follow her out the door.

———

THE RESTAURANT IS BEAUTIFUL. ROMANTIC.

Black walls. Flickering candles. Rose bouquets.

It's the perfect place for a date. Or a proposal. Or a declaration of undying love.

It's perfect for a panel. The happy moment where the couple falls in love or the miserable one where everything falls apart.

I swallow the lump that rises in my throat. There's only a week until Blake and I marry.

In one week, I'll be the wife of a man who will never love me.

It feels more real every day.

The hostess leads us to a private room in the back of the restaurant. It's just as romantic, though it's brighter. Ornate lamps in the corner offer plenty of illumination.

Meryl is sitting at the end of the table, nursing a glass of wine.

Blake is next to her, his fingers wrapped around a glass of whiskey, his attention on his mom.

She turns to us. "About time someone entertaining shows up." She looks to Lizzy. "You must be Kat's sister."

"Lizzy." She offers her hand.

Meryl shakes. "It's nice to meet you, sweetheart. You're just as pretty as Kat. Tell me there's some man desperate to scoop you up."

Lizzy laughs. "There have been a few."

"None good enough for your demanding older sister?" Meryl asks.

"How did you know?" Lizzy takes a seat. She turns to Meryl. Her expression gets bright. Animated. "None were good enough for me either. They're such... boys."

"And you want a man?" Meryl asks.

Lizzy nods.

"She's only eighteen," Blake says.

"But an old eighteen. Like you were." Meryl leans in to whisper in Lizzy's ear.

Lizzy laughs. She turns back to me. "I get it."

"Hmm?" Meryl asks.

"Why Kat was so... insistent about this... dinner." Lizzy pats the spot next to her. "She's been really excited for me to meet you."

"I've been excited too." Meryl takes a long sip of her wine. "Tell me, sweetheart. Are you an artist like your sister?"

Lizzy laughs. "No. I don't get art."

Meryl stage-whispers. "Me either."

"What's the deal with that one guy who does plaid paintings? I mean, those would look awesome on a skirt, but on the wall of a museum?" Lizzy shakes her head with distaste.

I can't help but smile. Even if Lizzy has no idea what she's talking about. The modernist movement—

"You look gorgeous." Blake's voice grabs my attention. He's staring into my eyes. "I've missed you."

"Me too. I've been busy." I take a seat next to my sister and look to Meryl. "College applications."

"Still?" Meryl plays with the stem of her wineglass.

"With art school, you need a portfolio. But nothing I draw feels good enough," I say.

"Her work is wonderful. She's underselling herself," Blake says.

"I haven't showed you anything." My cheeks flush.

"You leave your sketchbook open on the table. I see plenty when you're drawing." His voice is proud. He really does appreciate my skill.

But that only makes things more confusing.

He misses me. He wants the world for me. He's interested in my art.

And he's never going to love me.

It doesn't add up.

It doesn't make sense.

"And how have you been, Lizzy? How's your chess bot?" Blake asks.

She blushes. "Oh. It's okay. I mean, I'm trying something with Go, but it's impossible." She looks to Blake. "I spent a few hours testing the chat bot."

"You're more interested than I am," he says.

"Did you really program it all by yourself?" she asks.

"I did," he says. "It was my first time programming in awhile."

"It's amazing." Her voice gets loud. Excited. "I go into that room where you can play a game." She turns to me. "You have to guess if you're talking to a human or a chat bot, and the other person does the same."

"What if the other person is a chat bot?" I ask.

"Then it guesses. Sometimes it's two bots talking to each other. You can read the logs of that." Her eyes go wide. "It's so cool."

"Thank you," Blake says.

"Programming is his idea of fun, I think," I say.

Meryl laughs, but it's strained. She brings her fist to her mouth and coughs.

Blake leans closer.

She waves him away. "I'm fine, sweetheart. Just thirsty." She holds up her empty glass.

Right on cue, a server enters our room. He smiles at Meryl. "Another?"

"You're too kind." She hands him her glass.

He looks to Blake. "You too, sir?"

Blake nods. "A gin and tonic for my fiancée."

"You order for her?" Meryl coughs. "Really? Don't you think that's a bit old-fashioned?"

"You'll confuse the man." Blake's lips curl into a half-smile. He looks to me and winks.

He's making another joke. It's not a good joke—no server is so easily confused that the word *old-fashioned* would make him think he should fix an old fashioned rather than a gin and tonic—but it's mine.

It makes me warm all over.

"Yeah, it's weird. But I think they're into that." Lizzy looks to the server. "Diet Coke with a maraschino cherry."

"A second glass for my daughter." Meryl motions to the empty spot next to Blake. "She got held up discussing something with Trey."

The server nods and disappears through the doors.

Meryl lets out another cough. Or more like a fit. She clears her throat and forces a smile. "Lizzy, I heard you're going to school next year. Is that true?"

Lizzy takes a seat. She plays with her dress.

"Well, sweetheart, do tell. Have you decided?"

"Stanford."

My stomach drops. "Officially?"

"Yeah. I'm sorry, Kat. I should have told you sooner. But I already enrolled. Yesterday actually." She bites her lip. "I have a full scholarship."

"That's great, sweetheart," Meryl says. "Lovely campus. And California, well, it's not my taste, but the weather is lovely."

"Stanford grads do great in Silicon Valley." Blake takes a long sip of his drink. His eyes pass over Meryl.

There's something in his expression. He's worried.

God, if Blake's worried, it must be bad. Or it could be I've somehow cracked the code to his expression.

I look closer. No, that can't be it. The man is still a mystery. A beautiful mystery who makes me come so hard I scream. But a mystery nonetheless.

"I'll miss you," I say.

"Blake, honey, I hope you'll keep your wife too busy to miss her sister." Meryl lets out a light laugh and turns to me. "And aren't you looking at schools?"

"I won't start until the spring semester." I tug at the fabric of my dress. Same thing Lizzy was doing. "Most of them are in the northeast." None are anywhere near Stanford.

Meryl smiles at Lizzy. "At least you'll get the apartment to yourself for a few months."

"Oh, yeah. I guess you're not going to live here after you and Blake get married," Lizzy says.

"After the honeymoon." He looks at me with love in his eyes. The pretend kind. "We can pick out furniture tomorrow if you'd like."

Meryl shakes her head. "Please, my son has never picked out a piece of furniture. He has a decorator."

"Oh yeah?" I ask.

"You better take the reins, honey. His apartment and his office are so terribly utilitarian. Who can live like that? It's like a science fiction film," Meryl asks.

Lizzy's ears perk. "Which one?" She looks to Blake. "Don't tell me you have an intentional aesthetic."

"She hates art unless it's art direction in a sci-fi movie." I shake my head.

Meryl laughs. "She's a plebeian. Like me. You'll have to leave the art and literature to intellectuals like you and Blake. The rest of us need explosions and drama."

"True." Lizzy looks to Blake. "Where are you going? On your honeymoon?"

"Paris," Blake says.

Right. Paris. I knew that. I nod like it was my decision. It won't be so bad, fucking Blake in the City of Light. All that romance surrounding us…

"Paris. How lovely." Something in Meryl's expression changes. More serious. "I'm glad you two…"

"Mom?"

"You seem happy. I never thought…" She stares at her wineglass. "I never thought Blake would find something real."

Real. Right. I smile my biggest smile.

Lizzy frowns, but she doesn't say anything.

I think she gets it. How can she not? Meryl lights up the room. It's impossible to do anything but want her happy.

The server arrives with our drinks.

It's a perfect distraction.

Lizzy buries her face in her soda.

I drink half my gin and tonic in a single sip.

Meryl studies me the way Blake does, picking apart my intentions.

I'm not sure I can keep up my poker face. Between Stanford being official and our wedding in two weeks and Meryl coughing...

It's too much.

A loud hello interrupts my train of thought.

Fiona steps into the room. Alone.

We go through a round of introductions then she sits next to Blake. "You okay, Mom?"

"Fine. Stop asking," she says.

But Meryl doesn't look fine. Her skin has a slight yellow sheen. She's sweating. Her smile is strained. Her voice is shaky.

"Are you sure?" Fiona asks.

"I'd like to have one dinner that isn't about my condition. We're celebrating your brother's wedding."

"Of course." Fiona taps my shoulder. "I'm going to use the restroom. Join me, Kat?"

She isn't really asking.

But what could she possibly have to say with me?

She already offered me a small fortune in go-away money.

I look to Blake for a clue.

He nods *go with her*.

He knows his sister better than I do.

"Yes." I push out of my chair. "I need to fix my lipstick."

I follow Fiona to the restroom. It's quiet. Empty.

And beautiful. How can a bathroom be this beautiful? It defies logic.

She stares back at me. "I take it you're going through with the wedding?"

"Yes."

"I guess that's your decision." She looks to the mirror and adjusts her hair. "I have to admit, I admire it."

"Huh?"

"Your prenup. You only get a million dollars if you divorce."

Only a million dollars. What's wrong with these people?

She looks to me. "The offer stands. I know a hundred grand is a lot less than a million dollars, but it's a lot faster."

"I don't want money."

She looks me in the eyes. "I believe you."

My cheeks flush. "Then why are you—"

"I thought I was sparing Blake before. Maybe I was. If you were a gold digger, you'd have taken the money and run. Or demanded a lot more in your prenup."

"I told you—"

"I know. You aren't after his money. You want to be with him."

"Yes. Of course."

"I know my brother. I love him. He's my best friend. But he's another rich man. He thinks the world revolves around his desires."

"He won't—"

"Exactly. He won't. That's a full sentence. All those things you dreamed of as a little girl, the romantic walks on the beach, the candlelit dinners, the long, sweet kisses. He won't offer you that. He won't make time for it. And when you get sick of it—and you will, trust me—you'll leave him. And it will crush him. I don't want that."

"I won't leave. I love Blake."

The second the words are out of my mouth, I know they're true. I love Blake. I'm madly, crazy in love with him.

My stomach flip-flops.

I'm madly in love with him, and the best he'll ever be able to muster is *I care about you.*

My knees buckle.

Oh, God.

Talk about fucking things up.

I grab onto the counter to stay upright.

The bathroom door opens. Lizzy. Her face is the picture of concern. "Blake's mom collapsed."

Fiona goes white. "Is she okay?"

"They're calling an ambulance." Lizzy shakes. "We should— Kat? What do we do?"

Fiona rushes out of the bathroom.

I take a deep breath. "We follow the ambulance."

Chapter Thirty-One

The E.R. is an awful place. The air is stale. The tile is squeaky. The light is blindingly bright.

Fiona paces back and forth.

Lizzy sinks into the scratchy grey chair.

Blake leans against the wall, his eyes on his shiny leather shoes.

I press my palms into my thighs. What can I say? Meryl is dying. That isn't news. But now it isn't something far off in the future either.

Blake moves towards me. He kneels in front of me and looks up at me. His palm presses against my cheek.

He rubs my temple with his thumb.

"It will be okay." His voice is steady. Reassuring.

I believe him, even though it isn't true. It won't be okay.

She's going to die.

She's going to die believing this bullshit.

He wraps his arms around me.

I slide off the seat and sink into his touch. It's so

strange, Blake on the E.R. floor in his thousand-dollar suit. Bringing himself to my level. Comforting me.

He does comfort me.

He does everything to me.

We sit like that forever.

Eventually, Lizzy stands. "I'm going to get a soda. You want anything?"

Yes, but nothing out of a vending machine. I shake my head.

"Come with me anyway." She offers her hand and shoots me a *we need to talk* look.

I take it. I let her pull me up and lead me away from Blake. Into a quiet hallway. One away from the sounds of emergencies and screaming patients.

Lizzy finds a vending machine in the corner and digs a dollar out of her purse. "You okay?"

I shake my head. "It feels like last time. Not as bad, but the same kinda thing. I lost almost everything that day."

My sister hugs me. "I don't want to fight. You're my best friend. Always. And whatever happens with Blake, I support you. Okay?"

"Okay."

"I love you."

"Love you too." I hug her tightly. "I'm going to miss you so much."

"You can visit anytime."

"I will." I release Lizzy and turn my attention to the vending machine. I'm not big on soda. Too sweet. And I don't need the caffeine. I'm wide awake as is. "You should go home. You have school."

"It's Saturday."

"Still," I say. "Go home. Sleep. Study. I might be here a while."

Her brow furrows. "Are you sure?"

"Yeah."

"Tell you what—I'll stay another ten minutes. If you still want me to leave, I will."

I nod. It's nice having Lizzy around. Comforting.

We move back to the E.R. A doctor is talking to Blake and Fiona.

He holds strong.

She trembles.

Whatever he says must be good, because Fiona is sighing with relief.

We move closer, so we can hear their conversation.

"She's okay." Fiona nearly smiles. "She's okay."

The doctor nods. "She's sedated. You can visit in the morning."

He leans in and whispers something.

She shakes her head. The near smile falls from her lips.

"Can we see her?" she asks no one in particular.

He nods, whispers some directions, and turns back to the hallway.

I follow her and Blake to Meryl's room.

It's small. Private.

It's so much like that day three years ago.

We're separated by iron and glass.

I can see her, but I can't get close.

She's sleeping. Her heart rate monitor is steady. It's the same as Lizzy's was. It promises she's surviving.

But this time, she isn't.

My legs go weak. I clutch at Blake's arm, but, still I crumble.

He catches me and helps me to a bench. It's private. Sort of.

It's far enough away from everyone that we can talk.

He brushes the hair from my eyes.

It calms me.

It soothes every nerve in my body.

Of course it does.

I'm madly in love with him.

And he's looking at me with every ounce of concern in the world.

"I'll make sure you get your money," he says. "Even if she dies before the wedding."

"I don't care about the money."

"Let's do it here, tomorrow. There's a chapel down the hall. Your dress should be ready. Ashleigh can call the tailor. I'll offer him double to get it done overnight."

I take an easy breath.

Blake's expression is desperate. He needs control over this. He needs to go through with this lie.

But I need something he can't give me.

I can't marry him like this.

"No," I say.

"Kat, please."

"I'm sorry." A tear rolls down my cheek. Meryl is going to die and there's nothing I can do to save her.

There was nothing I could do to save my parents.

There's nothing I can do to fix this.

"Kat. Think about what you're saying."

I swallow hard. Just one last time. I lean in and press my lips to Blake's. He tastes good. Like whiskey and like Blake. "Goodbye." I push myself off the bench. "I'll visit her in the morning."

"Kat. You can't."

I shake my head. "I have to. I… I'll find a way to pay you back for the apartment. Somehow."

"It's only one day. Half an hour. Then she can die happy."

"I'm sorry." I pull the ring off my finger and press it into his palm.

"But why?"

"Do you love me?"

"Kat…"

"That's the only way you can change my mind."

And it's never going to happen.

He's never going to fall in love with me.

Chapter Thirty-Two

Room 302. A windowless room in the middle of the hallway.

Hospitals are always depressing, but this takes the cake. There's no life in this room. It's ugly. Still. Plain.

Meryl lies in her hospital bed. Her face is still a strange, pale yellow. She looks weak and tired, but she looks happy too.

"Sweetheart, what are you doing up so early?" she asks.

I pull up a chair next to her bed and get comfortable. I'm going to be here a while. "Visiting hours started three minutes ago."

"I'll forgive the delay." She looks me over carefully. Her eyes fix on my unadorned left hand. "You're no longer obligated to visit me."

"I was never obligated." I squeeze my purse handle. "You've been so kind to me. You really accepted me as your daughter-in-law. I'm sorry that I can't be... that Blake and I won't..."

Her brow furrows. "What happened?"

"I can't bother you with my relationship problems."

She scoffs. "Sweetie, it's not a bother. Anything is better than sitting here with everyone looking at me like I'm going to die." She grabs the bed's remote control and adjusts it so she's mostly upright. "I can help. I know my son."

"Then you know the problem."

Meryl frowns. "He said you got into a fight about the wedding. He wanted to move it up. You thought that was a transparent attempt to appease his poor dying mother."

I can't help but smile. She has a damn good sense of humor. "Did he really say all that?"

"I read between the lines." She sips her glass of orange juice. "He says it's a fight and that you'll make up soon. But from the look on your face…"

There's a look on my face? God damn Sterling ability to read people. I try to smile, but this time it's not coming naturally. "It's unlikely."

"Was anything he said true?"

Tension stirs inside me. I'm not lying anymore. Not to her. "It's his version of it." I stare at the white tile floor. "He and I never… he never…"

"Sweetheart, I know you were pretending."

My heart is beating so fucking loud. "What?"

Meryl offers a sly smile. "I don't know the details, but I can tell. It's almost sweet. I never realized he cared this much about making me happy."

"He does." My gaze goes right back to the floor. It's scuffed with ugly white lines. "And he's stubborn."

"Very."

I force myself to make eye contact. She has the same blue eyes as Blake. They're just as piercing. Just as good at picking me apart. "How did you know?"

"The boy doesn't have an impulsive bone in his body. If he really was seeing someone, I'd have known about it months ago."

Something in me relaxes. It's not that he's incapable of love. At least, she doesn't believe he's incapable of it.

I nod. "Part of it was true. We met when I was leaving an interview, and he offered me the job. If you can call it that." I pluck the stray threads from my purse's handle. "I feel awful about lying to you."

"Don't. You get something good in exchange for this?"

"Really good."

"Sweetie, as far as I'm concerned, we never had this conversation. Take Blake back, marry him, divorce him, and take him to the cleaners."

"We signed a prenup."

"And how much would you get?"

I hold my purse against my stomach. "A lot."

Meryl raises a brow. "He won't miss whatever he offered you." She pushes herself up so she can lean closer. "It's a hard world for women. You have to use whatever you have to get yours. You're beautiful, smart, and a damn good liar."

"You really want me to lie to your son so I can divorce him and take his money?"

"It was his idea."

"Apple doesn't fall far from the tree." I laugh. God, this whole thing is absurd. My life was a lot easier before I met Blake, but it was a hell of a lot less interesting. "I really wish I could."

She grabs my wrist. Her eyes get serious. "Honey, you can. And you should. You two would be much happier than Fiona and Trey are."

"Probably."

"Of course, she hasn't been happy since she was Homecoming Queen." Meryl shakes her head. "My kids, my problem. They don't know what it's like to grow up with nothing. Their father did well. He spoiled them rotten. And he was insured to the hilt." Her expression softens. "They're successful. What every mom is supposed to want. God. I'm a cliché, whining about the state of my children's marriages, or lack thereof."

My stomach is twisted and torn. This confession isn't exactly freeing us. Maybe Blake was right and it was better to lie. Better to die happy believing a lie…

I study Meryl's expression, trying my best Sterling stare. Her eyes are especially yellow but they're also bright. Alive. Her lips are turned into a smile.

She is happy, considering the circumstances.

"You want the truth?" I ask.

"Of course, sweetheart."

"I'm an idiot not to marry Blake. That money could be my ticket. I could spend ten years in school and another ten traveling the world. But I won't be able to do any of it with my heart broken."

Her eyes go wide. She leans closer.

"I love Blake. I love him, and he's never going to fall in love with me. I can't live like that, constantly wanting him in a way I'll never have him. It would kill me."

"Oh, sweetie." She pats my arm. "I'm sorry."

I prepare myself to blink back a tear—this whole love thing has me in pieces—but it doesn't come. I'm too tired, too numb, too something.

"You have to take care of yourself." Meryl studies me. She pulls her arm to her side. "Do me a favor and run down to the gift shop."

"Sure."

"You have cash?"

I nod.

"Get me the trashiest romance novel you can find. And get yourself a cup of coffee. You look like hell."

A laugh escapes my lips. "You got it."

"Blake would take great care of you," she says.

"He would." But it's not enough.

———

I BUY MERYL ONE COPY OF EACH ROMANCE IN HERE—there are only three—and buy myself a can of iced coffee.

It's a short walk to Meryl's room. I keep my gaze on the white tile floor.

Room 302. I reach for the door.

Shit.

Blake is here.

He's in jeans and a t-shirt. Messy hair. Bags under his eyes. He's undone. Not like the animal Blake, the one I understand.

He's some other version of Blake.

One I've never seen before.

I step inside with my best *I don't give a damn my ex is here* swagger. My shoes squeak against the tile floor. I force a smile.

Blake's eyes fix on mine. "Kat."

My name is a plea on his lips. But not for what I need. Not for every ounce of my love and affection.

I hand Meryl her books. "I should get going. I'll come back tomorrow."

Blake's eyes stay on mine. "Stay. Talk. I can come back."

"No, that's okay. I have a lot of work to do. Deadlines for my applications." I press the can of coffee against the inside of my wrist. It sends a chill straight to my spine. "I hope you feel better."

She nods. "You too."

I move into the hallway. I keep my eyes on the floor.

I'm not turning back. I can't. If he looks at me like that again…

"Kat, wait." Blake's voice booms in the hallway.

My intentions to avoid him crumble. That voice is intoxicating. I want it surrounding me. I want it any way I can have it.

"Forget about moving up the wedding," he says. "Let's do it as planned at the gardens. I wanted to marry you."

Those words are music. They're poetry.

They're bullshit.

I shake my head. "I can't."

His fingers brush my wrist. "There must be some way I can change your mind."

Warmth fills my body. Damn thing is against me. "There is."

"Well?"

I turn and take in his expression. It's the strangest mix of sadness and steel. The guy is going to hell over this, but he's still a goddamned automaton.

"It's not a possibility," I say.

His voice is strong and deep. "Anything is a possibility."

I shake my head. "This is one thing you can't negotiate." Small step backwards. "Let Meryl know I'll see her tomorrow."

"Kat."

"Take care of yourself."

"You too."

Chapter Thirty-Three

"Loverboy sent a gift." Lizzy points to a small package on the kitchen table.

"What are you doing up?" I ask.

"Heard you leave." She taps her fingers against the table. "So..."

I copy her annoyed tone. "So..."

She nods to the package. "I made coffee." She lifts her cup. "French roast."

I pour myself a cup and sit at the table.

"So..." Lizzy taps her toes. Clears her throat. Takes a long sip. "Are you going to open it?"

"It's more fun making you wait."

And I'm not exactly prepared for whatever this is.

It's a small package wrapped in plain grey paper with a pink bow on top. It suits him. It's exactly like his sleek, utilitarian office.

It's his life. Grey everywhere. The one touch of color is superficial. It's easy to tear away.

Even if it's my favorite color.

And the theme of the wedding.

Lizzy sighs. "I'm opening it."

"Don't you dare."

She raises her eyebrows. "I already read the card."

"And?"

She grabs the card—it's the same grey as the wrapping —and holds it to her chest. "Not sure if he wrote it before you dumped his sorry ass."

My stomach flip-flops. Fine. I'll read the damn card. I grab it from Lizzy's hands.

KAT,

I hope this gets your mind off things. If it's not enough, my way is a lot more fun.

Sincerely,

Blake

SINCERELY.

It twists the knife in my chest.

But it proves me right.

I can't be a *sincerely*.

I unwrap the present carefully.

It's hard. Slick. A book.

It's a hardcover copy of *Ghost World*, a special print with the entire comic and the screenplay from the film. I flip it open and—

It's signed.

It's perfect.

My heart thuds against my chest.

I'm a sincerely.

That's what matters here. Not that this present is perfect. Not that Blake seems to know exactly what I want.

I close the book and push it to the center of the table.

Coffee. I need to drink this coffee. I take a long sip. French roast. Black. Strong. Hint of vanilla.

Just like what was on his lips after the pool.

Fuck. It's not working.

"Hey… Kat…" Lizzy's voice is sing-song.

"Yeah?"

"Want me to get out of here so you can have a booty call?"

"No." I move the hardcover to our bookshelf. I'll look at it later. When it makes me think of something besides his strong hands and his piercing eyes. "I want to have brunch with my sister."

She smirks. "You want a booty call at his place."

"No, Lizzy. I broke off our engagement last night, and his mom is in the hospital. It's not the time for a booty call. Okay?"

She slumps in her chair. "I was just kidding."

"Sorry, I haven't slept."

"So can we go to the brunch place that doesn't card?" she asks.

"No way in hell."

———

BRUNCH IS QUIET. I EAT A FULL PLATE OF STUFFED FRENCH toast and spend the afternoon napping with my sketchbook pressed against my chest.

Lizzy makes dinner. She's not the best cook in the world, but neither am I.

We eat in front of the TV in silence.

Maybe she's reeling too. Her life is going to be different soon. She'll be on another coast. With all new friends and surroundings.

She resigns herself to studying.

I spread out on my bed with my sketchbook. I've been working on all these tiny little comics—four or six or even ten panels. When I lay them side my side, they fit together. They're kind of like *Ghost World*, actually. They're vignettes about life refusing to stay the same.

It's been changing all this time. It's not just before the accident and after the accident. Every day is different. Every day, I'm different. Meeting Blake…

That's just speeding things along.

I get to work on another six-panel comic. There's so much I want to capture, but I'm not good enough yet.

The images in my head don't come out right on paper. I need training. I need experience.

It's not too late to reverse my decision. It's not too late to take Blake's money to pay for school.

But that feels wrong. There are other ways. Need-based scholarships. Loans.

Working while I go to community college part time.

Between checking school deadlines and working on my comic, I lose track of time.

Lizzy wishes me goodnight. Promises to check on me before she leaves for school tomorrow. My phone beeps with a low battery warning. I go to plug it in when I see—

Blake: Kat, call me. I need to talk about Meryl.

It's only an hour or two old and there's a missed call to go with it.

I dial Blake and hold the phone to my ear. *Please be okay, please be okay, please be okay.*

"Kat," he answers. "You okay?"

"Yeah. Can you tell me what's going on?" I dig my fingers into the phone. "I mean, thank you for the book."

"It's supposed to be an early wedding present."

"Even so."

"You like it?" There's vulnerability in his voice. He really does want to make me happy.

"Very much." I clear my throat, but it does nothing to chase the light feeling from my limbs. "What's happening with Meryl?"

His breath catches. "Kat..." Every ounce of hope drains from his voice.

My heart sinks.

Blake is rattled.

He's never rattled.

There's no way this is going to be okay.

His voice is quiet. Soft. "She's going home tonight."

I take a deep breath and exhale slowly. "What does that mean."

"It's hospice care. She only has a few days."

Fuck. "Are you okay?"

His exhale is heavy. "Are you?"

I shake my head. Something he won't hear.

A tear rolls down my cheek.

How can something so inevitable hurt this badly?

Meryl deserves better.

She deserves more.

She's been so kind to me. Kinder than anyone has been in a long, long time.

I wipe my eyes. "I'll manage."

"She's staying at her house upstate."

"Oh, can I... I don't want to intrude."

"She'd love your company." His voice is steady again.

I take another deep breath. "I'll take the first train in the morning."

"I'm leaving in an hour. I'll pick you up."

My heart races. I manage a choppy breath. "Okay. Knock when you get here. Lizzy is sleeping."

"Sure."

"Thanks."

"Kat?"

"Yeah?" My stomach twists.

"It's gonna be okay."

It's not, but he's sweet to lie.

———

THE KNOCK IS SO SOFT I CAN BARELY HEAR IT. THAT WAS fast. My suitcase is only half packed. My clothes are a mess on the floor.

My head…

This is hard for me. How the hell is he holding on?

I move into the main room and pull the door open.

Blake is standing there in jeans and a navy Henley. Like this is a normal date. Like I didn't break off our engagement yesterday. Like his mom isn't dying.

His eyes find mine.

He steps inside and presses the door closed.

It's just us in here. Lizzy is in her room, but the rest of the world feels far away.

He brushes my hair behind my ear.

I lean into his touch as his fingers skim my cheek. It's soft and sweet, like he really does love me.

"You okay?" he asks.

"No."

Blake wraps his arms around me. His body is warm and hard, but there's something soft about his embrace.

He leans closer.

Rubs my shoulders with his palm.

"How the hell are you so calm?" I tug at his shirt.

He runs his hand through my hair. "I don't have a choice."

I take a deep breath and exhale slowly. I know exactly

what he means. Pulling yourself together is the only way to keep from falling apart.

"You do it, too." He runs his fingers over my cheek. "You're a strong person."

"Thank you."

"It does hurt me." His voice is steady. Even. "It's just I don't show it."

"You don't show anything. You're like a robot."

He laughs.

Oh, God, that laugh.

It cracks the wall around my heart.

It makes me warm all over.

And it convinces me this is going to be okay. One day. Somehow.

He steps backwards. "Sit down."

I do.

He pours me a glass of water. I drink it greedily. It feels like I've been thirsty for years.

Blake sits across from me. He leans closer, elbows on his knees, palm pressed against his cheek. He stares right into my eyes. "You're a very sweet girl."

"I'm twenty-one. I'm not a girl."

His lips curl into a half-smile. "Do you need some time?"

"Five minutes to pack."

He nods, reaches out, and brushes the stray hairs from my eyes.

He catches a tear on his thumb.

My legs go weak. Thank God I'm sitting. I'm spinning in too many different directions.

My body is desperate for his comfort.

But we're not together. Not even pretending to be together.

I can't ask that of him. No matter how badly I need it.

I press myself up and move into my room. It's a mess, but not out of line for a twenty-one-year-old.

I fold another pair of jeans, another t-shirt, another sweater. Extra socks and underwear. There. That's everything.

Worst-case scenario, well, best-case scenario, I can come back to pick up some extras. Hell, Blake probably has people for that.

There's a light knock on my door.

"Come in," I whisper.

He steps into the room.

His gaze focuses on my unadorned left hand. His eyes turn down. Almost like he really does want to marry me. No, he does. Just not for the right reasons.

He sits on my bed and pats the spot next to him. It's a tiny little bed—a full—but there's just enough room for the two of us.

I rest my head on his shoulder. He slides his arm around me.

His fingers brush against my back.

God, the man really is comforting. We could have had a perfect marriage except for the little matter of him not loving me.

"You're hurting," he says.

I nod. "I'm sorry. It's your mother. It's not fair for me to react like this."

He runs his fingers through my hair.

It wakes up every nerve in my body.

I turn towards his touch reflexively. It's the most comforting thing in the history of the world.

"I can get your mind off it." He drags his fingertips over my neck. "But you'll have to do things my way."

His breath is warm and wet.

I want his way.

I want to feel anything else.

His touch is so soft. My eyes flutter closed. My nerves stand on end. It's an itch, and he's the only thing that can scratch it.

"You'll have to surrender completely," he says.

Perfect. I nod. "Please."

He rises and presses my bedroom door closed. Slides my suitcase out of the way and surveys the bed. "You have any scarves?"

I grab one from my dresser and hand it to him.

Blake rolls his shoulders back. "Take off your clothes. All of them."

I slip out of my sweater, t-shirt, and jeans. Just a bra and panties now.

Blake's pupils dilate. His tongue slides over his lips. I unhook my bra and slide it off one shoulder at a time.

He stares at my chest like he's transfixed, groaning lightly as my bra hits the ground.

His gaze returns to my eyes. There's something in his gaze today—urgency. He needs this too. It's a release for him too.

My sex clenches as I slide my panties to my ankles.

Blake motions *come here*.

Hell yes. Two steps and my body is pressed against his. I'm on display for him. I'm his. He can use me as he pleases.

He runs his fingertips from the nape of my neck to my ass. His touch is light and patient. Much, much too patient.

He kisses me, slowly sliding his tongue into my mouth.

I grab his shoulders, hook my leg over around his hip, groan into his mouth.

Blake is kissing me. It feels so damn right. It's hard to believe there's so much wrong with this non-relationship.

He adjusts our positions so I'm a foot away from the

wall. Not the one that connects with Lizzy's bedroom. The one we share with the neighbors.

Blake guides my arm, placing my palm flat against the wall. He does the same with the other.

His hands close around my hips. He nudges me a few inches closer. My nose is six inches from the wall. There's barely any breathing room.

He pulls the scarf around my eyes, blindfolding me, and ties a tight knot. Everything is fuzzy but I still have a sense of the light in the room.

My body goes cold as he moves away.

The light changes. The main one is off now. Just the desk lamp. There's shifting behind me. Blake taking off some of his clothes. Everything inside me wants to turn around, to rip this blindfold off so I can drink in the sight of his gorgeous body.

He moves closer. His nails scrape against my back, trailing down my spine. He digs his fingers into my ass with a heavy groan. "What do you want?"

"You."

"How?"

That flutter below my belly goes into overdrive. I want him every way, including a million ways I'll never get him. But that isn't what he's asking. He doesn't care if I love him or not.

This isn't about love.

This is fucking, pure and simple.

I press my fingertips against the wall. Something to contain the desperate feeling in my body. "Inside me. So deep I can't breathe."

Blake groans as he slides two fingers inside me.

I press my palms into the wall. It's not enough. It doesn't contain the pleasure racing through me. I swallow a groan. I'm not waking up my sister. Not like this.

He fucks me with his fingers.

He brings his other hand to my breast and toys with my nipples.

I press my back against his chest, soaking up the feeling of his body against mine.

This is sex. Just sex.

But it's more too.

He wants me feeling good. Physically. Mentally. Emotionally.

"Blake." I slam my hand against the wall. There's the deepest, hardest tension inside me. It's perfect agony.

He draws circles around my nipple, sending pangs to my sex.

Almost…

I arch my back, shifting my body into his, pushing him deeper.

The tension in my core knots.

I arch my back.

I bite my lip.

There.

I bring my hand to my mouth to muffle my groans. My sex pulses as I come. Pleasure spreads out through my limbs. It pushes away all the storm clouds in the room.

Blake brings his hands to my hips and pulls me into position.

I shift my hips as he enters me. It's like I'm home, like I'm whole.

He brings his mouth to my ear. "You feel so fucking good." He groans, digging his nails into my hips.

He pushes deeper. Deeper. Deeper.

I gasp. It's so much pressure, so much it hurts. But that's its own kind of good.

He brings his hand to my pelvis and holds me against

him. All I can do is surrender to the feeling of him deep, deep inside me.

Pleasure whirs around inside me. "Blake," I groan. I rid my mind of conscious thought.

"Tell me you're mine," he commands.

"Tonight," I say.

"Always." He slides his fingers over my clit as he thrusts into me.

"Tonight." My legs shake. My breath catches in my throat. "I'm yours tonight."

He lets out a low, heavy groan.

He moves harder. Deeper.

I arch my back to meet him, rubbing my clit over his fingers like they're my personal sex toy. The ache inside me fades to bliss. I'm close.

"Don't stop," I moan.

"Like hell." He grabs my hair and pulls my head back, so my neck is pressed up against his mouth. "You're mine," he growls against my neck.

Tonight. I'm his tonight. It's the only thing I want to be.

He grabs my hips and pins me to the wall. I turn my head, arching my back to keep him as deep inside me as he'll go.

Blake kisses me. It's hard, hungry, desperate. He moans into my mouth.

Then, his lips are on my neck, and he's moving harder. Deeper.

IIis fingers slide over my clit with that same rhythm. Almost. Almost…

"Blake." I groan his name as I come.

The release is a rush. I go into free fall. I lose track of everything but the bliss spreading through by body.

He doesn't stop. He keeps rubbing me. Keeps thrusting

into me. It's too much sensation. It hurts like hell.

Blake nips at my ear. "Fuck. Kat."

Then it's not too much. It's perfect. This orgasm is fast and hard. It starts high. Builds and builds. Tighter and tighter.

Everything releases as his nails dig into my skin.

I come in waves. I shake. I lose my grip on the wall.

Blake grabs me and throws me on the bed face first. I hold on to my comforter as he pushes my legs apart and slides inside me.

He's mine tonight.

He pins me to the bed as he fucks me.

A few thrusts of his hips and he's there, shaking as he comes inside me.

My breath returns slowly.

Blake collapses next to me. He pulls off my blindfold and pulls me into his arms.

He's staring at me with all sorts of affection.

Like he really does love me.

"You okay?" His voice is soft. Sweet.

I nod. "Great." Physically, at least.

He presses his lips against mine.

It's not raw heat and desire.

It's need. Love. Something like love.

My heartbeat picks up. I get warm everywhere.

I let myself believe it. I let myself hold onto every drop of his affection.

"I hate to rush you, but we should head out." He brushes the hair behind my eyes.

I nod to the door. "You never gave me those five minutes."

He slides off the bed and waits in the living room.

I dress and run a brush through my hair.

Whatever it takes, I'm going to survive the next week.

Chapter Thirty-Four

No limo today. Blake drives a black sports car. It's spotless inside and out. It matches him perfectly.

Supposedly, he wanted to give Jordan the week off.

But I don't buy that story.

I think he wanted privacy.

I'd bet good money that no one has ever seen Blake cry, not as an adult, at least.

The drive is quiet.

This late, the roads are empty. Everything is a blur of asphalt and sky.

I rest my head against the passenger-side door and watch the stars fly by. The farther we get from the city, the brighter they are.

The suburbs sneak up on me. I blink, and we're parked in front of Meryl's house.

It's funny. This place is the picture of idyllic perfection. It's not the kind of place where someone dies.

Blake insists on carrying my suitcase. I let him.

The gesture is sweet. I need the warmth of it.

We move into the house quietly. There's a light in the

kitchen and a nurse sitting at the table with a cup of coffee. He nods to Blake like they know each other.

"Miss Sterling is resting," the nurse says. "She asked not to be disturbed until eight tomorrow."

"Thank you." Blake sets our suitcase at the base of the stairs. He turns to me. "You're staying in Fiona's room tonight. Last one on the right."

"What about Fiona?" I ask.

"She's coming up in the morning." He brushes the hair from my eyes. "You can stay in my room when she arrives."

I swallow hard. Sharing a bed with Blake is tempting. And dangerous. That's a quick trip to feelings-ville, that awful place where I'm crazy about him and he cares about me.

"I can't kick you out of your room." I slide my hands into my pockets.

"I insist." He nods to the bedrooms upstairs. "Let me put these away."

I take a seat at the table next to the nurse and offer my hand to shake. "I'm Kat."

"Vincent." He shakes.

"How are things? Is she okay?"

"I can't talk about that."

"Of course." Doctor-patient confidentiality. I know that. "You any good at chess?"

"Not at all."

"Me either. I might have a chance to win a game without a handicap."

Vincent checks his watch. "You're on."

I find the game and set it up on the table. I even give him white.

Vincent stares at the board for a minute then moves one of his pawns two spaces forward. Most of his attention is on his coffee. Well, most of his attention is somewhere else entirely.

Mine, too, but the game is a perfect distraction. I weigh every move like it's critically important.

The stairs creak. Blake.

He sits next to me, rubbing the inside of my wrist with his thumb.

Blake's touch is a perfect bit of comfort. I want to surrender to it. To soak up all of it.

But I can't. Not if he's never going to love me.

I win. Truth be told, Vincent isn't trying. But a win is a win.

Vincent excuses himself, grabs another cup of coffee in the kitchen, and goes to wait in the den.

Blake takes his seat and sets up another game. "You need a drink?"

I shake my head.

We play in silence. No queen handicap. He discards a rook instead.

I keep my eyes on the checkered board instead of looking at him. There's too much in his expression. It hits me someplace deep.

Blake puts me in checkmate. Figures.

"Play another?" he asks.

I nod. Focus on my pieces. They're little plastic things, cheap and flimsy. This is one of those chess sets you buy at the drugstore for five dollars, but then I'm not the type who needs to put a price tag on everything.

This chess set is a priceless distraction.

It's worth everything.

I'm more aggressive this game. We start trading pieces. I ignore my endless strategy contemplation and make the first move that comes to mind. It's pure instinct.

"Check," Blake says.

"What?"

"You have me in check," he says. "Didn't you notice?"

I look down at the board. Holy shit. How did I miss that?

"You won't get me that easily, Wilder." He laughs.

Fuck. That laugh. It makes my knees weak. It makes my stomach flutter. It makes me feel *everything*.

He moves his queen in front of his king. Figures the stupid king is sacrificing his wife. Asshole.

Well, fair is fair. I take his queen. "Checkmate."

"Now you're paying attention."

"I was too in the zone to pay attention to you and your wife-sacrificing ways."

"It was the best tactical move." His voice is light, joking.

"You always make the best tactical move, don't you?"

He takes my hand. "Not if it's a poor long-term move."

"But that's always it—it's always strategy."

"It's chess."

"But it's always strategy with you." I pull my hand into my lap. "Should we play again?"

"Kat."

"No. You're right. It's just chess."

"Reconsider." He stares into my eyes. "We don't have to rush."

"Yeah, right, as long as I mention it to your mom tomorrow?"

"That's not it."

He reaches for me, but I push his hand away.

I stare back at him. "I'm not marrying someone who doesn't love me."

He says nothing.

"Goodnight, Blake." I push off the table and walk up the stairs without looking at him once.

———

THE SUBURBS ARE QUIET. EVEN AT OUR PLACE WAY OUT IN Brooklyn, New York City is loud. There are taxis, pedestrians, subways rumbling underground.

Out here, there's nothing. Not even a fan for white noise.

I toss and turn. Sleep isn't happening. I shouldn't have spent the afternoon in a state of near unconsciousness.

There's a soft knock on my door.

I push out of bed and answer.

Blake is standing there in his pajamas. He looks normal. No, he looks hurt. Needy.

"Come to my room," he whispers.

"It's not a good idea."

"Do it anyway." He slides his hand around my waist and pulls me closer. "You shouldn't sleep alone."

"I shouldn't sleep with you."

He presses his lips to mine. "So don't sleep."

Warmth spreads through my body. It's a compelling argument.

But I can't.

I rise to my tiptoes and press my lips to his. "I'm sorry. For everything." I take a step backwards.

He nods with understanding.

Still, it breaks my heart closing the door and climbing into bed alone.

———

ONCE AGAIN, I WAKE UP ALONE.

The room is bright. The house is buzzing with conversation.

I brush my teeth, change, and head downstairs. The

kitchen and living area are empty. The conversation must
be in Meryl's room.

I pour myself a cup of coffee and hike up the stairs.

Soft knock.

Meryl answers. "Come in, dear. Watch your step."

I push the door open. The room is crowded. A nurse,
not Vincent but a woman in her thirties, is in the corner
replacing an IV. Blake sits on an ottoman. He looks perfect,
the way he always does.

The nurse makes a signal to Meryl and sneaks out of
the room.

Meryl pats Blake's hand. "Go eat breakfast."

"I'm fine," he says.

"And take a shower while you're at it." She makes a
gesture like she thinks he stinks. "Right, Kat?"

"Absolutely."

He kisses her on the cheek. "I'll give you an hour. I
love you."

"I love you, too," she says.

Funny, I've never heard anyone in the Sterling family
use those words before.

They sound good.

I move aside to give Blake room to pass. His body
brushes against mine, waking up all my tired nerves.

I steal his seat. "How are you feeling?"

Meryl motions to her IV. "Fantastic. This must be half
morphine. I'm very comfortable."

I let out a half-laugh, half-gasp. Take a long sip of
coffee to give myself time to think. "Your room is really
clean."

She laughs. "That's a nice look on the bright side. I like
that about you, Kat." Her voice softens. "You're so sweet to
come see me."

She motions for my coffee and I hand it to her.

"Even if you're in it for the sex." Her expression fills with delight as she sips her java. "You forget the little things in life. They're what matters—the taste of a good cup of coffee, the joy of sex with someone you're mad about—"

My cheeks go bright red. "Jesus."

She laughs. "Believe me, honey. Life moves so fast. You've been busy surviving, I know, but you can't forget the little things."

"Please, no more about sex," I say.

She returns my cup of coffee. "Okay, the cherry blossoms in the spring. You must love those to plan your wedding around them." She folds her hands. "Have you reconsidered marrying Blake?"

"I suppose this is what it would be like if my mom was around—she'd be pestering me about when I was getting married."

Meryl smiles. "I like you together, but you have to follow your heart. I should have done that. I never would have married Orson."

"You didn't love him?" I ask.

"No. I thought I did. But that was hormones talking." She looks out the window at the bright blue sky. "Maybe you're right to stick to your guns."

"I'm sure Blake will be happy." I press my fingers into the porcelain mug. "I hope he'll be happy."

"Make me a promise, sweetheart?"

"Not until I know what it is," I say.

Her expression gets serious. "Give my son another chance."

"Meryl."

"One date. One chance to change your mind."

"It's really not fair for you to ask." I stare into my coffee cup. "It's not like I can say no."

"Like I told you, you have to grab what you want and

hold on for dear life." She leans back into her bed. "Now, Blake told me you're applying to schools. I want to hear all about it."

I go over every single detail about my applications— the deadlines, the portfolio requirements, the different cities where I might end up. I even tell her I have no chance of paying without a scholarship.

She listens and responds thoughtfully. It's nice to have someone looking out for me. Even if she won't be around much longer.

We don't stop until Fiona arrives. I excuse myself and spend the rest of the morning working on another vignette.

Chapter Thirty-Five

Meryl sends us to lunch at a nearby restaurant, insisting she needs the time to visit with her lawyer alone.

Fiona excuses herself and disappears in her car.

Blake and I eat at a nearby chain restaurant. Honestly, I don't taste a thing. I'm not even sure what I'm eating.

We walk back home hand in hand. Blake squeezes my fingers until they're white.

I study his expression, but it doesn't help me put anything together. It never does.

At home, Meryl is sipping coffee on the couch with Fiona.

She mutters something about not wasting away in her bed. We all pretend like she didn't remind us she's dying.

We pass the afternoon with coffee and cake, reminiscing about easier times.

Meryl brings up every embarrassing moment from Blake and Fiona's childhoods. The room gets bright with laughter.

The sun sets. We order pizza. I taste everything. The

tangy tomatoes, the gooey cheese, the crisp crust. Perfect New York pizza. And rich red wine to go with it.

Meryl waves her night nurse away, asking him to wait in the den. She rearranges the chess pieces.

"Fancy losing to your mother?" she asks Blake.

"No, but I could stand to destroy her," he teases.

"I'll give you a fighting chance and take black."

Blake laughs.

It still makes me warm.

Blake is happy.

And there's love all around us. It's beautiful. Sweet.

Meryl wins every game. We stay at that table, talking and laughing until the wee hours of the morning. Even Fiona is nice to me. No sign she still wants to get rid of me.

Meryl hugs me goodnight. "Whatever happens, honey, it's been great getting to know you."

———

I KNOW SHE'S GONE THE MINUTE I WAKE UP. THERE'S something different in the air—an ugly stillness.

I throw off the comforter and rush into the hallway. Blake and Fiona are sitting at the kitchen table. She's crying into her coffee cup, and he's comforting her.

I squeeze the railing. "Is she... did she?"

Blake looks up at me. He nods. "She died around five this morning."

My stomach twists. I scratch at the railing. Tiny flakes of wood peel off under my fingernails.

Meryl is gone.

I force myself to breathe. It's not as hard as I thought it would be. She was happy. She was at peace.

And, whatever happens, it was great getting to know her.

It really is going to be okay.

Chapter Thirty-Six

Everything blurs together.

Blake takes over organizing.

I sit on the couch, staring at my sketchbook like it will offer some comfort. It does, but it's not enough.

Fiona is a wreck. She stays in her room so no one will see her cry. It's an admirable strategy.

I manage to sleep a little.

In the morning, I manage to eat a little breakfast. Drink a little coffee. Change into the black dress I brought for the occasion.

I even manage to listen to a few eulogies at the funeral.

Meryl told me to find what I want, and grab it, because no one else would give it to me. Because that was the only way I'd ever get it.

I owe it to her to try.

———

A MAN IN A SUIT TAPS ME ON THE SHOULDER. HE'S IN HIS fifties. He looks every bit the quiet suit.

"Miss Katrina Wilder?" he asks.

I nod.

"You're a named beneficiary of Miss Sterling's will. Please come with me."

"Yeah, sure." My senses catch on slowly. I'm a named beneficiary. That means Meryl left me something in her will.

I follow the lawyer through a crowded hallway, to an office in the back of the building.

Blake and Fiona are already inside.

Fiona isn't wearing her wedding ring.

Maybe she's okay with the divorce. She must know it's what her mom wanted.

Blake's eyes catch mine. They bore into mine. They demand everything I have to give.

I swallow hard. "Hi."

He nods back. "Hi."

The lawyer clears his throat. "Miss Wilder, please, take a seat." He motions to the empty chair.

I sit.

He shifts behind the desk and pulls out a contract. "Mr. Sterling, Mrs. Crane."

"Miss Sterling," Fiona corrects him.

"Of course, Miss Sterling. You know that your mother left most of her estate to charity."

They nod *of course*.

"But there was a last-minute change," he says. "To add Miss Wilder as a beneficiary."

"What?" Fiona's eyes go wide. She looks to Blake *really?*

He shrugs *how should I know?*

"Miss Sterling, your mother left you the house. With some instructions." He reads a passage from the will. "God knows, Blake isn't going to grace my home with children. Fiona, sweetie, it's yours. Enjoy it. Find a new man, one a million times better than your soon-to-be-ex-husband and fill it with love."

She wipes her eyes. "Thank you, Larry."

The lawyer, Larry, I guess, nods. "Mr. Sterling. I'm afraid Meryl left you nothing of material value. Only the chess set."

Fiona laughs but not in a smug way. It's more like she appreciates how much it meant to them.

"Miss Wilder—" he looks me in the eyes. "Let me read this." Larry looks at the will. "To my new friend Katrina Wilder, I leave two hundred thousand dollars. Sweetheart, I hope you'll use that money for your college education, but it's yours. Go out and grab what you want."

My heart skips a beat.

Two hundred thousand dollars. That can't be right.

"Miss Wilder." The lawyer is staring at me. "Are you going to be okay?"

I must be blushing. I must be beet red.

Everyone is staring.

And I'm not breathing.

I'm…

Two hundred thousand dollars.

That's ridiculous.

That's a fortune.

That's everything.

I force words from my lips. "Can you read that again?"

He begins. "It's two hundred thousand dollars, Katrina."

Two hundred thousand dollars. All the money I need for college.

Larry continues. "I can go over the details of the charities if you'd like."

"No, thank you." Fiona stands, brushing her perfect

black outfit smooth. "I should get to the house for the memorial." She looks at Blake. "Are you coming?"

"I'll meet you there." He waits until Fiona leaves then turns to me. "Are you okay?"

I adjust my dress. "I will be. Are you?"

"I will be." He stands and offers his hand. "Can we talk?"

I take his hand. "Okay."

Blake nods a goodbye to the lawyer and whisks me out of the room.

———

WE GO TO THE DINER AROUND THE CORNER. IT'S A GREASY spoon place. Vinyl booths. Checked tile floor. Big plates of fried eggs, hash browns, and bacon.

Blake holds the door open for me. He motions to one side of a long, red booth.

It's the next best thing to pulling out a chair. He really is a gentleman.

Somehow, he doesn't look out of place here. Even in his two-thousand-dollar suit.

He nods to the guy behind the counter like they're old friends.

I pull my cardigan over my chest.

His eyes meet mine. "Is that the winter formal dress you mentioned?"

I nod. "It's a funny chance to wear it."

"Yes, but it suits you."

"My chest?"

His laugh is sad. "Yes. But the rest too. It's—"

"Beautiful and understated?"

"You're already bored of my clichés. We're practically married."

My laugh is nervous. I unwrap my silverware and play with my fork. "It's weird wearing a party dress to a funeral."

"It wouldn't be. Not for Mom. She'd love that dress."

"Because of my boobs?"

"Yes. But because it's beautiful. Because it's for a party. That's what she wanted. She wanted us to celebrate her life instead of mourn it."

"A lot of people say that."

He nods.

"But it never really works that way."

"No. It doesn't."

Our server interrupts. "What can I get you?"

"Coffee," Blake says. "And the tilapia special." He half-smiles. "Best tilapia anywhere."

The guy nods *damn straight.*

"I'm sold." I hand the guy my menu. "And an iced tea."

"You got it." He looks to Blake. "I'm so sorry about Meryl."

"Thank you," Blake says.

"She was a great woman."

"She was," Blake says.

The guy walks away, shaking his head like he can't stand how unfair life is.

I fold my napkin into a triangle. "She was a great woman."

Blake smiles. Really smiles. It's not joy exactly. It's more like he's relishing his memories of his mom.

I feel the same way. It hurts like hell that she's gone. It's been three years since my parents died, and that still hurts.

But there's more than hurt in my gut.

There are happy memories everywhere.

For the last three years, I've been pushing everything about my parents aside—the pain and the joy.

I can't do that anymore. I need to feel it, all of it, even if it hurts as much as it feels good.

Blake's fingers brush my palm. "You okay?"

"I will be." I pull my hands into my lap. "I'm sorry you lost her."

"Me too."

He drifts into thought about something.

I play with the hem of my dress to keep my attention here. This might be the last time I ever see Blake. I'm going to remember it.

"Stay with me tonight," he says. "I'm going back to the penthouse after the memorial."

I hold his gaze. It's like he's looking deep inside me.

Usually, that makes me feel off-center. Picked apart. But not today. It feels okay. It feels right.

It feels like he really sees me. Kat. Not Super-Girlfriend, but the girl under the makeup and the highlights and the fancy clothes.

I stare back, trying to find the man under the expensive suit and the expression of steel. There are hints of him. He's hurting, and not just over his mom.

For once, I recognize his expression.

He's lonely.

I take a deep breath, weighing my options. "I'll be okay."

His facade cracks. "I know you will. I won't."

"Oh." My heart thuds against my chest.

"I don't want to be alone." He shakes his head "Fuck that. I'd rather be alone than with anyone else." He presses his palm against the table. "I want to be with you tonight."

Oh my. I take a deep breath and exhale slowly "You

mean for—" I swallow hard. "—sex? Or for something else?"

"Whatever you want." He presses his lips together. "As long as I can spend tonight with you."

I adjust my dress. It doesn't offer any clarity.

He's hurting and I want to wipe that away. I want to help however I can.

I want the comfort too.

I stare back into those piercing blue eyes. "Okay."

His sigh is heavy with relief. "Thank you."

"It doesn't mean anything. We're not together."

He nods. "Of course."

"Here ya go." The waiter drops off our drinks. "Sugar's at the end of the table." He turns back and he's gone.

I take a long sip of my iced tea.

Blake may be softening. He may have affection for me. But that's not enough.

I'm going to be with someone who is madly, passionately in love with me. Not just someone who finds me pleasant company.

Blake stirs his black coffee. He takes a small sip. His eyes focus on me. "I promised Meryl something that first morning."

"Did you offer or did she ask?"

"She asked."

"Of course she did." A laugh escapes his lips. He shakes his head like he can't believe how ridiculous she was. "You don't have to honor it."

"You don't know what it is."

"Still."

"I want to." Deep breath. "I promised her to give you another chance. One date."

Something flashes on his face. Concern. He shifts back

slightly. Wraps his fingers around his coffee. "I hope this doesn't count."

I shake my head. "Would be awfully tacky to do it the day of her funeral."

"She would have liked that."

"She would have liked it if I married you without a prenup, divorced you, and got half your shit."

He laughs again. A big laugh where his lips curl into a smile. He throws his head back. Slaps his hands against his thighs.

His laugh is still the best thing I've ever heard.

"No," Blake says. "She would have loved it."

"Did you tell her about our deal?"

"You did."

My chest tightens. How the hell does he know that?

"It's okay," he says. "In the end, it was for the best. She died thinking someone cared about me. That's what I wanted."

"Right. Of course." I bury my attention in my iced tea. Cared. I cared about him. If that's the story he wants to tell himself, fine. "What exactly did you tell her?"

He makes eye contact. "That I cared about you and wanted you to be happy."

There's that word again. *Cared*. God, what an ugly word. It's the worst word in the English language.

"Tomorrow," he says. "For our date. We can start in the morning." He watches me closely. "If your schedule permits."

That's another joke. I think. He's terrible with jokes, but I kind of love it.

I nod. "Tomorrow is perfect."

Chapter Thirty-Seven

Blake's apartment feels different than it did last time. It's colder. Sparser. More utilitarian.

This might be the last time I see it.

Or him.

He presses the door closed and clicks the lock. "There are clothes in the spare room if you'd like to change."

"Clothes or my clothes?"

"Ashleigh picked them out for you."

"No. I'm okay in this." And I don't really want to wear the clothes his assistant picked out. That only reminds me about the all business nature of our arrangement.

"You hungry?"

"A little."

"I'll make something." He moves into the kitchen.

I wander around the sparse living room. This one, huge room must be a thousand square feet. God, this place must cost a fortune.

It's a lot to give up for a little thing like love, but there isn't a doubt in my mind.

Gorgeous apartments are nothing compared to that perfect, safe feeling of someone's arms around you.

Damn. I'm waxing poetic. But at least I know where I stand.

I won't accept anything less than Blake being madly in love with me.

I study every nook and cranny of the room. The plush leather couch. The wide TV. The big, clear windows that lead to the balcony.

The cherry bookshelf in the corner. It's packed with rows and rows of science fiction novels. I haven't read any of them, but I do recognize a few names.

The shelf on the bottom is different. It's packed with graphic novels straight off a best-of list: *Blankets, Fun Home, Smile, Blue is the Warmest Color*.

As Lizzy would say, *boring girl stuff*.

Exactly what I like to read.

"Those are for you." His voice flows into my ears.

I turn to face him. He's standing in the kitchen, pouring whiskey into a glass of ice.

I nod. "Thank you." My heart speeds up. They're books, not a declaration of love. But they're a lot.

He understands me.

He knows what I want.

He wants to make me happy.

Maybe he is capable of loving me.

Suddenly, my black dress feels awkward.

I'm not mourning this relationship. Not tonight. Not tomorrow.

This is our last chance. That means it's my last chance too. These might be my last twenty-four hours with Blake. I'm going to enjoy them.

"Excuse me." I go to the sex room—I'm sure Blake

calls it his spare room, but let's get real—and change into a tank top, pajama bottoms, and a hoodie.

I'm tempted to linger here. It's familiar. Hell, this is certainly the room where I have the most positive memories.

I let my eyelids press together. I linger in memories of his body joining mine, his lips on my skin, his growl vibrating down my neck. The Blake I understand. Who understands me. Who gives me exactly what I need.

But then I understand this Blake.

And he understands me.

And we do want to make each other happy.

I swallow the thought as I move into the main room.

Blake is in his pajamas. It's still strange, seeing him casual and relaxed. Blake in a t-shirt and plaid pants is absurd. Even if he still looks like a sex god.

He nods to the coffee table. There's a plate of berries and dark chocolate. And two glasses. One amber. One clear.

"Gin and chocolate?" I move onto the couch.

He sits next to me. His fingers brush my cheek. My chin. "Would you prefer whiskey?"

I shake my head.

He grabs my drink and hands it over. It's just like the first time. The brush of his fingers lights me up.

I move closer, until the outsides of our thighs are pressed against each other.

His fingers trail over my back, pressing the soft cotton of my hoodie against my skin. He nestles his head into the crook of my neck. Slides his arms around my waist.

Fuck. My stomach flutters. My muscles go weak. This is exactly where I belong. In his arms. In his apartment. In his life.

But not if it's his life. Only if it's ours.

Blake's breath warms my ear. "Thank you."

"For?" I press my knees together. It does nothing to stem the electricity racing through me. I want his body, yes, but as more than a fuck. As everything.

"For being here."

"Of course." I want to be here. There isn't a single part of me that wants to be somewhere else.

I down half my gin and tonic in one gulp. Fresh with that hint of pine.

"Kat."

I grab a raspberry and plop it in my mouth. It's sweet, tart perfection.

"Are you alright?"

"Yeah."

He turns to me and runs his fingertips over my chin, tilting me so we're eye to eye. "Are you sure?"

No. Not at all. But I am sure I want to be here. "Let's watch a movie."

He stares back at me. His eyes fill with honest affection. "Anything you want."

"It's a little silly," I say.

"Same thing you said about your favorite book." He brushes the hair from my eyes. "Why are you embarrassed by the things you love?"

"I'm not embarrassed by them." I play with the zipper of my hoodie. "It's more that it's personal." My cheeks flush. This is really personal. But I want him to know. I want him to know all of me. "*The Matrix*."

He laughs. "You do realize who you're talking to?"

"Yes, I do realize you own a technology company, and you think you're a nerd. But that isn't what's personal. I don't really care about the movie that much." I finish the last half of my drink. "It was the thing Lizzy and I watched when she got out of the hospital. We must have watched the whole trilogy twenty times. She loves those fucking movies. Any movie where robots try to enslave humanity, she's all over it. *Battlestar Galactica* is her favorite show by quite a measure."

"What about you?" he asks.

"I root for the robots." I set my glass on the table. Fine. I'll answer the question he was really asking. "It's not my favorite movie, but it's the most comforting thing I can watch. It feels like… like love."

He runs his hand through my hair and rests it on the back of my neck. With the other, he tilts my chin so we're face to face.

His voice is soft. Sweet. "*The Matrix* is my favorite movie."

"Yeah?"

He nods.

I swallow hard.

I've seen *The Matrix* twenty times. More. It seems like it's a movie about rebels fighting a manufactured dream world.

But it's not.

It's about love.

Love is the thing that saves the day.

Love is the thing that saves the world.

Love is the thing that matters.

Chapter Thirty-Eight

I fall asleep on the couch and wake up in Blake's bed.

He's behind me, his arm resting on the curve of my waist.

It's so different than last time I was with him. When I woke up alone, I felt cold and empty.

Right now, I'm warm. The whole fucking world is warm.

My eyes flutter closed. One more minute to feel his arms around me.

I do my best to slide off the bed without waking Blake. He looks peaceful with his eyes closed, his chest rising and falling slowly.

I creep to the bathroom and brush my teeth. There's a sound in the bedroom. Then footsteps. He knocks softly.

I mumble a *come in*.

He does. His hair is actually messy. And he actually looks tired.

My lips curl into a smile.

His eyes fix on me. "What's that for?"

I spit out a mouthful of toothpaste. "For you."

"I make you happy?"

"Sometimes."

"I want to make you happy."

I turn to the sink and rinse my mouth. I don't know what to do with his words.

He moves closer. Waits until I'm standing then wraps his arms around me.

I bury my head in his chest. He runs a hand through my hair.

It's warm.

Comfortable.

"Relax. I'll make breakfast," he says.

"You make things?"

"I do."

"You? Not your assistant or a cook or a maid?"

He chuckles. "You're verging on insulting."

"You get insulted?"

"Only by people I care about." He reaches for his toothbrush. "I make an amazing breakfast. You'll eat those words."

"Or will I be too busy eating the delicious food?"

He laughs. "That's a terrible joke."

"That's why it suits you." I take a step backwards. "No offense."

"It's good to know your strengths and weaknesses." He turns back to the sink.

I slink to the main room, grab my sketchbook, and plop on the couch. I need to capture all the thoughts racing around my head. First, the funeral. Six panels. Starting with a closed casket. It's a little obvious, but it's necessary.

Then Blake, sitting in a cheap chair in his expensive suit, his eyes on the floor, his expression miserable.

And me, behind him, considering coming up to him.

A point-of-view shot of him standing.

Him at the podium.

The words *She was everything.*

"I like you lost in thought." Blake leans in to plant a kiss on my lips.

He tastes like mint toothpaste.

"Aren't you used to it?" I ask.

"I still like it." He takes a step towards the kitchen. "You want coffee?"

"Yes please."

He moves into the kitchen. I turn back to my drawing.

Slowly, the smell of java fills the room. That French roast with vanilla. The one he was drinking after the pool. I can't even smell vanilla without thinking about it.

I try putting last night into a panel, but I don't know where to start. At the diner? The drive here? My body pressed against his on the couch?

How can I put all my feelings about him into four or ten or even a hundred panels?

The smell of red peppers and olive oil fills the room.

I give up on work and move into the kitchen.

Blake pushes vegetables around a pan. He cracks eggs in a clean plastic bowl, whisks them, pours them in the pan.

He is a good cook.

At least if the smell of that omelet is any indication.

He turns back to me. Runs his fingers through my hair. Looks down at me like I'm the secret to all the happiness in the world. "Cream and sugar?"

"Please." I rise to my tiptoes to kiss him. This is so normal. So domestic. So sweet.

It's perfect.

He fills two mugs and adds just enough cream and sugar to one.

I steal the coffee from him and take a long sip.

It's perfect.

And it makes me think of him. Of vanilla on his lips. I get lost in my mug. And my thoughts. It's been less than two months, but it feels like it's been forever. Was it really me who ran into Blake? It feels like she was another person entirely.

"Here." Blake sets a plate in front of me. An omelet, avocado, two dozen raspberries.

"Thank you." I take a seat at the counter. This smells like heaven, but I force myself to dig in slowly.

Mmm. Fluffy eggs. And they're fresh. I didn't even know eggs could taste fresh.

The peppers are crunchy. The tomatoes are sweet.

"I admit it. You're a good cook." I shovel another bite of omelet into my mouth.

Blake sits next to me. He takes a patient bite.

His eyes pass over me.

I try to slow down.

"You don't have to do that." He sips his coffee. "I like you messy."

I wipe my mouth with a napkin. "That's hard to believe." I motion to the perfectly clean apartment.

"Who says I want it that way?"

"Twenty bucks. It says you spend plenty to keep it this clean."

He chuckles. "True. But it's too clean. I've had too much of clean." He stares back into my eyes. "I've had too much of uncomplicated."

I swallow hard. "Oh?"

"You remember what I said that first night at my office?"

"That was a long time ago."

He brushes his thumb against my chin, wiping off a

drop of coffee. "When you're with me, you won't want for anything."

Heat spreads through my body. I force myself to turn back to my breakfast. "I haven't." Mostly. There is one thing he can't give me, but Blake was always clear about love being out of the question.

I finish my eggs and coffee then get to work on the raspberries.

Blake watches me. He steals a berry off my plate and pops it into his mouth.

Ah, two can play that game.

I steal an orange slice off his plate and tear into it. Juice drips from my lips. Off my chin. Onto my chest.

Blake laughs. He catches the juice on his thumb and brings it to his lips.

He stares into my eyes as he sucks on the digit.

It shouldn't be sexy, but it is.

I slide off the stool and place my body in front of his.

He presses one hand into my lower back. The other slides through my hair.

He kisses me hard. Like he can't get enough.

No. It's not like.

He can't get enough.

I can't either.

I still can't say this with words. They've never been my strong suit.

But this—my body against his—I can say it like this.

I love you.

Be mine.

Be mine forever. For real. For everything.

I tug at his t-shirt. I slide my tongue into his mouth.

It isn't enough.

I need more.

I need everything.

Blake shifts off his stool. He presses his body against mine.

Everything in me relaxes.

This is exactly where we're supposed to be. Domestic bliss and sex and love and everything. In his kitchen. In the apartment that can be ours. In a life that can be ours.

He slides his hands under my ass and lifts me onto the kitchen island.

I wrap my legs around him.

He pulls my tank top off my head.

No teasing today. He brings his hands to my breasts and rubs my nipples with his thumbs.

He's giving me what I need.

I kiss him harder.

Arch my back to rub my crotch against his.

I comb my fingers through his hair, holding his head against mine, letting *everything* pour from me to him.

When he breaks our kiss, I'm shaking.

I pull his t-shirt over his head. "Now. Please."

He nods as he tugs at my pajama bottoms.

I place my hands behind my back, lifting my hips so he can get them off my ass.

They fell to my knees. My ankles.

I kick them off my feet.

He steps out of his bottoms.

We're naked in the kitchen.

But I don't feel exposed.

I feel seen. Like somehow I'm getting both versions of Blake.

Like maybe we can understand each other this well all the time.

I dig my hands into his hair and pull him into a kiss.

He brings his hands to my hips and guides me into position.

His cock strains against me.

Slowly, he enters me.

Fuck.

Heat floods my body.

But it's more than desire. I'm one with him. With *him* and not with the sex-crazed animal. This is the Blake with the sad blue eyes and the heart-stopping laugh and the tendency to pull away.

He's mine.

And I'm his.

And it makes sense.

The world makes sense.

He kisses me back.

I rock my hips in time with his. Taking everything he has to give me. Offering everything I have to give him.

Almost…

There.

With his next thrust, I come. My sex pulses around him. I dig my nails into his skin, pulling him closer, making him mine.

He groans back against my mouth.

He pulls me closer as he thrusts into me.

Then he's there, holding me tightly as he pulses inside me.

Mine.

We stay pressed together for a long, long time.

And it really is perfect.

Like I'm exactly where I belong.

Chapter Thirty-Nine

I give Blake the day.

We wander around the Met all morning, eat lunch at the cafe, wander around the park all afternoon.

It feels like spring. Bright yellow sun, brisk air, green grass, flowers blooming with pops of color.

The world is awake and alive.

And I am too.

This is what I want. Everything I want.

We walk around the park until the sunset streaks the sky orange.

Blake stops at a bench and pulls me onto his lap. He presses his lips into mine.

It's soft. Sweet. Perfect.

When we break, I try hard to keep my gaze on the sky.

It refuses. His face is a million times more captivating. Those blue eyes of his are gorgeous. And they're filled with every bit of emotion in the world.

He leans closer. One hand pressed between my shoulder blades. The other brushes stray hairs behind my ears.

"Come to Paris with me." His voice is vulnerable. Like my answer has the power to break him. "We can spend the week having sex. We can go to every museum in Europe. I already have my schedule cleared."

"It's convenient?"

His expression stays soft. "That isn't it." He runs his fingertips over my cheek. "I want to be there with you. I want the week with you."

Warmth fills me. It starts in my chest and spreads through my tummy. I take a deep breath. This is so close to everything I want.

But it's not enough.

"And then what?" I ask.

"Then we'll be together." His voice is sweet. Sincere. "I like having you around."

"Is that all—that you like having me around?" I dig my fingers into his shoulders. I force myself to stare back into his eyes.

His fingers skim my cheek. "I care about you, Kat."

The word makes my skin crawl. *Care.* I swallow hard. "Is that all it is?"

"We'd be happy."

Maybe. But that's not enough.

He runs his hand through my hair. It soothes me and lights me up in equal measures. It's everything.

But it's not enough.

"I'm in love with you, Blake." I make my voice as confident as I can. "I'm madly in love with you, and it drives me crazy. I can't eat or sleep. I can't think about anything else. I can't even draw anything else. I try, but somehow everything goes back to you."

I stare into his eyes, trying to find some reaction. There's only one thing I can see, and it's not love. It's not joy that I'm finally telling him this.

He's afraid.

He's afraid of my feelings.

"Kat."

"I understand you don't believe in love. You don't think you're capable of it. Whatever it is, fine. If that's really how you feel, fine." I squeeze the fabric of his sweater. "But I can't be with you unless you love me. Unless you're madly in love with me."

He goes to touch my cheek but I stop him.

"Don't do that." I stare into his eyes, but it doesn't help me understand what we're doing here. "You don't have to answer now. You can think about it."

"Kat." His voice sinks.

Deep breath. "If you are in love with me, then I will go to Paris with you. I'll go anywhere with you. But it's all or nothing, Blake. I can't be with someone who doesn't love me."

I try to shift off the bench, but he holds me in place. He grabs onto my shoulders, somehow sweet and controlling all at once.

I try to move again, but he squeezes me harder.

"There's no negotiating this," I say.

"I care about you."

"And that's not enough." I push off his chest, but there's still no good. Fine. Might as well use this once. "Chess."

He releases me immediately.

I grab my purse from the bench. I take one more look at Blake, at those gorgeous, impossible to read eyes.

There's nothing I can say, nothing left to do now.

I move backwards. His eyes are still on me, but he doesn't object. He doesn't ask me to stay.

I swallow hard. "I'll see you around, I guess."

I turn and I run. I run until the park is a blur. Until I'm sitting on a subway heading back to Brooklyn.

Chapter Forty

Lizzy hugs me the second I get home. I don't need a mirror to know the hurt is written all over my face. There's nowhere else for it to go. I'm bursting at the seams.

"Are you okay?" she asks.

I shake my head and hug my sister a little tighter.

"You want to talk about it?" she asks.

"Yeah, I do." For once, I really do.

We talk for hours. I tell Lizzy everything that's happened with Blake the last two months. I tell her about the will, about Meryl, about where I'm applying to school.

She listens with rapt attention. She confesses that Stanford was her first choice, that she was always planning to go there but was too afraid to tell me.

I send her to bed sometime after midnight. It *is* a school night. She mutters something about how she already got out of school for my fake wedding and there's no way she's leaving me alone.

Still, I head to my room. I draw instead of sleeping.

Everything is Blake. Or something to do with Blake. The guy is still the only thing I can think about.

And it's not like I can blame him. He was always clear about his intentions. He was always true to his word.

Hell, it's not like he said no. It's not absolute. There's still a chance. A tiny chance, but that's something.

———

LIZZY STAYS HOME FROM SCHOOL. I STAY LOCKED IN MY room, alternating between napping and drawing.

I turn my phone off. I can't handle an *I don't love you, I'm sorry*. I need more time to lick my wounds before I open myself up to that possibility.

At lunchtime, Lizzy knocks to ask if I've eaten. When I say no, she brings grilled cheese and tomato soup. Exactly what Mom always made on rainy days. I dip my sandwich in the soup so it soaks up the rich tomato flavor.

Lizzy sits on my bed, watching me carefully. "So, I was thinking…"

"Yeah?" I stuff another bite of cheesy goodness in my mouth.

She really tries to sell the enthusiasm. "We have the Botanical Gardens rented out tomorrow. Maybe we should go. It could be nice."

Nice isn't the right word. Not at all.

I stare at her, trying to figure out why she's suggesting this.

It's not like her.

She's smarter than this. I don't need a reminder of Blake's willingness to commit to a loveless life with me.

Lizzy plays with her jeans. "Kat. I know you're upset, but you love the park. I walked by yesterday and it's gorgeous. It's got to be the last few days the trees are in bloom. They're so pink and so full. Do you really want to miss that?"

Damn. She knows my weakness. "Okay."

"Good." She smiles.

It's too much of a smile. Like she has something up her sleeve.

She shifts off the bed. "I'll let you work." She closes the door as she leaves.

Music blares from her room, but I swear I hear voices. Like she's on the phone with someone.

Like she's planning something.

Chapter Forty-One

It's a beautiful day. The sky is bright blue. The air is warm. The sun is shining over the grass.

The cherry blossoms are perfect. Lush and pink and alive.

Lizzy talks to the woman at the admission counter. There's a sign that says *Park Closed for Private Event.* We're the event.

The woman nods and smiles. It's that *oh my God, congratulations* smile.

It makes me sick.

She unlocks the gate and ushers us inside.

Thankfully, she remains silent about our lack of wedding attire.

There's something on Lizzy's face—she's nervous.

It's strange.

Lizzy never gets nervous. At least, she never lets me know she's nervous.

We make our way through the rose garden—her favorite. Roses in every shade of red, pink, and purple. She checks if the coast is clear and plucks a deep red rose.

"Lizzy!"

"It's for you." She hands me the flower.

"You're defacing government property for me?"

"That's how much I love you."

"How sweet." I laugh. It feels good. It's still possible to feel good. That's something.

She grabs my free hand and runs forward. "Better get to those cherry blossoms."

Okay, something must be up. She hates running with a fiery passion.

It's only a few hundred feet to the cluster of trees.

They're even more beautiful up close. The soft petals flutter towards the ground, turning the grass pink.

"Um, Kat." Lizzy clears her throat. "So…"

Yeah, something is absolutely up.

I follow her gaze through the cluster of trees, all the way across the lake, to the place where we were going to hold the ceremony.

Blake.

He's standing there. I'm too far away to make out the expression on his face, but it looks like he's holding a bouquet of flowers.

My heart races. He can't be here. This can't be…

If he's here to let me down gently…

I swallow hard.

My feet move of their own accord. They carry me across the bridge, past the paper lanterns strung between the trees, onto the concrete.

He's twenty feet away. Fifteen. Ten. One hand is in the pocket of his jeans. The other is holding a bouquet of red roses. His long-sleeved t-shirt is hanging off his shoulders just so. The guy has aloof down to an art. I'll give him that much.

He's awfully good at driving me crazy. I'll give him that too.

He motions to the bouquet. "These are supposed to be for your sister. She helped me organize this."

"She would."

Blake drops the flowers on the ground. "Kat." He runs his hand through his hair. His cheeks turn pink.

Blake Sterling is nervous.

It's adorable.

"Did you mean what you said about Paris?" he asks.

"Yeah." My stomach flip-flops. That must mean... He... I... We... Deep breath. I can't get too excited. Not when he could crush me.

He takes my hands and rubs his thumb against my fingers. His eyes find mine. "I love you, Kat Wilder. I am, as you said, madly in love with you."

My knees go weak, but I manage to hold my ground.

"I think about you constantly. It hurts when you're not around. Something is missing. At first, it confused me. And I don't confuse easily." He squeezes my hands. "I tried working harder, but that didn't help. I couldn't stop thinking about you."

A petal lands on his hair. I brush it off and run my fingers through his hair.

His lips curl into a smile.

It still makes me melt.

It's still everything.

"I tried to deny it. That possibility of never seeing you again cut me some place I've never hurt before. That would have been the worst mistake of my life." He slides his hand around my waist. "I love you."

I hook my arms around his shoulders. Something to help me stay upright. Blake loves me. Blake loves me. Blake loves me.

I'm the luckiest girl in the whole fucking world.

"I love you, too," I say.

His lips find mine.

It's as hot as any of our other kisses, but there's more to it than heat. All his love is pouring into me. All my love is pouring into him.

He's mine.

And I'm his.

And it's perfect.

"Now, how about Paris?" he asks.

"A promise is a promise."

I squeal as he pulls me into his arms. It's just us in the park now. Lizzy is nowhere to be seen. Back at home already.

The park is ours.

The world is ours.

"How long until the flight leaves?" I ask.

"Three hours." He presses his lips into my neck. "But the private jet should be ready as soon as we arrive."

"Wonder what we'll do for three hours," I say.

He squeezes me. "You know exactly what we'll do."

I meet his gaze. "Say it again."

"I love you, Kat Wilder."

"I love you, Blake Sterling."

Epilogue: Part One

HER FIRST DAY OF SCHOOL

It's only two avenues and three subway stops from Columbia to the penthouse apartment. Barely time to feel the sweet relief of the air conditioning before I'm on the street again.

I run up the subway steps. Fuck. It's hot. Really hot. But it doesn't bother me.

My first day of college is over. The college part, at least. The school's art department loved my portfolio so much they offered me a spot in the fall class. A full scholarship, too. Meryl's money is still safely tucked away in my account, there for a rainy day.

God knows there will be plenty of rain soon. The city never relents. If it's not heat, it's rain, snow, wind. Still, I wouldn't trade it for anything.

Two blocks and I'm in the blissfully air-conditioned lobby. I wipe the sweat from my forehead as I wait for the elevator.

I'm not the picture of grace, but at this point, I've got nothing to prove.

"Good afternoon, Miss Wilder." The guard waves at me. "How is your sister?"

"In California. It's awful."

He shakes his head. Only a born-and-bred New Yorker can really understand. Who could leave the greatest city in the country for California?

The elevator doors open. I step inside and wave my key card for access to the penthouse floor.

The mirrors reflect my running makeup. I did my best college girl cat eye, but most of it has melted off. No matter. The only thing I want besides a glass of cold water is a shower.

Ding. I step into the hallway and dig into my backpack front pocket for my keys. It's silly that this door locks at all. The only way to get to the floor is with a key card. A lock is overkill. Three locks is insanity.

But it's so Blake.

There. I slide my key into the door, turn the lock, and step inside.

It's dark.

The lights are off.

The curtains are drawn.

Huh?

Something whizzes past me and bounces off the wall. Something small. A cork.

The curtains pull open.

Blake is standing in front of the window holding a foaming bottle of champagne. That explains the cork.

He points to the ceiling. There are a few dozen balloons in blue and white. Columbia colors. There's a banner hanging across the incredibly long main room. *Congratulations, Kat.*

And, my God, he's wearing one of those silly men's

racerback tank tops. Blue, with *Columbia* in big, white letters.

He catches me staring. "If you think that's something, you should see the matching boxers."

"Oh, yeah?"

He nods, takes three steps closer, picks up the champagne flutes on the coffee table, and hands one to me.

"Aren't you glad you started college old enough to drink?" he asks.

"You graduated too young to drink."

"Don't compare yourself to an old man." He smiles.

"Old at twenty-six?"

"Ancient." He pulls my backpack off my shoulders and sets it next to the couch. "Your shoulders aching from carrying that thing around?" He runs his finger up my arm.

Desire courses through me. Those are some amazing fingers. I clear my throat, getting ahold of my senses. "More like my neck."

He rubs my neck with his palm. Traces the neckline of my tank top with his other hand. "I don't like you wearing that to class."

"Would you feel better if I wrote *Property of Blake Sterling* on it?"

"Yes." He presses his lips against my neck. "But I don't suppose you're offering."

"Well, maybe if I hadn't bought the tank top."

He laughs. It's a hearty laugh. Ever since we flew to Paris together, I've heard a lot of that laugh.

I hear it every day and it still makes me melt. It's still the sweetest sound in the whole damn world.

He presses his lips to my neck and lets out a low groan.

Okay. That sound is a close second. A very, very close second.

I take a sip of my champagne. Sweet, fruity bubbles slide down my throat. Damn. It's good. I finish my glass with one long swig.

Blake places it on the coffee table. He brushes the messy hair from my eyes. "I got you something."

I fight my urge to clap. Surprise presents are always such a nice, well, surprise. "Let me see."

He laughs. His grin is ear to ear. His eyes crinkle. His cheek dimples. He shakes his head like I'm just so ridiculous, and he grabs a wrapped present from the bookshelf.

He hands it to me. "You'll like it."

"You're not supposed to say that."

"You're not supposed to say *let me see*."

"Oh, using my own words against me, are you?" I pull the wrapping off the present. It's a graphic novel. *Falling Petals*. The same thing I titled my portfolio project. And the cover image is one of my drawings. A self-portrait.

Right there where the author name is supposed to go it says *Kat Wilder*.

Shit. I'm the author. This is my portfolio project, the latest version of it.

"It's a mockup," he says. "You do like it?"

My jaw must be hanging open. It's a mockup of my portfolio project, and it looks like a real graphic novel. It looks amazing.

I flip through the pages. It's laid out perfectly. Each vignette is shaded with a different color and each one is just right, as vivid or muted as it was in my original drawing.

I let out all the air in my lungs. "I love it."

"It's meant to inspire you."

He picks at the pages, flipping to the vignette about Blake, well, inspired by Blake. It's all technically fiction.

He flips right to a page where the two characters are about to have sex. "I know it inspires me."

"Pervert."

Blake points to the panel at the bottom of the page— the one where the bedroom door shuts. "Cruel of you not to let your readers see what happens."

"Is that right?"

He nods. "Sadistic, even." He nips at my ear as he sets the book on the coffee table.

"It's not that kind of story."

"It could be." He works his way down my neck. His fingertips side over the waist of my denim shorts.

"Hey, Sterling. If we're going to do this, we're going to do it my way." There, I throw his words back at him. Though I am really fond of those words. And of his way.

He pulls back, straightening his Columbia tank top like he's my apt pupil. "And what is your way?"

I plant my hand on my hip. "Take off your clothes."

"Where have I heard that before?"

"Don't make me ask twice." I fight a giggle. I'm not pulling this off.

But he's indulging me anyway.

Blake pulls his tank top over his head. The light from the window streams over his body, highlighting all those deep, perfect lines. The man is cut. He's like a statue.

He slides out of his shorts and tugs at his boxers. He points to a label on the side. Columbia.

A laugh escapes my lips. "That's commitment. But take it off."

He slides his boxers to his knees.

Oh hell yes.

I motion *come here*. "Take off mine now."

We work together. I lift my arms as he pulls my shirt over my head. I shimmy my hips as he slides my shorts to my feet. He runs his fingertips over my calves, outer thighs, hips, stomach, back.

Want buzzes through my body.

His way or my way, we're doing this.

"I didn't tell you to do that," I say.

He unhooks my bra and pulls it off my shoulders. His fingers trail over my breasts. Draw slow circles around my nipples.

"I should give you a spanking for disobeying my orders," I say.

"You should." He pushes my underwear to my knees, grabs my ass, and pulls our bodies together.

His cock presses against my pelvis. I rise onto my tiptoes so it's pressing against my clit.

Oh, hell yes.

Blake kisses me. It's hard and hungry and sweet all at once. In one smooth motion, he lifts me. My legs hook around his hips. My arms slide around his neck. He carries me to the wall and presses me against it. Yes. Oh hell yes.

"Hold on tight." He kisses me hard.

His nails dig into the flesh of my ass as he adjusts me. A nice hint of pain. Just enough to feel good. To draw all of my attention.

His tip enters me. It's still as good as the first time. Still as good as every time.

I'll never get tired of fucking this man.

I kiss Blake, holding on for dear life as he thrusts into me.

Yes. Oh hell yes.

He presses me against the wall, rocking into me harder and harder and harder.

There. Perfect. He digs his nails into my skin, shifting my hips so every thrust goes deeper. My bare chest presses against his. Our bodies still feel so good together. We're so good together.

This is damn perfect.

His tongue slides into my mouth, exploring it like it still fascinates him. I do the same. God knows he still fascinates me. I want to know everything there is to know about Blake—about his mind, his heart, his body. Especially his body.

I dig my nails into his back, and he groans into my mouth. I squeeze my legs around his hips, rocking against him. My clit slides over his pubic bone. It's a delightful bit of friction.

Pleasure whirs inside me. It winds tighter. Tighter.

I pull my lips away, tilt my head back, groan his name.

His next thrust pushes me over the edge. Bliss fills my body. Free fall. It's everywhere, all around me.

He holds me tighter.

His breath hitches as he moves faster, harder. His eyelids press together. Groans escape his lips.

He's almost there.

He squeezes me tighter. Presses me against the wall.

There.

An orgasm overtakes him. He groans, digging his fingers into my skin as he comes inside me.

I collapse into his arms. Still, he holds me tight, pressing me against the wall. I unhook my legs and plant my feet on the floor.

Blake runs his fingertips over my chin, tilting it so we're eye to eye. "I love you."

I press my lips to his. "I love you too."

———

AFTER DINNER AT THE THAI RESTAURANT DOWN THE street, we climb into the limo.

Blake pulls a blindfold from the seatback pocket and places it over my eyes. "The next destination is a surprise."

"What kind of surprise?"

He kisses my neck. "Not that kind. Not yet."

I lean back onto the bench seat. Okay. Our destination is a surprise, and we're not spending the trip having sex. "Want to give me a clue?"

"No."

I shake my head. "You're so difficult. I shouldn't put up with you."

"You shouldn't."

"Why do I?"

"My body."

I laugh. "Not your money?"

"No. It's the sex."

"It helps."

"Only helps?"

"I also happen to adore you."

"Not as much as I adore you."

Blake slides onto the bench seat next to me, trailing his fingertips up and down my inner thigh, right under the hem of my skirt.

So, so close.

I yelp when the limo stops and he pulls his hand away.

"You can take it off," he says.

I pull the blindfold over my head, toss it aside, and step out of the limo.

We're in Midtown, in front of a tall building. The Empire State Building. It's blue and white today.

"For your first day of school," he says. "The whole city is celebrating you."

"It's celebrating the college, and it was purple for NYU yesterday."

He takes my hand and leads me into the building. It's past the hours for the observation deck, but a little thing like that would never stop Blake. He motions *hello* to the guard and steps into the elevator.

"Last time I checked, you're not afraid of heights," he says.

"Not at all." There's nothing like the rush you get from being up in the clouds.

He waves a key card at the elevator and presses the button for the observation deck. I don't even ask myself how he does these things anymore. It's some rich person trick.

It's just like when I was a kid. The elevator goes so many stories so fast that my ears pop. I swallow three time to unpop them. Ah. Finally.

The doors slide open, and we step outside. The entire observation deck is empty save for a lone security guard in the corner.

I press the double doors open and step onto the deck balcony. It's windy up here but the air is warm. Perfect September weather. Perfect for the city.

The sun is setting behind us. It sets so late this time of year. Blake slides his arm around my hips as I squeeze the guardrail. The city is all around us, and it's beautiful.

A smile creeps onto his lips. He brushes the hair from my eyes again. He laughs as the wind blows it back. "That shows me."

He pulls me away from the edge, so we're in the middle of the deck.

Blake's eyes find mine. He looks at the concrete. It's almost like he's nervous, but that can't be possible. Blake Sterling doesn't get nervous.

"Let's hope this goes better than last time." He takes my hand and drops to one knee.

Holy shit.

"Kat Wilder, I'm madly in love with you, and the only thing missing in my life—" he pulls a ring box from his pocket and pops it open "—is making you my wife."

I stare at the ring.

"It's the same one," he admits. "It really does suit you."

I reach for the words. My voice cracks. "Yes. Of course."

He slides the ring on my finger.

I tug at his hands, pulling him to his feet. He slides his arms around me, leans in close, and kisses me.

He kisses me like he never wants to come up for air.

Epilogue: Part Two

THEIR FIRST CHRISTMAS

December 22

There are only four blocks between my subway exit and the apartment. Today, they feel like four miles. It's not quite freezing, but the wind is heavy enough to send a chill through my wool coat. My boots are leaking. My jeans are soaked.

None of that matters when I see Blake. He's standing in the lobby, hands in his suit pockets, shoulders pulled back, hard expression on his face.

He softens when I step into the door. His eyes find mine. I can't help but smile. I can't help but throw myself into his arms. I'm sure my boots are dirtying his perfect grey suit, but I don't care.

Blake runs his fingers through my hair. "How was it?"

"Manageable. Good thing I had such an excellent physics tutor." I press my lips into his. Mmm. He tastes like vanilla. "I think I passed. Maybe even got a B."

"I'm sure it's an A. I'm proud of you."

I plant my legs on the floor. "Aren't you supposed to be at work?"

"Yes."

"You're ditching work for me?"

"We have something to discuss." His voice is heavy. Which means bad news.

I hate bad news.

I stop to admire the giant Christmas tree in the lobby. It's been here a few weeks, but I've been too focused on school to take a decent mental picture. It would look amazing in a comic panel— the image of untouchable, elegant decadence.

Even three feet away, I can smell the pine needles. I move closer, run my fingers over the soft red tinsel. This tree is huge. Ridiculous even. It's thirty feet tall and utterly flawless.

But not in that Beyonce kind of way.

In a lifeless, belongs in a magazine and not reality kind of way.

I imagine drawing it. I'd have to give it an entire page. I'd have to find a way to capture its majesty and its lack of soul all at once.

Blake runs his fingers over my chin. "Kat."

I turn back to him, examine the expression in his eyes. He's fighting something. "What's wrong?"

"We'll talk in the penthouse." Blake nods a hello/goodbye to the guard. His grip tightens around my wrist as he pulls me to the elevators.

It's rougher than usual. I know better than to ask. Blake isn't closed off when we're alone. But in public, he's a wall of steel.

Inside, the penthouse is as sparse as always. It's free of holiday cheer. If it weren't for the bleak white sky bleeding in from the floor-to-ceiling windows, it could be June.

Okay, that's not quite true. The trees in the park are barren, brown and gray instead of vibrant green, and all the people on the street are wearing heavy coats.

I kick off my boots and hang my coat on the rack. Blake sets my backpack next to the couch. That's where I sit when I draw. And he hates when my stuff is on the couch. He must know how much I want to sketch the scenery.

"Coffee?" he asks.

"Sure."

I watch as he fixes two cups and hands one to me.

The drink warms my fingers. Sweet, rich, vanilla. Like his lips. "I know it's cutting it a little close, but I was thinking we could get a Christmas tree tomorrow. Or even today. It's only noon. We have time to go to the lot on Fifty-Ninth or to grab a plastic tree at Target."

His expression hardens. He turns to the window, steps into the soft glow. Winter light is beautiful. I need to immortalize him. To capture the highlights and shadows and all the hurt in his eyes.

I move closer. Run my fingertips over his cheek. He leans into my touch, letting out a long, heavy breath. Not quite a sigh but close.

"What's wrong?" I ask.

His eyes stay on the window. "I don't celebrate Christmas." He takes a long sip of his coffee, breaking my touch. "Your sister will be here tomorrow. Celebrate here or use the company jet to take her to Aruba. I'll be at the office until the twenty-sixth."

I play with my giant engagement ring. It's hard, expensive, elegant. Like his apartment. Like his company. Like him. "Are you going to explain?"

His facade cracks. Hurt spreads over his face. His lip corners turn down. His eyebrows screw in frustration. For once, his posture isn't strong and impervious.

My voice gets soft. "You can run away if you want, but I need to know why."

"There are too many ugly memories."

I nod. Blake hasn't had an easy life. His father was a horrible, abusive man. Blake had to keep everything together for his mom and his sister, even when he was a little boy. "So you disappear into work?"

He nods.

"Every year?"

Again, he nods.

"And you waited until the twenty-second to drop this on me?"

"School comes first."

I don't know whether I want to hug him or slap him. He really does want my schoolwork to come first. Even before him. Even when he needs me desperately.

My fingers curl into fists. The anger is winning. "So, what, you're totally bailing on Christmas?"

Blake is stone even as he turns to face me. "Celebrate however you want. I won't get in your way."

"I want to celebrate with you."

His voice wavers. "I'm sorry, Kat."

Fuck this. I'm not going to let Blake lock me out. Not over something this important. "No." I press my heel into the hardwood. Only, it's a sock and the floor is just waxed. I slip, landing on my hands and knees.

Blake looks down at me. He smiles, endeared by either my clumsiness or my rejection.

I look up at him. "When is the last time you did anything to celebrate?"

His expression hardens.

"Ten years? More?"

He nods.

"Maybe you'll like it now. If you give it a chance."

He kneels, offering to help me up. I grab his hand but use it to pull him onto the floor with me.

He doesn't resist. And there's my untouchable CEO fiancé, sitting cross-legged on the floor in a three-thousand-dollar suit. Anyone else would look silly. Somehow, Blake still looks in control.

I meet his gaze. "Maybe happy memories can replace the old ones."

He brushes my hair behind my ear. It's soft. Sweet.

He wants this too. It's only a matter of helping him realize it.

"I love you," I whisper. "Let me help you."

"It can't be helped."

It can't be helped. Not *I* can't be helped. So he's not totally hopeless.

I press my fingertips against his. The intimacy of it sends a shiver down my spine. I drink in the high of skin on skin, safe and overwhelming all at once.

I intertwine my fingers with his and stare back at him. "No."

He stares back, totally unreadable. "Not many people tell me no."

"In a few months, I'm going to be your wife. And I'm not going to give up on spending the holidays with you without a fight." I press my free hand against his thigh and use it as leverage to shift onto his lap. "We'll make a deal."

Everything in his demeanor changes. Any hint of pain fades away. It's replaced by a perfect poker face. His posture straightens. His eyes turn to steel. "What are your terms?"

Crap. He's an intimidating negotiator. I swallow hard. I wrap my legs around him, pressing my crotch against his. It's a cheap move, sure, but this is too important for sportsmanship. "This year, we try Christmas my way. If you hate it, we never have to celebrate again."

He doesn't flinch. "That could be sixty years. Seventy even."

"That's how much it means to me." I pull my sweater over my head and toss it on the ground. Another cheap trick, but I don't care. I try out my best Blake Sterling look of intimidation. "And how confident I am."

I slide my free hand around his neck. He's warm, even with his expression as cold as the air outside.

I run my fingers through his hair. "Do you trust me?"

"Trust won't solve this."

"But you do."

He nods. "With my life."

"What if…" I bite my lip, suddenly shy at my unconventional addendum. I channel his negotiation skills. Time to close this deal. "If it gets to be too much, you can get back in control with me."

He runs his fingertip along my chin, tilting me so we're eye to eye. I hold his gaze. He's not hurt and closed off anymore. He's intrigued.

"I'll be yours, completely yours, and you can do whatever you want with me," I say. "Wherever we are."

He presses his lips into my neck. It's enough to send heat between my legs. His teeth brush against my skin. Soft, then hard, then so hard I yelp.

Oh God, how I want that mouth on me, how I want him to peel off these thick winter clothes.

"You are mine, Kat." He bites me harder. His hands go to the waist of my jeans. His fingers toy with the button. "Wherever I want, however I want, whenever I want." He looks into my eyes. "Don't pretend that isn't what you need."

My cheeks flush. "It is."

"You need me in control."

I nod.

"You need to submit to all of my demands."

He unbuttons my jeans. His hand goes to my ass. He pushes me up so he can tug my jeans to my thighs.

Blake runs his hands over the sides of my cotton panties. His touch is electric. It's been nearly a week since we've had sex. Longer since he's had me tied up and merciless. I've done nothing but study for the last two weeks.

My sex clenches. He's right. I love it when he's in control. And I need it now.

His hands stay on my hips. "What is it you're offering?"

Then his hands are on my ass. He brings my body toward his, so my sex is only inches from his lips. The panties are in the way, but they're no match for Blake's determination.

"You can use me," I say. "If that's what you need to feel better. If that's the only way you can get through how much it hurts."

His exhale is warm against my skin.

"Please." I take a deep breath, cultivating all my bravery. "I want to help you through this even if it's on my knees."

"I'm not going to use you." He drags his fingertips over the waistband of my panties. His voice gets rough. "Have I ever?"

"No. But…" I lean into his touch. "You can have a blank check. Whatever you want."

His fingers trail over the panties, lower and lower, until they're pressing the cotton fabric against my clit.

"Not until we agree on this."

My body is not on the same page. It's surging with pleasure, begging me to collapse in Blake's arms so he can throw me on the couch.

"If it's too much, we can stop, cease all holiday festivities, and take you someplace where we can be alone.

Where you can be in control." I stare at him, certain I'm going to melt under the weight of his gaze.

He says nothing.

"What do you think?" I ask. "Are you willing to try?"

I hold my breath waiting for his answer.

———————

Blake holds my gaze. "I already have you."

"But…"

"I'll try, Kat." He pushes up my tank top and presses his lips against my stomach. "But only because it matters to you." He kisses me just beneath my belly button. "Take off your top."

I hesitate.

His voice gets gruff and commanding. "Now."

Frustration breaks through his facade. He needs to be back in control. He needs to be the one place where the world makes sense.

I need it too.

I pull my shirt over my head and drop it on top of my sweater. His eyes fill with desire. I need that. I need all of it.

I go to unhook my bra but he grabs my wrist but pulls my hand back to my lap.

"Wait until I tell you," he commands. He looks me over, slowly, relishing every moment. "*Now* take off your bra."

I do it slowly, one arm at a time.

He runs his hands over my sides and up my shoulders. Then they're cupping my breast. Not teasing or toying. Not yet.

"How do you want me to touch you, sweetheart? Explain it to me." His voice is utterly in control as he runs his thumbs over my nipples.

A pang of lust goes straight to my core. How? Doesn't matter. As long as he's touching me. As long as he's making me his. "However you want. Whatever you need."

"What do *you* need, Kat?"

He pinches my nipples. His mouth goes to my neck. Without warning, he sinks his teeth into my skin.

Mmm. I gasp, digging my hand into the fabric of his suit.

"This is what you need, isn't it?" He pinches me until I pant. "You need me in control."

He bites me again. He drags his fingers over my stomach. No teasing, he slips a finger inside my panties and into my sex. I'm wet and ready for whatever he wants.

"Yes," I breathe. "Please."

"Explain it to me."

"Yes. I need you in control. I need to be at your mercy. Please."

He pushes my panties to my thighs. His voice gets soft. Sweet. "Come here."

It's a second, then he's back to the hard exterior. Blake in control. Blake the Dom. He hates when I call him that.

But I like it.

Love it even.

Fuck, I really do love him in control.

He pulls me closer, so my chest is in line with his head. His hands slide up my sides. He grabs my breast and brings it to his mouth. He eases me into it, sucking soft, then hard, then so hard I groan.

He bites my nipple. It sends a rush of pain to my fingertips. The next bite is harder. It hurts more, but that feels good. My sex clenches. I almost forget my purpose here.

I need to make him feel better.

But this is him feeling better.

There isn't a hint of frustration on his face.

Just the lust for control that makes my sex clench.

He moves to my other breast, toys mercilessly.

He doesn't stop until I'm panting. "Hands on my shoulders."

I do as I'm asked. It brings my body above his. He looks up at me as he tugs my jeans all the way to my knees. Then it's the panties. His fingers slide up my thighs. So, so close to where they need to be.

My gaze goes to the blinding white sky. It's not just bleak. It's beautiful.

"Eyes on me, Kat." He digs his hand into my hair, turning me so I'm facing him. "Watch what you do to me."

His hand brushes against my clit. I manage to hold his gaze, even as his pressure intensifies, even as bliss spreads through my thighs.

How can I possibly be doing anything to him? I'm the one at his mercy.

He strokes me. His touch gets harder and harder. I tug at his hair and he holds that pressure. It's just right.

The knot inside me tightens. I want to close my eyes, to do something to contain the intensity.

But I don't. I follow his commands. My gaze stays on Blake. I watch what I do to him.

His pupils are dilated. His mouth is open. He's hard. I can't feel it from this position, but I can see the erection straining against his slacks.

He strokes me until I can't take it anymore, until I let my eyes close, until my teeth sink into my lip.

He stops. "Open your eyes, Kat. I want you looking at me when you come."

I barely manage it.

"So you know you're mine."

I nod.

"And that I'm yours."

I bite my lip. He's not touching me. I hate that he's not touching me. My body is close to release. It's screaming for his hands.

"Tell me how you want me," he says.

"Touching me." I barely get the words out.

"Then?"

"I want you to fuck me."

"How?"

I fight my shyness. He's not going to touch me until I give him a specific answer. He's proving a point—it's ridiculous for me to offer myself to him when I'm so thoroughly his.

But the point hardly matters compared to how badly I need his hands on my body.

The angular lines of his tie catch my attention. Yes. That's what I want. I drag my fingers down his shoulder and over his tie. "I want this around my wrists, so I can't control anything but how loudly I groan."

His fingers brush against my upper thigh. "Why did you offer me carte blanche when you want this as much as I do?"

"I didn't know what else to offer."

He brings his hand to the back of my head and pulls me into a deep kiss. My body lights up with a mix of desire and affection.

When the kiss breaks, Blake stares into my eyes. His breath is heavy, like he's about to lose control. "You have no idea how much you much I need you." He takes my hands and places them on his shoulders, one at a time. "Eyes stay on me if you want me to fuck you. Understand?"

I bite my lip. That's an awful thing to lose. I nod. Yes. I understand.

He is painfully slow about dragging his fingertips up and down my thigh. They brush against my clit, so light I can barely feel them. The softness makes it more intense. I squirm to contain it. He does it again and I dig my hands into the thick wool fabric of his suit.

My eyes stay on his, even as his touch gets harder, even as the knot inside me pulls so tight I can barely breathe. I'm tempted to look away, to press my lids together, but I don't. I inhale and exhale slowly, focusing on every wave of pleasure pulsing through my body.

It's too intense. I'm at the edge, about to go over. I groan his name. It's the only way I can react enough to keep my eyes on him.

His next touch sends me over the edge. My orgasm is hard and fast. The pressure gets tighter and tighter then releases in a torrent of bliss. I'm desperate to close my eyes, to go deep into the feeling in my body. Instead, I hold his gaze. I go deep into the look of desire in his eyes, until I'm swimming in it, until it's the only thing I can feel.

Blake pulls me onto his lap. His lips find mine. He kisses me so deep and so hard I lose track of everything around us.

I'm vaguely aware that we're in his, well our, apartment a few days before Christmas. But the only thing in focus is the heat of his body, the vanilla on his lips, the hardness of his muscles.

He brings his hand to my ass and sets me on the ground. In one swift movement, he pulls my jeans and panties off my feet.

I watch as he strips. It's too damn slow. First his suit jacket. Then he loosens his tie and wraps it around his hand. He leans next to me.

I pull my arms over my head so he can bind my wrists.

He moves faster with his shirt, shoes, socks, slacks,

boxers. The soft white light casts such a wonderful glow over the hard lines of his body. He's still too good to be true, like a statue cut out of marble.

He kneels between my legs and pries my knees apart. It's needy but gentle. He isn't proving anything. He's giving me what I want.

What we both want.

Blake brings his body onto mine, his hands outside my chest. His cock strains against my sex. It's a tease. It isn't enough.

My body lights up. I'm so, *so* desperate to get him inside me.

His presses his lips to mine.

Slowly, he slides inside me.

I groan against his mouth. I arch my back, my wrists straining against their binding.

The weight of his body presses me against the hard-wood floors. They're still slick, and with my hands bound, I can't do anything to keep from sliding.

There's no more tease. He thrusts into me, hard and fast. I wrap my legs around him. It's the only way I can hold him, the only thing I can do that will keep us from sliding all the way across the room.

Every thrust presses me against the floor. My head and shoulders ache. Not the good kind of pain, the kind he gives me, but a strain I don't like.

I bring my eyes to his. He's lost in this. He pumps hard and deep. He feels good inside me, but I want him here, staring at me the way I stared at him.

"Blake," I groan. I shift to meet him. "Look at me."

He blinks. His gaze meets mine. He looks at me funny, like he doesn't know where he was.

And then he kisses me. I kiss him back, focusing on the sensations of his body. How warm he is. How hard he is.

How his muscles tense the closer he gets. His mouth goes to my neck. I turn my head to offer myself to him. This is how I want him, feeling so good he can't help but mark me.

Every scrape of his teeth pushes me closer. There's not far to go. I'm almost there.

The heat coursing through my body collects in my legs. Desire turns to a deep, desperate pressure. So tense and so tight that I can't do anything but groan.

His next thrust sends me over the edge. I come again, pressing my wrists against the bindings of his tie to contain the heavy wave of pleasure.

Blake does nothing to slow. His movements get harder, more intense. His teeth sink into my neck. His cock thrusts deep inside me. His breath strains.

I groan his name. After coming twice, any more sensation is hard to bear. But I need to feel him go over the edge too. I need him to be mine too.

The next time he bites me, he's there. I can sense it in his breath, in the way his shoulders tense. One more thrust and he's groaning, his cock pulsing inside me as he comes.

Blake waits until he's emptied himself, then reaches over and undoes my bindings. He examines my wrists, one at a time.

"You got lost for a minute there," I say.

"Yes, but you found me." He leans down to kiss me.

I soak it in for a moment. "Can we pick up a tree today?"

Blake shakes his head. He shifts so he's sitting next to me. "Tomorrow."

The affection is draining from his eyes. He's closing off. I push myself up and place my body next to his. I run my hands through his hair. I stroke his cheek. But nothing brings him back.

"It will be okay," I say. "I promise."
He looks away like he doesn't believe me.

————

For lunch, we go to the Thai restaurant down the street. The Christmas tree in the corner does nothing to boost Blake's mood. Thankfully, there are no holiday decorations around our booth, just the usual photographs of tropical beaches, Buddhist temples, and mango trees.

It's a quiet meal. I try to come up with some words to soothe Blake, but I know they'll feel hollow in his ears.

At home, he excuses himself into his office. He expected three days of uninterrupted work, quite the luxury for a man who has to weigh in on every one of his company's decisions.

Two cups of coffee do nothing to ease the tightness in my chest. He's been better about working shorter hours. We have dinner every night, spend every Sunday together. But he loves work so much. It would be so easy for him to disappear into it forever.

I spend the afternoon drawing. After a few rounds of sketches, I fall into a rhythm. Draw a dozen panels, fix a cup of coffee, repeat. I'm working on a new graphic novel, my first attempt at pure fiction. It's a simple story about falling in love during a New York City summer. The imagery is supposed to be warm and vibrant. The feelings are supposed to be big and overwhelming.

But, today, it isn't coming. I'm cold and muted and small. Everything outside is bleak and gray. Everything in here is hard and empty.

Blake is dealing the only way he knows how. I tell myself this every time a doubt creeps into my head, while I eat dinner alone, while I shower alone, while I watch TV alone.

Sometime past midnight, I go to bed alone. He's still working, his office door locked, the walls around his heart creeping so high I might not be able to climb them.

The bed is cold without him. I toss and turn, trying and failing to fall asleep.

He's dealing the only way he knows how.

The words don't warm me.

December 23

───────────────

Blake is not in the bed when I wake. He's in the kitchen in his pajamas, sipping a cup of coffee and staring out into the bleak white sky. It's uglier today.

His gaze turns to me.

"Are you okay?" I ask.

"I'll tell you if I'm not."

"But—"

"Don't ask again."

He's clearly not okay, but I won't get anywhere by pushing it. I go back to the bathroom, brush my teeth, apply a touch of makeup, and change into jeans and a wool sweater.

When I return to the kitchen, Blake is dressed in a similar outfit.

His eyes find mine. "Are you hungry?"

"I'll grab something at Starbucks."

"You want to go to Starbucks?"

I nod.

"Why?"

He stares at me like I'm crazy. Most New Yorkers take

pride in their hatred of Starbucks, only stopping at the chain coffee shop if it's particularly convenient. And I certainly don't make a point of visiting chains when there are so many independent shops to choose from.

But, dammit, we're getting into the holiday spirit and that's going to start with a sugary espresso drink.

For a moment, I reconsider my plan. Blake drinks his coffee black. He'll order a black coffee, hate it, and start the day off grumpy. But he does like chocolate. And when it's mixed with mint, it's so sublimely seasonal.

At the very least, he can taste it on my lips.

"For the holiday drinks," I say.

He looks at me even more curiously.

"I know you like chocolate syrup." I fold my arms over my chest. "Don't pretend otherwise."

"Is that a request?"

My cheeks flush. "Maybe later."

He moves closer. His hands go to my wrists and he unwraps my arms then places them around him. I squeeze tightly, breathing in the smell of his soap.

He runs his fingers through my hair. "Today, you're in charge."

A thrill passes through me. I need to bring my A-game. I nod and press my lips into his. "Are you hungry?"

"I ate."

"Then get your coat so we can go." I find my boots and step into them. "We'll walk to the lot. We can take a cab home."

He raises an eyebrow like he's not sure about my plan, but he doesn't object. It's true, cabs don't always look kindly on strapping Christmas trees to the roof. But I'm not about to shove an evergreen into Blake's limo.

Outside, the wind is cold and the air is heavy. Those clouds mean snow. If not today then tomorrow. My breath hitches. Real snow would be amazing. A white Christmas is like something out of a dream.

It's only a few blocks to the closest Starbucks. Blake squeezes my hand, no protests, no demands, no sign he's anything but okay. He looks around the chain coffee house with amusement.

I order a peppermint mocha, no whipped cream for him, and a gingerbread latte and an egg sandwich for me. He tries to pay, but I beat him on the draw. No way is Blake paying for any of this holiday stuff. That's all on me. I've barely touched the two hundred thousand dollars Meryl left me. My scholarship covers tuition, books, and a meal plan.

We take a seat at a tiny table in the corner. Blake looks so tall in the little chair, but he still fits in.

"Was there anything you ever liked about Christmas?" I ask.

He drags his fingertips over my palm. "When we were very young, Meryl sent me and Fiona to stay with our grandmother."

"You liked her?"

Blake shakes his head.

I really can't catch a break with this holiday thing. "What did you like about the trips to your grandmother's house?"

He nearly smiles. "The chocolate."

Right on cue, one of the baristas calls out our drink orders. At the counter, my sandwich is up. It takes two trips to get everything back to the table, but I insist on doing it myself.

There's affection in Blake's eyes. He holds the cup under his nose, smelling it the way most people smell wine. He takes a small sip and his face screws in surprise.

"This is all sugar," he says.

"Of course. That's the point of the holiday drinks. Massive amounts of sugar to temporarily boost your mood and energy. Then caffeine to keep it boosted." I practically inhale my sandwich. It's not the best thing I've ever tasted, but I'm damn hungry.

"You've thought about this."

I sip my gingerbread-flavored drink. It is awfully sweet, so sweet and so artificially flavored that I can barely taste the coffee.

He takes another sip. There's no surprise on his face this time. There's also no sign he's enjoying his beverage.

His eyes find mine. "You're sweet, Kat—"

"But you hate it?"

He nods. "Coffee is meant to be bitter."

"Like you?"

"Of course." He half-smiles as he offers me his drink.

I take the cup and take a tiny sip. Despite its obscene level of sugar, it's delicious. Comforting, creamy, warm. A wonderful mix of cocoa and mint. Much better than the gingerbread.

"I'll keep this one." I toss the other drink in the trash on our way out the door.

The cold air is in sharp contrast to the warm drink in my hands. I pull my coat a little tighter.

I squeeze Blake's hand, running my thumb over his first two fingers. "What did you like about the chocolate at your grandma's?"

"We never had candy at home. Meryl was strict about eating well."

"Really?"

He nods. "Vegetables with dinner. Fruit for dessert."

"But she…" I struggle to come up with an explanation that isn't *but your late mother was a lush*. A very sweet lush, but a lush who died of liver disease nonetheless.

"Was an alcoholic. You can say it." He stops at a red light. "She said it openly."

I look both ways. No cars. We're still deep in the upper East side. I jaywalk across the street. Blake follows me.

"Okay. Yes," I say. "She was an alcoholic. She loved all sensory delights. I can't imagine her depriving you of candy."

"She wanted better for me and Fiona. She was happy when she met you."

"She saw right through me," I say.

"That's why she liked you." His gaze goes to the ground. "She had to drink. It was the only way she knew how to survive."

I bite my lip. All things considered, an aversion to Christmas and a habit of working sixty hours a week—down from a hundred—are pretty functional coping mechanisms. Better than turning to booze or running off to a loveless marriage.

But I don't care.

Blake isn't running away on my watch.

I'm afraid to ask my next question, but I do it anyway. "Why did you go to your grandma's house for Christmas?"

His expression steels. He pulls his hand away from mine and shoves it into his pocket. For three blocks he says nothing.

When he does speak, his voice is unsteady. "My father was the worst during the holidays."

There's this tightness in my chest. I'm terrified to ask him to explain. I can't do it here. Not yet.

Instead, I lock my arm with his and stay as close as I can. We only talk when we stop in a local cafe and order him a black coffee.

He's stuck in a bad memory, but I'm not about to let him stay there. I check the maps application on my phone.

Perfect. There's a Duane Reade five blocks and one avenue over. It's a little out of the way, but it's worth the extra walk.

"Follow me." I lead us out of the cafe and away from the park.

Blake looks at me curiously, though not as curiously as when I suggested Starbucks. Still, he follows without protest, even as I walk into the drug store.

I go straight to the candy aisle. "I'm sure your grandmother had some kind of fancy chocolate, but there must be something close here."

He scans the shelf. His eyes fall on a pale yellow box of inexpensive truffles. He picks them up, examining them carefully. "Meryl's mother was poor. She couldn't afford to spend money on candy."

He leans down to pick up another bag of chocolates—a holiday blend with peppermint flavor and candy cane pieces. Without a word, he hands it to me. His eyes meet mine. They're filled with confidence like he knows I'm desperate for the holiday themed chocolate.

"Thank you," I say. "That looks great."

His lips curl into the tiniest smile.

"Do you want anything else?" I ask.

He shakes his head and takes a long sip of his coffee as if to say *I only want this.* Then he presses his lips against my cheek as if to add me to the list of things he wants.

I buy the chocolate at the register. The cashier thanks us with a Merry Christmas. Blake cringes but stays silent. He follows me outside where I tear off the chocolate's plastic then pull open the lid.

I offer him the candy. "Did you have a favorite?"

He picks a picks a chocolate-covered truffle, bites it in half, chews, and swallows. "Not quite as sweet as your drink." He offers me the remaining half.

I take it and pop it into my mouth, much less graceful than he was. It's not as good as the dark chocolate in his kitchen, but it's not half bad. "Thank you."

"Do you plan on eating the entire box?" he asks.

"You had good memories of chocolate. You're eating another chocolate."

His lips curl into a half smile. He nods and does as he's told. This time, he picks something filled with caramel. Of course, Blake manages to avoid getting a single bit of caramel on his face.

He points to the box. "And one more for you."

"I'm going to collapse of a sugar overdose."

"I'll make sure you use the energy."

My cheeks flush. I scan the candies and pick one at random. A raspberry cream. It tastes artificial. A year ago, I'd be enamored with the flavor. Blake has ruined me for normal food.

"Thinking about anything?" I ask.

"Only that you're sweet."

Okay, that's a start. A new, holiday adjacent memory— the time his fiancée forced him to eat cheap drug store chocolates. One memory down, a thousand to go.

I press the lid over the box, slide it back in the plastic bag, and sling the bag around my wrist. We make the rest of the twenty minute walk in silence.

Finally, we reach the Christmas tree lot. It's small, about a thousand square feet, and surrounded by a metal gate. The trees are so close together that there's almost no room to move around them. Everything smells like pine, like Christmas.

There are lots of other people here, couples and families mostly, but they all fade away. My attention goes to a tree in the corner. It's on the shorter side, missing a few branches. By all accounts, it's ugly, but that imperfection is charming.

"What are you thinking?" Blake asks.

"That tree." I point to it. "It reminds me of my first Christmas with Lizzy after the accident."

His voice softens. He drags his fingertips over my neck. His skin is so warm. It melts all the chill around us.

"Tell me about it," he says.

I turn to Blake to look into his eyes. He's hard to read, as usual, but he seems okay.

"She hated being in a car. She still does. I wasn't about to lug a tree back to our apartment, so we looked for something at the drug store. They only had one tree, and it was about two feet tall and metallic purple."

"It sounds charming."

"It was." I lean into his chest. "We didn't really know what to do. Our parents had always been big on the holiday. They were schoolteachers and winter break meant they had a lot of time to celebrate. I was lost without them."

He plays with my hair. "You miss them."

"Of course." I bring my gaze back to the charming little tree. "The pain was fresh, but it helped to move forward. We did everything differently. We ordered Chinese food instead of cooking a big dinner. We decorated that tiny tree with exactly three candy canes. And we each bought a single present. I got a *Star Trek* sweater for Lizzy. She bought me a manga from the used book store at the library. And we stayed up all night to watch *The Matrix Trilogy* for the eight millionth time."

He sighs. "Kat, you have no idea what you do to me."

I meet his gaze, totally unable to read his expression. "What's that?"

"The world is beautiful through your eyes. I wish I

could use them all the time."

"The world *is* beautiful."

His eyes fill with affection. He brushes the hair behind my ear with a soft touch. "You've been through so much and you're still idealistic."

"No." I bite my lip. "I just… look at these trees—" I point to a tall evergreen, lush with pine needles. "They're beautiful. And the park. And the streets. And the sky." My gaze goes back to his eyes. "And you. When you smile or laugh."

His expression changes. Almost like he's overwhelmed. But Blake doesn't get overwhelmed. And certainly not by me.

His fingertips skim my chin, sending warmth straight to my belly. He tilts me so we're eye to eye. "I love you."

"I love you too."

He pulls me into a tight hug then releases me. I give him space to sort out whatever it is that's going through his gorgeous head.

There's a family picking out a tree. The parents are in their thirties. They have a daughter about four or five years old. She's wearing a bright pink coat and she runs around like doesn't believe anything will ever hurt her. When she trips, she picks herself up like it's nothing.

She runs straight to the tallest tree in the lot. Then she tugs at it like she needs it right now. She's adorable and she's happy.

Everyone here is happy.

Everyone except Blake. He has a frown on his face. He's watching another family, a man in his thirties and a little boy who can't be older than ten. The man is yelling at his son. The kid is holding an empty cup and the man's jeans are stained with hot chocolate. It's such a small thing to yell over, but the man is angry.

And then the man reaches out and grabs his son so hard the child cries.

Blake's expression hardens. His hands go to his pockets. He doesn't have to say anything. I know what this means. He needs to get out of here and now.

"I'll call your driver," I say. I grab Blake's hand and drag him to the street. It's tough to dial one-handed, but I make do.

Jordan picks up. "How can I help you Ms. Wilder?"

"Can you meet us a Fifty-Ninth and Fifth? I'm going to start walking from First."

"You're not far from Blake's place—"

"Please hurry." I hang up the call and shove my phone into my pocket. I bite my lip, cursing myself for sounding so obnoxious. I worked in a restaurant for three years. I always hated when people asked me to hurry as if I wasn't already going as fast as I could.

I look into Blake's eyes. It's like I'm losing him. He's going off somewhere far away, to something that rips a hole through his gut. I know that feeling, not to the extent he does, but I know it. Every time I hear about some horrible car accident, I can't breathe and I'm sure I'm about to break in two.

The only thing that keeps me functioning is knowing my sister is okay.

The limo meets us around Third Avenue. Jordan got here fast. There's no forced decorum. I pull the door open for Blake and wait for him to climb inside.

Everything eases once we're alone. Or as good as alone. I offer Jordan a friendly nod. "Back to Blake's place."

Blake shakes his head. "You need your tree."

"Okay. How about we get a plastic tree at Target?"

He nods.

"The one in Brooklyn if there's not too much traffic." I

go to roll up the partition.

"It should be about twenty minutes if you'd like some privacy." Jordan's tone is unreadable, but his implication is clear. There are twenty minutes to fuck.

Blake presses his back against the seat. There's less tension in his shoulders. There's less pain in his expression.

"Are you sure you want to stay out?" I ask.

"I told you not to ask if I'm okay."

I scoot onto his bench seat and move as close to him as I can.

He's still tense, turned away from me like he's lost in some well of agony deep enough to drown him.

I go to take his hand, but he pulls it into his lap.

"Talk to me," I say. "Please."

"Not now."

"Please."

"That man. He looked like Orson. Handsome, charismatic, and vile to the core."

"You don't know..." I hold my tongue. There's no sense in arguing over whether or not a stranger is vile. We'll never see him again. "Tell me about it."

His gaze goes to the tinted window. It's a charcoal color and it's totally opaque. It can't be an interesting view.

I squeeze his hand. "Please."

"My father kept it together when he was sober, but alcohol brought out all the hate inside him. One night, he came home drunk. Meryl had lit candles. She tried to keep things normal, even when we were old enough to understand exactly how despicable he was."

I squeeze him tighter.

"He knocked over one of the candles. The presents caught fire. Then the tree. He stood there, laughing as we tried to put it out. There was a fire extinguisher under the sink, but by the time we put the tree out it was charred and black. When I tried to take it down—" Blake's gaze drifts to the floor.

"He hit you?"

Blake nods. "It was the first time I kept him from hurting her."

My heart pounds against my chest. "How old were you?"

"Ten."

God, I can't breathe. I can't think. The limo feels darker and colder. Blake has to live with these memories every day. How many are there? How deep do they go? He's quiet about his father, but I know there were years of abuse.

It might be better to let him disappear. It's only a few days.

"Don't feel sorry for me, Kat. I can't stand it."

"Are you sure you can do this?"

His expression hardens.

He shakes his head. He turns, his eyes passing over me slowly. He brings his hands to my shoulder and traces my neckline. "You have a bruise."

I look down. I do have a soft purple bruise next to my collarbone. From yesterday, though from the regret in Blake's eyes I'm sure he realizes this.

"I hurt you," he says.

"I like it. I feel marked."

The car stops. Must be a red light. I go to stroke his hair but he turns away.

"You're not like your father," I say.

"He took control by hurting the people around him."

"You don't take anything, Blake. I give you control because I want it that way. Don't you remember what you said about how much I want that, how much I need it?"

His gaze goes back to the dark window.

"Was that a lie to seduce me?" I ask.

His voice is clipped. "No."

"It's barely more than a hickey," I say.

"If we keep this up, I might not be able to stop the next time you ask."

"You will."

"I'll hurt you."

I run my fingers through his hair, grabbing him hard and turning him to face me. "You won't. I trust you."

He presses the top of his forehead against mine. That sense of closeness overwhelms me. He's not a million miles away. He's here with me, in this tiny limo.

"I trust your judgement," he says.

But the truth is I'm shaking. I'm not so sure I trust myself to pull this off.

———

Fuck me. The mall that houses this particular Target is the image of Christmas spirit. The walls are decked with wreaths and string lights. The music is a constant loop of overplayed holiday songs. Everyone is wearing red and green.

The store is better. Its yellow fluorescent lights and shiny white floor give it a certain timeless, placeless quality. But the decorations, God, the decorations. There are cardboard cutouts of trees and smiling kids unwrapping presents.

I grab a big red cart and lead Blake straight to the Holiday section in the back.

Blake is behind me, but he's not really here. He's off someplace far away. Why do I put up with his stubbornness? I should have forced him to go home.

There are about a dozen different plastic trees on a

display three feet off the ground. Truth be told, I love all of them. None of them smell like pine, but each is a pleasant shade of forest green. There's something nice about building a tree, picking exactly where the branches go and how they turn. Maybe it's enough to make Blake feel in control again.

His expression is inscrutable. I take a deep breath, willing myself to give up on understanding what's going through his head.

I point to the tree in the back corner. It's the smallest option. "How about that one?"

He nods. Without a word, Blake finds the large box containing the correct model, lifts it, and places it in the cart.

"Is there anything you want to talk about?" I ask.

"You need ornaments."

True. Those are in the next aisle. There are dozens of choices, from *Star Wars* figurines to baby angels. Blake picks out a set of round ornaments in bright, metallic colors. They're much more electric than anything in his apartment, but the slight silver sheen will fit in well.

His gaze goes to a cracked ornament on the ground. He picks him up and examines the pieces. It's broken, absolutely, and it's sharp enough to cut someone pretty badly.

Something flares in his eyes, a memory, but this time, I don't push it. I offer my hand and he takes it.

"That should be enough," I say.

Finally, our gazes meet. There's a lightness in his eyes, like he's pushed past the part that hurts.

"Candy canes," he says. "And string lights."

"You're very thorough given that your assistant does all your shopping."

"Who do you think gives her the list?"

He drags his fingertips over my cheek. It's as comforting as the first time he did it. I lean into his touch, soaking in everything I can about him. He's hurting, but he's still so concerned with making sure I'm okay.

He presses his lips to my forehead. "What else do you need?"

"Stuff for cookies. A mix, a rolling pin, cookie cutters, sprinkles, icing."

He softens. "If we're making cookies, we're making cookies from scratch."

We fill the cart with necessary ingredients and tools. It's completely normal, like the thousands of times I came here with Lizzy.

After I pay, we meet Jordan on the street outside the mall. There's plenty of room in the trunk for the plastic tree's box, which means the limo is all ours.

Instead of talking, I rest my head on his shoulder, nestling my body into his. He runs his fingertips through my hair with a soft, gentle touch. It's a perfect respite. I can feel his heartbeat and hear his breath. He's close, and he's warm, and he's mine.

The drive is over too fast. Jordan insists on helping with the bags. After everything is on the sidewalk, Blake shakes his hand.

"You're off at midnight tonight for three weeks. I don't want to hear a peep from you," Blake says.

Jordan nods.

"Did Ashleigh speak to you about your bonus?"

"Yes, sir. It was very generous. Thank you. Merry Christmas."

Blake doesn't frown. That's something.

Jordan turns to me. "And Merry Christmas to you, Ms. Wilder. It's been a pleasure getting to know you this year."

"Merry Christmas." Suddenly, it occurs to me how

often people utter these two words. Every time I've been in a store in the last two months, the cashier thanked me with a *Merry Christmas*. Every other person I've seen the last two weeks said goodbye with a *Merry Christmas*.

Even in a city filled with people who celebrate other religious holidays, *Merry Christmas* is everywhere.

It must be hard to hate everything about the holiday.

There's no signs of displeasure on Blake's face. No anger or frustration or sadness. If anything, he's happy.

He leans down and kisses me. "We have cookies to bake."

I fight my urge to jump up and clap my hands. Screw it. I clap my hands together and whisper, "Yay."

He smiles, his eyes filling with affection.

It's a pain lugging everything into the elevator then into the living room. Blake scans the apartment like he's trying to figure where the tree will be the least offensive. I point to the corner behind the dining table. He nods and leaves the box there.

I get to work unloading the baking supplies and measuring the dry ingredients.

In minutes, the counters are already coated in a white dust, a mix of flour and sugar. Blake takes in the mess with a look of horror but he doesn't make a verbal objection.

"Did you ever bake cookies?" I ask.

"Never."

"Really?"

He nods.

"Preheat the oven to 350. And dust the cutting board with flour. The wood one."

"At your service."

I have to clear my throat to keep from groaning. I'm getting all sorts of mental images and not the kind that fit on a panel.

"Something on your mind, Kat?" His lips curl into a smile.

"The only thing on my mind is the delicious taste of cookies."

Blake's eyes go to the bowl. "I'm not an expert, but I believe you need eggs and butter."

"And vanilla."

His smile spreads until it's ear to ear. He presses his lips to mine. They don't taste like vanilla anymore, just like Blake. Heat rushes through my body. My knees buckle. I have to grab onto the counter to keep my balance.

When the kiss breaks, Blake follows all my commands. I add the wet ingredients and stir the batter until it's smooth. He steals the spoon from my hand, scrapes a bit of batter onto his finger, and holds it out to me like he's offering a taste.

I wrap my lips around his finger, lapping up the batter with my tongue. It tastes like sugar and vanilla. Then like his skin. My head swims with ideas.

Blake drags his finger across my lower lip. The touch sends a spark straight to my core. I want him now but I'm not about to abandon my task.

I clear my throat. "You really shouldn't eat raw batter. The eggs can give you salmonella poisoning."

He laughs, a big full belly laugh. It lights up something in me. It lights up *everything* in me.

"I appreciate your caution." He digs his finger into the bowl of batter and brings his finger to my mouth.

I lick the batter off him then suck on his finger. His eyelids press together. A tiny groan escapes his lips. But he stays in control, dragging his fingertip over my lips then down my neck.

I take a deep breath to contain the desire coursing through my body. "I take it that you enjoy baking cookies."

He nods.

"Then get to work." I fold my arms, trying my best look of intimidation. "Dust the cutting board with flour so we can roll out the dough."

"Yes, ma'am."

"It's Miss Wilder, not 'ma'am.'"

"It's not 'Miss' for long." He traces the outline of my engagement ring.

He sprinkles flour over the cutting board. I plop the cookie dough on top of it and grab the rolling pin. Blake positions himself behind me, placing his hands over mine, leaning into me as I roll out the dough.

My hands go forward. My torso follows. It presses my ass against his crotch. We could easily be having sex here if it weren't for the clothes and the flour.

It's very hard to stay focused on cultivating holiday spirit, but I manage. I find the cookie cutters and make three sugar cookie snowmen. Blake cuts out two stars and places them on the baking sheet next to my snowmen.

There's just enough room for a few more. I press the scraps of batter into a ball, roll it flat, and reach for the Christmas tree-shaped cookie cutter.

Something pierces my skin. Ow. My thumb is bleeding all over the clean white batter. I bring it to my mouth and suck on it. It eases the pain.

Blake looks me over with caution.

"It doesn't hurt," I say.

"I'll get you a bandage." He takes a step toward the bathroom. "You've found a unique way to avoid food coloring."

The batter is stained red. There's something familiar about it and about his words.

My mom said something like that. It was a long time ago. I was helping her bake. Lizzy had the snowman cookie cutter and I didn't want to wait my turn. I improvised and used a knife to cut a crude snowman shape. Only my grip slipped and I cut my finger so deep we had to go to the ER.

Every step of the way, my mom was sweet and attentive. My dad was out on some errand. He must have rushed to meet us at the ER, but he was still calm.

I was never scared, not really. I knew it would be okay, that my parents would protect me.

My eyes flutter closed. I'm back in the ER again, only it's right after the accident. I'm not calm. I'm terrified. The nurse is giving me the bad news, that mom and dad are gone, that Lizzy is in the ICU. I'm running down the halls without any awareness of my legs moving, then staring through the glass window watching her heart rate on the monitor.

I was terrified she was going to die. Not just for her sake, but because I couldn't bear to lose her. I couldn't bear to be alone.

My legs go weak. I press my back against the fridge and slide down, all the way to the floor. I'm still here, in Blake's apartment, but I'm powerless and terrified all the same.

It's too easy to lose everything that matters.

What if I lose Blake too?

A tear stings my eyes. There's no use in fighting it. I pull my knees into my chest and dig my fingers into the rough fabric of my jeans.

There are footsteps, but I don't look up. Then there are arms around me. Blake slings his arm under my knees, carries me to the couch, and lays me down on my back.

He runs his finger along my collarbone.. No words. What good would words do? They won't bring back my parents. They won't bring back Meryl. They won't ease this.

I finally manage to blink my eyes open. He's staring at me protectively. He holds up a bottle of anti-bacterial cream. I nod as if to give him permission.

Blake is tender as he cleans and treats my minor wound. He does it with ease, like he's treated plenty of wounds before.

He *has* treated plenty of wounds before.

The thought tears at my gut.

His fingers brush my cheek. "What are you thinking?"

"I'm scared."

"Of what?"

"Losing you." I throw my head back to see out the window. It's still blinding white. "I lost almost everything once. I don't know if I can do it again."

He slides onto the couch next to me. His fingers go to my chin and he tilts me so we're eye to eye. "Would you like to discuss it?"

I shake my head.

"How about get your mind off it?"

His eyes flash. He's not offering to watch a movie or play a game. At least not a conventional game.

"We need to put the cookies in the oven," I say.

He smiles. "How are you so able to put other things ahead of what you want?"

I've been doing it a long time. Not as much anymore, but it's a hard habit to break.

"I'll put them in the oven after I take care of you." He presses his lips against my forehead. "Do you want to rest?"

"No."

"Do you want a release?"

I don't hesitate. "Yes."

"Then sit up straight and unzip your jeans."

I move as fast as humanly possible. Faster even. In a flash, I'm upright and my zipper is down. I don't dare do anything else to my jeans.

Blake kneels in front of me. "Ass up."

I do as I'm asked.

He pulls my jeans over my ass then down my thighs. He does it slowly, revealing one inch at a time.

An ache builds between my legs. I need him touching me properly. And I need to touch him. I only hope he can tell how desperate I am to feel all of him.

Finally, he pulls the jeans off my feet. His fingers trace his work, up my calves and thighs. They settle on my hips and tug at the sides of my panties.

These are a much sexier pair. Black lace boyshorts that make my ass look fantastic. Blake licks his lips, pleased. It takes everything I have not to pull off my sweater to show him the matching bra.

"Did you wear those for me?" he asks.

"Yes," I breathe. "In case it was too much. I wanted something that would grab your attention as quickly as possible."

His expression is heavy with lust. It worked. I can't say that I have any desire to brag.

I spread my legs, shifting closer to the edge of the couch.

Blake grabs my knees and holds me in place. "Patience."

His fingers trail up my thighs again. My breath picks up. My heart races. My body is not patient. It needs him touching me. It needs something to chase everything else away.

"Stand up." He pats the ground in front of the couch. "Feet here."

I shift off the couch. He's right in front of me, his head about two inches from my sex. My thighs clench in anticipation. Yes, please. I want that mouth on me.

He digs his hands into the flesh of my ass. Then his nails. The burst of pain calls all my attention. My concerns about holidays, my memories, my desperate fear of losing control— all of that fades away until there's nothing but his nails against my skin.

Blake grabs the sides of my panties. Slowly, he pulls them off my ass, down my thighs, all the way to my feet. His hands close around my ankles like he's warning me not to kick the underwear out of the way.

His breath is warm against my skin. I shake. I have to dig my hands into the outside of my hips to keep from moving.

He goes slow, tracing his way back up my leg. He brings his arm around my ass and uses it to push my body forward. It's almost impossible to keep my balance, especially with his breath sending shockwaves over my sex.

"Don't move," he says.

"But—"

"Not until you come."

He presses his lips against my pelvis. Then an inch below. Then his lips are against my clit.

Don't move? How the hell am I supposed to manage that? He slides between my legs and licks me from top to bottom.

It takes every ounce of attention to do anything but collapse. I press my calves against the front of the couch. It's the only way to keep my balance as Blake licks me.

His tongue is soft, wet, and so, so warm. Every flick of it sends a wave of pleasure through me. Usually, I'd grab his hair and clench my toes. Without an outlet, I go deep into the ecstasy. It's so intense that I lose track of the entire world.

All I know is Blake's tongue on me. It works magic, soft and flat then hard and pointed, fast and greedy then slow and patient. He moans into the inside of my thigh. He needs this as much as I do.

"Blake," I groan.

It urges him on. He brings his free hand to my thigh. It's two inches away. Then one.

His finger teases my sex.

I gasp. My knees buckle, but I manage to stay upright. If I move, he'll stop. I may not be bound, but I'm still at his mercy.

And God, how I love being at his mercy.

"Blake." It's a plea as much as anything.

It doesn't work. He runs his finger along me, making zig zags but not going inside me. His tongue slides over my clit, focusing in on just the right spot.

Pleasure bursts through me. It's hard to stay upright. I close my eyes to focus on the sensation. The pressure inside me is deep. A few more moments and I'll be at the edge. Then I'll be coming so hard I can't breathe.

But I'm getting ahead of myself. I need to be here, right in this moment, soaking in the feeling of Blake's soft tongue.

Heat builds between my legs with every lick. He brings his hand back to my sex, teasing mercilessly. I fight my desire to beg. He won't leave me without.

Just when I want it enough to scream, Blake slides his finger inside me. I sigh in relief. Yes. I need him inside me, even if it's his fingers and not his cock.

He brings his teeth to my thigh, nipping at my skin as he fucks me with his finger. I groan. I shake. I squeeze my fingertips together. Anything except moving out of this position.

He adds another finger. His teeth sink hard into my thigh.

It's too much. It feels too good. My knees buckle and I fall right back on the couch. So close to the edge but not quite there.

Blake's eyes are on fire. He pulls off his sweater and his t-shirt. I scan his body like it's the first time. Broad shoulders, strong chest, perfect abs, soft tuft of hair above his jeans.

My body is aching, desperate for release. "Blake," I groan. "Please."

"You're not coming yet." He digs his hand into my hair. "On your knees."

A spark ignites inside me. That's almost as good. Better even. I shift off the couch, on my knees in front of him, so I'm face to face with his crotch.

His hard cock is pressing against his jeans. I want to drag my fingers over it, but I have to wait. He's not taking this away from me.

"Unzip my jeans," he says.

I do.

"Do you want to touch me, Kat?"

"Yes."

"Do you want to suck my cock?"

"Yes."

He pushes his jeans off his hips. Then the boxers. I press my hands against my thighs to contain my desperate need to touch him. Not until he says.

He digs his hand into my hair and presses lightly, bringing me closer. My lips brush against him. I look up at him as if to ask permission. It's there, in his eyes.

I grab onto his hips, using them for leverage as I take

him into my mouth. It's just as much of a release, pressing my tongue against him, sucking on his tip.

A low, deep groan escapes from his lips. It pushes me so, so close to the edge. I wrap one hand around him and stroke him as I take him deep.

I flick my tongue against his tip, teasing him the way he teases me. His touch gets rougher, desperate. He presses against the back of my head, urging me to go deeper.

I look up at him as I take him in. His eyes are still commanding but they're also filled with desire. His whole face is wrecked with desire, like he can barely control himself.

He tastes good and he feels better. I suck on him untilhis thighs clench. Until he's shaking.

Blake tugs hard at my hair, pulling me off him. He shakes like he's at the edge, like he's desperate for release.

"Turn around, hands on the top of the couch, knees on the cushion," he says.

I do it as quickly as possible. He brings his hands to my hips, positioning his body behind mine. His cock strains against my sex. I let out a deep sigh. His follows.

"Come with me." He slides inside me.

I gasp, digging my hands into the soft leather fabric of the couch. Blake moves fast. His nails are sharp against my hips as he pumps into me. It's hard and deep. Within moments, I'm at the edge. The pressure inside me is so intense I can barely contain myself.

My thighs shake. I groan. "Blake. I'm almost there."

He scrapes his nails against my skin. The burst of pain shoots through me, mixing with the ecstasy and forming a much more powerful combination. My body is desperate for release, like it's been waiting a million years, but I need another moment of this.

His hand comes down hard on my ass. Yes. There. He

does it again, and again. The rush of pain pushes me forward, until my thighs are shaking.

I lose control of my breath. All I can do is embrace the sensations he's creating in me. A burst of pain. A rush of pleasure. A tension growing tighter and tighter.

There. I'm at the edge. I groan as I come, my sex spasming around his cock, pulling him closer.

He spanks me again—I went before him. I disobeyed his orders—but it only spurs me on. The pressure releases and builds up. I'm about to come again already. I sink my teeth into my lip, desperate to come with him this time.

Blake drags his nails over my back, from my neck all the way to my ass. He thrusts into me harder, deeper, faster. He groans, almost there.

I close my eyes, soaking in the feeling of him inside me, the pulsing in his cock as he gets closer to the edge. The pressure inside me builds to a crescendo. One more thrust, and he's there, pulsing and groaning. It pushes me into another orgasm.

Pleasure fills my body as I come down. It's harder, deeper, all the way to my toes.

Blake slides out. He wraps his arms around me and pulls me onto the couch next to him.

He strokes my hair as if he's asking *feel better?*

I nod. Much better.

———

After we catch our breath, Blake takes me to the bathroom and runs a bath. He strips off my sweater and tank top. His eyes go wide like he's taking me in. He clearly appreciates the bra, even if the matching panties are in the other room.

He traces the outline of the bra, then runs his fingers

over the lace. The fabric strains against my nipple, filling me with a desperate desire. How can it be possible to want him so quickly?

"You wore this for me too?" he asks.

"I don't have any other fiancé to wear it for."

His lips curl into a smile. He runs his fingers over the bra, starting at the outline and working his way down the cups. I gasp when his fingers skim my nipples. The fabric is creating all sorts of delightful friction.

"Can you stay still this time?" he asks. "You'll hurt yourself if you slip on the tile."

I shake my head. "Still" is unlikely with the way he's touching me.

He grabs a towel and lays it on the floor. "On your back."

"But—"

"Do you want to come again?"

I nod.

"Then now."

I do as I'm asked. The towel provides little cushion against the hard tile, but I'm so keyed up I don't mind.

Blake lies next to me. "Arms above your head."

I raise my arms. He holds me in place just above my elbows. Then he presses his lips into mine. The kiss is long and deep. My arms struggle against his. He maintains control, pressing me hard against the tile floor.

He works his way down my neck and collarbone. To my chest. To just outside the edge of the bra. He pulls one cup down so my breast spills out. It's enough to make me gasp. His tongue flicks against my nipple, sending a wave of pleasure down my stomach. I've already felt so much, but I still want more. Am I greedy or blessed with a sex god for a fiancé?

He sucks on my nipples one at a time. It's hard but not

enough to hurt. His free hand trails over my stomach and between my legs. No teasing this time. He slides his fingers over my clit, then inside me.

I go to tug at his hair. He holds me in place. It's different than being tied up, but I'm just as powerless. If I didn't trust him so deeply, I'd be terrified of the feeling of being overpowered.

But I do trust him, and that makes this so much better. He hooks his leg over my knees, increasing the force of his hold. My eyes flutter closed. I sigh, relaxing completely into his control.

I'm his. Utterly his.

He teases my nipples as he finger-fucks me. Every motion of his hand and every brush of his lips pushes me closer to the edge. I surrender to the sensation, so the only thing I can feel is the pleasure building between my legs.

His breath strains. I open my eyes to look at him, so I can see all the desire on his face. He's in control of his expressions but hints of want break through.

He doesn't have to ask. I hold his gaze, staring into him, the man who makes me feel so good I could die, the man who means everything to me.

A few more thrusts and an orgasm wells up inside me. I groan his name. Almost. His eyes close as he sucks on my nipple. The pressure of his mouth sends me over the edge. I come, pleasure pulsing through my body.

Blake releases me. He gets up to turn off the running water. Somehow, the tub is perfectly filled. Magic powers or just Blake? Sometimes it's hard to tell the difference.

———

We take a long, slow bath together. Blake washes and conditions my hair and rubs me down with a bottle of vanilla scented body wash. The only thing that can convince me to leave is my appetite.

It's well past a normal lunch time. We order Thai delivery then bake and decorate cookies while we wait. I make a mess of every bowl in the kitchen in my attempts to mix the perfect icing colors. It's worth it for the lovely shade of pink I make. I get to work on a star, painting it white then adorning it with cherry blossom petals. Not Christmas-themed, but I don't care. They make me think about Blake. They make me think about why this kind of thing matters.

Life is short and I want to spend it running to the beauty in the world instead of running away from the pain.

Blake is less creative in his decorations. He paints the snowmen white, the trees green, the stars blue. I add ornaments to his trees, scarves and hats to his snowmen, neat patterns to his stars. He watches me with affection.

Lunch tastes damn good. I eat my entire bowl of red curry shrimp and still have room for two sugar cookies. They're as good as the ones I made with my parents so many years ago. The memory still stings, but mostly it feels good.

I offer Blake his choice of Christmas movies, any movie in the entire world. He picks *Die Hard*, of course. What is with men and movies where things blow up?

It's entertaining enough. Better than watching *The Matrix: Revolutions* again. I have no doubt Lizzy will subject us to all seven hours of *The Matrix Trilogy* sometime in the next few days.

The movie isn't quite my scene. I rest my head in Blake's lap with every intention of staying awake. Just a few minutes with my eyes closed…

It's a few hours later when I wake. The sky is orange. Sunset. Blake isn't here, but there's a note on my phone.

Blake: Went to pick up Lizzy at the airport. We should be home by six. I'll order a pizza for dinner.

I smile. Blake and Lizzy don't see eye to eye on much, but they agree violently when it comes to two things: how amazing programming is and how much New York pizza blows California pizza out of the water.

I find my sketchbook in my purse and set myself up on the couch to draw. Something in the corner of the room catches my eyes. A flash of green.

It's the tree. It's up. And it's decorated with exactly three candy canes.

My heart melts.

———

Lizzy bursts in through the door, a bundle of energy. "Sterling, if you are teasing me, I will throw you off this balcony." She drops her suitcase on the floor and throws her coat on top of it.

Blake slides both out of the way. He closes and locks the door. "I don't tease anyone but Kat."

Lizzy sticks her tongue out in disgust. "Jesus, please keep that to yourself. I don't need the mental images." She scans the penthouse, her eyes wide. "Is there any place here you two haven't— Ugh. Don't tell me."

"At the very least, he'd take you on as an intern. You're better than anyone out of a hack school."

She glares at Blake. "Is that supposed to be a compliment?"

He smiles.

"I'm better than most junior programmers. Not in Silicon Valley, but in New York, fuck yes. Have you seen what passes for code some places?" She folds her arms over her chest.

I cut in. "How many cans of Diet Coke did you drink on the plane?"

"It's free. It's a bad value if you don't drink until your bladder explodes." She turns to me. Her face softens as she bounces over and hugs me. "I missed you." She steps back. "Your hair looks cute. When did you get lowlights?"

"I felt weird all blonde."

"I dig." She tosses her hair back as if to compare styles. Her expression shifts back to Blake. "You're less greedy than I always figured."

He doesn't blink. "How so?"

"Well, you stay in New York even though you should be in Silicon Valley. Because Silicon Valley blows and New York is the greatest city in the entire world." She goes to the fridge, scans it and frowns. "No soda? Don't tell me you buy into that Bloomberg soda ban bullshit? Only sixteen ounces at a time. What a—"

"It's bad for you." My voice is stern, like a lecturing mother.

Blake rubs my shoulder. "We can order soda with the pizza."

"Oh, he's the permissive parent." Lizzy takes a seat at the kitchen island. "Wouldn't have guessed that."

"You were explaining my lack of greed," Blake says.

"Yeah. You're sacrificing a lot of potential profits to stay in New York." She makes eye contact with me. "That's the only reason why I trust him at all."

Blake is unfazed by her talking about him as if he's not in the room. It's no secret that Lizzy only trusts Blake as far as she can throw him. But she must be willing to put it aside. She's helped him arrange a number of surprises, including his marriage proposal.

Lizzy runs her hand over the counter, scraping off a fine layer of sugar. "You made cookies without me?"

"Let's make more now." I nod to Blake. "You order the pizza. We'll make a mess."

His eyes connect with mine. "I'll punish you for that later."

Lizzy screws her face in disgust. "I'm going to pretend I didn't hear that."

I go to help Lizzy bake. She has a massive sweet tooth and knows every ratio without consulting a recipe. This time, I'm extra careful with the cookie cutters.

Blake orders dinner then excuses himself to fit in a half hour of work.

We catch up on silly things—her recent hairstyles, the terrible weather in San Francisco (it's cold in August), the news about the most recent *Star Wars* film. There's a sadness underlying her caffeine-induced energy high. I get the sense she's not happy on the other side of the country.

Before I have a chance to probe, the pizza arrives. We eat together, on paper plates, while watching the first Matrix movie. Then the second. Despite drinking an entire two liter bottle of diet soda, Lizzy falls asleep on the couch.

"Would you like me to put her in the spare room?" Blake asks.

I shake my head. "She'll wake up here and finish the trilogy. Then we don't have to watch *Revolutions*."

"I love all the Matrix movies."

"A third thing you have in common. You're almost best friends."

Blake pulls me off the couch. "Are you ready for bed?"

For bed, yes. But I'm not ready for my sister to wake up to the sounds of us having sex. He didn't offer, but I still don't want him to get the wrong idea.

I squeeze his shoulder. "I don't want to do anything while she's here."

"She's here for three weeks."

"I'll meet you at the office sometime." I bite my lip. "And she'll be out a lot. She gets stir crazy easily."

I brush my teeth, wash my face, and change into pajamas. Blake is already in bed in a very cozy gray pajama set. It's the kind of thing that makes him look casual and effortlessly put together at the same time.

It has a monogram.

A monogram.

After a few minutes with a sci-fi novel, he turns off the light and pulls my body close to his.

I fill with warmth. "Is it okay, all this Christmas stuff?"

"For now. The twenty-fifth was always the worst."

"Oh." I take a deep breath. "You might still bail."

He says nothing.

"When will you let me know?"

"Tomorrow. After dinner." He rests his hand on my stomach. His voice is even. "Fiona will join us. We can order Chinese food and watch *Lethal Weapon*."

Another action movie that technically takes place on Christmas. That part is fine. I'm willing to watch anything if it means I get my holiday with Blake.

I pull my blanket tighter. "Which way are you leaning?"

"I want to be there."

"But you're not sure if you can handle it?"

He presses his lips against my neck. "I'm going to take care of some things tomorrow. I'll be home for dinner."

"But—"

"I've had you for three-and-a-half months. She can have you for half a day."

I nod. Lizzy will want to go shopping. She's always been last minute about buying gifts.

I press my eyes closed, willing my worry to melt away. But it sticks with me. I need Blake here on Christmas. I need him here, with me.

Christmas Eve

Blake is gone when I wake. Sure enough, Lizzy is on the couch with a cup of coffee and a bowl of cereal, watching *The Matrix: Revolutions.*

"I'm shocked that Blake has cereal," she says. "It's normal for him."

"He's very normal."

"Neither are you, so it works." She finishes her coffee with a long sip. "I hope you cleaned this couch after the last time you made sweet, sweet love on it."

My cheeks flush. I always wipe off the couch after sex. Can't ruin the gorgeous apartment.

"Have you always been such a pervert?" I fix myself a cup of coffee and stay in the kitchen.

"Mm-hmm."

"You need to shower before we go shopping, or do you want to leave when I'm done with my drink?"

"Are you using his credit card?"

"No."

"Good." She stands up, stretching her arms over her head. "I don't want any of his money."

"You drank that soda he bought pretty fast."

"Thirst got the best of me."

———

We take the subway to Thirty-Fourth Street and spend the morning at Macy's. It's packed to the brim. The shelves are picked over. None of that bothers Lizzy. She pushes past anyone in her way, honing in on deeply discounted winter clothing.

Lunch is more pizza. I consider lecturing her about healthy eating but decide against it. She hasn't gained any of the Freshman Fifteen and she looks perfectly healthy— clear skin, shiny hair, muscle tone in her shoulders. That car accident did a number on her back. She has to exercise aggressively to keep it in check.

After lunch, it's back to shopping. We stop in a dozen different boutiques. She buys a scarf for Blake. It has a reference to a TV show I've never heard of, but she's certain he'll love it. She even buys something for Fiona. It's a fairly generic gift, a bottle of gingerbread scented lotion, but it's something.

The pizza isn't providing me with the steady energy I need for this. By three, the excess carbs has me in a major crash. It doesn't help that I skipped breakfast.

I stop in a cafe for a coffee and a salad.

Lizzy eyes my snack with distaste. "You lost weight. At least five pounds."

"How can you possibly notice that I lost five pounds?"

"You admit it."

"I started running again."

"Around the park?" She sighs wistfully. "Must be nice having it across the street."

"You can stay with me and Blake if you want."

"Stay with my sister and her fiancé? There's no way that will be awkward. Or that I would be a painfully unwanted third wheel."

"Awkward, maybe. But I… wait. You're not going to leave school, are you?"

She sips her vanilla latte. "That's my decision, you know."

My stomach drops. "Are you?"

She makes eye contact, fierce and unwilling to back down. "No. But if I want to, I will. And don't even think about offering me any of Blake's money to go to school in New York. Or his scholarship. That is so unethical—"

"What about the money from renting Mom and Dad's apartment? I don't need it—"

"I'm not taking your money."

I squeeze my fork. "It's our money."

"Not. Taking. It. Offer it a million times, but it's not happening." She runs her finger over the plastic lid. "You've given up a lot to help me already. I can't take anything else."

That's not how it is, but I know better than to argue with her. If she doesn't want help, fine. I'll find a way to help without her realizing it.

She steals a grape tomato. "It's possible I'll be in New York next year. An internship here."

"What Blake was talking about yesterday?"

She nods. "But I don't want his help getting it. All he did was point out the application."

At this point, she's being obscenely defensive. I open my mouth to object.

She cuts me off. "Did you want his help getting into Columbia?"

"Okay. Fair. I won't offer you anything. Not even a bite of my salad." I stab a piece of lettuce with my fork.

"You have any more shopping to do?"

"One place."

She raises her eyebrow.

"You'll see."

We chat about nothing while I finish my salad.

Outside, the sky is blue and the sun is shining. Midtown is gorgeous—a mix of tall buildings and frosted parks.

I turn over Blake's words in my head. There's a chance he won't be there when I wake up tomorrow, that I'll spend the entire day alone.

Lizzy isn't going to take this well.

I take a deep breath, adopting my most *it's totally okay* voice. "Blake might not be here tomorrow."

She clears her throat.

"He might have an emergency meeting."

"Either he has a family you don't know about or you're lying to cover something up." She doesn't waver. "Should I spend the last of my shopping money to buy you a clue?"

"He has a lot of bad associations with the holiday."

She scoffs. "And?"

"His dad was abusive, Lizzy. That doesn't heal overnight."

"Are you happy with him?"

"Yes."

"Good." Her voice gets serious. "But that's a load of crap. He can't bail on Christmas because he has a few bad memories."

I turn on Thirty-Sixth Street. The light is red and cars are whizzing by the avenue.

Lizzy taps her toe. "He can use all his sweet words or his beautiful money, but that doesn't matter. What he does matters."

"You've never been in a relationship." The light turns green and I step into the street.

She follows. "I understand. He says he loves you. He promises the world. Then he leaves on Christmas." She walks in front of me. "Anything I'm missing?"

"No." Deep down, I believe he'll be there tomorrow. I believe he'll do this for me. But what if he can't?

"If he hates it so much, how did you get him to put up a tree?" She steps onto the sidewalk, racing into the shade. "Actually, don't tell me. Those details will scar me for life."

She's kidding, but what if she's right? He only put up the tree after we had sex. Doubt passes through me. He was doing that for me, because I was hurting. There's no way I convinced him to put up the tree, not by screwing him.

"Do you think about anything besides sex or computers?"

She shakes her head. "You promise he's treating you okay?"

"Better than okay. He's amazing."

She stops to lean against a concrete wall. "And it's not just…" Her eyes find mine. "Don't take this the wrong way, because you're the least materialistic person I know, but are you sure it's not his money?"

"Yes."

"Or his amazing cock. I only assume it's amazing, but—"

"What is wrong with you?"

"Because I wouldn't blame you. Marry the billionaire, live the lux life, draw whatever your heart desires. You deserve the break, but you're better than lying to yourself."

"I'm not with Blake for his money." No way am I discussing the latter point.

"How do you know?"

"I don't love when he spends money on me. I love

when he washes my hair, when he makes me breakfast, when he holds me all night."

"In his ten-million-dollar penthouse apartment."

"It could be anywhere."

She pushes off the wall, waiting for directions. I nod to the avenue in front of us.

She walks quickly. "Does he really wash your hair?"

"It's nice."

Lizzy finishes her drink and tosses it toward a trash can. It misses.

She kneels down to pick it up. Her expression strains as she stands, like her back is bothering her again. "Thank you for not adding 'when he makes me come like a waterfall.'"

"Where do you come up with this?"

The lingerie shop is around the corner. It's cozy with pink walls, red carpet, and oodles of adorable underwear.

I scan the walls. "Are you having sex?"

"Not regularly." She says it casually.

I know my sister. She's taunting me on purpose. No way am I taking the bait.

"As long as you're safe." I move to the next row. "When you say regularly—"

"There was only one guy in California." She folds her arms. "One guy, one time. It was nice. I used a condom. I don't expect I'll ever see him again."

"Great." Not great. I take a deep breath but my chest feels tight. My sister is nineteen. She's going to have sex. It's normal behavior.

"Doesn't bother you at all."

"Of course not." I grab a pink bra and panty set. "Just like it doesn't bother you hearing about my sex life."

She sticks her tongue out. "That's different. I'm

disgusted by the details. You want me to be your innocent baby sister."

I admit nothing.

"I'm going to wait outside. I love you, Kat, but I don't want to picture you in lingerie. And I really don't want to picture Blake— Ugh." She groans like she can't avoid a mental picture. "You have twenty minutes until I get bored of my smart phone."

The bell rings as she leaves the store. I turn back to the wall, all my attention focused on finding the perfect piece of lingerie.

It has to drive Blake out of his mind and hint at the holiday spirit. A positive association with Christmas.

Of course, there's a chance that it will keep him from touching me, but that's a risk I'm willing to take.

There. I find a red bra and panty set. It's peekaboo style. I try the bra on in the dressing room.

When I check my reflection, I gasp. The red band lifts my breasts. It stops a few inches below my nipple. The straps make a triangle-shaped outline. It does nothing to limit access to my breasts. Blake won't even have to remove it.

A rush of heat passes through me. I'm sexy and ready to be touched.

Hopefully, I'll get to make use of the feeling.

———

Lizzy and I spend a few hours on the couch, recuperating from our shopping marathon with popcorn and bad TV.

Around eight, Blake and Fiona arrive together. He's holding takeout bags. She's holding two neatly wrapped presents and a bottle of wine. She places the presents under the tree, for us to open tomorrow.

The takeout isn't the greasy Chinese food of my past celebrations. It's healthy stir fry from a fusion restaurant. Rich people takeout. The vegetables are fresh and crisp. The seasonings are perfectly mild. No excess of salt or sugar, just flavor.

Conversation starts stiff but relaxes. Lizzy has nothing in common with Fiona and she's not too happy with the way Fiona tried to bribe me to leave Blake. Thank God, my sister is polite. She manages to talk about a TV show they both like.

By the time we're on dessert—sticky rice and mango, plus sugar cookies dotted with sprinkles—everyone is having a good time. Not a family yet, but something close.

Fiona leaves after dinner. I go to help Blake clean up.

"I'm going to get out of here." Lizzy looks at Blake like they're sharing a secret. "Blake told me about the Sterling Tech hotel suite. It's empty and it sounds really nice."

"Stay here."

"It's fine. I'm sure you two need to… talk." Her eyes light up mischievously. "And other things. I'll be back in the morning. I'll bring coffee." She hugs me goodbye. "Merry Christmas, Kat. I'll see you tomorrow. You're going to love your present."

"Goodnight." I kiss her on the forehead and squeeze her as tightly as I can. It's been miserable having her halfway across the country, but I can't deny how independent and self-assured she seems.

"Do you want me to call a car?" Blake says.

"I hate cars. But thank you." Lizzy looks at me. "He really is polite." She waves on her way out the door.

And then it's me and Blake alone.

This is it, time for his answer. I take a deep breath. But, before I can start, he wraps his arms around me.

He pulls me close. "I have a surprise for you. But you can't have it until after we go up to the roof."

I like the sound of this. "What kind of surprise?"

"No clues." He squeezes me tighter. "Get your coat."

We don our outerwear and climb the stairs to the roof. It's snowing.

Perfect white snowflakes blow around in the wind. Better than anything I could ever draw. Better than any snow I've ever seen.

Cold air nips at my nose and mouth. I stick my tongue out and catch a snowflake. Blake is staring at me with wonder, the way he always does. You'd think he'd be used to me by now.

"What are you looking at?" I ask.

"I love when you get that look in your eyes," he says. "Like you can't believe how amazing the world is."

"Because I can't believe how amazing the world is."

I squat down to pick up a clump of snow. There's actual powder on the roof! We never get powder in New York City. The well-tread sidewalks mean the snow melts into slush.

Blake watches me pack a snowball. It's messier than the ones I made as a kid, but it's still completely marvelous.

"Not everyone sees it that way," he says.

I hold up my arm like I'm going to deck him with the snowball. He sees past my bluff. He doesn't even blink.

"Yes, some people are cynical tech CEOs who have too much money to appreciate little things like gorgeous views and perfect snowfalls," I say.

His lips curl into a smile. "It would be awful to know someone like that."

"Truly awful."

I toss him the snowball and he catches it. He stares at it like it fascinates him. Was his childhood really so awful he never got into snowball fights? A pang hits my chest. He's had such a hard life. It's a miracle that he's ever happy.

"Don't go feeling sorry for me, Kat. I'm the happiest man alive."

"Really?"

He moves closer. "Every day, I get to see the world through your eyes." He leans down to press his lips into mine. "Every day, I get to wake up next to you."

"Is it really that great?"

"Better." He holds the snowball over my head. Then he smashes it on my hat. "And I always win."

Oh, it's a snowball fight he wants, it's a snowball fight he'll get. "Not this time."

I lean down to pack another snowball. Blake moves fast. He darts to the door behind the stairs, no doubt packing an armory.

I get busy making snowballs and carry them around in my hat. I move as quietly as I can, but I can't manage to sneak up on him. He darts to the open area and hurls a snowball at me.

It smacks my chest with a light impact. I squeal in delight. It's been years since I've done this.

I launch a snowball at Blake. He dodges it. But he's not lucky for long. My next throw hits him right in the chest. His neat wool coat isn't so neat anymore.

He laughs. Still the best sound I've ever heard. Still makes me feel warm all over.

We get lost in our snowball fight, racing around the roof and pelting each other. When I'm out of snowballs, Blake tackle-hugs me to the ground. There's enough soft snow that it doesn't hurt.

He kisses me, his tongue sliding into my mouth, his body sinking into mine. That warmth turns to a desperate, coursing heat. Even with my head pressed against the snow, I'm burning up.

When our kiss breaks, I stare straight into his eyes. They used to be impenetrable. But I've learned how to read them.

And they're just as filled with desire as I am.

"Let's call it a draw," I say.

"Rematch soon." He pushes himself to his feet and helps me up. He brings his mouth to my ear. "I hope you won't miss the snow."

"It's going to be freezing until March. Always is."

Blake leads me to the staircase. "Not in St. Barts."

I turn to look at him. "What do you mean, not in St. Barts? I've seen your work calendar and there's no St. Barts on it."

He shakes his head. "We're leaving Friday and we'll be there for two weeks."

"But Lizzy will be alone for New Year's."

"It was her idea," Blake says.

"Was it her idea to leave us alone tonight?"

He nods.

"But last time I mentioned vacation you said that a three-day weekend was the best you could do. That Sterling Tech would fall without your capable hands at the wheel."

Thoughts of sun and sand dance around my brain as we climb back to the penthouse floor. Blake watches me the whole time, smiling like he's sure he's got me exactly where he wants me.

He unlocks all three locks to our apartment. "I'd rather have my capable hands on you."

All of a sudden, I'm scorching hot.

"But what if the company falls without you?" I ask.

"Then it falls. You're more important."

"Say it again."

Blake rubs my arms. His hands stop at my shoulders and he looks me in the eyes. "You're more important than anything, Kat. Even my company."

"Even..." I hold his gaze. "Does this mean you'll be here tomorrow?"

"You'll have your answer in two minutes." He points to the bedroom. "Follow me."

Christmas

According to the clock on the microwave, it's 12:05. I'm so anxious waiting for Blake's answer that it registers slowly. It's Christmas.

He pulls me into the bedroom. Not the sex room/extra guest room but the bedroom where we sleep every night.

It's transformed, decked in holiday adornments that are very, very Blake. Red silk sheets. A plush striped comforter. String lights hanging from the walls.

And mistletoe right on top of the headboard.

Blake enters holding a neatly wrapped present. It's about the size of a shoe box. Shiny red paper. Soft white bow.

"But," I take a deep breath, "you hate Christmas. You can't put it in your bedroom if you hate it."

I turn and stare into his eyes. They're soft. Like he's happy.

"You were right. Running away didn't help. It only gave my father power over me." His expression softens. "It's terrifying, but I have to face those memories if I want to move on. I do want that, Kat. I want to share all my life with you. Even the parts that hurt."

"Every single part?"

He nods. "You really have no idea what you do to me."

"How could I do anything to you?"

"You've given me the world."

What? If anything, he's given me the world. I shake my head. "But you're—"

"Rich?"

I nod.

"There's more to the world than money." He runs his fingers over my cheek. "Before we met, I spent all my time in my office. I was so desperate to stay in control that I wasn't open to anything that wasn't my way. But you… you've showed me how beautiful the world can be. You've forced me to open myself to that."

I swallow hard.

"Do you remember when we went to Paris?"

"Of course. We spent more time in the hotel than out of it."

"True." He smiles. "It wasn't the first time I'd been to Paris, but it was the first time I enjoyed it."

"Because we were—"

"No, Kat, though I adored the part in the hotel room. It was because it the first time the city seemed beautiful."

"But, it's Paris. How could it not be beautiful?"

He pulls me close. "How did I get so lucky to have you?"

"But it is beautiful. How could you see it otherwise?"

He offers no explanation. He doesn't have to. I remember the Blake I met last spring. The world was something for him to control. He didn't see it as beautiful. He didn't see it at all.

Blake steps back. "I have a present for you."

"Those are supposed to wait until tomorrow."

"You won't want to open this one in front of your sister." He pulls a wrapped box out of the dresser and hands it to me.

I unwrap it slowly. It's an unmarked box. Inside is a sleek velvet pouch. I study Blake for a clue. His expression is demanding—the look he gets when it's time for him to take control.

My breath strains. My hands are totally unsteady as I open the pouch. It's a vibrator. Heavy. Silver.

Oh my God. It's actual silver. Sterling silver. I almost laugh. Blake Sterling bought me a sterling silver vibrator.

It must have cost a fortune.

His eyes find mine. "Don't worry about the price." He shifts into the arm chair across from the bed. "The show I'm about to get is worth every penny."

Tension builds between my legs. He wants to watch me. We've never done that, not like this.

"Put it on the bed," he says.

I hesitate.

"Kat, do you want to do this?"

Hell yes. I nod.

"Good. Now set the vibrator on the bed."

I do.

Blake's eyes are glued to mine. "Take off your sweater. And your jeans."

I shimmy out of my clothes. I'm wearing nothing but a tank top over the peekabo red bra and panty set.

Blake's eyes scan my body. They stop at my chest and my crotch. Seems that my present to myself is working just as well on him.

His breath hitches, but he stays planted firmly in the chair. "Take off the top."

I pull it over my head. His eyes go wide. He's looking at

me like he wants to consume me, like the sight of me is enough to take him all the way to the edge.

His gaze goes to my bra. "Did you buy that today?"

"Yes."

"I like it."

"Thank you."

"Turn around, so I can get a better look."

I turn slowly. My cheeks flush. A hint of nervousness rises up in my chest. Then Blake groans and it all melts away. I'm not nervous or shy or anything but desperate to reveal myself to him.

Whatever he wants to see.

Back to my original position, my eyes meet his.

Heat passes through me, collecting between my legs.

"Touch your breasts," he says.

I go to rub my thumb over my nipples.

"Slower. Cup them first."

I cup my breasts, pressing my palms against my nipples. He's going to torture me making this take forever, but I really can't complain.

His eyes are fixed on my chest, wide with desire.

He leans back in his chair, spreading his legs to take up as much space as possible. "Play with your nipples."

Finally. My fingers waste no time. Every touch and pinch sends a shock wave to my core. I can barely keep my eyes open. It already feels so good.

My breath picks up until I'm panting. I squeeze my nipples hard, the way he does. My sex clenches, desperate for a build-up and release. Desperate for Blake.

He's watching me with rapt attention. "Keep your panties on while you touch yourself. But do it slowly."

My hand goes up my thigh reflexively. I look to Blake as if to ask permission. He nods. I almost sigh in relief.

I slide my fingers over my clit with a soft touch. It's not as good as if it was Blake, but there's a thrill to him watching me. Tension builds inside me. I'm already keyed up.

His voice gets heavy. "Sit on the bed now."

I do.

"Spread your legs."

I do.

"Wider."

I spread my legs as wide as they'll go. My breath catches in my throat. That same shyness threatens to derail this. The flush in my cheeks spreads to my chest and stomach.

I inhale slowly. It's enough to calm my nerves. There's still all this electricity buzzing through me.

"Don't you want to join me?" I ask.

"After I watch you come."

Blake's eyes find mine. The look that passes between us is enough to melt the last hint of nervous energy.

I want to give myself to him, whatever he wants.

"Turn on the vibrator," he says. "Then come for me."

I pick up the new toy. It takes a few moments of playing with the buttons to get it on. Then it's buzzing in my hands, the way my cell phone does when it's on vibrate, only harder and without ceasing when the call goes to voicemail.

I drag the toy down my stomach. The cool metal warms slowly, until it's not quite so shocking against my skin.

My heart races. Every nerve in my body wakes up as I press the vibrator to my clit.

Holy shit, that's a lot of sensation. More than I've ever felt before.

The knot inside me tightens so damn fast. I'm seconds

from coming. I have to move the toy. This can't be over yet. Not until Blake is panting and groaning too.

Deep breath. I press the toy against my clit again. Pleasure shoots through me. Almost too much. I have to do something to contain it. I slide it down. The sides of my knees strain against the bed.

Blake is staring at me with such rapt attention. He wants this as much as I do, even if he has the self-control to sit all the way over there.

The silver toy nudges at my sex. I'm wet already. It slides inside me with no force at all.

Wow. Not as good as Blake inside me, but amazing all the same. I fuck myself with the toy, taking it as deep as it will go then pulling it almost all the way out. Every time, I get a little closer to the edge. The knot inside me pulls tighter, until it's so tight I can barely take it.

When I finally manage to pull my eyes open, they go straight to Blake. His mouth is hanging open. His pupils are dilated. For once, he's completely at my mercy.

I'm not about to lose this opportunity. I'm going to give him one hell of a show.

I lean back, until I'm flat against the bed. I spread my legs wider. And I fuck myself with the toy. Harder and deeper.

His breath gets heavy. He groans like he can't stand watching without touching.

It all feels good. My body is buzzing with electricity, somehow desperate for more and racing toward an orgasm all at once.

My eyes close. I can't wait anymore. I bring the toy back to my clit and slide it in slow circles until it's in exactly the right spot. Every vibration tightens the knot, sending me closer to the edge. I squeeze the sheets to maintain control, but they're too smooth.

"Blake," I groan.

He's not even touching me and he's making me come.

An orgasm rises up inside me. I need to show him how good he makes me feel. And not just now, but all the damn time. I groan and pant. When that's not enough, I groan his name again and again.

I go over the edge. All the tension inside me unravels, sending waves of pleasure to my fingers and toes. I come so hard I can barely breathe.

I try to turn off the toy, but the buttons are too confusing. I drop it on the ground instead.

Finally, Blake gets out of his chair. I can't see him, but I can hear him. He reaches down, picks up the toy, and turns it off. Then he sits on the bed next to me.

He leans close and strokes my hair. "You're beautiful."

"Thank you." My cheeks flush. "Is that what you meant about the world being beautiful?"

"Not quite." His lips curl into a smile. "Come here."

He slides his arms around my waist and pulls me into his lap. I slide my legs around him, straddling him. He looks up at me, the same way he did when we first made this Christmas deal. Only this time, there's no need to negotiate in his eyes. There's nothing to prove. There's nothing except love.

Pure, deep, true love.

I kiss him hard. It's like his feelings are pouring into me. His words are sweet, but his body says more than words ever could.

He pulls his sweater and t-shirt over his head. I run my hand over the strong muscles on his chest and stomach. Then over his jeans.

The sweetness shifts to something a lot more demanding.

I rub Blake over his jeans. He groans, pressing his lips

against my neck. There's a vulnerability in his eyes. He's not used to me in control.

We shift up on the bed. I press my hands against his shoulders to push him flat. Then I kiss my way from his shoulders to his stomach. Soft skin against hard muscles. He's warm and he tastes so damn good. I unzip his jeans and tug them down his hips. Then the boxers.

I slide my tongue over his tip then take him into my mouth. It's so different than last time I was in this position. Right now, he's at my mercy.

I suck on him until he's groaning and tugging at my hair.

His nails dig into my shoulders. "Get on top of me."

An amazing idea. I shift, straddling him. My hands on his chest, I lower myself onto him.

It's like I'm home.

Blake slides his hands up my sides. They meet between my shoulder blades and he pulls my body onto his. We're pressed together, stomach to stomach, chest to chest.

The skin to skin contact is enough to push me to the brink of an orgasm. My sex clenches, desperate for another release. I dig my hands into his skin to contain myself.

He kisses me hard, sucking on my lower lip. His hands dig into my ass. He holds me in place, shifting his hips to thrust into me.

I melt into his motions. Bliss rises up inside me. How can anyone see the world as anything but beautiful? Everything is in its right place. Everything is perfect.

My eyes flutter closed. I soak in the feeling of his skin against my fingers, his lips against my lips, his cock in my sex. We fit together perfectly, here, there, everywhere.

With his next thrust, I come. My sex spams, clenching him tighter. I moan into his mouth so I don't break contact. He kisses back—hard—his tongue plunging into my mouth like he's claiming it.

In one swift motion, Blake slides his hands around my stomach and shifts us so I'm under him. I hook my legs around his waist. I wrap my arms around his chest.

The weight of his body sinks into me. On the plush foam mattresses, it's perfect.

His lips go to my neck. He bites me gently. His breath speeds up. His arms shake. He's almost there too.

I open my eyes to watch him come. It's such a beautiful thing to see. His teeth sink into his lip. His forehead relaxes. A shudder goes from his forehead all the way to his stomach and toes.

His next motion sends him over the edge. His cock pulses, filling me. I dig my fingers into his skin to hold him close. And I watch the expression of pure bliss form on his face.

He collapses next to me and pulls me close, so I'm his little spoon and he's my big spoon. My eyes close. It must be late now. I'm exhausted, ready to fall asleep in his arms.

We lie together for what feels like an hour.

He breaks the silence. "Are you hungry?"

I nod. "For something small."

Blake shifts off the bed. I take a moment to change out of my lingerie and into a pair of flannel pajamas.

He's in the kitchen, fixing two mugs of hot chocolate. When our eyes meet, he smiles.

"Kat, look." He points to the window.

It's snowing.

Those perfect white flakes from the roof fill the air. A white Christmas. It's an actual white Christmas.

He hands me a mug of cocoa and wraps a blanket around my shoulders. Then he finds a blanket for himself.

Blake leads me out to the balcony. It's freezing, but I

don't mind. It's Christmas and it's snowing and I'm here with the man who is going to be my husband.

Everything in the world is right.

Blake slides his arm around me. "Merry Christmas, Kat."

"Merry Christmas, Blake."

———

Want More?

Thank you so much for picking up *Dirty Deal*. I hope you love Kat and Blake's story as much as I do. Want more of Blake? <u>Sign up for my mailing list</u> to get an exclusive alternate POV scene.

Dirty Boss, featuring Lizzy Wilder and her own mysterious billionaire Nick is <u>available now</u>. Lizzy needs a job if she wants to stay in New York, but her new boss is the man who shared her bed three months ago. He says he never mixes business and pleasure, but some things are too tempting to resist…

Turn the page for a sample.

Dirty Boss

EXCERPT

Chapter One

Buy *Dirty Boss* Now

The elevator doors slide open. I take a deep breath, cultivating every ounce of badass I can muster. Either I nail this interview and get this internship, or I slink back to Stanford for dull classes and three thousand miles between me and everything I love.

Here goes nothing.

The woman sitting behind the reception desk is pure New York City cool. Slick straight black bob. Sleek red dress. Perfect makeup.

"You must be Elizabeth Wilder. I'm Jasmine Lee, the office manager." She shakes my hand with a strong grip.

"Lizzy."

Jasmine smiles. "We mostly go by last names here. It's a lot more formal than the Bay."

She leads me through the modern office. It's sleeker than a typical San Francisco startup. Modern art hangs next to huge windows. The room glows with the soft January light.

We stop in a corner office.

Jasmine motions for me to sit in the leather executive chair. "I'm going to leave you with this programming test. Then Mr. Marlowe is going to come in and ask you a few questions."

My stomach twists. Phoenix Marlowe is the company's CEO, a billionaire programming genius. How am I supposed to impress him?

"He's excited to meet you. He couldn't stop talking about your AI projects." She points to the monitor, now displaying a programming test. "Good luck."

She nods a goodbye on her way out the door.

The second it clicks shut, my attention shifts to the computer screen.

I get lost in the hard but doable questions.

Until I hear his voice.

That same voice I heard that night in San Francisco.

"I hope I haven't surprised you," he says.

That's him. It can't be possible, but that's him. I spin in my chair so we're eye to eye.

What the hell is Nick doing here?

"No," I say. "It's fine."

He closes and locks the door. His gaze drifts to the résumé in his hands. It's like he doesn't recognize me. Maybe he has one-night stands all the time. Maybe it meant nothing to him.

My head fills with the feeling of his body sinking into mine, the taste of whiskey on his lips, the smell of his cologne.

He's wearing the same cologne today.

His eyes flash with something. Anger, I think. He's hard to read.

It's something. Something bad.

He does recognize me. He must.

His voice is rough. "Who is Marie?"

I take a deep breath. "My middle name. And Nick?"

"Phoenix. My friends call me Nick."

"I didn't realize." I press my hand against the slick surface of the desk. "I'm sure this kind of thing has happened before."

His eyes narrow. "No."

"But you're very—"

"I don't go around fucking college students." He places my résumé on the desk and takes a seat behind it.

"I don't go around fucking billionaire programmers." My nostrils flare. My heart pounds. Anger fills my veins. As much as it hurts, meaning nothing to him, I need this opportunity. It's the only way I can stay near Kat. And Kat's the only person I trust. I clear my throat. "Can we start over?"

Frustration spreads across his face. "This project means everything to me."

"Your assistant, Ms. Lee—"

"She's not my assistant."

"Whatever she is, she told me how impressed you were by my board game bots. Is that true?"

"Yes." He stares at me like he's expecting me to back down.

I don't.

"Your programming skills are not up to the standards of Odyssey Industries. Your code is sloppy and inefficient."

"You didn't even look at my programming test."

He taps the monitor.

"You can see the test on your computer, can't you?"

Nick nods. His eyes meet mine, and his expression shifts. It's softer. "You're stubborn and overconfident."

"I am not." Objecting doesn't help my case. But he's wrong.

"I'd like to hire you, Ms. Wilder. You're the only candidate with any grasp of artificial intelligence." Nick stares back at me. "But there are other issues to consider."

"I fucked the boss, so I'm shit out of luck?"

His expression is impossible to read.

"Are you even going to deny it?" I will myself to stay logical. This is a good opportunity. Not worth wasting over a romantic connection, not when there are three million men in Manhattan.

It doesn't help.

I can't look at Nick for another second. How can this be the same man I met last September? That man was calm and collected, but there was warmth in his eyes. His voice was stern and strong, but it was caring too.

This guy is a narcissistic asshole.

I push myself out of my seat. "I'll spare you the awkwardness of explaining it to HR." I sling my purse over my shoulder and march to the door.

"Lizzy, wait."

That's not happening. Not when there's a tear welling up in my eye. This opportunity is everything to me and it's nothing to him.

There's no way I'm staying in New York.

Dammit, I'm not crying in front of him.

Head down, I rush to the elevator. Jasmine says a frantic goodbye, but I pretend I don't hear her.

There are footsteps behind me. I can't bring myself to turn and find out if they belong to Nick. I duck into the staircase and race all the way to the first floor.

I disappear into the Wall Street subway station.

MY SISTER, KAT, LIVES WITH HER FIANCÉ BLAKE

Sterling on the Upper East Side. He's wealthy. If I tell him about this internship, he'll offer me the money to stay in New York.

But I'm not accepting help from either of them. Kat spent the last four years taking care of me. For once, she's going to live her life. I'm going to stand on my own two feet. Even if it kills me.

I collapse on the modern black couch and scan my streaming options. All the sci-fi movies make me think about Nick's project. The Haley Bot (named for Hal, the evil computer in *2001: A Space Odyssey*) is a virtual assistant far beyond any of its competitors. It's an amazing AI project. It's the best opportunity I'll ever have to learn about AI.

This internship is the only way I can stay in New York without dropping out of school.

I can swallow my pride, apologize, and convince Nick to keep our relationship professional.

But I'm not so sure I can be around him without melting into a pile of desire.

<u>Buy *Dirty Boss* Now</u>

Acknowledgements

My first thanks must always go to my husband, who not only tolerates but loves all my weird quirks (even my rants about grammar). Kevin, I couldn't do it without you. And the second goes to my father for always encouraging me to follow my dreams and especially for taking me to the book store when I was supposed to me grounded.

This book has had many covers. And while my latest cover is my favorite, I'd like to thank all the designers who have worked on the series: Aria, Melissa, LJ, and Hang Le, thank you so much for the gorgeous covers! To my editors, Dee and Marla, thank you so much for the quick turn around with this manuscript. It looks amazing. My beta readers—there are too many to name--thank you for helping me make this book the best book it could be.

And my biggest thanks goes to all the readers for taking a chance on a new book.

Stay in Touch

Sign up for my mailing list to get an exclusive alternate POV scene from *Dirty Deal*.

Dirty Boss, featuring Lizzy Wilder and her own alpha CEO is available now.

If you enjoyed the story, please help other readers find it by leaving an honest review on Amazon or Goodreads.

If you love to review and want to get books before anyone else, join the Crystal Kaswell ARC team.

Want to talk books? Awesome! I love hearing from my readers. Like my page on Facebook, join my fangroup, follow me on Instagram, follow me on Twitter, or friend me on Facebook.

Also by Crystal Kaswell

Dirty Rich

Dirty Deal - Blake

Dirty Boss - Nick

Dirty Husband - Shep

Dirty Desires - coming in 2020

Sinful Serenade

Sing Your Heart Out - Miles

Strum Your Heart Out - Drew

Rock Your Heart Out - Tom

Play Your Heart Out - Pete

Sinful Ever After – series sequel

Just a Taste - *Miles's POV*

Dangerous Noise

Dangerous Kiss - Ethan

Dangerous Crush – Kit

Dangerous Rock – Joel

Dangerous Fling – Mal

Dangerous Encore - series sequel

Inked Hearts

Tempting - Brendon

Hooking Up - Walker

Pretend You're Mine - Ryan

Hating You, Loving You - Dean

Breaking the Rules - Hunter

Losing It - Wes

Accidental Husband - Griffin

The Baby Bargain - Chase

Inked Love

The Best Friend Bargain - Forest — coming 2020

The First Taste - Holden - coming 2020

Standalones

Broken - Trent & Delilah

Come Undone Trilogy

Come Undone

Come Apart

Come To Me

Sign up for the Crystal Kaswell mailing list

Made in the USA
Middletown, DE
27 December 2021

57119588R00274